. . . when he drew his tongue along the seam of her closed mouth and dared to part her lips. He was pushing her to touch, to taste, to breathe in every inch of him. His lingering scent, that pine and supremely masculine essence of him.

He tasted of everything forbidden. He tasted of man.

She was lost somewhere in the dales between Derbyshire and Yorkshire, lost in a powerful stranger's arms and losing, with every passing moment, her reticence.

This was not the kiss of a gentleman.

It was not respectful or chaste or decent. It was molten and lush and harsh.

And Grace loved every moment of it . . .

Romances by Sophia Nash

LOVE WITH THE PERFECT SCOUNDREL
THE KISS
A DANGEROUS BEAUTY

Sophia Nash

Love
With the
Perfect
Scoundrel

AVON
An Imprint of HarperCollinsPublishers

This is a work of fiction. Names, characters, places, and incidents are drawn from the author's imagination or are used fictitiously and are not to be construed as real. Any resemblance to actual events, locales, organizations, or persons, living or dead, is entirely coincidental.

AVON BOOKS
An Imprint of HarperCollins*Publishers*
10 East 53rd Street
New York, New York 10022-5299

Copyright © 2009 by Sophia Nash
ISBN 978-0-06-149328-7
www.avonromance.com

First Avon Books paperback printing: March 2009

Avon Trademark Reg. U.S. Pat. Off. and in Other Countries, Marca Registrada, Hecho en U.S.A.
HarperCollins® is a registered trademark of HarperCollins Publishers.

Printed in the U.S.A.

10 9 8 7 6 5 4 3 2 1

To Helen Breitwieser,
a literary agent whose diplomacy, confidence, and
great vision astound

Acknowledgments

Greatest thanks to Executive Editor Lyssa Keusch for her extraordinary editorial guidance. Her encouragement and insightful advice are such wondrous gifts.

And to Anne Kane and Cybil Solyn, endless appreciation for providing critiques of early drafts.

Thank you also to Arthur Huntington Nash and Kim Nash for supplying inspiring ancestral ideas as well as research materials concerning the equine industry in early-nineteenth-century Virginia.

To Ingrid Lindquist, thank you for nurturing my early love of horses via Sioux and all the others.

Nancy Meyer and the Beau Monde provided advice regarding entailed lands and missing heirs, and for that I am grateful.

And as always, special thanks to my family for tolerating life with deadlines and making it all worthwhile.

Love
With the
Perfect
Scoundrel

Chapter 1

Nobody could really explain the reasons behind the failed engagements of the beautiful Countess of Sheffield.

Oh, there was speculation. Oodles of speculation, and none was kind.

But that was to be expected.

For the aristocracy of England was unparalleled in its ability to knock one of their own off the fragile ladder of rank—with merely a look or an emphasis on a single syllable of a word. And they accomplished it with relish—especially during the little season, when few of the amusements of town were in the offing.

Yes, during those cold days of December, Grace Sheffey often wondered with dark humor if it had something to do with all the falsely elegant variations of boiled mutton and prune pudding that coddled lords and ladies endured following autumn's cornucopia.

Whatever the cause for the malaise coursing London's ballroom jungle, the countess knew that the traditional method of clawing out survival involved an iron jaw and a tin ear. For if a lady possessed an "of" in her name, she had best armor herself well against the vicious jaded humor prowling about Mayfair's upper ten thousand.

And so, after fleeing her circle of friends in Cornwall on the heels of her second engagement debacle, Grace tightened her corset and valiantly tried to brazen out the sting of rumors in London.

And failed.

Quite miserably and quite alone, for there had not been a single invitation addressed to her for a single event during the upcoming holidays, nor had there been a single acceptance to a small soiree she had meticulously planned.

There were only regrets. Regrets from everyone she had invited and her own regrets for ever thinking she should attempt a return to London in the heat of such ferocious gossip.

That was why she next chose to do what she did best: to leave. *Again*. Grace Sheffey decamped from this newest disaster in the making, as far and as fast as she could. Little did her kindhearted traveling companion know of Grace's ultimate plan.

"Put your feet on the hot brick, lass," Mr. John Brown pleaded, his bushy salt-and-pepper eyebrows rising over faded, owlish eyes.

"I'm perfectly fine, thank you," replied Grace softly, taking care to keep her back perfectly arched, her lustrous pearls and dress perfectly elegant, her expression perfectly blank. "Forgive me, Mr. Brown, but do you think we'll reach York before nightfall?"

Silence and their frosted breath mingled inside the cold, cramped space.

"Perhaps," he said across from her as he rubbed at the tiny window and glanced at the leaden sky. "But perhaps no. Roman is an excellent driver, but I see patches of ice forming. Well, at least there's no snow. My old bones tell me it's too early in the season. But it might have been better to secure rooms at that last inn."

She put aside her book. "I'm sorry I asked that we continue on."

It was the longest stretch of conversation they'd had since leaving town. And it was the first time she'd offered anything other than a response to a question.

"No, Lady Sheffield, 'tis I who am sorry. I shouldna have presented you with the chance to go north with me. The dowager duchess will no' forgive me for taking you from her. But then again, she'll no' forgive me for anything else." He muttered the last under his breath. "Take this, Countess."

Grace grasped the heavy horsehair blanket but it slipped from her stiff fingers. Mr. Brown unfolded it and arranged it to cover both their laps.

"Lady Sheffield, I know you willna like me for it, but may I have a word? You've stewed too long. I know now you're no' going to crack and—"

He stopped cold when she dared lift her eyes to his. She then took care to draw the lacy veil of cool elegance back into place.

Mr. Brown would not be deterred. "Perhaps we

should speak about your future, about the past, about your—"

"No—"

"—recent ill fortune."

She exhaled sharply and her ghostly breath swirled into nothingness. "Do you mean to propose we examine all the details that led up to my being thrown over by one gentleman and jilted by the next, Mr. Brown?"

"There's no need to—"

"You're absolutely right. There's no need to discuss any of it. It's the most tedious story in the world. If you really want to help, perhaps you can give me your opinion concerning two bonnets I saw at Locke and Company. Shall I order the one in pale pink satin with grapes dripping off the ends, or should I reconsider the lace creation with the blue bird of happiness tipping drunkenly to one side? What say you, Mr. Brown? Are fruits or birds the thing this winter?"

He refused her well-baited trivialities like a cunning, seasoned old trout. "I admire you, Countess. More than you know. I've always thought you gentle, sweet, and full of feminine sensibilities. But I do believe I might have misjudged you on the last. I came prepared for this journey with three dozen handkerchiefs and yet they remain as dry as a Scotsman's throat when gin runs thin."

"Tears never change the facts, Mr. Brown."

He scratched his balding pate, returned his hat to its place, and refused to drop the matter. "After Ata is through with me, the marquis and the duke will probably drag my bones through all of England for taking you to Scotland."

"And I shall tell them that this was the only solution," she continued. "I will not ruin my friends' happiness by staying and becoming an embarrassing reminder of past expectations."

"Is that what you call ruptured engagements now? *Past expectations*?" He snorted. "The dowager duchess calls them something entirely different, and unforgivable. But that's not fit for your ears."

Grace knew his pride was still bruised from the dowager duchess's stalwart refusal to reconsider a life with him.

"So, it appears we're both running away." Grace stared unseeing out the smudged window of Mr. Brown's small carriage.

"No, lass," he replied. "*You* are running away. *I* am giving up."

"Well, Mr. Brown, we shall have to make a bargain then. I shall promise not to call you a fool for giving up a lady who obviously still loves you, if you will promise not to utter the obvious—that I'm a coward for running away."

"You are anything but a coward, Grace Sheffey. You've proved to be a lady of great fortitude and character. You didn't have to release Lord Ellesmere from his promise."

She pursed her lips. "There's no need for false praise. I've never found virtuous behavior all that rewarding."

"Perhaps, but wrongdoings never improve one's lot in life, either." The older gentleman sighed and stretched his aching limbs as much as the interior of the small carriage would allow.

"Are you suggesting we're damned to be unhappy whether we're respectable or sinful, Mr. Brown? Hmmm . . . I hadn't guessed our view of life so similar."

"Och, what a muck I've made of cheering you." He leaned back against the hardened leather squabs of his carriage. "You're entirely wrong, my dear. You've forgotten the great benefit of youth. You've the whole of your life ahead of you. I'm the only one allowed to feel sorry for myself. When you're staring at seventy years in your brittle dish, then—mind you, only then—may you seek peace after failure."

"Well, it's a bit different for females, as you well know, sir. Most everyone would argue that a widow of seven and twenty is as firmly stuck on the shelf as mildew. But please, Mr. Brown, never think I'm complaining. I've had my second chances. And I was blessed with an enormously kind husband for a short while—"

"A very short while," he interrupted. "Och, Countess, Sheffield was a great man, but, forgive me for saying, he was too old for ye."

"You're very wrong, Mr. Brown. Age has nothing whatsoever to do with attachments of the heart. But, now I want"—she paused and smoothed a wisp of hair back in place with her cold, stiff fingers—"no, I *need* to go away for a short while. But have no fear. I'm certain I'll return to the whirl in town very soon. I can never stay away for very long. It's just that everything is too fresh. We never should have stopped in London.

I should have waited until a new scandal made my failure look like moldy old news." Distractedly, she rolled one of her long strands of pearls between her fingers. "Fortunately for me, I have the wherewithal to feel sorry for myself far, far away from all painful conjecture."

"If it were not so cold, I would argue with you. Why, you're but a spring chick. I'll endeavor to do better once we thaw before a good fire on the other side o' the border." He tucked the loosening corner of the blanket under her. "I'm only sorry you didn't urge your maid to continue along with us. You're too softhearted by half."

"Not at all. Sally doesn't tolerate the cold—has never been more than ten miles from Cornwall," Grace replied. "I never should have asked her to come. But I've arranged for her return to London. When I'm settled, I'll engage a maid who is more hardy to the vagaries of the northern climes."

She remained silent for a moment, her hands folded demurely in her lap, then cleared her throat. "Mr. Brown?"

He stopped tapping his fingers along the edge of the bench.

"I'm glad we've been frank with each other. I've wanted to tell you that I've decided on a small change of plans."

Mr. Brown shook his head. "I don't like changing plans."

"I would ask you to deposit me in Lancaster. When we arrive in York, it will be a simple matter to take the crossroad to the coast."

The elderly gentleman opened his mouth like a carp, then clamped it shut when Grace continued, "I decided several days ago that I will not go on with you to Scotland. I'm going to the Isle of Mann—where I spent my childhood. When my cousin inherited, he invited me to reside there anytime I choose. He's never there—too desolate to his taste, I suppose."

"The Isle of Mann? You must be joking. I can't let you go there, not at this time of year. Why, it might very well storm. The Irish Sea is treacherous in the best of weather."

She raised her eyes to his, and apparently what he saw quickened his speech. "I won't let you go alone, Lady Sheffield. I'll go with you, see you settled. Perhaps even stay on for a while if I'm honored by an invitation. Maybe through the winter? Or longer. Yes, much longer."

"You're not my nursemaid, Mr. Brown. I only asked to take a detour—to be left at the port in Lancaster. I know the village there well, and shall arrange for passage. Then you are to continue to—" She stopped at the sound of an eerie, mournful moaning outside the carriage. "*What* was that sound?"

"Just the wind, my dear. It's more than a mite wicked in the vales."

"But it sounds like a child crying most piteously."

"Some say it's the lost heir of the moors."

"I beg your pardon?"

"Just a sad tale told by—"

The carriage bounced out of a frozen rut and lurched to one side. Grace became stiff with the ill feeling of disaster. And in one suspended instant in time, everything changed.

Rounding another sharp turn, the carriage careened across the ice-slicked lane. Mr. Brown levered his aged frame into the space beside her and braced her shoulders as the old, ill-suited carriage floated on a long skid to the far side of the road. The driver shouted, and with an awful creaking sound, the tiny single-horse-drawn carriage teetered sideways before losing its fight with gravity, and tumbled onto its side. The loud crack of a wheel or axle rended the air at the same moment Mr. Brown's heavy form fell on top of her and a pain lanced her ribs.

In that moment, Grace envisioned the distraught, pitying expressions of her two former fiancés, the Duke of Helston and the Marquis of Ellesmere, as they searched the wreckage. Mr. Brown and she would appear like frozen herrings in a tin under a hedgerow.

For a few seconds there was blessed silence before the carriage horse whinnied and the ruined vehicle slid a few inches forward. The old carriage's off-kilter frame creaked in outrage and cracks snaked down the joints.

"Lady Sheffield? Lord, I'm crushing you," Mr. Brown croaked.

"No," she whispered. "I'm perfectly fine."

"Thank God." He awkwardly reached for the door, which was now above them. Maneuvering, he wrenched it open and a blast of cold wind rushed inside the tiny carriage, which had never been meant for long-distance travel.

"Roman? Roman, are you there, man?" When there was no response, Mr. Brown toed a buckled bench and heaved himself through the opening, muttering a Scottish oath.

Breathless, Grace righted herself despite the tangle of her gown's skirting and the blankets, and then knelt on what had once been the side of the carriage. She collected all the objects flung about—her book; Mr. Brown's ledger; her embroidery bag; and her large jewelry pouch. The latter she put in her voluminous pocket.

"Lady Sheffield, can you hear me?"

"Yes."

"Look, we've a dilemma. Mr. Roman is knocked senseless and his head is bleeding. At least the horse is unharmed. You're going to ride pillion—behind Mr. Roman, holding him—toward the last town. I'll walk. Give me your hand and I'll help you out."

"Mr. Brown, I'm afraid I can't do that."

"What? Come along now. I've wrapped Roman's wound but we have to make our way out of here straightaway. The wind is up and—"

"Mr. Brown, I cannot ride astride with this narrow gown." She prayed it would be an acceptable excuse. "And I certainly won't be able to prop up Mr. Roman if he's unconscious—especially without a saddle. He's a very large man, is he not? You must take him. I'll wrap myself tightly with these blankets and wait until you send someone back for me."

Mr. Brown muttered another oath. "Lass, you will get out o' this wreck and mount the blasted horse now. And I'll hear no' another word about it."

"Mr. Brown," she replied calmly, "if you don't do what I suggest, you might very well find yourself with two injured people on your hands without any sort of shelter—not even a wrecked carriage—and then what will Ata do to you? Especially when I tell her that I begged you to send help. And I could also hail the mail coach when it passes. The man at the inn mentioned it was traveling this same road, did he not?"

She heard him climb down the outside of the carriage while mumbling something about ladies and their *blooming* ability to make men bow to their ill thought out ideas. Then a heap of clothing was tossed through the door. She swaddled herself in a mélange of thin shawls taken from her trunk strapped to the rear of the rickety carriage.

Mr. Brown draped his torso through the opening and thrust a flask into her fingers. "Here's a bit o' false fire." He cradled her cheek with his gnarled hand. "I don't like this at all, mind you. No' one bit. But you've got that look about you. That mulish look I'm thinking Ata taught you. Och, I know it too well." Mr. Brown's Scottish burr always became more pronounced when he was agitated.

"You're correct. Go on, now. I don't want Mr. Roman to suffer a moment more than necessary. I shall be perfectly fine. I'm stifling under all these shawls. And I have the basket of food from the inn."

Mr. Brown was remarkably good in a crisis, and even better at taking direction.

He shook his head. "Don't you dare set one foot out o' this carriage. I promise I'll return for you." He glared at her until she shook her head once. Then he shut the carriage door above her.

Within minutes, the sounds of Mr. Brown and the carriage horse muted and she was surrounded by silence. It was the first time she'd been alone for days—no, months. Actually, she realized, it felt like the first time she'd been truly alone for *years*.

She exhaled in one long, almost endless breath, and became lightheaded. For the last month she'd thought she might burst from the pent-up emotion. She'd not dared to show an inch of sorrow, even around her sweet Cornish maid.

During the journey, she'd been so grateful for the cold. It had numbed her limbs, which had been screaming at her to get away from Cornwall, and then London, as fast as possible. The chill had also allowed her mind to see everything with crystal clarity.

She was not meant to be living with other people. She was completely different from other ladies. And the thing of it was, she would be entirely happy living alone as she had done most of her childhood. Her friends often mistook her love of solitude for loneliness; they didn't understand the contentment that could be found by leaving one's heart sheltered and one's mind to quiet reflection. She tried to breathe, but again felt a hitch in her side from the effort.

There—she'd admitted it all to herself. Mr. Brown had been wrong. She possessed a great defect in her character—in her moral fiber. She was weak and she approached everything in life tentatively and without any sort of passion. It was the reason she had not secured the affections of two fiancés.

She was a retiring coward in the fruitful garden of her pampered life. And running away from her disappointments was something of an art form she had perfected. But sitting here, growing dizzy, she accepted the truth. She was never going to be able to run far enough away this time—for she could not run away from herself.

Agony darkened the edges of her vision before she struggled against all the binding layers of impractical thin clothing. Pain hit her rib cage like an avalanche gaining momentum at the same moment she noticed a small streak of blood on her glove.

Glancing behind her only to find the broken glass of the carriage sconce, she guessed she'd fallen against it during the accident. Now scared, she refused to examine the wound; instead she wrapped a silk mantlet around her ribs and bound it as tightly as she could bear.

Grace knew she should be worried about her predicament, but instead she could only feel tired. And she was grateful. She hadn't been able to sleep more than an hour or two at a time since leaving Cornwall. Then again, she'd never slept well. Surrendering to exhaustion, Grace Sheffey's mind sloughed off her worries and flew out of the confines of this wreck of a carriage all the way to the oblivion of a deep, dreamless sleep.

The fragile strands of consciousness lay just out of her grasp for Lord only knew how long. With a strength she hadn't known she possessed, Grace clenched her fingers repeatedly to waken. She lay there a long time before she forced down some of the contents of Mr. Brown's flask and coughed violently against the burn.

Her mind blurry, she wasn't sure if she had swooned or fallen asleep. But she wasn't foolish enough to succumb to it again. This unnaturally dark, frigid cocoon frightened her.

The hinges creaked as she shoved at the door above. In a rush, the door fell from its moorings, taking a portion of the carriage siding with it. Clumps of snow littered her as she toppled over from the exertion.

The silence of the snow showering from the ever more gloomy sky clawed at her. When had the storm started? Surely, it would stop soon. Mr. Brown had said it never snowed this early in the season.

What had happened to Mr. Brown and the driver? Lord . . . Perhaps they'd met with ill luck. Mr. Brown would've returned for her by now if he could.

Well, she had to get out, had to start walking. No one was coming for her. She would perish if she remained here. Yet it was hard to make her limbs obey. Tears of frustration almost froze inside her eyelids as she twisted herself from the wreckage.

Bent with weariness and the edge of pain furrowing her side, she leaned into the wind, into the gloaming, and trudged toward the main mail coach road—away from the direction Mr. Brown had taken. It was her best chance. She was certain she would find a house or village around the next bend.

The world around her became ghostly, the flakes falling on a slant, drifting onto the heavy branches of the trees, hedgerows, and the lane, softening the ugly ruts in the road. She shivered and drew the blankets more tightly about her.

Snow cascaded from a nearby conifer and the tawny shadow of an enormous owl emerged from the branches, its wings spread in flight. How she wished she could fly away too.

Icy flecks invaded the tops of her inadequate half boots while Grace trudged onward. Only the crunch of her footsteps on the new snow breached the silence of the northern Peak District. Her breath crystallized in the blanket near her mouth as she tried to regulate her thoughts and her breathing.

Just past the first turn, she realized there was no house, no village in front of her, only a long stretch of whiteness bordered by snow-powdered hedges without a telltale rise of smoke in the distance.

She didn't dare look up again for a long while.

Time lost all meaning as she walked onward, her cheeks stinging, then without feeling, as hints of eventide crept in behind the melancholy December sky.

It was then that Grace Sheffey murmured an almost forgotten prayer from her childhood . . . a little something to her guardian angel begging an entree to paradise.

Chapter 2

Michael Ranier tugged his brushed-beaver hat lower on his head and was grateful for the protection against the heavy snowfall. An eerie calm had settled on this land, despite the outpouring from the heavens. He loosened the reins and gave his powerful mare her head so she could choose the best path in this sudden, wretched blizzard. He wouldn't have pressed onward from the last village if all the physical features of the landscape had not proved he was close to the first view of his new beginning . . . Brynlow.

Then again, the fast-forming drifts were quite effectively covering any trace of his passage. It helped quell the ill ease that had dogged him since the moment he had stepped onto the filthy English docks less than a week ago.

Only a few miles now separated him from the mysterious property his childhood friend had left to him in his will. Poignant memories tinged his thoughts. Who would have guessed that little Samuel Bryn would one day tempt Michael from the hard-won productive life he'd cobbled together in the colonies during the last decade and a half or more?

Michael rounded another turn in the road, grateful for the guide of the hedgerow blanketed in snow, and hoped more than anything that Sam had left him a huge pile of split wood, for it was going to take a cord of well-seasoned red oak to ease the cold from his heavy bones.

Michael began to hum in an effort to calm and encourage his mare. After eight long hours on the road, her strength was not waning nor her spirit, but he knew she liked it when he sang to her. She whinnied and shook the melting flakes from her heavily muscled black neck.

Michael chuckled. "Sorry sweetheart, pipes are damned near frozen."

He stroked his mount's shoulder, then clucked to urge her to turn onto the northwesterly route, a long, straight, desolate roadway.

There was something moving far in the distance. A stag, most likely. He squinted.

He had imagined it. There was nothing there. Michael continued onward, leaning into the brunt of the storm. The effort to encourage his horse with song was stripped from him by the increasing gusts of the tempest.

The mare raised her head and stopped, her ears pricked up. She sidestepped and her neck swung around before she snorted.

A small hooded form leaned against an ancient, towering hemlock, its huge branches shielding the figure.

Good God.

He called out, "Hey . . . you there."

The hood moved toward him but the effort appeared too great to bear. His heart lurched. Everything screamed this was a person poor in spirit and material goods, two things he knew all too well.

Without hesitation, Michael eased his weight onto his left stirrup and swung off, landing in a quagmire of snow.

"Hey, are you all right? Caught by the storm, were you?"

He reached the shelter of the tree just as the pitiable, blanket-covered sod raised his head again.

Two soft blue eyes, drowning in the wisdom of the ages, stared straight into his soul, piercing his heart. He staggered backward.

Why, he'd stumbled across something from heaven. No earthly eyes or flesh possessed such translucence. Beyond the fringes of the dull, worn blanket wrapped about her, pale hair shimmered silver in the fading light.

Her gaze faltered not. "For—forgive me for being so ridiculous, but are—are you an illusion?"

A deep chuckle rumbled within his chest. "I was about to ask you the same, miss."

"Well, this is a f-f-first. My prayers have n-n-n" —her teeth chattered uncontrollably—"never been answered before."

"I've never been the answer to anyone's prayers, sweetheart." Michael scratched his jaw and smiled. "But I'll try my damnedest to live up to your expectations."

He wanted to ask what in hell she was doing out

here, alone and facing the elements, but knew the importance of helping her keep whatever shreds of pride her obvious poverty allowed—and so he remained still and silent, waiting for her.

She darted a glance around his body, spied his horse, and shuddered.

"Shall we, then?" He held out his hand. "You would be doing me a great favor by coming with me. My ears are like two blocks of ice and I see you've a muffler trailing behind you I might ask to borrow." He'd say anything to gain her trust and get her to come with him.

"Thank you, s-s-sir." The wind howled through the branches and she braced herself against the tree. Gathering her strength again, she reached for the thin shawl at her feet and placed it in his outstretched hand. "The carriage I was in slid into a ditch."

"I see." He hadn't seen any carriage and he would swear her eyes flicked. "Are there others?"

"My companion went for help l-l-long ago, but he didn't return. I was waiting for the mail coach."

Hmmm. He wasn't sure he believed her story. No gentleman . . . No. No *man* would leave a woman behind to fend for herself. "There won't be a mail coach in weather like this. In any case, I believe we'll find shelter nearby."

"Are you lost too?"

He smiled. "Will you trust me if I tell you the truth?"

She tilted her head and was apparently too polite to utter her opinion.

"Perhaps, a trifle," he admitted. "But I've good directions and an excellent horse, who has yet to fail me."

He had a nearly primal urge to pick her up in his arms, get her in front of a fire, offer her warm food, and comfort her. "Let me help you onto my mare."

She appeared vastly embarrassed. "I don't ride very well. Actually, I never learned."

This was no surprise. Many poor could not afford the luxury of a horse. "You've nothing to fear. My horse is gentle despite her size. She doesn't bite and she's always well behaved. The same cannot be said of me, however—when someone is stalling." He offered his hand once again to help her negotiate the deep snow.

"I'm sorry to be so craven."

"It's the cold. It scrambles the mind. But we mustn't waste any more time." He looked about. "The weather is getting worse by the minute." He hoped she wouldn't scuttle away like a feral animal in distress.

She glanced at his outstretched hand again and finally grasped it; his great paw engulfed her tiny one. Two steps forward and she floundered in a small drift, her balance as offset by the frost-filled air as her mind.

Without a word, he leaned in, grasped her about the waist and under the knees to haul her delicate form against the wall of his chest.

Her breath left in a rush. "Really, this isn't necessary. I'm perfectly capable of—"

"I have it on the best authority that not walking another step was part of your prayer. Well, I know it would be part of mine—if I was in your position." God, she was so wraithlike in his arms, and an animalistic surge of protectiveness flooded him. She was dangerously light and would freeze to death if he didn't get her out of the elements in short order.

She struggled when he approached his mare. "Put me down. I can walk very well here on the road, thank you." She climbed out of his arms onto her own two feet and rearranged her blankets. "I will follow the trail you blaze."

He stared at her and then shook his head. "I'm sorry."

"For what?" Her eyes bloomed with fear.

"You'll have to keep your voice low."

"Whyever for?"

"You're hurting her feelings." He tilted his head toward his mare, praying humor would help.

She glanced at the animal then raised her eyes to meet his. He was sure she would refuse again.

"Oh, for goodness sake," she said quietly, her face drawn. And suddenly he noticed, despite the fading light, a slick, dark area on her snow-dusted blankets . . . a place that was *blood red*. The time for polite cajoling was over.

In one easy motion he regathered the reins in one hand and grasped the saddle's cantle to remount. Before she could utter another word, he leaned down and hauled her up to sit in front of him, her legs dangling to one side. He didn't dare try to examine where the blood was coming from—the elements were too harsh and she was too cold.

He should have seen the signs. Clearly, her mind was half lost to a freezing daze. In fact, she was now an inch closer to oblivion thanks to her obvious fear. He unbuttoned his heavy, long coat, deeply slashed on the sides for riding, and pulled her close to his heated body while refastening the closures.

"Put your arms around me, sweetheart," he whispered into her temple while he turned her to face him better. "Hold on tight, now."

She was making sounds of distress but tentatively grasped his sides. Michael transferred the reins to one hand to gather her more firmly against him.

His horse remained as rock steady as he knew she would. The mare was smarter than most humans alive, and he would trust her with his life. Hell, he already had, on numerous occasions. He'd never considered even once the thought of leaving her behind when he'd returned to England.

His horse lurched forward, plowing through the mounting layer of snow, while the woman now held onto his sides with a death grip.

"That's it. Get closer—as close as you can. There now. No need to talk. We'll be there in a trice." He kept up the stream of comforting commands as his mare negotiated her steps.

An enormous blast of wind barreled down the long roadway and momentarily stole away his breath. He hunkered inward and grasped the waif closer still. It was then he noticed the most evocative scent emanating from her. He lowered his head and breathed deep, letting the heady fragrance wash through his senses.

There was the hint of spring, of lilies of the valley, and the rains of March, and something else . . . of femininity—and of luxurious *affluence*. Who in damnation was this young woman? He exhaled and realized he didn't even know her name. She slumped against him then, in exhaustion, or from loss of blood, he knew not which.

For Christ sakes. What had he gotten into now? He was lost within the eye of a blizzard near Yorkshire with an injured, mysterious woman. Actually, if he was honest, this was nothing more than the usual madness fate had always tossed his way. Fate was surely a woman determined to flummox him at every twist in the uneven road of his damned life.

Sioux neighed and tossed her head. "I know, sweetheart, I know. It never fails . . ." He clucked encouragement, and at the haunting sound of the wind, he sang low—a song from his childhood.

The last thing Grace heard as the black veil of unconsciousness overtook the riot within her mind was the most beautiful voice singing above her, surely from the heavens. For once, she slumbered in peace—not tossing and turning like a leaf caught in the battering winds of autumn. How ironic it was that this could occur on the back of a mammoth horse while lost within the powerful grasp of the most daunting, immense man she had ever encountered.

He held not the carefully cultivated, jaded countenance of a lord. He appeared carved from the raw brawn of daring, with a side helping of rugged instinct. And those eyes . . . those audacious, lion-like eyes that fronted verve and intelligent cunning in the wicked ways of the world.

She should be terrified. She should be on her guard. But she was too weak to feel any of it. Her heart filled with the most illogical sense of security given her predicament, and it warmed her all the way down to her marrow.

Chapter 3

Finding Brynlow required greater fortitude and patience than Michael had anticipated. The barkeep at the last inn had not been jesting when he had said it was lost in a forgotten corner of Christendom. Yet, it was perfect. By the hazy radiance of a waxing crescent moon behind cloud cover and the still falling snow, Michael discerned the pale stone house tucked away in a stand of silver birch trees, the pastoral scene warming his heart.

He weaved his mare through the branches to find two large barns hidden beyond. Crystallized ice cracked and broke free as he dismounted and slid the woman off in one long motion to prop her against the stable's door once inside. She moaned when he disengaged her from his warmth.

Carefully lighting a nearby lantern, Michael made short work of rubbing down and settling his horse in the comfort of a stall, then hefted his saddlebags and the semiconscious form of the woman to make his way to the dwelling.

It was obvious from what he could see of the inside of the small manor that Sam had had the wherewithal to establish the place with many creature comforts. Stopping to reposition the woman within his arms, Michael noticed a note on the small table beside the front stair.

Dear Mr. Ranier,

Begging yer pardon sir, but I'm for the village to look in on the missus who's feeling poorly and staying with her sister. I've left the larder and animals in the barn well stocked. Don't know if you'll arrive on the day you wrote in yer letter but I'll look in—in a day or two. I've left our eldest, Timmy, in the room above the stable.

Yours respectfully,
Bertie Lattimer

Well. The day was bringing nothing but good news, he thought dryly. He ducked his head and negotiated his way up the long, creaking staircase before nudging open the first door along the short hall. At least the bed was made up and wood lay in the grate. Carefully placing the woman on the bed frame, he turned his attention to the fat wood and flint box to nurse a fire.

There was a host of surprises awaiting him as he removed his fur-lined gloves, peeled off his wet coat, and rolled up his sleeves to unwrap the many-layered mystery of the beautiful woman before him. Beneath the dull blankets, Michael encountered a ragtag assortment of shawls. His calloused hands snagged the delicate silks, some marked with blood, until he removed the last impractical outer garment.

She truly was an ethereal creature. In the glow of the lantern light, she was a study in pink-hued femininity. Her cloak gave way to a rose silk gown stitched with silver thread. Four lengths of pearls lay draped in a heavy tangle around her delicate neck and entwined in her pale blonde hair.

Who in hell was she?

His gaze hooked on the red stains on her gown and dread corroded his veins. There was too much blood.

Well, rich or poor, aristocrat or waif, a wound was a wound.

He cursed each of the tiny, silk-covered buttons of her gown as his brutish, scarred fingers worked past the impractical lacy tapes of her chemise. Drawing aside the flimsy fabrics, he sucked in his breath when a good portion of her exquisite breasts were exposed.

Her flesh was too smooth and unflawed, leaving him hesitant to mar her in any way. Pink silk swirled around the tiny rosy tips and he swallowed. He concentrated on removing the corset and remnants of the chemise underneath.

It was a maze of whalebone and lace and like nothing he'd encountered on the no-nonsense women on the other side of the ocean. He snorted in disgust at the impractical, torturous nature of the beast and retrieved a pocketknife from his bag. With a few deft moves, he sliced through the stained layers and pulled apart the contraption and chemise beneath. Blood gushed from a deep gash below her breast and she moaned once. He pressed a shawl against the wound. Well, at least the blasted overly tight corset had helped staunch the flow of blood. And the injury wasn't mortal—but it would need stitching.

He would have to rouse her from whatever state of frozen exhaustion to which she had succumbed, for she would have to be near death not to feel the pinch of the needle when he stitched her.

He juggled between pressing against the wound and reaching for a small kit in his bag.

Michael covered her breasts with another shawl and stroked her hair. "Blue Eyes . . . hey, wake up." It was no surprise there was no reaction. Hell, if she hadn't woken from his cutting through her corset . . . "Come now, sweetheart." He shook her shoulders and she inhaled harshly. "That's it. Look, you've got to wake up." He jarred her again.

Her eyes slit open slightly.

"Good. You've nothing to fear. You're safe. We've arrived, but we've got to see to your injury."

She closed her eyes.

He sighed, then spied the gleam of a flask within the folds of her velvet cloak. He pulled off the stopper and splashed some of the contents between her lips, cursing the fact he'd sworn never to swig a mouthful himself. He had enough to atone for without adding another vice.

She coughed violently and tried to rise.

"That's it. No, no. Don't sit up."

Grace's eyes watered from the brandy fumes in her tight throat. But at least, for once, when she could breathe, it was without difficulty. Ill ease growing with each second, she glanced down and realized her state of undress. With horror, she grasped the shawl tighter to herself. "Good Lord . . ."

"I'm sorry, sweetheart. Looks like you've hurt yourself." The towering giant's slumberous golden eyes contrasted with the harsh angles of his face. "I'm afraid we'll have to stitch it."

She tried to hold back a cough, her voice faint. "Did you undress me?"

"Yes. But, uh, I didn't look." A fleck of humor warmed his expression. "Well, perhaps I did look. Once." His eyes flickered. "All right, maybe twice."

He was immense, hovering over her, taking up all the space in the small room. And yet . . . Why was it that a man could possess a stubbled face and weary eyes combined with disheveled hair and lines of exhaustion, and it all served to make him supremely handsome in a beastly sort of way? If she hadn't been in so much pain, and lightheaded to boot, she would have been mortified down to her stockings given the situation.

As she watched him rifle through his bag, the awful feeling of helplessness invaded her in the face of such overwhelming masculine vitality. She had been determined never to leave herself vulnerable again. Frailty was the trait she most despised in herself.

"So, what happened to you, sweetheart?"

"Please stop calling me that." She tried to still her shivering limbs with no success. "I fell against the carriage lamp during the accident." He was glancing at her clutched hands and the heat of a blush overtook her.

"There's no need to be bashful." He drew a needle and a length of thread from his kit.

"That's easy for you to suggest when you're sitting there fully dressed, Mr. . . . ?" She focused on the needle and a long shiver worked its way through her body. For some perverse reason, she was chilled to the bone now that she was out of the elements.

"Ranier. Michael Ranier. I'd offer to let you see me in the altogether, but then" —he winked— "I'm doubting that would make you feel less awkward, would it, Blue Eyes?" He deftly knotted the thread and leaned in closer. "Now then."

"Now then, what? How do you know I need stitches? I could just bind it. I really think we should wait. Have you ever done this before? Surely there's a surgeon, or even an apothecary we could send for . . ." *An ancient, learned man who looks like a grandfather instead of a colossal, powerful archangel with enough distilled charm to steal the feathers off a chicken with nary a squawk.* Her gibberish of questions slowed with each passing word when she realized he wasn't going to argue. "Look, you already know I'm hen-hearted, so any attempt to goad me to your way of thinking won't work, Mr. Ranier."

"Perhaps you should call me Michael."

"Absolutely not! In cases such as these, it's vitally important to preserve every last measure of civility, sir."

"Am I at least permitted to know your name?"

"Of course." She sighed. "Grace Sheffey." She tried to offer her hand but quickly lowered it when she saw how it fluttered.

"Such a lovely name, Duchess."

"I most certainly am not a duchess."

"Baroness?"

She shook her head, exasperated. "You may call me Mrs. Sheffey."

He disregarded her. "Viscountess?"

"Does it matter?"

"I have it," he uttered with a knowing grin. "*Count-ess* . . ." He placed his hand on top of her clenched one still shaking with cold.

When she didn't reply, he smiled again. "No denial? Well, then. And your husband is the Earl of . . . ?"

"Sheffield," she replied, lifting her chin. She was not hiding anything from him. She had no reason to feel defensive and could not understand why she did. It was just that this man's immense presence completely shredded her nerves.

"And where is the good earl?"

"Why do you ask?"

"You know, if you keep evading simple questions, I'll start thinking there's something you're trying to hide, Countess." He gathered another shawl and pressed it against the wound more firmly. "I'm asking because I'd like to know if a herd of lordly relatives led by an over-wrought husband will come crashing in here at any given moment."

She swallowed. "I'm a widow."

He raised one slashing brow a fraction of an inch.

"I think I told you about my traveling companion, Mr. Brown. He'll be very worried, and will come for me if he hasn't met with disaster himself." She stopped short, caught in misery at the thought of elderly Mr.

Brown in peril. She watched the great chest of the man in front of her rise and fall steadily for a few moments and was abruptly worried about the appearance of impropriety. "My maid was not well and remained behind at the last village."

He didn't appear to believe everything she said. "Countess, I suggest you drink as much of this brandy as you can manage, and then I'll be as quick as I can."

"This is entirely improper. I can't possibly allow you to—"

"Sweetheart, there was nothing proper about you traveling alone with this Mr. Brown fellow, or the way I rode to this house with you, or the way I hauled you up the stairs. And there was certainly nothing proper about the way I undressed you, or the fact that I will have to stitch you—no, I see that look. But I will be doing it. Look at it this way—all of it is insignificant to how you will feel if you waver longer and I'm forced to remove every last article of clothing on both of us and climb in this bed to take the chill from your bones."

She shrank back, horrified. No one had ever spoken to her in such a coarse manner.

His eyes softened and he stroked her head. "I've had plenty of practice at this. I promise you."

He must have learned on the battlefield. Lord knew he looked large enough to take the place of half a battalion. Grace grasped the flask he offered and drank two small sips before gasping. Then she loosened her hold on her favorite silk shawl, now quite ruined, and eased it up, keeping her breasts covered. A rush of pain flowed through her at the same moment she looked down to see a warm trickle of blood stream down her ribs.

He tilted her chin up. "No. Close your eyes or look at me, but don't look down." His tone and his eyes had turned serious. As serious and implacable as a man who knew what he was doing—and knew it well. "I'll not lie to you. This will hurt. You may cry out if you'd like, but don't move. You'd best take a deep breath."

She did as he bade and sharp pain lanced her side before it changed to an awful pulling sensation.

"You may curse if you'd like," he murmured, breaking the tension.

"I do *not* curse." She exhaled roughly. "Ever."

One corner of his mouth rose slightly. "All right, Countess. Now take another deep breath."

Deep breath? Why, she couldn't breathe at all, especially when he leaned over her again to peer at her bared flesh.

"That's it," he said after a moment. "I'm sorry, but there's something imbedded. I'll remove it now."

She cringed, but then stilled when she saw the intelligence deep in his eyes. She nodded and a nearly unbearable probing pain engulfed her for long moments.

"Got it." She heard the clink of a piece of glass hitting crockery. Another round of shivering wound through her body. She just couldn't control the cold, which had seemed to take up permanent residence in her body.

Another stitch. More drawing up of the thread, and

more concentration. The edges of her vision blurred, and blackened. She clenched her fists so tightly she was certain her nails would pierce the thin leather of her gloves.

"Steady now. Three more I think—just a little higher here."

To her complete mortification, he raised the shawl and she could feel the chilled air on one breast. His bare forearm brushed the sensitive tip as he leaned in at an awkward angle. She had never felt so exposed in all her life.

"I'm sorry," he murmured, his eyes trained strictly on the thread and her injury. She concentrated on his face, partially covered by the many layers of dark hair. One lock was a whisper away from her breast. The warmth of his breath bathed her bared flesh and she could feel the tip of her breast tighten involuntarily. The relentless tension in the room was leaving her lightheaded, until he casually broke the silence by low melodic humming.

She exhaled slowly.

Her vision cleared as his hands appeared to be tying a knot.

And then another.

And, blessedly, a last one.

"Finished." He cut the last of the threads and tucked her shawl back into place. Placing the needle in the dish, he turned to her. The light of humor was gone from his face, and Grace spied something very like sympathy in his expression.

She closed her eyes against the feeling it evoked.

From behind her eyelids, a shadow passed over and she felt him lean in again and stroke her hair.

Flustered, she inhaled, only to notice a potent woody scent. Ferns and moss, combined with a smoky pine fire, and mountain wind invaded her senses. He smelled of raw male essence washed clean in a crystal clear lake. It was the aroma of undeniable masculinity. She opened her eyes.

"You are a surprise," he said quietly at her temple as he rearranged the pillow.

"How . . . so?" she whispered unevenly.

"You're a fraud. Your avowed cowardice is outrageous. You could have at least thrashed a bit, or swooned, or at the very least shed a few tears."

"Sorry to disappoint."

He cocked his head and revealed an irresistible smile, one corner slightly lower than the other. The stubble of his beard carved a dark pattern on his face.

"You're the bravest patient I've ever had the privilege of serving, sweetheart. Of course, I suppose I had the benefit of reason in your case." He chuckled. "My other patients almost always refused to do what I wanted until I brought out a twitch."

She jerked away. "A twitch? Whatever are you talking about?"

"All my other patients were horses."

"Horses?" she asked faintly.

"Or sheep. A cow or two on occasion. Went with the territory."

"And what territory was that?"

"With smithing."

"You're a blacksmith?" Her voice sounded reedy and thin to her own ears.

"And most recently a farmer. Does that pose a problem?"

"Well, I would have liked to have known—"

"There's one last thing I should do. Hold still."

"Now wait a moment, Mr. Ranier. I must know exactly what—"

He uncorked Mr. Brown's flask again with his teeth and his hand snaked out to snatch the shawl from her clenched fist.

"Don't you dare—"

"I don't have to find my twitch now, do I? Just when you were behaving so well, Countess."

"I do wish you'd stop interru—"

He dashed some brandy on her injury and a splash of fresh pain washed over her side.

"I can't believe you just did that," she said hoarsely.

"Just a bit of Indian lore concerning firewater. A medicine man I once knew was a remarkably skilled healer as far as I could see."

Indian lore? Dear God. Could her current world become any further removed from what she knew? "So now I am being treated in the manner of horses *and* pagan ritual?"

"I suppose you could say it's your lucky day, Countess." He deftly secured a bandage.

Grace wished she could conjure up a nice long faint. She closed her eyes and shivered involuntarily. While some people often thought they were dreaming when bad things happened to them, Grace had never mistaken her actual world for reverie.

It had happened too often.

"You're too pale, angel. You've lost more than a little blood. We've got to get you warm."

"W-w-w-would . . ." She clenched her jaw to stop her chattering teeth, and hissed, "Would it be too much trouble to ask for some tea?"

"I'm sorry, but I doubt there'll be any tea here— knowing its previous owner." He crossed to the grate and added two logs to the fire, which crackled approvingly. "But, I do think we've got to face facts."

"I think I've had about as many facts as I can stand for one day, Mr. Ranier."

He continued without pause. "A cup of tea is not enough to warm you at this point. Let me see your hands."

She stared at him.

"To check for frostbite."

She couldn't make her fingers work properly and he finally took over the job of unbuttoning the ivory heart-shaped buttons at her wrists and peeling off the sodden pink kid gloves.

Her hands appeared so small in his work-worn palms, the size of butter dishes. Faint streaks of scarlet marred her pale hands and fingers, which felt like wooden pins.

He shook his head.

"What?"

He muttered something that was probably an Indian curse. She winced.

He gave her his back and tugged off his boots. This boded ill. She couldn't help but notice his massive shoulders strained against the seams of his rough-hewn shirt. Grace wondered how tall he truly was. Surely, it was just her low angle of hazy vision that made him appear to stand at almost six and a half feet.

"Isn't there another bedchamber, Mr. Ranier? I'm not in a position to complain, mind you. But, oh dear Lord, you're not going to . . . Don't you think it would be—"

"No."

There was no clarification while he proceeded to strip off his damp shirt and woolen stockings and lay them near the fire. "Let me assure you, Countess, the effects of frostbite are too high a price to pay for modesty."

Grace bit her lip and looked away. He wouldn't dare take off all his articles of clothes.

Under her lashes she discerned he was sporting some sort of heavy buckskin leggings, low on his hips. She tightened her body to halt a long shiver. Perversely, she could not seem to stop shaking.

Mr. Ranier extinguished the flame in the lantern and advanced toward her by the flickering light of the fire, his bare chest fully revealed. Unlike her beloved husband, this man was a fortification of defined, corded muscle. A vast expanse of golden skin shone in the flicker of firelight with only a hint of dark hair that trailed to his leggings.

He took up the entire view in front of her, leaving her nowhere to look but at his tawny eyes if she wanted to keep any semblance of dignity in this impossible situation.

"Your turn."

It was absurd to pretend ignorance of what he expected of her, and so she did what she knew how to do best. She remained silent.

"It would seem that you have two choices before you, Countess. You may either remove your wet clothes by yourself or allow me to help you." He cocked his head in that already familiar fashion. "Look, I'm mortally exhausted, and could use the sleep. And it's an age-old method to get someone warm. It's a fair exchange, Blue Eyes."

She bit her lip. "Mr. Ranier, I would be most obliged if you would use my proper name instead of all those" —she searched for a suitable word— "those . . . those ridiculous endearments." She knew her tone was a touch peevish and she was not sorry for it.

"Sorry to offend." He smiled, and his eyes twinkled. "No one's ever complained before, *Mrs. Sheffey.*"

That name, the one John Sheffey had used for her in private, sounded more like an intimate caress than all those silly other endearments he had uttered. Well, it would have to do. The quivering refused to be repressed.

"Oh, all right," she grumbled. "Turn around."

He gave her a long-suffering look but complied. Grace removed her torn, wet garments as quickly as her numb fingers would allow. She stopped short of lifting away her damp linen shift. She'd have to be dead before she'd remove that.

"Will it be so insufferable, really?" A chuckle followed.

She turned in time to catch a magnificent view of his backside as he eased off his leggings by the light of the fire. She'd been so flustered she hadn't realized he would dare to remove the only article of his clothing which had promised a small—but very vital—degree of decency.

She nearly choked. There had to be terms to describe the acre of raw strength displayed before her, but she was too shocked to find the words in the tangled swirl of thoughts churning her mind in between the violent quaking that spun up her spine every few minutes.

He was still facing the fire. "I mean, we're both made of the same simple, God-given flesh, blood, and bone," he continued, then turned to catch her staring at him.

Mortified, she snapped her eyes shut and turned her head to pray for deliverance from . . . from . . . from something she could not remember for the life of her. *Sin*. That was surely part of it. She prayed for deliverance from something she knew far too little about.

Right. *The same simple, God-given flesh, blood, and bone.* Had he really suggested that drivel? Christ, this was going to cost him.

He raised the layers of bed coverings and eased his body close to hers. She flinched and scooted away. Her wet shift had to be removed and his patience was wearing thin.

"Easy, now," he whispered. Michael draped his heavy arm around her waist to trap her, and then lifted her garment over her head despite her choked words of protest. He pulled her into the heat of his body.

Christ, she was cold. And he would soon be burning up. He prayed for distraction. "Give me your hands," he murmured in her ear. He caught her icy fingers between his own and advanced his legs forward until he felt her feet. Opening his knees slightly, he urged her freezing limbs between his.

A long shiver snaked down her slim frame and a small strangled sound came from her before she swallowed it.

"It's all right, sweetheart. Here, get a little closer now . . . Let's try and get some sleep." He tried to cover a few more inches of her slender body with his own. "Don't worry, the worst is over." *For her.* The worst had just begun for him.

He felt her shaky exhalation, and a series of unsteady breaths followed for a long time before they formed a pattern. Apparently, she was too shocked or exhausted from the ordeal to say another word. Time passed and the tension finally drained from her.

He smiled, and finally nuzzled the back of her neck, reveling in the luscious, complex scent. Her skin was so soft here, as silky as the feathering of her hair, which gleamed silvery gold in the firelight.

He'd never beheld anyone like her—part prim shyness, part refined elegance, and all feminine mystery. What in God's name was a blue-blooded countess doing all alone in the back of beyond?

As her fingers became pliable, he transferred them to one hand and wrapped his other around her until his fingers cradled the soft curve of her hip.

He was certain he wouldn't sleep. Bloody hell. Well, his body might be reacting like any other male in creation capable of breathing, but he wasn't a damned lecherous bastard. He'd led a disciplined life due to necessity, and no one—no female—had ever shaken him from his simple, well-ordered world.

He forced himself a half inch away from her and thanked the stars above that she was asleep and could not feel his reaction to the soft essence of her body. He cursed the fate that had put her in his path, yet denied him someone of her ilk.

She was a goddamned *countess*.

And he was a blacksmith. And a farmer. A former lowly stablehand. Oh, and a *fugitive*, for Christ sakes.

Chapter 4

Grace awoke to the luxurious feeling of warmth. It was an anomaly. She had always tossed and turned at night, which inevitably led to the bedclothes ending up on the floor by first light, and nothing covering her other than her thin night rail. This morning, a thick layer of heavy blankets was tucked all around her naked form.

Last evening's events flooded her mind and she quickly turned her head to see if Mr. Ranier was still abed beside her. The impression of his head on the adjoining pillow confirmed her memories.

She turned onto her back and stretched, only to have a torrent of pain unleash under her breast. She stopped in mid-stretch and then remembered waking numerous times during the night.

She'd been amazed she'd been able to sleep at all. When she awoke each time, she'd been disoriented, until she heard his whispered, calming words. It had been the way of it all night. He'd kept up a steady flow of reassuring phrases, and insisted on keeping her close to him—to give her body the heat it so desperately needed.

Except that one time.

She'd woken much later because she was warm—overly warm, in fact. And he was finally asleep, his arms still binding her to him, possessively. And she had suddenly become aware that he was aroused. That part of him was pressing against her. She'd been thoroughly shocked, unaware that a man's body could do that in sleep, and more to the point, that a man could become quite that . . . well, that *intimidating*.

Oh, she was no virgin. John had regularly engaged in conjugal relations with her. It had made her feel very married, and secure, and content that she could offer this to her husband, who had delivered her from her former spartan existence on Mann, of which few of her friends knew. But John had always been apologetic about his needs, which had left her confused. She had wanted to please him, wanted to be proud. Yet his words had dimmed her womanly self-esteem.

Mr. Ranier had drawn in a series of short breaths, clearly in the midst of a dream, and unconsciously pressed himself against her. *What would it be like to* . . . As soon as she had the wicked thought, she tried without success to lock it out of her conscience with a vengeance. Unlike other ladies, she'd always been unsettled by the jovial, dashing young gentlemen parading in packs about London's entertainments.

Yes, ladies of her same age, especially several of her friends at the heart of a secret widows club, never failed to rise to the challenge of wordplay between the sexes. But where others were bold in words and actions, she was not. It just wasn't her nature.

A knot of pitch exploded in the fireplace, sending

a cascade of sparks up the flue, and Grace focused on the day at hand. She eased to a sitting position, pressed one hand to her injury and grimaced. Lord, could this last day have been any worse? Could this *month* get any worse?

Quite obviously, it could.

She wondered with additional discomfort if he had watched her sleep when he had risen and folded her garments, which now lay at the base of the bed. Well, she was not going to bear the distress of his returning to find her barren of clothes in this bed, no matter what sort of pain it would cost her. Clenching her teeth, she reached for her gown and noticed the bodice was damp but free of bloodstains. He had obviously cleaned the article, knowing it was the only one she possessed. She swallowed, her mortification complete. The fine lawn shift and corset were nowhere to be found, which was just as well since the latter was too painful to contemplate. Grace donned her gown as quickly as the injury allowed, and wrapped two shawls about her shoulders. Only her dearly familiar pearls reminded her of the opulent life that had been hers until yesterday. She never went anywhere without them for they were tangible proof of security and freedom from being dependent on anyone else ever again.

Before making her way downstairs she pulled aside the striped curtains to find the snow still falling, unchecked. Dear God . . . Mr. Brown. She sent up a prayer as she descended the stairs, hoping against hope that her elderly friend had somehow found shelter, and would not be so terrified for her safety that he would risk everything to find her.

At the bottom of the stairs, a small sitting room fronted the southern aspect of the dwelling. A small blue settee faced another blazing fire, and two intricately tooled chairs sat opposite each other. Oddly, every square inch of wall was covered with drawings and paintings, some framed, some not. Many were likenesses of furniture, of all things.

She turned, determined to locate the kitchen with the great hope of finding it deserted. She just could not face Mr. Ranier until she had had a little more time to order her thoughts. And tea would help. Dramatically. Nothing would provide more comfort to her than tea at this moment.

But it was not to be. For as soon as she found the kitchen in the back, the unmistakable sound of a door opening broke the silence. She whirled about to find Mr. Ranier's large, snowy figure ducking inside the room's low doorway moments later.

He straightened and looked down at her, his eyes flashing with amusement while he dusted off his hat. "Well, it appears countesses are not the fragile flowers I'd assumed." He removed his overly long, outer garment without the many capes of a gentleman's great coat.

"How are you feeling this morning, madam?"

Thank God he was preserving the illusion of propriety. His knowing expression, however, did the reverse.

Grace lowered her gaze. "Very well, Mr. Ranier. Thank you." She rushed on. "And I must be allowed to again tell you how grateful I am to you for coming to my aid yesterday. I realize now the grave danger I was in when you found me. I'm afraid I wasn't thinking very clearly. I'm so sorry for trespassing on your time and for all the trouble I've caused you."

His large strides ate up the distance between them. He raised one corner of his lips, and then he stripped away any and all notions of decency. "Sweetheart, troubles of your sort are always a pleasure." She dared to fully meet his laughing eyes, which were as pure and clear as the Irish whiskey Mr. Brown had favored on occasion.

"Come," he insisted, retrieving the pails he'd carried in. "Let's get you closer to the stove. Can't have you catching another chill. There's no tea or the sort of breakfast you are probably accustomed to, but I've cobbled together something."

The warm glow from the new-looking four-plate stove chased away winter's effects in the kitchen. A long wooden table with turned legs dominated the center of the cozy room.

He was a study in efficiency, heating milk from the pails and arranging a place for her at the end of the table nearest to the heat source. Within moments he retrieved crockery and honey from a larder.

She hated feeling so inadequate. Inadequate in so many ways, mostly to the necessary tasks that bespoke a purposeful life. But then, she knew the sensation over well. Since marrying the earl, it had crept up and become a common theme in her life. "May I help in any way?"

"No, no." Moments later, he poured a stream of hot milk into a bowl before her and ladled something into a second bowl. "I should warn you, we shall have to do for ourselves. The storm scared away most of the people employed here."

She leaned in. *Porridge.* Grace smothered a giggle. She hadn't had porridge since her girlhood on Mann. "This looks delicious," she murmured, meaning every word as the long-forgotten nutty scent reached her senses.

"I'm glad for there's a limited variety of goods in the larder." He moved the honey toward her and she dribbled the sweet concoction into her hot milk and porridge.

"I'm the last person to complain, Mr. Ranier." She had so many questions, she didn't know where to start. "Surely, I would be frozen under a hedgerow if not for you."

"Perhaps only half frozen." He grinned.

She sipped the fresh milk from the simple earthenware bowl. "So, where precisely are we? Is there a town or village nearby? Perhaps York?" she asked with great hope.

He shook his head, and she noticed the shadow of last night's beard was gone. "As far as I know, we're somewhere between Derbyshire and Yorkshire, about five miles from the nearest village and about three miles from a grand estate by the name of Beaulieu."

"So, this is an acquaintance's property? Not your own?" The man had ridiculously long eyelashes, she observed, as he glanced sideways at her. It was so incongruous, considering the harsh geometry of his features—all chiseled planes and angles.

"No, it's mine. Brynlow was recently left to me." He abruptly stopped.

A wave of sympathy wound 'round her and she changed the subject. "Do you suppose it will stop snowing soon?"

"Hard to say, precisely."

She began to tap her foot nervously. "Have you always lived in Yorkshire, then? You've an accent I'm not quite familiar with."

"You ask a lot of questions, Countess." He silently offered more steamed milk which she refused. "But not the right ones."

"What should I be asking?"

"Perhaps you should ask if your fingers were frost-bitten last night or how many days' worth of food are in the pantry."

She looked down, discomfort drenching her.

"Now don't look so frightened, Blue Eyes. I've enough cows, sheep, and chickens in the barns to keep us for a year or more. The pantry goods will only hold us for a week or so. But cheer up—the storm will let up long before then."

"One would hope," she said, trying to hide her ill ease. "I must ask if there is anything I can do to help. I've been nothing but a hindrance so far."

"No. You're to crawl back to bed after you finish here." He glanced at her fingers and captured one to examine it. His touch was sure and warm and he looked pleased by her hand's appearance. "You're very lucky. Do they tingle? If not, I'm thinking you'll keep these pretty fingers, every one."

She disengaged her hand from his, but felt very self-conscious and inadvertently knocked against the sticky honey pot, tilting it.

In a flash he righted it, then recaptured her hand to wipe her knuckles with a damp cloth. The action left her feeling like a helpless child. "Mr. Ranier, I'd prefer to sit in that cheery front room, if it is all the same to you—or to help you in some way."

"Sweetheart"—a slow smile graced his face—"I'm happy to examine your injury in there, or even here in the kitchen if you'd prefer. I'd just thought you'd be more at your ease above stairs."

She started. "The wound is healing perfectly. There's absolutely no need for you to trouble yourself. I promise to examine it most faithfully," she added quickly when she saw his features change. "*Hourly*, if need be."

His eyes crinkled in the corners from withheld mirth. "I'd no idea a widow could be quite so modest. The ones I've known never seemed to share your sensibilities. Quite to the contrary, actually."

Her patience deserted her in a rush. "That speaks volumes about the women you are acquainted with, Mr. Ranier." She stopped with horror. Had she really just insulted him in such an outrageous fashion? And after everything he had done to save her.

He tipped back his head and laughed. "You're entirely correct, Mrs. Sheffey. Now, come along. I see I've not a chance of herding you upstairs. I think we can postpone the examination for now, but I insist you rest. It'll take a day or two before you feel more the thing." He rose and collected his hat. "Well, I've much to do. There's a barn full of sheep to see to, not to mention the other animals, and I've but a wide-eyed lad of five and ten to assist me."

"Please allow me to help in some way," she pleaded softly, not rising.

He straightened and looked down to examine her appearance. "Such determination. Well then. Shall I count on you to start dinner after you rest a bit? But only if you are truly feeling up to it, Countess."

Her throat tightened in panic.

"I'll just retrieve the bit of mutton from the cold storage before I take my leave. The vegetables and flour are in the larder's bins—all good for a stew. I even spied a round of butter and apples if you favor a pie. I'll return with Timmy, say, 'round about two o'clock?"

"Of course," she managed to reply with what she hoped was a facsimile of a smile glued to her face.

He grinned, smoothed his wild dark mane of hair before donning his hat, and crossed the small room, only to turn back toward her. "Are you certain you're feeling well enough? You don't have to do this, you know. I could get it started in a trice."

"No, no. I'm perfectly fine."

He nodded once and was gone, with only the sound of presumably an entire mutton carcass being dropped inside the side entrance a few moments later.

Perfectly fine. Right. Perhaps it was time to strike those two words from her vocabulary.

Good old Sam. Michael couldn't believe his superior fortune as he looked over the barns and the animals within. There was just a tickle of disquiet lurking in his mind. Good fortune had never found its way to him, and so he distrusted it.

"That's the last of the water for the sheep, Timmy," Michael said to the lad, teetering on manhood, who stood beside him. "Let's see to the horses next."

"Yes, sir," the boy said with reverence and a bit of fear in his eyes.

Michael had tried to put the boy at ease upon meeting him, with little success. People were often in awe of his stature and did not easily forget him—not a good trait for someone attempting to blend in.

"Never heard such a din, Timmy. Are you certain English sheep don't make more noise than those in other parts of the world?" That finally brought a grin to the eager-eyed lad's face.

"No, sir."

"Well, my horse would beg to differ with you, I'm certain."

"She be a real goer, sir."

He leaned down conspiratorially. "It's a good thing you said so. I'll tell you a secret. Like all females, she responds well to compliments."

His eyes widened. "Yes, sir."

Michael clapped the young man on the shoulder and laughed. It was going to take some doing to extract conversation from the boy.

The tack room, which also housed the grain bins, was across from them, and Michael headed toward it. Just before opening the door, Michael spied Timmy out of the corner of his eye.

"No!" Michael's heart pumped frantically as the blood drained from his head. "Stop!" He spun and grabbed the pitchfork from Timmy's hands.

Timmy was now as terrified as Michael, his back against the stall door.

Michael tried to regulate his breathing. "I'm sorry. It's my fault. I should have explained how we shall go about it with the horses."

Timmy nodded, red-faced.

"I want you to always remove the horse from the stall first, before you muck it out. Then, fill the buckets before you return a horse to its stall. Is that understood?"

"Yes, sir."

"And I want to have a look at every lantern here before the day is done. No one is ever to leave one unattended."

"Of course, sir."

"Right. Now I'll see to the grain while you start with the plough team. I shall always see to Sioux, myself."

"Yes, sir."

"Oh, and Timmy?"

"Yes, sir?"

"You did an excellent job overseeing the animals by yourself yesterday. I don't know many men who could have maintained relative order with this large a group under one roof."

"Thank ye, Mr. Ranier."

Michael smiled at the boy and took a deep breath before he headed into the tack room.

His quick glance last night had been correct. Sam had left him a veritable windfall. Rows of well-tended leather goods decorated one long wall of the chamber.

Oiled bridles, saddles, girths, and harnesses draped from pegs while gleaming bits and other assorted metal goods hung nearby. The bins were free of dirt and filled to the brim.

A thorough inspection of the assorted side buildings revealed a well-stocked establishment for farming the land and breeding stock. It would take time to fully determine the merits of the horses, sheep, and cows, and to learn if the land was fertile, but hope filled his veins for the first time in many years. Sam had planned well, and Michael was filled with an aching gratitude for his childhood friend. Who would have guessed that kindness to a young boy would lead to this?

Michael opened Sioux's stall door, and the mare's large, supple neck swung toward him. She whinnied low, and nuzzled his side, searching. "You know it's there, sweetheart." A cloud of her exhaled breath surrounded him and he stroked the mare's shoulder. She retrieved the half carrot visible from his voluminous coat pocket and chomped on the treat. "Come along, now."

His mare dropped her head and followed him to the center aisle. Once she was in cross ties, Michael curried her flanks while Timmy cleaned the stall.

The peaceful sounds and smells of the barn soothed his spirit as they always did. It was more than good to be set free from the confines of that storm-tossed ship's cabin he'd endured for many weeks. If the rough crossing from England to the colonies all those years ago hadn't proved it to him, this last journey, aboard a Jamaican privateer's ship dodging the Royal Navy bent on war, certainly had. There was something about being trapped on a bobbing, creaking, leaking vessel with a fleet of English commanders hungry for promotion on your tail, or worse—a pirate hungry for bounty of any kind—that left the taste of bile in Michael's throat.

Whatever it was, he'd have to be trussed and chained before he'd leave solid ground again. He'd risked his life when he decided to return here, and he hoped he could eke out a simple existence. For this was surely the last, and only, opportunity he would ever be given on a platter.

He felt a sudden relief from the worries that had weighed on his mind for more than a decade and a half. He was finally in a place where he didn't have to spend half the day or night in the blasting heat of a furnace, while also trying to work and protect his meager strip of land from starving British or colonial troops bent on raiding. Trading his hardscrabble life for the risk of discovery in the dales between Derbyshire and Yorkshire seemed more than fair.

Methodically, Michael's mind ran through the rest of the chores that would have to be seen to today. Chickens, eggs, more milking, evening watering and feeding. And then, of course, there was the question of the mysterious, elegant lady inhabiting his new residence. He began to hum as he brushed out his horse's tail and thought about the strangely haunting beauty in Sam's manor.

It was painfully easy to sense she was hiding or running from something. He should know. She was as skittish as an unbroken yearling, and as prim as the spinster schoolmarm in the village nearest his tiny farm in Virginia. It was a good thing, too. He could not afford to dally with a woman of consequence, or really with any woman here, if he was honest with himself. It was just too damned dangerous. It would up the risk of exposure and might ruin his chance for a better life.

He lifted one of Sioux's forelegs, cleaned the hoof and examined the frog for rot. Satisfied, he started on the next hoof. He felt her warm muzzle nudge his backside and he smiled. Yes, the only females he was going to concern himself with, as soon as he could help the countess on her way, were the ones with four legs. This new home of his was not to include any sort of golden-haired beauty wearing pearls that were worth more than any property he would own.

His mare snorted with something that sounded remarkably like disapproval.

Michael stomped his snow-covered boots inside the side entry to the house and Timmy followed suit. The storm showed not a single sign of letting up. It was but a moment before the unmistakable scent of burnt stew assailed his nostrils.

He stayed Timmy's progress and set a finger to his own lips. "I trust you'll grin and bear it?"

The boy wrinkled his nose, shrugged, and nodded.

An alarmed protestation sounded from the kitchen, followed by the clatter of crockery. He made his way down the hallway.

Huge blue eyes flew to his as he paused at the doorway with Timmy. An enormous apron splattered with numerous stains was wrapped twice around her tiny waist, and flour dusted her arms and face.

"Mrs. Sheffey, allow me to present one of the best stable hands in the North Country, Mr. Timmy Lattimer. Timmy, Mrs. Sheffey." He had no intention of revealing her stature in society to anyone. There was too much at stake and he had no intention of tarnishing her reputation just because two people of differing sexes were forcibly stranded together for a short period.

Timmy tugged on his forelock and looked everywhere but the countess's face. "Ma'am."

"Mmmm," Michael murmured. "What is that delicious scent? I should warn you we're as hungry as two bears after a long winter."

She bit her soft lower lip and drew a fallen strand of hair away from her face. "Of course." Her voice held the beguiling, cultured musicality of an angel's.

"Come along, Timmy. Let's help Mrs. Sheffey by setting out the table goods." He filled Timmy's outstretched hands with dishes and cutlery and then loaded his own with a wheel of cheese and a large loaf of bread he spied, with relief.

He called out, "I hear tell that Yorkshire cheese is a delicacy not to be missed. Shall I toast a bit for the table?"

"Oh, please do," the lovely countess said, with something more than desperation in her voice.

He smiled. Toasting fork in hand, he speared a block of cheese and placed it before the fire, expertly turning and catching the melting sections with chunks of bread while she ladled stew from a pot and placed the shallow dishes on the table with ill ease.

Michael seated the countess and came around to his place across from her. He looked at the dish in front of him and it was all he could do not to make a sound. A glutinous quagmire of grayish matter was before him. He regarded the enticing platter of melted cheese and bread but for a moment before he resolutely picked up his spoon.

It not only resembled something one might find mired in a bog after a century, but he imagined it tasted like it too. It took a mountain's worth of determination to swallow a mouthful and to take another. "Delicious, Mrs. Sheffey," he rasped. "Absolutely delicious." He glanced at Timmy, whose face had turned as ashen as the color of the stew. His estimation of the boy's character was rising by the minute.

"Oh, please stop," she moaned. "It's revolting. No, worse. I beg you to stop eating this instant."

Timmy's spoon stopped in midair and he gratefully looked at Michael and replaced it in the morass of burnt stew. Michael silently offered the cheese and bread to Grace and Timmy before taking a portion for himself.

"Oh, I don't understand. I put everything in the pot as you said, the mutton, the flour, the carrots, and potatoes. I added some water and then put it over the fire. And, and—"

"And it's a rare cook who can turn out a meal in an unfamiliar kitchen." He clamped his lips to stop them from trembling with laughter.

"I had a difficult time carving the mutton, it was partially frozen."

"Of course."

"And I think I added a bit too much flour."

He nodded, his eyes smarting with held-back mirth.

"The vegetables seemed to melt after a few hours."

"It appears so." He offered the platter to her and to Timmy again before surreptitiously wolfing down three more pieces of cheese and bread.

"Oh stop it!" she said, her face drawn from fatigue. "Go ahead, and say it. I'm useless. I'm so sorry I made such a horrid meal and a huge mess in the process."

"That's all right, ma'am," Timmy spoke up. "Me mum always makes one o' us clean the pots after dinner, and that's nothing I haven't seen afore wot with seven brothers and sisters tryin' their hands at the cookin'." His accent was poor, but Timmy's heart was rich, and that counted more than anything at that instant.

At that exact same moment Michael noticed a pattern of blood seeping through the front of the countess's gown. He abruptly stood. "Thank you, Timmy. I'll join you for evening chores in a bit."

"No need, sir. The barn looks better than it 'as in months. I can do the milkin'." Pride laced Timmy's plain words.

Michael nodded and offered his arm to the countess. "May I beg a moment of your time in the front salon? Straightaway?"

She looked up at him, her face pale and her eyes reflecting the edge of pain in their deceptive blue depths. "Of course."

As soon as he had escorted her past the kitchen door, he scooped her up into his arms and headed for the stairs.

"What are you doing? Put me down, Mr. Ranier!"

"You know, I think this is becoming a habit. Not that I'm complaining, mind you."

"I don't see why you feel the need to—to carry me about like some sort of child. I was disentangled from leading strings more than two decades ago!"

He bounded up the last of the steps, taking care not to jar her. He kicked the bedchamber door shut with his boot heel. "I know, sweetheart, I know. But humor me, will you?" He glanced at the jumble of the unmade bed and placed her in the padded leather armchair next to the fire, which had gone out.

"I meant to straighten everything, but there wasn't time," she said, defeated.

"Never seen the point of it, really," he lied, yet again. "It only becomes undone." He flashed a grin toward her.

With a few quick movements, Michael expertly arranged the linens and placed her in the middle of the large bed, completely ignoring her pleas to stop carrying her about.

He met her annoyed gaze and glanced pointedly toward her bodice. She looked down and inhaled sharply.

"So," he said and stopped.

"So," she replied. "You will leave me and I will bind

my . . . the *area* with greater care. The bandage has evidently slipped."

"Evidently."

"Yes."

"Look, sweetheart, if you think for a moment that I'm not going to take a look—right now—then you're a greater fool than I would take you for." He put up a hand when he saw her open her mouth to disagree. "No, it's no use. Now you can either voluntarily submit, or we can do it the other way."

"And what way is that, Mr. Ranier?" she asked sourly. "Are you threatening me with a twitch?"

"Something like that."

"Really?"

"Actually, I was thinking more along the lines of tying you up like a calf before we snip off its, ah—well, you get the idea." He stopped and chuckled, unable to continue after spying the look of horror in her eyes.

"You wouldn't dare," she breathed.

Silence was his answer.

"Well!" She narrowed her eyes.

"Look, angel, it's not like I haven't seen you naked as a jaybird already."

She sputtered and tried to rise but his hand on her shoulder stopped her.

"All right, all right. My apologies." He wasn't sure what it was about her, but he couldn't stop himself from uttering completely outrageous things around her. It might have been because he enjoyed seeing a spark of fire to her otherwise cool expression. When annoyance filled her, her eyes became as vibrant as the bluebells in Virginia on a clear spring morning.

"So . . ." He drawled the word expectantly.

"So . . . what?" She asked with a measure of exasperation.

"We're back to waiting for you to unbutton your gown," he replied. "Would you like me to help?"

Her eyes flared with panic. "Absolutely not! Oh, for goodness sakes, allow me some degree of privacy."

"Of course, Mrs. Sheffey." He set about stacking wood in the grate and restarting the fire while he heard the unmistakable rustling of a woman undressing behind him.

It was ironic, he thought with a grin. In the colonies, he'd taken great care not to overly entangle himself where it concerned women. For some godforsaken reason he couldn't figure, almost all of them, wide-eyed virgins to lazy-eyed harlots, were attracted to him like moths to a flame. The more experienced, daring ones had fluttered toward his blacksmithing furnace in the heat of the night, and he'd sometimes given pleasure and taken it in return. Never with a promise of anything more. But in the end, he'd learned it wasn't worth the corporal relief. For invariably, they wished for a future with him and became overwrought when dreams were denied. And so he'd learned to employ every evasive trick imaginable to sidestep advances.

It was probably for that reason that Michael took such pleasure in wearing down the countess's defenses with humor. It warmed his soul to watch this tiny, soft package of femininity wrestle with him over the notion of decorum.

He poured water into a basin on the washstand, and then turned to find her under a hill of blankets, her face turned away from him.

The floorboards creaked under his measured strides and she inched the covers higher.

He stared down at her even, refined profile resting against the pillow. A pulse fluttered frantically along the delicate column of her neck. He uncovered her as gently as possible and found her arms rigid at her sides.

"Two of the stitches have come loose." He grasped a wet cloth and squeezed the excess water from it to dab the injury. "But at least it isn't festering."

Her eyes clenched shut. She was using every effort to remain silent. He glanced fully at her beautiful torso, and felt like the worst sort of peeping sinner. It was just that he'd never seen one like her—so perfectly proportioned and angelic, so ethereal and pure. She was more beautiful than he remembered from last night.

Her breast would fit in the cup of his hand, and he had an irrational desire to test the contemptible thought. "It's no wonder this happened," he continued on an exhalation, "what with all your efforts downstairs."

She said not a word.

The devil on his shoulder reminded him she was a rich, pampered widow whose aristocratic husband had probably purchased and swaddled her in those long strands of pearls pooling in the hollows of her neck. The good earl had obviously followed the tradition of many peers of the realm by consecrating his wife's body with his own and then marking his exclusive use with jewels from the vast family coffers. This was an elegant woman who expected everything in life, while Michael was a coarse rotter who was content if he could just fill his perpetually empty belly and survive. They were as alike as those lustrous pearls of hers to dross.

"I don't think you need new stitches, provided, of course, you promise to spend tomorrow in this bed."

"Anything," she said tightly. All at once she turned her head and opened her eyes, which were shiny with withheld tears.

The devil in him withered away at the sight of her obvious pain and it nearly broke his heart. "Oh sweetheart . . ."

Her expression changed to horror. "Don't look at me like that," she whispered.

His gut twisted with guilt. She'd obviously witnessed his raw male response to her beauty. "Sorry."

"You don't appear sorry at all." She covered her breasts with her slim hands.

"I *am* sorry, sweetheart. But all men are scoundrels. Didn't the earl warn you?"

Her eyes flared again but this time with uncertainty. "What on earth are you talking about?"

"What are *you* talking about?"

"No," she replied. "The person wearing the clothes should have to answer first."

He dragged a hand through his hair. "Hold off. I should see to a new bandage." Perhaps there would be something on the shelves. That would buy him a few moments to gather his wits.

With little thought, he ripped a frayed sheet he

found into long strips. "All right then, let's get this out of the way. Can you sit up? Here, let me help you."

Before she could reply, he gritted his teeth and dug his arm under her tiny waist and dragged her into a sitting position. Her head fell into the crook of his arm, and she was forced to drop her hands from her breasts as he draped her lower body with a blanket. He knelt in front of her and found himself inches away from her heavenly, creamy flesh.

A little trickle of blood slipped past her ribs, and he grabbed the cloth to stop the flow.

"I can do that," she said.

"Good." His voice sounded hoarse to his own ears.

He anchored the bandage on her lowest rib, and continued to wind the white flannel upwards. "Raise your arms now," he gritted out.

She inhaled, and God help him, she followed his directions. The faintest note of her heady, expensive scent reached his nose and resonated in his sensually starved mind. The lovely tips of her breasts tightened right in front of him and his groin followed suit to a painful degree.

Michael placed an extra bit of padding over the wound and continued binding the injury, inadvertently brushing one breast in his haste.

She made a sound of distress.

"Sorry," he bit out.

The moment he tucked in the end of the cloth, she dropped her arms and wrapped one of her shawls about herself.

"Thank you," she said with a small degree of desolation in her words.

An awkward silence filled the room as he stood and moved the basin.

"I shall leave you to your rest," he said.

"No."

He turned back from the doorway. "I beg your pardon?"

"I said, no."

He returned to her bedside.

"You didn't answer my question."

"And which one was that, sweetheart?" He had a sinking feeling.

"Why did you say all men are scoundrels?"

Hell. "Sorry, Countess, I should've held my tongue."

"As long as it wasn't about pity, I don't really care what you meant."

"Pity?" He looked at her amazed. "Why would I pity you? Certainly, you're hurt. But you'll heal. And the snow will melt and you'll be on your way soon enough."

She was scrutinizing his face as if she doubted his words. "I'm something of an expert at recognizing that expression. I saw little else in London. And when you looked at me before, I read it all over your face."

"And why is pity so very bad, sweetheart? There were some times in my life when I would have welcomed compassion."

"Well, I *loathe* it." Her voice hissed with tamped-down emotion.

He waited for her to continue.

"I've found pity is always tinged with hidden glee in the other person's misfortunes."

He raised a brow. "And what great misfortune have you suffered, Countess? Your husband's death, is it? I find it hard to believe that anyone would be so cold-hearted as to take pleasure in that."

"No, of course not. But you have quite cleverly changed the subject, Mr. Ranier. We were talking about you, not me."

"Really?"

"Yes. If you were not looking at me with pity then what was it?"

"You know, if you cannot figure it out, Blue Eyes, I think it would be best for both of us if we just forget all about it."

"It's all right, Mr. Ranier. You can tell me. I already know there is something about me that deters gentlemen when it comes to the point." She had looked away from his face. "But actually, you would do me a great favor if you could explain it fully to me. I mean, as you said, the snow will soon melt and I will take my leave of you. And I doubt I'll have such an opportunity again for brutal honesty, and a full assessment of my flaws."

What on earth? Her flaws? He looked at her exquisite profile for long moments, dumbstruck. He shook his head slowly, but knew without question that this bizarre query had come from somewhere far beyond the elegant countenance she presented to the world. She had forced the words into the air, exposing a great vulnerability. But it was just plain ludicrous . . . "Your faults, eh?" He scratched his jaw. "Well, darling, if you're looking for brutal honesty, the only one I can see is perhaps, just perhaps, mind you, you could learn a thing or two about cooking."

She raised her eyes to his slowly. "Do not patronize me." Her gaze held such pain he nearly fell back.

"What happened to you, Countess? Who put the idea in that pretty head of yours that there was the slightest thing wrong with you? If it was the earl, I'd be happy to dig up his carcass and brand an *S* on his forehead for stupidity."

She gaped at him. "Do you know the Duke of Helston?"

That was not what he was expecting. "Who in hell is he? Blacksmiths don't exactly rub along with nobs. Is he the blackguard who put these ideas in your head?"

"No, it's just that the duke and his friends often like to describe inventive methods of torture."

"Now look who's changing the subject," he said after a long silence.

She plucked at the twisted sheet. "Look, you don't have to be kind. I just want your opinion. It would also help if you would give me a blunt perspective on the qualities gentlemen are most attracted to in a lady."

"How can I give you my perspective without knowing what we're talking about?"

She rolled her eyes. "You are worse than the Duke of Helston's grandmother, and she's something of an expert when it comes to evading questions."

"If you want an honest assessment, sweetheart, then I'll give it to you. But fair is fair. I want to know what has happened to make you come to these" —*asinine*— "uh, *interesting* conclusions." He disengaged her small hand from the material.

She seemed to have come to some sort of decision as she took a deep breath and began to speak quickly.

"Two gentlemen cried off from marrying me in the last twelve months. Both fell in love with other ladies—both good friends of mine—actually, the best of friends. I'm very happy for them, really. I don't want you to get the wrong idea. It was for the best, I know. I'm much better off the way it is. It's just that these gentlemen . . ."

"Go on," he encouraged, while the word *idiots* took up residence in his mind.

"It's just that they were very different from each other. One was a brilliant, powerful duke, a former commander in the Royal Navy with a fiery temper. And the other was a cool-headed diplomat . . ."

"And?"

"And I thought they'd be attracted to very different ladies. But they were not. Actually . . ."

He waited.

"Actually, I had thought I was similar to my friends. But, recently . . . very recently, I've come to realize I am very different from them."

"The difference being?" *That you are the most beautiful, gentle, good-hearted angel on this godforsaken earth.*

"I don't want to say. I don't want to influence your opinion. I, I want to know if you can sense it."

"You know, I'm no good at flowery compliments. I can tell you the good points on a ewe or a mare but probably not on a woman. But that doesn't matter. I don't think compliments will drive out whatever it is that makes you think there's something wrong with you, will they?"

"No."

"All right, then I'll tell you what I think."

She looked at him expectantly.

"All females base their worth on their desirability to the other sex."

She pondered the thought. "Yes, for the most part, you're probably right."

"But men base their worth on what?"

"I don't know."

"Yes, you do. Think about it. They base it on their fortune and station in life, which is more realistic."

"So?"

"So, perhaps you should start thinking like a man, sweetheart."

Her face drained of all color. "Are you telling me my desirability lies solely in my fortune?"

"No. I'm telling you that your true worth is not based on your ability to attract a gentleman. And by the by, you seem to draw in those lordly sorts well enough. You've had two offers in the last year and now there's this damned Brown fellow, although he seems to be somewhat wanting in brains and good character, if you ask me."

She pulled her hand from his.

"Well, I can see I haven't helped you. But then again, you should know better than to trust anyone, sweetheart. The sooner you learn not to count on anyone, be it a gentleman or not—the sooner you'll stop wasting your time with these confounded questions. It's like I told you. All men are scoundrels."

He had said it deliberately. He knew that no amount of sense would dispel the doubts she had about her allure. In fact, there was only one sort of man who could help her, and he didn't have the gold lining his pockets to do it. Clear, rational thought ruled him, and the pronouncements of a blacksmith would not make a lick of difference in allaying her convictions.

The paleness of her face proved she had withdrawn from the conversation, and he was glad.

"Mr. Ranier, I want to know how long it will be before I can get word to my traveling companion. And no, I don't want to hear that that isn't the right question. I just require your best guess."

Michael had a deep desire to darken the daylights out of Grace Sheffey's companion, whoever the dog was. "Missing him, are you?"

"Do you always answer a question with one of your own?"

"Only when I'd prefer a different question," he replied. "Sweetheart, I'm sorry the conditions are not what you're used to, but we're stuck until the roads are passable, so let's make the best of it."

"No, Mr. Ranier, you misunderstand . . . I appreciate—"

He didn't hear the rest of her words for he had already left, bounding down the stairs, grabbing his coat to return to the life he knew . . . in the stables, surrounded by animals, the creatures who had brought him more comfort than any person ever would. . .

Until the following day, when he found the heart-wrenching efforts Grace Sheffey had expended on him.

Chapter 5

G race woke the following morning to find another steaming bowl of milk and porridge with honey on a tray beside her. Shame filled her. After a lifetime of repressing every last provocative thought, she was possessed with equal parts horror and embarrassment over what she had revealed last night to a man who was so purely masculine, so purely distilled capable male that he made her feel like an awkward young girl all the time.

She tried to be kind to herself. Surely, what could one expect after sustaining the death of a husband, two failed engagements, one carriage accident, an injury and nearly freezing to death under a hemlock tree?

Well. She could not stay in this bed all day with these morose thoughts. But she wouldn't risk further injury, for she could not suffer more scrutiny by Mr. Ranier. She spied her torn fine lawn shift folded on the end of the bed, as well as her ruined corset. Thoughts of his large, capable hands washing these intimate garments brought only more mortification. It seemed she was to be stripped bare of every last dignity.

And then an idea came to her as she finished the porridge. A wonderful, calming idea. The former owner—or the housekeeper—must have some sort of sewing basket. A short search produced the well-stocked basket, and much more.

Six hours later, she was surrounded by stacks of mended goods, her own and those of the other occupant of the house. It was the only way she could think of to show her gratitude. Timmy Lattimer had interrupted twice, first with a delicious, simple dinner tray of roast mutton with potatoes and carrots, and the second time with a small hammered-copper hip bath and three pails of hot water.

"Mr. Ranier said ye might fancy this ma'am." Timmy had blushed to the roots of his black hair.

She couldn't think of anything she wanted more. "Thank you, Timmy. Thank you ever so much. And, ah, where is Mr. Ranier?" She couldn't stop the question from tumbling from her lips.

Now the boy was adding more wood to the fire, sending a shower of sparks up the chimney. "In the barn. One o' the ewes has gone and started birthin' early."

"Really . . ."

"Yes, and he's got his hands full of her now." The boy's face turned a shade of crimson when he realized what he had blurted out. "I mean, he'll pull the young 'un out soon. It's a good thing Mr. Ranier's got so much experience with those animals he tended in the colonies."

So that's where Michael Ranier was from. That was the elusive accent she sometimes heard. "You're very right, Timmy. So how does Mr. Ranier know the former owner of Brynlow?"

The boy gave her a measured glance before continuing quietly, "Well, the ways I understand it from me pa is that Mr. Bryn met Mr. Ranier in town."

"So he was from London originally?" she tried to keep her voice light.

"Mr. Bryn was in a foundling home there afore 'e was taken in by that fancy furniture maker and his wife. That's how 'e came by this place." He swung a glance toward the door. "Mr. Bryn used to tell me how lucky I was to have me ma and pa like the ones he got late in life. Uh, ma'am? It's been a long day. I think I'll see to heatin' Mr. Ranier's bathwater now. I'll fetch the tub in a half hour if that suits ye, ma'am."

Well, she'd drawn more information from Timmy Lattimer than she would have extracted from a month of Sundays with Mr. Ranier. She wondered if Michael Ranier had been an orphan too and met Mr. Bryn at the foundling home. It would explain his reticence about revealing his past. All of it made her want to bury her head in shame. How dare she feel sorry for herself. She only wished she knew if her assumptions were true or not.

She pondered when and why he had gone to the colonies as she took advantage of the hip bath. True luxury, she decided a short time later, was hot water sluicing away the thick froth of country soap she had lathered over every square inch of her body, taking care with her injury. She'd even washed her hair, luxuriating in the simple, clean scent.

With a sigh, Grace combed the last of the tangles before the fire, and then gathered up the mended garments. She stood at the doorway, listening for any telltale sounds. When a rush of water echoed from the lower level of the house, Grace tiptoed down the hall to return Michael Ranier's articles to his finely turned bureau, crafted by Mr. Bryn's company, at first guess.

Grace returned to her room, now deliciously relaxed from the bath, and her fingers less stiff from the needlework. She was gloriously at peace, taking comfort in the industriousness of the day. She'd even forgiven herself for her lack of restraint the evening before.

She had but to face Mr. Ranier one time to beg his forgiveness for plaguing him with her outrageous questions, before she would put it all behind her. And now that the snow had stopped falling . . . Well, all would be right in her world soon. One long prayer of hope for Mr. Brown's safety followed by one short one thankful of her blessings, and she fell asleep . . . blissfully asleep.

Grace woke three times that night. The first time, she was alone, shivering, the bedcovers lost in a deep puddle on the floor, where she had to retrieve them as usual. She was plagued by strange dreams of her last fiancé, the Marquis of Ellesmere, on one knee begging her forgiveness while her dear friend Georgiana, his bride, whispered something to their other friend, Rosamunde, beside her. The Duke of Helston made up the group, along with Ata and Mr. Brown. They all rushed toward her, a flood of pity unleashed on their faces, and she began to run. She ran so far and so fast that she was back on the Isle of Mann, running on the high cliffs, dangerously close to the edge and not really caring.

The second time she woke, Grace heard the door close and noticed the fire revived and crackling in the grate. She was freezing, but oddly enough the bedcovers surrounded her. She was so tired of always being cold.

The third time she was roused from her horrid dreams, she was hotter than the fires of Hades. A mountain of hard flesh surrounded one side of her, and all reason was lost.

There was not a chance of sleep now. And so she lay awake, drinking in the delicious heat of Mr. Ranier, and praying he would not wake up and initiate a conversation. Silence, indeed, was her consolation.

His heavy arm shifted under her, and suddenly, inexorably, he was turning and pulling her closer, face to face, into the cradle of his body. His lips pressed against her temple; the bristle of his bearded face sanding her cheek.

"Sweetheart . . ." he murmured on an exhale.

She stiffened.

And then he fell back into the grip of slumber. Grace knew this because she heard the long, slow catch in his breathing.

She was now trapped in his solid embrace, her mind spinning with that provocative male scent of his. Her one hand was caught between their two bodies, but her other had involuntarily come to rest on the long line of his hip when he had pulled her to him.

She had never touched a man's naked body really. Each time John Sheffey had come to her chamber, he'd extinguished the candle, popped under the covers and raised her night rail to her hips before positioning himself between her limbs, taking care to touch her only where it was absolutely necessary. In the four months of her marriage, she'd never touched John's bare body. She had always lain on her back, her arms at her sides, as she assumed other wives did.

Grace's one hand, resting over Michael Ranier's heart, rose and fell ever so slightly with the regular, strong pumping beat below the thick layers of muscle. His hard flesh was devoid of the patches of hair her husband had had. Mr. Ranier's breathing continued, even and slow, and she finally relaxed. Relaxed so much that she tentatively circled one fingertip on his chest and realized the difference in texture was that she'd encountered a flat male nipple. His skin was softer there, and yet such power rested below in the sinuous network of muscles and bone.

A large brand of rigid flesh jerked against her hip and jarred her to her senses. *Oh God, oh God, oh God . . . Oh, please let him fall back asleep.*

"Darling," he rasped, his voice filled with gravel, "are you trying to take advantage of me?"

"Pardon me?" She frantically tried to think of a plausible excuse.

"Perhaps that's why those other idiots rejected you. You're too fast by half. By God, Countess, I've only known you a day or so, and here you are trying to seduce me . . . Brazen is what you are."

Dear Lord, he was laughing at her. "I'm nothing of the sort. You just pulled me into your arms, and—and I didn't give you permission to enter this bed."

"You're making it damned difficult to keep the chill off you, sweetheart."

"I'm perfectly capable of keeping myself warm."

"Is that so? I beg to differ. You moan in your sleep and wake me every hour on the hour. And each time I come to look in on you, the blankets are on the floor. I was getting tired of being roused from my bed."

"Don't you ever wear a nightshirt?"

He chuckled. "No."

She didn't know what to do with her hands so she tried to lower the one that was trapped between them and he groaned.

"Look," he said, putting more space between them, "since it appears I won't get another lick of sleep, perhaps now would be a good time for you tell me more about your Mr. Brown or . . . "

"Or what?" she whispered.

He lowered his lips, leaving a whisper of space between them. "Or tell me exactly what you plan to do to me."

She inhaled.

"I find detailing every touch in advance always heightens the pleasure, don't you?"

She exhaled roughly and tried to pull away, which he would not allow. Grace prayed for rational thought. "Mr. Brown is—"

"Good," he cut in, "I was afraid you wouldn't come to your senses. Continue."

"Mr. Brown is one of the most wonderful gentlemen in this world. He is witty, and kind, and—"

"Rich and handsome?"

She stifled nervous laughter at his assumptions. But if this thread of conversation could place a measure of decorum between them, she would grab it. "Not handsome in a conventional way, but I think that makes him even more interesting."

He snorted. "Stop. I've changed my mind. I don't want to hear any more about Brown. He was a fool for leaving you defenseless and alone."

She could not think of a single retort.

"I'm just pointing this out so you don't travel another inch of road with this fellow without taking a brawny carriage driver who has more chivalry in his little finger than that gentleman fop has in his entire white-livered hide."

She smiled to herself. "All right."

"What, no argument? I hadn't known you to be so biddable."

"I have my good points."

The bedcovers rustled again and she felt the warmth of his large hand brush past her shoulder to rest on her bandaged rib cage and then lower. His palm seemed to envelope her entire hip and she could barely breathe.

"By the by, Countess, I must thank you."

"For what?" she whispered.

"For mending every last article of my clothing. I'm not fond of darning and have put it off for months. You did me a great favor, and I must say you are a fine seamstress."

It had been so long since she had felt the warm glow of pride, and his simple words pleased her more than any of the false compliments she had heard over the years. "I'm so glad I could do something for you after everything you have done for me," she whispered.

He rested his chin on the top of her brow, and his deep voice rumbled through her. "I've been dreaming of you."

"An effect of the burnt stew, surely. Probably causes naught but nightmares," she said nervously.

Grace was certain he would change the subject because he remained silent for a few moments.

"I dream I'm riding toward an apple orchard in paradise."

She swallowed, unable to make her mouth work.

He brushed a wisp of hair from her face. "And you're lying under one of the trees, a book in one hand, an apple in the other—lost in thought . . . but obviously waiting."

"Stop. I've heard this story before."

"Really?"

"This is when Eve is in league with the snake and tempts Adam."

She had managed to put even more space between them, and chose this moment to try and brush his hand from her hip. In doing so, her fingers slid past his groin and touched . . . *Good Lord.*

He made a pained sound in his throat. "For the love of Christ, woman . . ." His words were but the merest rasp of a whisper. His teeth gritted together, "Tempt me again or tell me I am a callous ox. Remind me you are hurt or that you're in love with that stupid

Brown fellow. But for Christ sakes, sweetheart, do something—anything—before I'm forced to jump out the window and wallow in the snow."

Her hand had stopped, paralyzed when she brushed against his staggering arousal. She knew, without a single doubt then, that he would not caress her without her unconditional absolution, which made her position all the more difficult.

Intuitively, she knew she was being given the chance to learn the answers to some of the sinful questions that had bedeviled her. Once she left this stranger's hidden corner of Christendom, those answers might never be found.

Yet, it would be so much easier if he hadn't thrown down the gauntlet and allowed her a choice. She had thought he might just lower his lips to meet her own and she would passively accept what he did to her. Just as she had done in her marital bed. And then she would finally understand what relations would be like with a man who was not elderly or ill—a man whose virility was unequalled and whose plain, bald words she trusted more than any of the eloquent witticisms she'd heard in town.

Oh, this was all wrong. It was sinful.

What was she supposed to do? She certainly could not put into words that she might welcome this. It was just too far beyond the propriety that had been instilled in her since the day she was born.

It was then she noticed his colossal frame was shaking. From the sharp exhalation of warm breath on her shoulder, it appeared he was in pain. And abruptly, she threw off all the many layers of modest decorum that had always bound her. "I'm sorry if I hurt you when I touched . . . Well then." Mortified, she stopped, raised her chin a fraction of an inch, and kissed him chastely—just the merest brush of lips against stubbled cheek.

It was, quite possibly, the most daring thing Grace Sheffey had done in her entire life.

"Oh sweetheart," he murmured roughly. He pulled her back into the heat of his body and nuzzled her neck, sending little shivers of tension down her body. His presence was overwhelming. She felt like a mouse caught between the huge padded paws of a lion whose soft fur surrounded her face while he sniffed her, trying to decide how best to enjoy the morsel before him.

The barest edge of his teeth nibbled the column of her neck until he reached her mouth. He paused, the tension unbearable.

In the flicker of the firelight, he was staring at her, his amber eyes grown dark, almost black in their intensity. "Are you certain?"

She nodded once, very slightly.

"I must warn you I'm not like those chivalrous fops who would stop at the first sign of hesitation—or the ones who make promises. I'm not that sort of man. And I don't fancy morning regrets or tears, mind you."

"For someone who gave the impression you might welcome this," she said quietly, "it appears you are doing everything you possibly can to change my mind. I assure you I harbor no expectations, and I won't have hurt feelings if you don't want to . . . " she inhaled, "to . . . In fact, I'm quite used to stopping or reneging or whatever you call it." She pushed against his wall of a chest. "I told you I have that effect on gentlemen, so I'm inured to it."

"Really?" He tightened his massive arms around her again and allowed his heavy arousal to fully fall across her thighs. "Dolts. Complete dolts, the lot of them, if that Brown is any example." He lowered his lips to hers with infinite care and . . . and she was lost in a whirlpool of heat. Heat like the flames licking from the fireplace. And if she had thought she was hot then, a moment later, she felt like the center of the sun.

This was not the kiss of a gentleman. It was not respectful or chaste or decent. It was molten and lush and harsh.

And Grace loved every moment of it.

She nearly fainted when he drew his tongue along the seam of her closed mouth and dared to part her lips. It was such an invasion. This man was pushing her to touch, to taste, to breathe in every inch of him. His lingering scent, that pine and supremely masculine essence of him lay beyond the scent of the soap he had used. He tasted of everything forbidden. He tasted of man.

And every so often, just when she was losing her head and falling, falling, he would murmur a word or two into her ear, the rumble passing from his chest to hers, and she would be brought back to the startling reality of the moment.

She was somewhere in the dales between Derbyshire and Yorkshire, lost in a stranger's powerful arms, her reticence melting in the face of such wanting.

"Mmm," he purred. "That's it, sweetheart. Touch me."

She realized she was stroking his immense shoulder while he rained kisses all over her face.

"I've spent hours wondering if . . ." His mouth drifted to the hollow of her neck. " . . . if you are softer here," he trailed lower, " . . . or here."

He eased himself on top of her, keeping his weight on his forearms, and then lowered the edge of the bandage to kiss the top of her breast, shockingly close to the ruched, sensitive tip.

"But then," he murmured, "there are a few other choices to consider . . . perhaps a bit later."

She had no earthly idea what he was talking about, but then he moved his mouth a fraction of an inch, to her nipple, and she could not make sense of a single thing he uttered.

Her pent-up breath left her in a rush as he dragged his large hand across her breast while he tugged the tip of the other between his lips in a motion that released a deep pull of longing within.

"Tell me if I hurt your injury," he insisted.

The almost unbearably sweet pain of desire rushed through her, and she gripped his shoulders unconsciously. She just could not believe this was happening to her, and she had the absurd urge to laugh when she looked down to see the long sweep of dark lashes splashed on his face as he reverently suckled her. She'd never imagined a man would want to do that. As if he could read her thoughts, he glanced up at her, his mouth on her flesh, and slowly winked.

She stopped breathing when he did something sinful with his tongue.

Oh God. She just wasn't prepared for this. For one thing, she didn't know what to do with her hands. For another, she was scared she would not be able to keep her voice clogged in her throat. Oh, what he was doing to her.

He reached for her palm, then pressed his lips to it, allowing cold air to touch the peak of her well-kissed breast. "Talk to me, sweetheart. Tell me what you like, what you want me to do to you."

Oh, she could not do this. She couldn't stop the trembling in her throat. "I don't know what you mean. Don't you know what to do?"

The deep rumble of laughter echoed from him. "Darling, there are just too many options." He lazily trailed his tongue around the tip of her breast. He looked up. "Won't you help me narrow the possibilities?"

"No," she whispered, wishing but far too shy to ask about the possibilities.

He grinned at her. "Well, then we'll just have to explore them all." He had rolled to the side and was now stroking his hand down the dale between her breasts, past the bandage, all the way to her navel. Her sensitive skin registered the rough calluses of his palms and she shuddered. And suddenly his fingers were sliding lower, perilously close to the jointure of her body. She stiffened.

"Mmmm . . . You're as soft as a kitten here," he mused, tangling his fingers in the sparse blonde hairs.

Grace had always known she was physically different from other ladies. On several occasions she had seen hints of the lush womanly virtues of her friends in the secret club. The other ladies were more voluptuous than she, had dark thatches of hair in their most intimate places, where she was nearly bare. She clamped her legs together at the thought.

A large warm hand closed over one of her own, now frozen on his shoulder. He brought it to his lips and then returned it to below his chest. The hard planes of his abdomen were sleek and molded like silk over iron. Her hand trembled and she couldn't make it stay still.

"Sweetheart . . ." His voice rumbled like a purring lion.

"Yes?"

"You're not a virgin by any chance, are you?"

"Of course not. I told you I'm a widow."

"Just wanted to be sure." His hand stroked from her hip to the side of her breast and back down. "You're awfully quiet. And still."

She rolled away from him and curled to her side. "I should have warned you I'm not very good at this."

Silence invaded the room. She felt like crying. She just was not like other women. She never had been and she never would be.

And then the bed covers lifted slightly and his body settled along her back as he found her hand. "Just how long were you married?"

"About four months."

"Only? And were you happy with this fellow? Tell me about him. Was he anything like this Mr. Brown?"

"I was very happy. My husband was a wonderful, kindhearted man."

"Hmmm."

"What is that supposed to mean?"

"Well, sweetheart, I'm trying to figure why you think you're no good at this."

"I think it's a bit obvious. I mean . . . well, look at us. Nothing's going to happen now. I've ruined the moment. I've none of the natural passion required. Cannot inspire it, either." She forced herself to continue. "I once spied a newly married couple—good friends of mine, actually. And it was stark daylight, and . . ."

"And?"

"And there was a billiards table . . ."

He chuckled. "And?"

"And it was scandalous, what they were doing."

"And?"

"And," she swallowed. "I could never do that."

"I see."

He released her hand and she felt the softest brush of his fingers stroking her head.

"What are you thinking?" she asked, unable to stop herself from asking.

"Well, I'm thinking"—he grinned—"I'm glad Sam didn't install a billiards table here. Ah, sweetheart, let me put a small part of your fears to rest."

She didn't move, still curled away from him.

"Will you turn around?"

When he tugged at her waist, she slowly complied.

He urged her closer. "That part about not being good at this? The part about not being capable of inspiring passion?"

She finally dared to meet his gaze.

"Well, it's just not so." He brought her hand to his groin, and she was overwhelmed by his shocking size.

He made a sound deep in his throat as if he was in pain. "The thing is, a man can't pretend interest like a woman. I think you can safely forget all that nonsense about not inspiring a man now, can't you? But sweetheart, you need to tell me if I can keep touching you, if you'll allow me the privilege. If you don't feel passion, that's my fault, not yours. Let me try a bit harder, will you?"

She was too afraid that if she spoke she wouldn't be able to keep the wobble of emotion from her voice, and so she whispered just two words. "All right."

"Well then . . . you'd best turn your back to me again. Otherwise, if you keep your hand where it is, I'm going to be more embarrassed than you."

His words formed the smallest sliver of warm pride inside her as she complied, unsure of his assertion. His lips nuzzled her ear while his hands slid over the rise of her hips, then lower to the edge of her most intimate place. She bit her lower lip.

"You know, I was right. I was sure this was going to be the softest place on you. Like spun silk."

Grace could feel the iron length of him against her bottom, and noticed with alarm the wet warmth between her thighs.

And then his large hand dipped lower, into the slickness, and Grace was unable to stifle the sound in her throat.

"Ah, sweetheart . . . Yes, that's it. Let me hear you." And then there were no more words, only his fingers stroking her with such wickedness. Yet he evaded a maddening peak she hadn't known would crave his touch.

Her hands bunched the sheet and she was lost for many minutes in her desire to scale some imaginary space to reach something . . . something. When she thought she couldn't bear another measure of this silken torture, he plunged a finger into her at the same moment his palm closed on the elusive crest and pressed with sure precision. "Ah, sweetheart," he groaned. "Yes . . . do you feel me? Don't worry, I'll never stop . . . never want to stop."

"Oh . . ." she whispered. "Oh," her breath hitched and she moaned, lost in a violent spiral of heat rushing from where he touched her all the way to the tips of her extremities. Grace was filled with a pulsing elation so pure it ached. She arched her back in pleasure.

Michael felt her body contract and pulse in waves, but before he could let any sort of joy reach his heart at her heady reaction to his touch, his arousal jerked against her deliciously soft bottom and he reared back, his length slipping between her slender thighs. His breath caught in his throat and he groaned yet again as she relaxed against him. The promise of what lay beyond so much heat and essence was too much temptation. And it had been too long. "Stay still," he ground out. With a curse, he wrapped his arms under her breasts, and prayed for control.

She breathed unevenly. "What is it?"

"Sorry," he exhaled. "I need a moment." But the problem was, he knew, that no matter how many tasks he tried to line up in his mind, his thoughts would drift right back to the bloom of femininity touching his length, and the tight sheath his fingers had found, and he almost lost control again. Michael screwed his eyes closed and clenched his jaw.

That was when he felt oozing wetness on his arm. The cool edge of reason returned. "You're bleeding," he said with a rush and broke away.

"I'm perfectly fine." She reached for him. "Oh, that was . . . astonishing. What you did. I never knew that could . . ." In her obvious shyness, she couldn't seem to look at him.

He peered more closely at the bandage, which had come loose again, and found the telltale dark stain of blood. "God, look what I've done to you."

"No," she insisted. "I don't care about that. It doesn't hurt. Please, please don't worry. Please come up on me. I want to ease you. I know how to do this part." Her arms passive by her sides, she opened her slender limbs and the primal urge to possess her engulfed him.

The ache in his tight ballocks radiated all the way into his belly, and the selfish beast in him saw himself roll on top of her and force his entire thick length into her until his hip bones fully clasped hers. "No," he ground out, squeezing his eyes shut again.

A puff of her breath brushed his skin before he felt her soft lips press against his shoulder. He jerked in response, then forced himself still. Her fingers tentatively trailed down his side, the small nail crescents tracing a pattern. With the smallest hint of boldness, she tried to pull his hips toward hers, without budging them.

"You're hurt, for Christ sakes. I'll not be the cause of you losing any more stitches. I'd have to get my kit again and I promise you won't like it."

She continued to trail innocent kisses along his chest. "Show me, then," she whispered. "Is it possible for me to do to you what you just did to me?"

"Oh God, sweetheart . . ."

She dropped her hand to his length and he was almost undone. They were lost together in their own private world, deep into the night, deep into each other and he just couldn't—wouldn't—deny himself. Forgotten were their polar opposite stations in life, the danger of discovery, and everything he was and his past. There was just this one beautiful angel and one starving man. "Just touch me, then. Oh Christ, yes, sweetheart, that's it." He covered her slender fingers with his own and guided her to the blunt ridge that promised a quick end to his torture. Her touch was as light as a bluebird's wing fluttering against a summer breeze. Michael checked his movement as the sensation peaked to an excruciating degree. With a mighty roar, he jerked in her gentle grasp and exploded in an endless flood of shuddering spasms.

And for one brief instant in time, Michael Ranier, Michael Ranier de Peyster, *the long lost Earl of Wallace* . . . absolutely, completely, and finally tasted the temptations found only in paradise.

Chapter 6

I n the bluish, harsh light of a new winter day, Grace recollected the events of the last night. Heat curled along her spine as she remembered what Mr. Ranier had said to her and how he had touched her. Oh . . . it had all been so *wicked*. And yet . . .

So wonderful. So wonderfully wicked.

Surely, pious people did not do that sort of thing. Mr. Ranier was a blacksmith and a farmer. Perhaps that was how it was done in the colonies. It was a war-ravaged wilderness on the other side of the ocean.

And then she remembered the Duke and Duchess of Helston stretched across the edge of a billiards table, Luc's hands deep inside her bodice and Rosamunde's . . . well, hers were deep inside his *breeches*. And they had been laughing. And gasping. And Luc had called her a witch, and Rosamunde had called him the devil. And Grace had fled to her chamber, before she died of mortification.

Well. Perhaps affairs of this nature were not conducted so very differently in the colonies after all.

Grace's fingers clenched on the sill as she stared out

the front window to the snow-blanketed scene before her. The whiteness reflected the sun's rays to such a degree that it was almost painful to view, and she dropped her gaze to the gleaming brilliance of the cluster of her many ropes of pearls that always comforted her.

She should be grateful for the sun, but she was not. She had wanted an escape from her life, and here in this modest country manor, she had found it. And now that she had, she admitted she craved just a little bit more, before she continued on to the Isle of Mann. She didn't want to think about the future. She'd been thinking about her future for so long, because that was what a lady of lineage was supposed to do.

This was obviously why temptation was to be avoided. And yet . . . would the private actions of a widow and a blacksmith lost somewhere between Derbyshire and Yorkshire really be sinful?

She straightened her posture and looked forward. She would not be here much longer, if the harsh sun had any say in the matter. And Mr. Ranier had made it patently clear that what happened last night was merely an unexpected short dalliance. He was a man who obviously had very little time for trifling affairs of the flesh, hard labor being his primary employment given his circumstances.

She imagined him swinging and striking at a fiery hot horseshoe on a pitch anvil, his bare shoulders gleaming with sweat, and smiled despite herself. What would her friends in Cornwall think of her if they knew she had spent the last few nights in the bed of a former smithy bent on relieving her of the perpetual cold that had taken up residence in her veins and in her heart?

They'd never believe it. Not in a thousand winters.

And that was when she saw something that made her hand freeze in midair.

A drip. And then another. Her gaze darted to the eaves covered with snow, which was melting. And her heart sank.

Her eyes refocused on a movement to the side. Michael Ranier was making his way in giant steps around the side of the house, shovel in hand. He looked up, his eyes squinting against the brightness of the snow's reflection, and seeing her in the window, nodded to her.

The scrape of the shovel pierced the winter stillness as he cleared a path to the front entrance. She watched him stomp his feet and went to meet him.

A smile overspread his features and he winked at her. "Looks like a thaw is settling in, doesn't it? Just in time, too."

"In time?"

"Well, I don't know about you, but I'd welcome a bit of sunshine. I'd forgotten how dreary winter could be in the northern climes."

She tried to relax. He was acting so very normal, as if nothing so momentous had happened between them last evening. It had meant so very much to her. But obviously, it meant nothing to a man like him.

"Have you had your porridge, Countess? Got to keep your strength up." He scratched the shadow of his beard on his jaw. "Especially after last night."

She felt an unflattering mottled flush rush her neckline.

"I like how you do that."

"Pardon me?"

"When you blush." Humor danced in his eyes. "It matches your gown and your pearls."

"I don't see how that—"

"It's a compliment. Well, I've got to get back to Timmy. One of the yearlings kicked out a stall—probably as tired of being cooped up as we are—and I've got to go after him. I just came in to make sure you are faring well. How are those stitches this morning? Perhaps I should—"

"No, no. It looks much, much better. I think it's finally healing. *Really.*"

He smiled and looked at her with a tinge of wry disbelief. "Glad to hear it. Well, I'd better—"

"Wait." She reached her hand out to rest on his heavy coat's lapel.

He looked down at her hand and then grasped it in his glove. "Yes, sweetheart?"

Oh, his eyes were so warm and expressive. And knowing. "I'm going to go stark raving mad if I have to spend another day inside. I've nothing more to mend. Would it be all right if I just took one short tour outside? I see you've cleared a path."

"I don't see why not—as long as you keep it short." He gently squeezed her fingers. "Besides . . ."

"Besides, what?" she asked.

"It'll be devilishly good fun to chase the chill from you after."

She sucked in her breath and then, with a chuckle, he was gone.

As Sioux's hooves broke through the thin layer of ice covering the snowdrifts, Michael gave himself over to the pleasure of thinking of the soft femininity of Grace Sheffey.

Like the first crocus of spring, she was a fragile beauty amid the harsh bleakness of what his life had been until now. He shook his head. But like that first blossom, her stay would be short.

Yet, he could acknowledge that. If there was one thing he had learned, it was to accept and enjoy any brief joys fate tossed his way. It made the rest of it that much more bearable.

It wouldn't be long now. In another day or so, the snow-covered road a half mile away would give way to the wheels of the sturdier coaches. And soon, Michael would have to make an effort to find that idiotic Mr. Brown to allow Grace Sheffey to go back to a life among her own kind. And he would continue on this new, promising land before him. Just looking at the vast fields made him eager for the planting season. It had taken him more than a decade to clear three acres of wilderness along the Potomac, and here there was not one damned, stubborn stump to contend with. There were only people to worry about. Curious, gossiping people. He was glad this trifling corner of the world was tucked into a mostly forgotten piece of England.

As it was, he suspected it was going to be more than a little difficult to watch her leave with some pam-

pered dandy. He glanced at the azure sky above, a lone
cloud meandering across the expanse. Yes, it was but a
day or so before she would be gone. He urged Sioux to
cross over an icy stream.

A day. And one night. One time to construct a few
unforgettable moments to last him through many winters to come. But there was nothing to be done about
it and he knew very well how to accept truth. Thank
God she did too.

And then he saw him. There in the distance, on
the top of a small hill, the missing dark bay horse
stood looking down at him. Michael loosened the
makeshift halter looped over his saddle and was
about to dismount when his mare nickered. After a
brief pause, the gelding dropped his head and came
toward them.

Michael knew how the bay felt. It was just too bad
he couldn't follow his own instincts.

An hour later, the yearling on a lead behind Sioux,
Michael negotiated his way through the last of the
melting drifts in front of the barn. As he dismounted,
a late-afternoon wind rushed through the withered
brown leaves still stubbornly clinging to the branches
of an oak tree next to him, and he saw himself in
nature. He refused to give up his grasp on the old until
new life budded. It would be a long time before he felt
safe here—if ever. Perhaps it would have been better
to remain in Virginia instead of dodging all his true
countrymen here.

He clucked to the animals and with purposeful loose strides headed for the warmth within. The
peaceful sounds of animals well fed greeted him. A

cow lowed in the milking stall, its tail twitching as Timmy's happy face glanced toward him.

"There ye be, sir. And you got him, too." The boy grinned. "Me Pa says he's a rare one, that one is. Won't be easy to break to saddle. Got the taste of the wild in him, he does."

Michael chuckled while he led the animal to a newly turned out stall. "Sometimes it's not wise to take it all out of them, Timmy. You lose their heart that way. Then what use is the animal to you?"

Timmy stopped milking. "Never thought of it that way, Mr. Ranier. I'd be much obliged if I might watch when he's backed for the first time."

"Of course. Now what's left here? How's that lamb faring?"

"Well, sir, funny thing that." Timmy placed the half-filled bucket of milk beside him and stood up. "Mrs. Sheffey came out 'ere a few hours ago and asked for a tour o' the barn. Doona think she much liked the manure pile out back, but then she spied that lamb, and, well . . ."

"Yes?"

"Sir, there weren't anything I could do to persuade her to leave it be when she learnt the ewe hadn't survived."

"Where is she?"

"In the kitchen. But, she keeps coming back every hour begging more milk. I'm trying to keep up with her, sir. But she wouldna listen when I told her I doubted a lamb would do well on cow's milk."

Michael suppressed a smile.

"She's not from about here, is she, sir?"

"No."

"She sure is pretty."

Michael laughed.

"If'n you'll pardon me for sayin', I think she's taken a fancy to ye, sir."

He stilled, then swung his head toward the boy. "And why would you get such an idea in your head?"

"Well, she keeps asking me questions. And they're all about you, sir." He appeared bashful. "I thought I should tell ye since I doona know how to natter with fancy ladies. Never sure what to say."

"I've always thought men should discuss ideas, not people, don't you think, Timmy?" Michael gentled his voice.

"Yes, sir," Timmy murmured.

He ruffled the boy's hair.

"And, Timmy, let me know if you ever figure out how to talk to a woman, will you?" Michael removed his hat and ran his hands through his itchy scalp, hoping his next words would guide Timmy's future course of action. "In the meantime, I suggest you leave as much to mystery as you can. The questions never stop, no matter how many answers you give them."

Timmy Lattimer drank in the many truths Michael had to offer as they finished the last of the stable chores. The boy had had dinner, so he bid Timmy good evening and carried a wire basket of eggs to the house.

She was just as he expected, sitting in front of the kitchen fire, the tiny lamb swaddled in her arms, and for the briefest instant, when her bonny blue eyes met his, he imagined her holding a child, not a lamb, and he nearly cursed. What on earth was he thinking? Absurd was what it was. Michael turned away to place a pan of water on the new-fashioned stove, and set the eggs to simmer.

"Well then." He cleared his throat. "Trying to teach a lamb to be a calf, are you? And how are you faring?"

"Not very well, I think."

Michael lowered himself onto his haunches in front of her. A tiny black nose poked out of the blanketing, the lamb fast asleep. "And why do you say that?"

"She sleeps too much, and hasn't taken enough milk." Her slender fingers stroked the soft white curls of wool.

"I see." He surreptitiously cupped the soft underbelly of the lamb for a moment and then withdrew his hand.

"Her face is so very sweet." She appeared anxious. "I've named her Pearl, if that's all right with you?"

He nodded, resisting the urge to smile. Her knowledge of anatomy was appalling.

"I tried to feed her with a tiny spoon, but she wouldn't take it, so I dipped this piece of cloth in the milk, and she took it then."

He peered into the small bucket, which was nearly full.

"She drank about one half of the first bucket. Actually, she took precisely an inch more than one half of a bucket. I measured it. But she won't take any from this new bucket. And, and . . ."

Michael covered one of her hands with his own to still the trembling. "And?"

"And I think she's dying." Her voice strained to continue. "I couldn't bear—"

"Sweetheart," Michael said unable to keep a smile from his lips, "that lamb's not dying. It's doing exactly what I would expect it to do when *drunk* on cow's milk—sleep."

"Are you certain?"

"I'm surprised you got the lamb to take as much as you did." He didn't tell her the animal's stomach was probably twice as full as any other newborn's. "If Pearl lives, it will be because of your ministering."

Such transparent joy, with a tinge of uncertainty infused her face. It was almost painful to witness. Like a child long denied great happiness and still disbelieving. Like the rare child at the orphanage who left arm in arm with a new mother or father. Like Sam.

"Do you think the cow's milk will hurt her?"

He scratched his jaw. "I've seen odder things. I once saw a whelping hound adopt a piglet. But, you mustn't get your hopes too high. Nature always has her way, as everyone knows. It's the strongest who survive."

"I know that lesson well."

"Do you now, Countess?" He eased to his full height, refusing to give in to the urge to lean forward and kiss her. She was just so damned beautiful.

"Yes."

Michael retrieved bread, the remaining cheese, and butter from the larder. "And where did you learn this? I hadn't thought you were raised long in the country."

"Oh, it's worse in town. One of the tenets of society is that aristocrats always manage to weed out the less vital offspring of their peers—innocent or not—to keep the upper ten thousand to its proper number."

He shook his head, "And why must it stay at that particular number?"

"Well," she said wryly, "I suppose everyone thinks upper *eleven* thousand does not sound nearly so fine."

He laughed. "Obviously they have too much time on their hands, if they're wasting it on such nonsense. But I remember it thusly." He went still, shocked he had let the words spill from his mouth and praying she was too engrossed in the lamb to have taken notice. "Come, the eggs are ready."

He carefully deposited the sleeping lamb in a nest of blankets despite her protestations.

"You once lived in London?" She seated herself at the table.

His neck hairs prickled. "Yes. Like many." He cracked open a coddled egg in a swift motion.

"Why do you avoid telling me about your life?"

"Nothing interesting to relate, unless you want to discuss smithing and farming, that is."

He could almost feel the wheels turning in her mind, and he stymied her efforts by changing the subject. "Where were you raised, Countess?"

"The Isle of Mann and a few seasons in London. Generations of my mother's and father's families lived on Mann. I was actually on my way there when the accident occurred."

"That explains it."

"Explains what?"

"You're heartier than you appear at first glance," he murmured, quickly polishing off three more eggs before turning to the bread and cheese.

"I'm sorry?" Her spoon stopped in midair.

"Viking blood."

"I beg your pardon."

"Wasn't Mann raided and settled by Vikings? You certainly look like a blonde, blue-eyed norsewoman, albeit a petite one. Do you have any hidden desire to go raiding that I should know about, Lady Sheffield?"

Her eyes had widened with each word. And then she let out her breath. "Oh, for goodness sakes."

"Your oaths show little variation."

"Well, yours would too, if you were a lady." The warmth in her eyes had returned, and his tension over her questions eased. Too soon.

"I've told you about my childhood. And yours?"

He stood up, his chair's legs raking against the floorboards. "A little here and there."

"So you spent part of your youth near here?"

She was never going to quit. "Yes, and as you know, in London and Virginia too." Their plates clean, he removed everything from the table. She drifted to his side.

"What was it like there?"

"Virginia?"

"Yes." Her voice was tentative and soft, obviously afraid of being cut off.

"It's a land of much raw beauty. The life there is new, and uncertain. You can't imagine how red and boggy the clay mud becomes during the March rains—especially in Georgetown, a drummed-up trade village. Makes the bogs here look tame," he said, meeting her eyes. "But in Virginia, the woods and mountains go on forever and a day. The wild flowering trees of spring—especially the redbud—make up for the harsh winters, but the fine weather of fall does not make up for the hordes of summer mosquitoes."

She was silent next to him. She'd finally learned how to move about the kitchen with ease. While he washed, she dried.

"Thank you," she uttered.

"For what?"

"For describing it to me. I can see it perfectly."

There was such gentle goodness to her, he longed to lean down and kiss her senseless, and remind her exactly how ungentlemanly he could be when provoked by her generous spirit and beauty.

"Well," he said, seizing the chance to turn the conversation. "This is the first moment we've had with nothing to do but amuse ourselves. What shall it be, then? And no, Pearl is going to be looked after by Timmy tonight."

"I would prefer to see to her myself. It's no trouble, really." She arranged the two cups in the cupboard and moved to the other dishes to dry.

"I'll extract a promise from Timmy to watch over her as well as you have done. You know, you've such a rare gift with animals, I'll have to give you horsemanship lessons next."

Her expression froze and he grinned. "I can see you're delighted by the prospect. But I'm certain you'd make a fine horsewoman." He chucked her under her chin. "It's your luck there's too much snow to consider it. Hmmm. Let's see. We could play cards. Wagering has always been a favored vice of mine." He chuckled at her raised eyebrows. "But not my favorite."

"You're a gambler?" she asked, her voice strained.

"What's wrong, sweetheart? All men, even gentlemen, enjoy a wager here or there. Indeed, it helped me gain my supper many a fortnight."

"But it can also worsen your lot in life if you're unlucky."

"Well, one does what one has to do to survive."

"I detest gambling."

"And why is that, sweetheart?"

Her gaze rested on her hands as she continued to rub the last plate even though it was already dry. "My father won and lost our family's wealth twice over. The first time I was young and we were on Mann. I remember the servants leaving and the bare spots in the rooms where furniture and paintings had once been. The second time, another foreign canal scheme . . . Well, I was nearly twenty and . . . and it's a common-enough story."

"And?" he encouraged.

"And I had just been paraded about London with a promised dowry in excess of thirty thousand pounds."

"Is this when you married Sheffield?"

"No." She halted and appeared to waver in her decision to tell him more. He refused to urge her to continue.

"Our townhouse in London and all items within were sold at auction along with the gowns, the horses, and the carriages. And now you are going to say that you feel certain I didn't really care about the horses."

"No, Countess. I would not say that." He hated her wretched story. There had been too much sadness in his own life, and he preferred not to dwell on misery in any corner.

She had become silent, but then continued. "Before then, I'd been declared a vision and the catch of the season. I'd found it amusing to be compared to a fish. Yet after a while it had been hard not to feel like one when eight gentlemen tried to reel the fat dowry into their coffers," she glanced at her hands. "I don't know why I am telling you this. I need to write a few letters to my friends in Cornwall. They will be very worried."

"Whatever you'd like, Countess."

Her lovely blue eyes looked to his. "I am boring you."

"You have yet to bore me." Her expression told him everything she did not. "Go on."

"When we retrenched, I was abruptly remeasured, came up short, and was declared a bit old. The ton's new opinion was best expressed by the Countess of Home, who dismissed me as *ordinary*. This was worse than being a complete failure. I was packed back to Mann before my parents fled for yet another foreign city, in search of yet another grand scheme."

"And how came you to marry the earl?"

"When my parents died a few years later, my cousin,

the heir, arrived on Mann with his good friend, the Earl of Sheffield. And while many assumed I married him for avaricious reasons, for he was much older—"

"You did not do that. I'm certain of it."

She bowed her head. "John Sheffey was one of the finest gentlemen I have ever had the honor to know," she finished.

The countess knelt before the lamb and stroked its head. "We returned to London, but while my husband's will was strong, his heart was not, and he succumbed to a fever shortly thereafter. Many whispered I was lucky to have secured a solid foundation of financial security locked behind the doors of London's most venerable banking institutions—all in four short months." Her glittering eyes met his. "They were right."

"Sweetheart," he shook his head. "You can try to convince me all you like that you were a conniving female on the hunt for a fortune, but unlike those fools in town, I'll never believe it."

"It's a well known fact that fear of destitution breeds motivation. But I was indeed lucky—very lucky—to have been granted the happiness I found with Lord Sheffield." She said it so quietly, he had to lean forward to catch it.

"I'd bet my last farthing that the earl would have given you his wealth twice over again just for the pleasure of being with you those few months." He couldn't stop the heat from entering his words.

When she didn't reply, Michael leaned over and collected the lamb to return it to the barn. "Come, we're finished here."

Her attention fixed on the creature, she changed the subject. "If you don't mind, I would very much like to write those notes."

"Hmmm." If he had cared less for her, he might have suggested something more to his liking. Something that would involve sheets of linen instead of sheets of pressed paper. "All right. I've a mind to glance at the books in the library after I return the lamb. Shall we?"

He gallantly offered his arm to her but she arose unaided. She clearly had no wish to continue what they had begun last night.

An hour later, Michael rather thought he might go mad. The silence of the library was broken only by an occasional snap from the fire, and the faint scratching of her quill on the paper he had found for her. Distraction, in the form of the delicate beauty before him, ruled his thoughts and his imagination. He tried yet again to concentrate on an excellent book describing the various types of sheep to be found in England and Scotland.

He'd always devoured books whenever he'd had access, which had been rare. Apparently, Sam had loved books too, given the overfilled bookcases. Michael imagined many comfortable yet solitary nights ahead, spent in this room.

The gloaming shrouded the view beyond the heavy drapes. Michael pressed his aching shoulders into the padded leather chair and tried to resist glancing at the woman before him, without success.

He studied her elegant profile as she applied words to the page. Her loveliness was boundless, her heart no less. And he wanted to pound to hell and back all those nobs in London who'd suggested she was a callous fortune hunter. Good God, she was everything innocent, everything fine, and everything a man could want, and so much more. And for him, she was everything he would dream of and everything he could never, ever hold on to.

He would go after Brown tomorrow.

She sanded the note and carefully cleaned her fingers with a cloth. He trained his attention on his book. The smoky scent of molten sealing wax curled in the air between them before he heard her chair push back from the small escritoire.

She held the missive before him silently, and he gazed at the extraordinarily beautiful script of the directions she had written. Of course she had taken as much care in forming the letters as she had making the delicate stitches in his clothes, feeding the lamb, and touching him last eve. He placed the letter on the side table next to him.

"The snow will have melted by half in the morning at any guess. I'll take this to the village then and also make inquiries." He rubbed the ache between his eyes. "You shall be on your way soon after."

Unexpectedly, he heard the rustle of silk and he realized she was kneeling in front of him.

"I've been uncertain how to say something." High color crested her cheekbones.

"Yes?"

"My injury is much improved, and—and I'm feeling much stronger. Must be the porridge, or the excellent care you've—"

"I'm glad to hear it," he cut in.

There was a long pause before she continued. "Well—that is—I just thought I would assure you . . ." She stopped, the crackling of the pitched pine in the fireplace deafening in the silence.

Her eyes skittered away from his scrutiny, but she soldiered on. "Last night you said you didn't like regrets and couldn't offer any promises, and—and . . ."

"And?" he prodded.

"And I said I held no expectations."

"Yes."

"Well, do you think it would be very wrong—or truly *sinful* to . . . I mean to say, I'm a widow. I still revere the memory of my husband, and have mourned him. But do you think it would be disrespectful to . . . That is—if you would even still be inclined to—"

He cut off her stream of nonsense with his lips and drew her into his lap in one long motion. There was a rushing in his veins each time he touched her, making it very hard to think in an orderly fashion. He tried to regulate his thoughts before he was consumed by her.

"I think it would be safe to say I'm inclined," he rasped out. "But, sweetheart, soon you will return to your world and I shall continue on here. Most would say it's evil—say it's wrong. But I want it." He had to force himself not to clutch her arms in his urgency.

"I want it too," she said very quietly.

"Well then." The enormity of it crashed in on him. It had been one thing to find himself in her arms in the middle of the night in bed. But here and now they were fully dressed, caught in the lengthening shadows of the library.

He refused to let her out of his sight to precede him above stairs to undress and wait for him. It would give her too much time to change her mind. And he was overly selfish to allow for the possibility. There had been just too many times in his life when the promise of happiness had been snatched from his fingertips.

And so he dared her to avoid his eyes as he unbuttoned her gown and drew it from her. Her mended shift was so fine it was almost translucent. The shadows of the small rosy peaks beneath caused his fingers to tremble. God, he wanted her too much. Touching her last night and the feel of her hesitant, soft hands had only served to inflame him like no other.

Those same hands were grasping his coarse shirt, and he leaned forward to urge her to pull it over his head before leaning back in the large chair.

Firelight danced across her lovely face, her light eyes grown darker, like the stormy winter skies in Virginia. He reached for one end of the delicate bow gathering the front of her shift and tugged at it, taking care not to touch that which lay below. Without a word, he lowered the material and the bandage and with relief found the cut dry and healing.

"Satisfied?" she murmured shyly.

"Relieved," he returned.

Letting the last of his fears slip into the evening, he grasped her tighter and rose from the chair only to gently, ever so gently, place her on the thick carpeting in front of the fire.

"Aren't we going above?" she choked out.

"No. Won't waste a moment." He tossed the large pillows of the settee to the floor in between the economical movements needed to divest himself of his clothes to join her.

And then he was lost. Lost in the sensation of touching her, stroking the silk softness of her.

Kissing her was like diving into a pool of sun-warmed water and coming up gasping. She was the element he couldn't describe but knew without a doubt was vital, and the shock of that knowledge made him hold her tighter to him, desperate to imprint her form on his, knowing all the while the futility of the effort.

He couldn't stop kissing her, her lips, her throat, her breasts—and then his lips followed the fast-beating pulse down to the curve of her hip and the hollow of her soft abdomen. She was like a decadent dessert, all spun sugar and temptation immortal.

As he inched lower still, her voice became a satiny ribbon, knotting his mind, that grew tighter until he became conscious of her words.

"Oh, please wait . . . Wait! What are you doing?" Her voice was reedy, confused; her hands unsteady on his shoulders.

"Kissing you," he murmured. His lips trailed near her navel, and he inhaled the marvelous mysterious scent of her, so different from his own. "You're not going to ask me to stop, are you?"

There was uncertainty in her expression, maybe

even fear. He leaned on one forearm and stroked his other palm down her too slender side to behind her knee.

"No," she said on an exhale. "It's just that I'm alone up here, and I'm not sure what I should be doing."

"Oh sweetheart," he said, easing back up to her face to kiss her forehead.

"And . . . well, I was beginning to form the idea that you were going to . . ."

"Going to do what?"

"Nothing—nothing. Forget I said anything."

"Really?"

She nodded slightly.

"I hope it wasn't anything *wicked*," he said, hiding a smile while he dipped down to taste the tips of her exquisite breasts. A shuddering sigh escaped her lips. He reached for her hand and brought it to his lips. "Because I daresay I'll have more than enough to atone for before dawn." He rose up and looked down into her dazed eyes. "You did propose a night of sin, did you not?"

"But I didn't mean to suggest—"

"And I plan to make the most of it." He was sure she was going to argue, but then, inexplicably, her eyes became a deeper, softer blue, and she uttered but one word . . . one magical word.

"Please . . ."

He closed the gap between them, his hot flesh molding to her cooler body. He took care to envelope her within his arms until he had chased all her fears away to replace them with yearning.

He dragged his fingers to the traces of angel hair at

the apex of her body, which tempted him in the low light. Marveling at the fine texture, he stroked her restlessly. Her eyes were closed and she was breathing with effort; her hands tentatively tunneled through his hair. Michael urged her thighs apart and delved deeper.

And then, there was nothing that could have stopped him from doing something he'd never desired before. He couldn't explain this starved feeling she engendered within him.

With a groan, he edged his heavy body down hers and before she could say a word against it, he lowered his head and stole a taste of her. And then, just as surely as instinct engulfs a Virginia mountain lion after the first sampling of his own kill, the male hunger in him roared to life, making him deaf to every single last one of her choked protestations.

His shoulders bunched and strained to get closer until, without thought he curled an arm under each of her limbs and tilted her to suit him. The slow and thorough tempo of his ministrations rhymed with the beat of his arousal, leaving him maddened with a stark need to cover her, hold her, possess her. God, it had never been like this. Never would be like this again. He roared with need and prowled back up her delicate form.

"Hold on to me," he groaned, his desire radiating from every pore of his body. "No. Tighter."

He grasped his length and sweeping between her plush folds, he became all raw instinct as blood pounded in his veins and roared through his head.

His arousal felt like an anvil, hot and unforgiving, and she was so trusting and soft beneath him. The animal in him had robbed him of his power of speech and he would not be denied any longer.

He sucked in his gut until it ached with fatigue and then let himself loose on her, regret for his inability to hold back instantly flooding him. He plunged deep, deeper, like a rutting bull, overwhelming her beneath him. Worry warred with intense pleasure as he struggled to harness his desire.

Burning . . . his immense hard length bore into her, and she was powerless to stop it. He held absolute dominion over her and she finally understood the difference between quiet intimacy with her dearest husband and carnal possession by a man in his prime.

It was so very different from anything she had known; it was undeniably more than a little frightening given its primal nature. But seeing the wild hunger in his eyes, she reveled in the pure feeling of being intensely desired—without apology.

He had stopped after one powerful, endlessly long thrust, and was now shaking, his entire body as hard and immovable as a tree trunk. More than anything, she wanted to offer him all the pleasure she could after everything he had given her during the last few days. But he seemed to be waiting for a sign from her.

She eased the tension from her fingers, which clutched his shoulders, and whispered into his hair, "Yes . . ."

A harsh groan reverberated from his chest and like a great wave from the sea, his body undulated, surging deeper inside her.

Her hips ached from the massive body clasped between them, but still she urged him, sensing his concern for her and his desperation. "Don't stop . . . *please, Michael.*"

He tipped back his head and roughly drew in a large lungful of air. As if controlled by another force, he seemed to unleash himself, hurtling his hips against her, filling her, stretching her until the intensity overwhelmed them both. Her breath caught the same moment he opened his eyes and stared at her, his golden eyes darkened with undistilled desire. The intensity she saw in those glittering depths was too great a promise, and she lowered her gaze.

"Look at me," he insisted as if she would one day forget him. "Don't look away."

In that moment, Grace recognized the voracious passion within him and knew she returned it measure for measure without fear. She fully bloomed from the nourishment.

Wordlessly, their eyes enraptured by the sight of each other, their bodies and minds trapped and still, Grace felt a pulsing grow from her depths. And as if he read her need, he surged forward until her vision tunneled. Her body stiffened and spiraled wildly to completion, until finally, she could breathe once more.

With a harsh gasp, he withdrew and spilled himself in great pulsing shots. Arms shaking and with deliberate care, he lowered his lips to hers and kissed her tenderly, reverently.

He rolled to her side and swiped at the wetness before pulling her into his arms; his breathing still uneven.

Dazed and overwhelmed, Grace tried to regain her composure. Desperate to end the piercing, sudden stillness after the storm, she latched on to her first disordered thought. "Are you all right?"

"Shouldn't I be asking *you* that?" His voice was nearly gone.

She stroked an unruly lock of hair from his face. "Are you suggesting I'm still asking the wrong questions?"

She felt his arms squeeze her closer. "No. I'm just that worried."

Grace reveled in the warm strength of his arms, and wished she could tamp down the welling desire to never leave this illusionary bubble of happiness. How was she going to manage it? "You shouldn't be," she assured him.

"I crushed you, hurt you."

"No." She nuzzled under his iron-like jaw. "Just the opposite."

He didn't appear to believe her. "And you might find yourself with child, despite my efforts. God, you must promise me—promise me faithfully that you will write to me immediately if there is a child."

"You mustn't worry. I rarely . . . well, I almost never experience what other ladies complain about."

"But you must promise me." There was a hollow tone laced in his words. "I couldn't bear the thought of a child of mine walking this earth without me being there to protect . . ." He leaned back, unable to continue.

"Of course I would tell you. I would never deny you your own child." She rushed on, knowing she was ruining the intimacy of the moment. "You were an orphan, weren't you? You met Mr. Bryn at a foundling home. Did you ever know either of your parents?"

His eyes searched hers. "My father," he began, then stopped abruptly.

She reached up to stroke his head. "Will you not tell me what happened?"

"Nothing unusual. There was a fire when I was a child and, well, all was lost to me, and I was taken to Lamb's Conduit Fields."

"The hospital for foundlings?" she continued when he nodded slightly. "You didn't have any other relations?"

"None," he said with overt finality.

"I've no real family left either. No brothers or sisters," she murmured.

She sensed his keen desire to stop examining his painful past. "Michael?"

"Yes?"

"Thank you."

"For what?"

She pulled away from his arms and eased up to kiss his cheek. "For confiding in me again. And for showing me."

His heavy arms pulled her to him and rolled her on top of him. "Showing you what, sweetheart?"

"That I'm perhaps not so very different from my friends after all. That I'm not—well, that I'm not what I overheard in London."

"And what foolish thing was that?"

"The 'Countess from the Isle of Ice.'"

A warm, slow smile overspread his face. "Sweetheart, everyone knows Vikings lived in the northern climes for a reason—"

She laughed and shook her head. "I am *not* a Viking."

"—Their passionate blood runs too hot to live anywhere else." He tugged her head down to rest in the comfort of his immense chest. "Idiots, all such bloody idiots, in town. Although . . ."

"Yes?"

"I'll admit your wee feet are of a cold I've never encountered before. Come." He sat up with a groan and lifted her in his arms. "Let me wash you and get you settled for the night. You need to rest—you made me forget how much blood you lost."

Grace encircled his neck with her arms. The poor man. He had no idea. If he thought for a moment that she was going to waste one of the last few nights she would ever have with him by sleeping, he was about to learn differently.

She smiled to herself. *Viking blood.* He had said she had Viking blood coursing through her veins.

The rest of the night was filled with short intervals of unconsciousness followed by painfully intense roiling emotions and actions, instigated always by her. But they shared few words between them. It seemed that while their bodies could not stop the pull of attraction, their minds would not allow the chance of any words tearing them apart. That is, until the first pink streaks of dawn colored the walls of the simple chamber.

Michael caressed the back of her neck, sad to see the red chafe marks from his night's growth of beard on the slender column. Her words interrupted his reflection.

"You never did tell me the end of your dream the other night," she whispered, her eyes still closed.

"I'm not sure I can remember it now," he said gruffly. He dipped to kiss the top of her head.

"You said you saw me under a tree with a book . . . waiting."

"Did I?"

"Yes. Who was I waiting for?"

He paused, determined not to go down this path. "Well, it certainly wasn't for Mr. Brown."

She rose up on her forearm and looked at him. "Why do you do that?"

"What, sweetheart?"

"Turn the moment with humor."

He stared at her. "Because the truth of it is better left unsaid."

Her expression played havoc on his good sense, more so than any words ever would. He brushed back the lush gold hair that had tumbled over her shoulder and could not stop himself from saying what should not be said.

"Why, you were waiting for me, *Grace*." The first taste of her given name on his lips was unbearably intimate. And as intoxicating as the potent yearning and happiness exposed now in her vibrant blue eyes. Ah, he shouldn't have told her. It would do nothing toward bringing her a lasting happiness that was not his to offer.

And it made everything that would occur in the next hour all the more bitter.

Chapter 7

His head heavy but his body drained, Michael knew as he was roused from slumber yet again that he had rarely experienced such profound emotion or exhaustion. Grace lay curled beside him, and he lifted his head, which weighed five stone, to reverently gaze at the astonishing woman beside him. In this twilight of wakefulness, the poignant memories of her tentative and oh-so-achingly tender invitations to take her—over and over again—during the night unraveled in his mind.

And then, with a muffled sound below, all the devils from hell attacked their lost corner of heaven.

With a vengeance.

Long after, Michael wondered which of the two sensibilities he experienced had been worse; the pure terror of discovery, or the flood of relief that a brigade of Bow Street runners hungry for blood money had not found him. Of only one thing he was certain. None of it compared to the feelings he would endure in the weeks to come.

From instinct borne of experience, Michael jumped from the bed with a curse and dragged on his buckskin leggings. "Countess," he shook her, "wake up." The sound of many footsteps echoed from the stairs.

He reached for his saddlebag and the pistol he always kept there, but hesitated. He couldn't risk it. Couldn't risk inciting an exchange of gunfire that might harm her. He would just have to go without a fight. He envisioned the entire affair in a moment: they'd place him in shackles and drag him down the stairs and she would run behind them, begging to know what he had done. *Good God.*

He tossed Gracie's crumpled shift toward her and roughly pulled her from the bed when she didn't respond. Her garment slid past her surprised expression when the chamber's door shuddered and violently gave way to a rash of humanity, none of whom bore the telltale signs of the Bow Street bloodhounds.

Her eyes wide, Grace grabbed her gown and clutched it in front of her as Michael tugged his shirt over his head and attempted to help Grace find the arms of her garment.

"Looks like your lucky day, Ellesmere," said the dark devil leading the troupe to the unruffled gentleman beside him. "It appears the pleasure of peeling off your sodding hide for letting Grace go will have to be deferred. We'll draw and quarter this rotter first."

A tiny old lady dressed in dull black from the tips of her high-heeled boots to her jaunty hat rushed through the gap and grasped Grace so tightly Michael could see the fragile bones through a misshapened hand.

"Oh my dearest, dearest . . . Oh Grace, I was so worried. We scoured every last dwelling in this parish. I thought you were—" The lady promptly burst into tears.

"Ata," Grace said, leaning down to accept her into her arms, "I'm perfectly fine. I was very fortunate to be—Oh Mr. Brown, thank goodness you are safe. I—"

A balding old coot stepped forward.

"Brown?" Michael cut in, staring at Grace. "*He's* Mr. Brown?"

"Why, yes I am," the gentleman said. "Although I didn't realize my name was said with such infamy in these parts."

The tiny virago muttered, "Your name is now synonymous with disgrace throughout the British Isles, you old codger."

"We all know who he is," the infuriated dark-haired bloke said loud enough to shake the rafters. "But who in bloody hell are *you*?"

"Perhaps it would be even more interesting to learn, Helston, why he's lurking about the countess's chambers in his smallclothes." Worry lined the brow of the more reserved gentleman.

The darker man gave the other a sour glance. "I don't give a bloody damn about any of his answers, actually. The only question is whether we bury him alive now or flay his lecherous hide first."

"Luc, please," Grace said, mortification warring with relief in seeing Mr. Brown unharmed. "Stop, all of you. Mr. Ranier saved my life. I'm greatly indebted to him."

The devil-like nob examined Michael's form with disgust. "Ranier, is it?"

Michael nodded once.

Grace rushed forward. "Mr. Ranier, please allow me to introduce the Duke of Helston, Luc St. Aubyn. Luc, Mr. Michael Ranier."

The man actually scowled as he tipped his head a fraction of a degree. She'd ruthlessly butchered etiquette by introducing an aristocrat to a blacksmith instead of the other way around.

"And this is my dearest friend Merceditas St. Aubyn, the Dowager Duchess of Helston, Luc's grandmother. Ata, may I present Mr. Ranier?"

Michael grasped the elderly lady's good hand and bent to hover his mouth above skin as thin as parchment. "Your Grace."

The countess continued, "And may I present the Marquis of Ellesmere, Quinn Fortesque and also Mr. John Brown?"

Michael nodded briefly to Ellesmere and turned to shake the elderly man's aged hand. "It appears I owe you an apology, sir," Michael murmured.

"Really? I can't imagine why," Brown replied with a gummy smile. "And here I wanted to express my undying gratitude. Lady Sheffield," he turned to Grace, "I don't mean to burden you, lass, but I believe you took ten years off my life when I returned to that blasted carriage to find it empty."

"And well you deserved it for leaving my dearest Grace to freeze to death," the duchess added, her visage drawn with fatigue.

The older man's face drained of color.

Grace shook her head. "Ata, you're entirely mistaken. Mr. Brown, I hope, in time, you will forgive me. I was chilled and I fear I wasn't thinking clearly. And well, if not for Mr. Ranier—"

The Duke of Helston interrupted with a disgusted sound. "There is far too much fawning about to my liking, and not nearly enough thrashing. Now Grace, you are to go belowstairs with Ata for the moment while Ellesmere, Brown, and this Mr. Ranier and I converse. Then you are to gather your affairs. We'll not presume to take up Mr. Ranier's time any longer than necessary."

Grace looked at him and then at the other assembled personages. Michael gave her credit. Any other lady of consequence would have been blushing and stumbling with embarrassment for having been caught in the bed of a stranger.

Instead, she calmly walked to Helston and grasped his hands. "Luc, I'm sorry to have caused you such trouble and worry."

The hotheaded hellion pulled her into his arms and crushed her to him. A lethal desire to wrest her from that bloody aristocrat engulfed Michael.

But in that brief moment, Michael spied an intense combination of relief and something else overspread the duke's features, before the man hid his face in her hair and whispered something to her.

Grace pulled away slightly and stared into Helston's eyes, then shook her head.

The duke's tiny grandmother grasped Michael's arm. "You're very tall."

"Yes, ma'am."

"Very large all over."

"So I've been told."

"I like tall men."

Mr. Brown snorted.

Michael looked down into her wrinkled face. The dowager had the most remarkable dark, penetrating eyes with penciled eyebrows, and a mass of iron-colored hair that threatened to come undone and tumble down to her shoulders. Her lips were shrewd.

"It's the short ones you can't count on," she shared.

Mr. Brown made an exasperated sound again and rolled his eyes.

Michael glanced at the last man, the one named Ellesmere, silently brooding at Helston's elbow. The unmistakable air of guilt lurked in his expression. Ah, the jilting bastard in the flesh.

"Quinn," Grace pleaded, "I must ask you, as the one who possesses the coolest head here, to exert a measure of rational thinking. Mr. Ranier is not to be blamed for what I know must appear, at first glance, very odd. But, you see, the fault is all mine. I was injured and near to frozen when he found me. We were forced to share . . ." A deeper color rose along her neckline.

"Hush," Helston said, releasing her. "Grace, you are not guilty of a single bloody thing. Now, please allow me to escort you to—"

"No. If you think I'm going to leave you here to bash each other's heads, you're quite mistaken."

"Ah, lass," Mr. Brown said, "look at it this way, we'll all be on our way much faster if you go belowstairs now."

The dowager held her hands out to Grace. "Come, Grace. Neither one of us has a chance of putting a dent in their stubborn, ill-conceived notions."

Grace sighed with exasperation.

"Just think of the pleasure we'll take in reminding them later of their stupidity and how much they deserve every last bruise for not listening to you. Oh, and Mr. Ranier?"

"Yes, ma'am?"

"I think it only fair to warn you, since it's three to one, that my grandson possesses a nasty left hook. Although, I would not underestimate Ellesmere's right jab—it's called an uppercut, isn't it? Well, whatever it is, it left a rather impressive mark on Luc's jaw last summer."

Helston glowered darkly, while Ellesmere appeared vastly uncomfortable.

"Grace, fear not," the dowager continued. "Remember they were similarly idiotic about that affair, but it considerably shortened the end result, don't you agree?"

Grace was biting her lip, it appeared, to keep from laughing. "Mr. Ranier, I'm so sorry. And after everything you've done for me."

Helston glared at him.

"This is impossible," Grace continued. "I don't know what to say."

"Go on now, Countess. The jack-a-dandies are correct. We do need to parley," Michael said, keeping his expression deceptively unconcerned.

Grace glanced at the sullen faces and appeared to give up by addressing the elderly duchess. "Do you like porridge? I shall prepare breakfast for all of you."

The lady's small mouth *V*'d into a sly smile. "Actually, I'm thinking frozen beefsteak will be more the thing for some of the party."

Grace linked arms with the dowager. "Ata, I've acquired a new art while waiting out the storm—the art of cooking. I've quite taken to it."

If he hadn't been so ill at ease, her comments would have provoked a curl to Michael's lips. As it stood, he was lucky to be able to breathe given the tension in the overcrowded room.

Grace collected a few articles and took her leave, the other lady clucking behind her. With the loud click of the door engaging, Helston paced a circle around him.

"You *are* on the tall side, Ranier."

Michael remained silent.

Helston's scorn was palpable. "Great in stature, but short in honor. But then, one can never count on that when facing a . . . a . . . what *are* you, anyway?"

"Not a tarted-up dandy."

Helston sighed. "Oh, there was never any doubt of that. Just tell us you're not the bloody footman or gamekeeper here."

"I suppose it was too much to hold out hope for a cit, at the very worst," Ellesmere said, a reasonable undercurrent in his words.

"So, he speaks." Michael half-shuttered his eyes.

The Marquis of Ellesmere stepped forward. "What in hell are you inferring?"

"It means that while my attentions toward the

Countess of Sheffield were dishonorable in every way imaginable, they did not break her heart. Your original attentions were honorable in every way, I am guessing, but you, *my lord*, broke her spirit quite recklessly."

He should have paid closer attention to the dowager's advice. Helston's left hook was indeed as vicious as she'd suggested. Michael gripped his hands behind his body, refusing to engage the three men before him. He deserved every bloody fist they sent his way.

"Oh, you're good," Helston purred in his ear after several blows. "But if you think playing the stoic pillar will gain you an inch of respect after you've admitted to dishonoring her, you're about to be proven quite, quite wrong. You see, there was something about that uncooperative, cowering boy in your stables which bespoke of hasty lies and secrets."

Michael took a step forward, colliding into the duke on purpose. "I don't care if you're the bloody King of England. If you laid a hand on Timmy Lattimer I shall strangle you with your lacy neckcloth and stuff that ornate quizzing glass down your throat."

Mr. Brown chuckled. "Now wait a minute, lads. This is pointless. Shouldn't we be discussing Lady Sheffield's—"

"Stay out of this if you treasure the last few hairs on your head, old man," Helston bit out.

"Brown's correct," Ellesmere insisted.

"Spoken like a true diplomatic bore," the duke muttered.

"I know I can always count on you to remind me of my place," Ellesmere replied dryly, "just as I must remind you that a naval commander's tactics bear little fruit on dry ground."

Helston looked like a ship's cannon, ready to explode. "Do we or do we not want to get to the bottom of this?"

"Of course," Ellesmere replied. "Mr. Ranier, let us state the facts. We could really care less about what you might be hiding. But you've compromised a lady high above your touch when she was at your mercy."

"I say we flog him," Helston muttered.

"You have precisely thirty seconds to explain yourself, lad," Mr. Brown warned.

"I never suggested I had an explanation."

"Did you or did you not seduce the Countess of Sheffield?" Helston barked. "And if I understand it, she was injured, to boot." He had completed a new circle and was now standing a fraction of a breath away from him.

Michael's three-inch advantage in height did little to unnerve the bastard. "I see few advantages to commenting on your theories."

Helston sent him a look filled with daggers. But under it, Michael was certain he glimpsed a similar expression to the one he'd spotted earlier in the marquis. "Ah, I understand the way of it now. *You* are the bloke who jilted her the first go-round, aren't you?"

Mr. Brown and the marquis grabbed the duke's arms as he fisted his hands.

"Dash it all," Mr. Brown muttered. "The lad 'as a bloody death wish."

"At least have the courtesy of telling us if you own this property or are you just a lusty servant after all?"

"I hold the deed to Brynlow."

The three gentlemen expelled their collective breaths.

"But I am sorry to inform that I have come into this property but lately. Until now, I shod horses and farmed a strip of land."

Pain of the acutest kind crossed the gentlemen's faces and Michael's throat tightened. If he had meant to cause them lifelong regret, he had accomplished it quite effectively.

He had taken advantage of her. A lady who was injured and at his mercy, during a snow storm. He had encouraged her to engage in wicked lust with a stranger.

In an ominous, strangled voice, the duke continued, "And how does a man such as you come to possess property such as this?"

"A will."

The Marquis of Ellesmere was still stunned by Michael's pronouncements. "Well, there is that. At least he's a landowner, if it comes to the point."

"And why does that signify?" Michael said through tight lips.

"I daresay they're trying to decide if it wouldna be better for the countess to marry you or if they should go with their first intention to bury you," Brown said.

"Grace Sheffey has no desire whatsoever to marry

me. She told me her intention is to travel to the Isle of Mann."

A look of relief washed over the gentlemen's faces.

"You will, of course, offer her marriage before she leaves. As a courtesy," the Duke of Helston stated.

"And we will do everything in our power to make sure she doesn't commit the greatest mistake of her life," Ellesmere continued, *"as a courtesy."*

Michael scratched his bristled cheek. "It appears I place a higher value on the countess's wishes than you. And since there's the fact that I possess none of your sort's manners—well, I feel absolutely no compunction to take part in your *undemocratic* charade."

Helston's face blanched. "By God, that's it. That accent. He's a murdering traitor to the crown. You are, aren't you? An ungrateful heathen from the *colonies.*"

It was the comment that broke Michael's self-discipline. It was too bad for them that they had not the advice of his cronies in Virginia in advance. It was clear within a few moments that these lords knew little of tactics practiced in London's finest gutters and Washington's muddiest ditches. Tactics that included a fury of elbows, knees, and teeth.

"Grace, my darling girl," Ata murmured, grasping her hand as they sat in the kitchen. "Luc found traces of bloodstains in the wrecked carriage."

"It was a small cut. There's no need to worry, Ata."

"Don't you dare lie to me, Grace Sheffey." Ata searched her exposed skin without success.

"Rosamunde and Georgiana, they did not join you?"

"They insisted on leaving Cornwall to see you in town as soon as Georgiana wed Quinn. But we arrived there the day after you left again. We determined to follow you when your servants told us you were gone with Mr. Brown to his home in Scotland. But Rosamunde and Georgiana remained in London for it was too hard on Quinn's daughter and the infants. The rest of us continued on, only to find ourselves stranded in the most wretched inn when the storm broke. We left yesterday despite the roads and found the wrecked carriage and Mr. Brown soon after."

"And Sarah and Elizabeth?"

"The other widows are waiting for us at a lovely estate not three or four miles from here—Beaulieu Park. The Duke of Beaufort's principal seat." Ata appeared flustered. "A very accommodating gentleman, the duke. Grace, what is that on your neck? You are very red there. Were you burned? Is there no salve to be found here?"

Grace jumped to the stove and stirred the bubbling porridge. "Nothing. Just an ill effect of the cold I suppose."

The sound of Ata's finger tapping the table broke the silence. "Grace, you must tell me. Did he hurt you? I promise I won't tell Luc or Quinn. He doesn't look the sort, but then he's so very intimidating. I must know. I can help you, you see. I know very well what it's like to have a man—" she interrupted herself. "That is . . . Oh Grace, I am so, so happy to see you well. But you are altered, or perhaps it is that you are acting differently.

I mean, cooking? Where are the servants? Oh, you are blushing . . ."

"Ata, Mr. Ranier did not ravish me."

"I see," the tiny dowager said, not seeing at all. "He's a very large man."

"You remarked on that already."

"But very gentle, I am guessing," Ata said with a knowing smile.

Grace could not utter a word. Instead she arranged the articles on the table.

"You must marry him. He's so very dashing and, well, *virile*. You will make us all so relieved to see you happy."

"I beg your pardon? I never meant to suggest I would wed Mr. Ranier."

"Well, in my day, a lady did not engage in an affair with a gentleman without benefit of marriage. Oh, the very bold might anticipate the vows by a week perhaps, but even so . . ."

"I am sorry I cannot make you and the others happy, Ata." Grace poured warmed milk into two bowls and pushed forward the honey pot.

Her older friend gazed at her for a long while and then murmured. "Well, I had to try, didn't I? Had to make it appear romantic. You know, Grace, unlike Luc and Quinn, I don't care if he is the gamekeeper. If he pleases you, that is all that matters. And no one would have to know. You could sell the townhouse the earl left you in London and purchase property in Cornwall—near all of us, and we'd concoct a history for Mr. Ranier. Oh, it would be perfect. You probably could not really show your face in town, since we both know peers are better at sniffing out a person's pedigree than hounds on a hunt. But, then, who needs town when—"

"Ata, Mr. Ranier and I agreed from the start. He is single-minded in his desire to work day and night to make this property, this new windfall of his, a fruitful one. And while he would never say it, he does not desire the added worry of a wife or—"

"But men never know what they—" Ata tried to interrupt, without success.

"No. I must finish." Grace examined her chapped hands. "I chose to take advantage, for a moment in time, of the freedom widowhood allows."

"It was never allowed in my time," Ata snorted as she pushed away the cooling milk. "Females were kept under lock and key, I tell you."

Grace's stiff smile wavered.

"And what is this business of returning to the Isle of Mann? You can't be serious," Ata said, a hint of fear in her expression. "Grace, you should never have tried to brazen it out in town by yourself. Why didn't you let us help you?"

"I think it should be obvious. Did you really think I would want to ruin Georgiana's sudden happiness by hovering about as the awkward, cast-off fiancée? Perhaps Georgiana shouldn't have hidden her great love for Quinn from me, but I understand why she did. Did I not do the exact same thing with Luc for years?"

Ata suddenly looked older than she ever had before in that moment.

"Oh Ata, I am sorry. But I realize now it might have

been better if we had spoken about it then instead of my running off to Italy when Luc married Rosamunde. Look, I left Cornwall last month to prove to myself that I could reenter society and refashion a new life all by myself. I wanted to do it alone, but in the end, I just didn't have the fortitude to do it." She looked down at her hands, folded in her lap. "The society columns were full of wild speculation and I received not a single invitation after I put my knocker up. And so, I begged Mr. Brown quite shamelessly to take me up in his carriage when he announced he was continuing on to Scotland."

For once, Ata did not try to interrupt her.

"Again, I tried to run away from disappointment. But I realize now that I'll never find lasting happiness there. I'm only running away from myself. And I enjoy the vast diversions of life in town. I always have. I like the vibrant excitement of it. And I love to be surrounded by my friends. By you, Ata, most of all."

"Oh my darling," Ata uttered, gripping Grace's hand tightly, tears glinting on her withered cheeks. "I can't bear what you've endured. I think if Luc were not related to me I would have put a pistol ball through his heart last year. And Quinn . . . but that is too new. My only consolation is knowing they suffer more than you, I assure you."

"Ata, I am certain you understand that I cannot support everyone's pity." Grace returned to the pot to stir the porridge, which she knew neither one of them would eat. "In fact, I pray Mr. Ranier will tell Luc and Quinn the bare truth of the last few days. I am very grateful to Mr. Ranier. I assure you I vastly prefer the role of a scandalous widow bereft of morals rather than a wretched, jilted bride twice over."

"Grace!"

"Well, it's true. We both know it."

"I don't think the peers of the realm will see it quite that way," Ata added dryly.

"I know."

"Well, what are we to do?"

It saddened Grace to see the dowager duchess in such a state. Ata had never, in all her life, not had a plan. She was a force of nature when it concerned her wishes. "I suppose we shall just have to do what will bring all of us the most ill ease and the greatest potential for disaster—return to London."

"Oh." A gleam appeared in Ata's shrewd brown eyes. "And I know just what to do. No one will ever learn of what happened here. You shall give an enormous ball in Quinn and Georgiana's honor. That will keep the gossip-mongers in check. Do you think we stand a chance of enticing Mr. Ranier to attend? If you dance two waltzes with him, why, he's so very masculine in that animal-like way that everyone will forget all about that talk regarding you and Quinn."

Grace closed her eyes. Would she always have to endure such situations? The stark manor on the desolate lands of Mann really did appear much more inviting.

The muffled sounds of Luc, Mr. Brown, and Quinn's voices and footfalls echoed from the stair, yet the gentlemen did not enter the kitchen. They were hiding something. Luc's gruff voice called from the door leading to the stables. "Ata . . . Grace? We'll see to the carriage. We depart for Beaufort's at a quarter past the hour. That should be sufficient time for you to collect your affairs, Grace. Ata, you are not to leave her alone with that . . . that bloody heathen."

The duke did not wait for an answer. The slam of the door proclaimed to the world what he really wanted to say.

A gleam appeared in Ata's eyes and it eased Grace as nothing else had. "Insolent puppy. Always was. Always will be."

Grace smiled. "You love him."

"Well, how can I not? I sadly recognize my obstinate blood runs thick in his veins. And I have no one else to blame but myself."

Grace smiled, so happy to see her friend's humor returned.

"Now go on, child. Don't be a fool. I don't need to tell you to ignore my grandson. If you are half the lady I know you to be, you will stop all this nonsense and grab onto that monstrously large man upstairs and compromise him again within an inch of his life."

"Ata!"

"Oh, botheration. Do you want me to do it for you? I've taken a sudden liking to this era's customs."

Tears of laughter filled Grace's eyes. "Enough!"

Ata leaned in close to confide in her. "You know, I've never told anyone but I actually tried to do something similar fifty years ago, although it was perhaps not quite so bold. Unfortunately, the man I chose was too hen-hearted to go through with it."

Poor Mr. Brown.

A creak from above stairs interrupted and they both glanced up. Ata grasped Grace's shoulder. "Go to him. I could see he cares for you, Grace. You've nothing to fear."

"I never said I was afraid of him, Ata. In fact, he might just be the only man I don't fear."

Grace moved the porridge pot from the fire and left before Ata could say another word. She knocked on his chamber door once and didn't bother to wait for a response.

He was standing before the fire, his hands on his hips. When he did not turn to face her, she began. "I've come to take my leave. And to thank you. Thank you for rescuing me and for, well . . . everything else. I'm only sorry my friends did not understand the enormity of how much I am in your debt." He still refused to turn around, and his silence made it very awkward. "And I also wanted to inform that I've decided to return to London after all. I was a fool to think I'd find happiness on Mann. Everyone knows the home of your childhood never turns out to be the way you remember it."

"Actually, sweetheart, sometimes it's exactly as you remember it." He slowly swung around and she rushed to him.

"Oh, you're bleeding." She felt for the handkerchief in her pocket and reached for his face.

"Stop. It's naught but a scratch."

"Don't be ridiculous. Here, let me—"

He caught her wrist in midair. "Don't, angel."

So they were back to the impressive list of impersonal names he used to address her. Well, perhaps it was better that way since it was good-bye.

"It's nothing," he continued, "and we've more pressing things to discuss." His face was tight and very white and it didn't appear to be due to the cut on his chin.

"Mr. Ranier, if you offer a single word about marriage, I shall not forgive you." She forced levity into it. "I might even prepare your dinner for a month as revenge."

Michael's expression relaxed a small measure. "Now Blue Eyes, did I ever complain about the meals you so lovingly prepared?"

"No. You were too polite to utter a word. But I do think I'd take great delight in watching you squirm through a few more if you suggest the joys of connubial bliss. I will know it's the work of Luc and Quinn."

"Connubial bliss? Is that what your sort calls it?" He'd moved closer to her. Unbearably close.

The scent of him jolted memories of passion shared and passion about to be lost forevermore. "Don't. Please," she whispered raised her eyes to his. "We made a bargain. And I will consider it a grave insult if you dare to offer a single insincere wish."

"With you, my dear Countess, the notion of *connubial bliss* holds much appeal . . . although I might call it something altogether more interesting. Ah, sweetheart . . . what happened last night. What I will dream about for the rest of my natural—"

She put her hands out to stop him. "No. Don't say it."

For the barest instant, his expression revealed the strain of withheld emotion before it closed off again.

It was so horribly unfair. The temptation was just too great. She had to know if he spoke the truth or if he was like all the rest . . . a man who uttered sentiments all in the name of chivalry. It was easy for him to pretend emotions when she had promised to reject him. But what would he do if she did not keep her end of the bargain?

Grace ignored her ill ease and took her decision before courage deserted her. And she would do it on her own two feet, without the easy comfort of his arms. "Michael . . . you once told me men base their self-worth on their fortune and station in life. I just want you to know that I care not a jot about those two things in a man—or in a future husband."

His eyes filled with pain and something else. Something very like fear.

Grace's fingers moved unconsciously to her pearls. "Look, the truth of it is that I possess a fortune great enough to keep several peers and their families in lavish comfort for longer than one lifetime."

He paused before he asked quietly, "Are you proposing that your future husband will live off of your generosity, Countess?"

She tried to inject humor in her tone but knew she fell flat as she cared too much for the outcome. "Well, did you not suggest my desirability lies in my fortune?"

"No. I suggested you should start thinking like a man, Countess."

"Well, you must know the gentlemen of England never hesitate to elevate their stations by marrying ladies for their fortunes. Wives are actually the primary contributors to the gaming houses in town. It's truly extraordinary, the largess gentlemen fish for in the well-lined pockets of heiresses." She took one long last look at his closed-off expression, and the pain of rejection filled her, yet perversely encouraged her to continue on, toward complete and utter humiliation. "Unless, of course, there is something irrevocably off-putting in the female. Then, I've found lately—very lately, that is—that the man will decide to become noble and too proud to accept that sort of windfall."

He grabbed her arms and shook her. "For Christ sakes, if last night didn't prove to you how much this godforsaken blacksmith desires you, then there's just no hope for it."

"Well then, is it your pride that . . ." She just couldn't voice the rest of it.

An odd light appeared in his eyes before he tamped it down. "Is that what you call it when a man refuses to fawn over and feed off a rich woman?"

"Yes."

"Well then . . . yes, it must be bloody pride."

"There's no need for blasphemy."

"Damnation, this is exactly the time for blasphemy. I warned you I'm not a man of pretty words, even if those silk and satin lords in London do well by them. You're correct. You should go back there, sweetheart.

It's where you belong, not mucking about the northern shires."

Emotion surged through her. "I will not apologize for my life—for the riches my husband left me. Your acquaintance bequeathed this house to you and you accepted it."

"True. But you'll never find me at the end of a leash in London, dancing about like a *prize stud*. Go back to your world where dreams are bought and sold on a whim. I've no place for you here."

With a strangled sound, Grace cracked her hand against his cheek with enough force to snap his head to one side and then whirled toward the door. She was two steps from freedom when strong arms gripped her waist and turned her into his arms to kiss her quite senseless, despite her resistance.

He shouldn't have pulled her into his arms. He knew it. But he couldn't bear the last memory of her to be one of anger. He was just too selfish. And so for one short moment before she could react further, he poured out every last drop of his passion for this perfect woman in his arms.

His eyes still closed, she shoved hard against him and dashed through the door before he could see her clearly. Damn, his eyes were leaking. All this mingling with dapper nobs was rubbing off on him.

Michael moved to the fire again and listened for the sounds of her departure. His feet felt like they were mired in a bog.

God, he had hated saying what he did. But it was better for her to think him a crass idiot than for her to understand the truth of the matter. What was it about confounded aristocrats and their stupid pride?

He would never allow the deadly threat of discovery and vicious truths to ruin the life she deserved. A life beside a true gentleman with everything and the sun to give her.

Panic surged inside of him. The clinking of the traces on the duke's carriage horses penetrated the fog of his mind. He didn't even know her direction in London. Perhaps it was better that way. She had promised to tell him if there was ever a child. Hell, if there was a child, he had no doubt those two lords joined at the hip would track him down.

He closed his eyes, listening hard until nothing could be heard except the sparks crackling before him in the grate. And suddenly, the memories of another fire, so long ago, obliterated all thoughts of Grace Sheffey.

Chapter 8

Grace wasn't sure what force pushed her to go down to dinner at Beaulieu Park that evening. Perhaps it was that she knew she might just go mad if she indulged in another minute of reflection.

He had said he didn't want her—didn't want to be a *prize stud at the end of a leash*. Good God. The bile rose in the back of her throat and she stopped on the stair. She knew of such women. There were several very rich, slightly aged widows in town who were whispered to welcome the attentions of handsome gentlemen with pockets to let.

His words echoed repeatedly in her mind and balled themselves into a black fury growing within her.

The unmitigated gall of Michael Ranier.

She pushed back her shoulders to continue down the wide carpeted stairs of the Duke of Beaufort's extraordinary castle. She concentrated on the magnificent fresco on the domed ceiling above, and the gold leaf applied to almost every surface of relief. Elegant antiquities had apparently dripped from the family tree for centuries. Everything reflected painstaking refinement. The pathos of the ages echoed from the violent battle scenes depicted on nearly every enormous canvas buffeting the walls.

Grace encountered two motionless footmen dressed in pale blue and silver livery at the foot of the stair.

"Good evening," she murmured.

Both servants appeared flustered to be addressed without a request attached. "Your Ladyship," they replied in unison and bowed.

She followed the drift of voices farther down the wide main hall to peer from the shadows outside the salon's doorway.

They were all assembled, Luc, Quinn, Ata, and Mr. Brown, as well as Elizabeth Ashburton, Sarah Winters, and their host, the Duke of Beaufort. The latter held the rapt attention of all of his guests as he told an absurd story concerning a poacher found on his land.

"I told the man this morning that he had two choices. I would either give him over to the constable in York or he could save both of us quite a bit of trouble by allowing me to shoot him straightaway," the tall, elderly duke said.

"Pray tell, what did he choose, Charles?" Ata was hanging on his every word.

The duke chuckled. "He relieved himself into my care as well as the tangle of fur and feathers and informed me as cool as you please that I was touched in the attics."

Ata dissolved in laughter while Mr. Brown remained unmoved.

"Ah, Lady Sheffield," the elderly duke said, spying her. "Delighted you joined us after all, my dear. Shall you take a glass of ratafia before we dine?"

"Thank you, but no, Your Grace."

"No, no, my dear. You must call me Charles. Makes me feel young again to have all of you address me so."

Two shadows fell on either side of Grace and she turned to find her friends, Elizabeth and Sarah, beside her. Grace took comfort in their silent companionship.

"Charles," Ata said, laughing, "you are entirely too free with us. And we shall never be able to repay you for taking us in at a moment's notice."

"It is I who am grateful to you"—he stared down intently at Ata—"for relieving the tedium here. I hadn't known I was bored until you quite effectively removed the blinders from my eyes."

Mr. Brown coughed while Luc and Quinn appeared vastly amused.

The butler chose that moment to enter and announce dinner.

"Come, my dear Ata, you must sit beside me again and tell me more about this Cornwall of yours. Is it really as warm as you say? Does such a place exist in England?"

All of them fell into two orderly lines as they strolled into the dining room. The racks of generations of horned beasts adorned what seemed to be every square inch of exposed wall between tapestries depicting all manner of hunters and their prey. Candlelight reflected from the crystal and porcelain placed with precision on the vast table covered with crisp white linens. The duke lived the life of a man who enjoyed the privilege bestowed by generations of kings and barbarians before him.

And it left Grace cold. Colder than all the layers of ice to the north and all the frozen caverns below. But at the same time, she was comforted by the familiar feeling. Had not cool reason been the guiding hand throughout her life?

Mr. Brown held her chair as Grace eased onto the elegant embroidered seat. He leaned down to whisper, "The man tells too many stories by half. Don't trust him an inch."

Grace smiled and waited till Mr. Brown seated himself beside her. "Perhaps you should do something about it."

He raised his gray eyebrows, as thick and unruly as gorse bushes. "What do you suggest?"

Elizabeth Ashburton leaned from his other side, her melodic laughter turned to a whisper. "Don't waste your breath, Grace. He wouldn't take any of our suggestions."

"Eh? What's that you're saying?" The Duke of Beaufort asked from the head of the table.

Grace gazed at the overabundance on the table as a servant placed a steaming bowl of turtle soup in front of her. For a moment she was reminded of nutty porridge before she firmly pushed away the thought and proceeded to engage in what she did so well—banal conversation. It was just too bad the duke would have little of it.

"Your hospitality knows no bounds, sir. How did you come to meet my friends?" Grace unfolded the napkin, stiff with starch.

"Why, I was hunting in the westerly corner of the Park yesterday and spied them clustered about that wreck of a carriage. Not surprised it fell to splinters. Why the thing should have been taken to the chopping block two decades ago. Not safe. Not safe at all."

Grace's hand found Mr. Brown's arm and he cursed under his breath.

"Charles invited us all to stay as soon as he heard of our predicament," Ata said, gazing at the duke.

"Of course I did," he replied. "And I hope you'll stay a fortnight at the very least. The countess must regain her strength, after all."

Grace looked at the faces around the elegant table. Such a comical array of expressions. Luc and Quinn were very ill at ease each time they glanced at her. "You are very kind, sir, but we shall not inconvenience you. There are two ladies in London who are probably very worried, and their husbands should return to them," she said. "*Tomorrow.*"

Mr. Brown squeezed her hand.

"This will not do at all," the duke replied. "Ah, but I have it, by Jove." He appeared vastly pleased with himself.

"What is it, Charles?" The outlandish glint of flirtation shone in Ata's dark eyes.

"I have the famous idea of joining you. Hate town . . . but I have an enticement, now. And there is something to be said for spending Christmas among friends."

Mr. Brown muttered something not fit for female ears. Grace only wished she knew what it meant.

The rest of the meal passed without much participation from her, the Duke of Beaufort's garrulous ways a blessing in disguise. With the exception of Ata and the duke, each of the others at the table appeared to have not the slightest interest in conversation. Quinn Fortesque most of all. She was going to have to make an effort in that guilt-stricken corner.

Much later, as she sat before an ornate looking glass in the lovely bedchamber she had been assigned, Grace stared at her reflection. She was surprised to see the same visage staring back at her. She felt as if a lifetime had passed and she thought it should have at least marked her in some fashion.

Suddenly, her many layers of soft nightclothes, recovered from Mr. Brown's carriage, seemed for the first time suffocating. She rose from her perch and flung open the window. A vast expanse of starry sky filled her vision. She stared to the east. Just three miles away stood a very small manor, tucked into a cluster of trees. *He* would be reading again in the cozy library, which would appear far too small for a large man such as he. Or perhaps he would be in the barn with Timmy Lattimer. She wondered in a rush if the lamb had survived the night, and sent up a small prayer for Pearl's sake. Oh, she was being such a stupid little fool about all of it.

Everyone knew that lamb was going to end up in a stew pot in the coming months, or forced into a lifetime of annual birthing before ending up in the stew pot. She exhaled. They had agreed it was but a simple joining of bodies. Mutual pleasure.

But for her it had proved to be something else entirely. It had been an awakening. The world appeared cold and raw and new, instead of sedate, ordered, and comfortable.

She should be grateful to Michael Ranier. But she

could not be. The time with him had been too poignant, and the breaking away had not been done well.

She just had not known how to go about it. She never should have dared utter a hint that she might welcome sharing a life with him. Her throat tightened in remembrance. How on earth did people conduct affairs with any sort of decorum?

She knew time and the comforts of her well-ordered, easy life would ease her as they had done in the past. Soon, she would be able to untangle the disorder of her thoughts and feelings and put them into organized compartments. Under lock and—

A soft tapping at her door interrupted her thoughts, and Sarah and Elizabeth slipped in on tiptoe around the edge of her door.

"Oh, you *are* still up," Elizabeth whispered. "Sarah and I couldn't sleep."

Grace looked at the other two widows, and wished she had the gift of easy intimacy with other women. "Nor could I. I'm glad you came."

The two women drifted to either side of her and Sarah pulled back the curtain to gaze into the night sky too. "Oh, it's not as cold tonight, thank goodness. What a lovely night, is it not?" Sarah said.

"Yes," Grace agreed. All three ladies gazed mutely at the stars until awkwardness crept in.

"Grace," Elizabeth began tentatively, "will you not tell us what really happened—what is wrong?"

"Why would you think something is wrong?"

"Luc is limping and Quinn appeared very ill at ease when all of you returned," Sarah said, "and throughout dinner both kept staring at you."

Before she could respond, Elizabeth took over. "When you left Cornwall with Mr. Brown, Sarah and I wanted to come after you right away. And we would have, if we'd owned a carriage. We thought you might have liked to confide in us."

Grace rubbed a finger along the edge of the window frame. "I'm sorry I didn't seek you out. I shall tell you the truth of it. I just wanted to lick my wounds in private. It all seems so silly now. I wouldn't have been truly happy with Quinn." She turned her gaze from the stars to look at her two friends.

"Oh Grace," Elizabeth breathed, "there's something different about your eyes now. They are . . ."

"*Bluer*," Sarah finished hesitantly.

Grace returned the lady's smile and linked arms with them for the first time since she had known them. Surprise warred with pleasure on their faces. "You know what I've decided?"

They glanced at her expectantly.

"I think the Duke of Beaufort is directly descended from the murdering heathens of the Dark Ages, when whole villages lived in this castle, and entire families slept in each of these huge beds. With this forest of beheaded beasts staring at me I'll never get any sleep. What say you? Shall we all get under this heap of blankets on this monstrous bed? Perhaps we can debate how long it will be before Mr. Brown tries to hang the good Duke of Beaufort from one of these fallow deer racks."

Elizabeth, the tallest and most exuberant of the widows in their club, flung her arms about Grace and hugged her to her breast. "Oh, I prayed you were having a grand adventure. You did, didn't you?"

Grace looked at the impetuous young widow with her lion's mane of hair haloing her lovely face, and smiled. "Perhaps."

"Oh, I knew it. I was the only one who had faith in your endurance. Did I not tell you, Sarah?"

"You did, indeed." Sarah Winters was the eldest of them. Two wings of soft brown hair framed her clear gray eyes. Of all the ladies, Grace had found Sarah to be the kindest, and the most reserved.

Each of them rearranged the covers of the massive sleigh bed and propped the huge pillows along the head board. Inelegantly, they crawled under the covers like children.

Elizabeth leaned forward and grasped her hands, her eyes sparkling. "Tell us precisely what happened . . . Do not gloss over a single detail."

Grace glanced from one expectant face to the other. If she could not trust these two ladies, there was no one on the face of this earth whom she could trust. And so, for the first time in her life, Grace confided what had happened. Oh, she was not so bold as to convey every last shocking detail. But her blushes probably explained what her words did not.

Sarah patted her hand. "Oh, but he will come after you. And he will come on bended knee, uttering a mound of apologies, too."

Before Grace could disagree, Elizabeth continued. "Sarah is correct. Gentlemen don't easily forget." Elizabeth twisted a corner of her plain white dressing gown. An unusual hint of fear glinted in her eyes. "Indeed, sometimes, they never forget." Elizabeth Ashburton had never said a word about her past, and

Grace was certain there was something much deeper to her words.

Grace glanced at the earnest faces on either side of her. "I thank you for allowing me to confide in you, but you are both absolutely mistaken. In fact, given my rare history with gentlemen, I'd sooner expect to recklessly wager my fortune than to ever see the day Mr. Ranier came up to scratch. But I don't want you to worry. I know precisely what to do now. We shall all go to London. Together . . . with our hearts united as we dance foolishly toward disaster."

A smile returned to Elizabeth's pretty face. "Ummm, Grace?"

"Yes?"

"Could you please relate again exactly what happened between you and Mr. Ranier? You seem to have gained an unholy love of the ridiculous, something we'd not known you to possess before."

Grace hugged a pillow to her breast and smiled.

Michael sat at a table in a room he had not previously occupied in Sam's house, the small chamber fashioned for formal dining. It was the only room which was not fully furnished. For some odd reason, Michael had the distinct impression that Sam had halfheartedly gone about decorating it, only to give up when he'd decided it was an awkward chamber, too far from the kitchen, and too cold and dark.

Michael toyed with the excellent roast beef and the boiled potatoes and carrots Timmy's mother had prepared for him within hours of Mr. and Mrs. Lattimer's return that afternoon.

He would have given just about anything for a taste of burnt stew instead. Had it really only been three days?

The gloomy chamber made Michael lonely, a sensibility with which he was not well acquainted. It was the only room he could tolerate this evening. Every other place in Brynlow held memories of Grace.

He tossed his knife and fork onto the plate with a clatter.

Michael rose from the table and fisted his hands. He'd been itching to punch a wall all day. That was certainly a first. He'd always taken pride in his even nature.

Aside from two very specific events, he'd never regretted any action in the whole course of his life. Tonight, he did.

He wasn't sure how he could have accomplished it, but he should have severed his connection with her in a better fashion. He had counted too much on her desire to rejoin the fabulously rich Mr. Brown he'd concocted in his mind. And he'd been certain she would want to return to the luxuries of her life with her friends.

He had guessed straightaway that all her talk of trotting off to Mann had been a desire for temporary sanctuary. If she had gone there, she wouldn't have lasted a fortnight before becoming bored out of her mind on that desolate island.

She was far too good and kindhearted for her friends to abandon her to a lifetime there. She was a lady who was meant to return to the dazzling amusements found only in town. And if he forced himself to guess, within a month or two at most, a slew of richer-than-Croesus swells would pluck her out of her roost, place a very tight jeweled ring on her finger, and install her in a Mayfair townhouse dipped in gold and swathed in servants who would answer to her every beck and call.

He rubbed the ache between his brows. *Ah, hell.* Grace wasn't like that at all. That was the crux of the problem. He would wager she would be willing to give up a good deal. He envisioned the cozy cocoon she would have created at Brynlow. He could even imagine her lovely voice falsely insisting each year that she wasn't interested in spending the season in town with her friends.

And all the time, she would think he refused to go to London because of stupid pride. And for years, he would have let her think that. And there would have been always . . . *always, damnation,* the risk of exposure.

The risk of coming face-to-face with Rowland Manning's vengeance and the utter ruination of anyone caught with him. It was not dancing in the air at the end of a hangman's noose he feared so much as the stain it would leave on her name and his family's name. He would be relegated to a footnote in history as a cowardly, lying murderer—true or not. He would be proclaimed the single failure among generations of heroic, illustrious Wallaces.

He shook his head. And worst of all, Grace would be forever cast aside by society.

And suddenly he was mortally tired of living this half life.

A footfall echoed in the hall and he turned to find plump Mrs. Lattimer in the doorway. She glanced at the heaping remains on his plate and appeared crestfallen. "Shall I bring you somethin' more to yer likin', sir? Timmy tells me yer right fond of our cheese."

"No, no, Mrs. Lattimer. The roast beef was delicious. I, uh, I'm feeling a bit off, that's all."

Concern lined her forehead and she plucked at the practical cap covering her tightly coiled hair. "Half the village is abed with a digestin' complaint. A fine welcome to the North. I'm sorry, sir."

He waved away her concerns and rose from the table. "Never been ill a day in my life, ma'am. I'll be as right as nine pins on the morrow."

She grinned, revealing an uneven but endearing smile. "Shall I bring you a drop o' tea in the library, sir? I bought a bit in the village in case you liked it. Mr. Bryn never asked for it. But perhaps it would ease you. Mr. Lattimer built up the fire for you."

They were determined to coddle him, which amused Michael to no end. He'd never employed servants before and it was clearly going to take some getting used to. He realized, oddly enough, the luxury of poverty—of never having to put on a show of good humor. "Tea would be just the thing," he lied.

He urged her to enter the short hall before him, and she trundled ahead, stopping inside the library. "Oh, and Mr. Ranier? I took the liberty of going through the chest of drawers, as it be wash day tomorrow." Her face colored and she couldn't meet his eyes as she placed something on the edge of the desk. "Found this pretty shawl, and wasn't sure if'n it be from the lady Timmy said you rescued. And, sir, it appears she knitted these mittens. She used a bit of the brown wool in the basket Mr. Bryn kept filled fer me."

He would not rush forward. "Thank you Mrs. Lattimer."

Blessedly, she departed and in two strides he was at the desk. Without thought he crushed the pink silk shawl to his face and breathed deeply. A rush of heaven sang in his mind and settled in his heavy bones. He gulped in the scent like a drunken fool. With each successive pull, images of Grace Sheffey floated in his consciousness. Her graceful hands, the arch of her back as she sat perched on a chair, the gold spun softness of her hair in the glow of firelight, her silken skin, and lush, tentative lips. And her eyes. Those blue, blue eyes of hers. Eyes that became lost in passion when he encouraged her to—God . . . he had to stop. He would lose his sanity from it.

He dropped into the leather chair, clutching the shawl like a bloody infant and then noticed the huge mittens. What on earth . . . Good God. She'd knitted them for him. Her scent was even in these too. Perhaps they had been her way of thanking him for rescuing her. She would have done it for anyone. Or perhaps they were for something else. She had mentioned something about the approach of Christmas and Boxing Day when they had spoken freely in the darkness, wrapped in each other's arms. He hadn't had the heart to tell her that Christmases at the orphanage had brought only the paltry joy of an extra portion of coarse bread if they were lucky, which did little to dispel the sadness of life without a most beloved parent.

God Almighty.

And he had given her nothing. Had only taken.

Staring into the leaping flames of the tidy fire in the library, flashes of her rooted around his mind again and again. It was a sign of weak character. Of pointless longing. He'd heard tell of it. Had thought it was something for idle, rich folk. Well, he'd no time for it. Surely, it was a temporary ailment, probably brought on by soft living—with servants, no less.

Mrs. Lattimer bustled inside with a tray and after a flurry of inquiries after his morning hours and needs, disappeared. Damn temptation. She'd placed a bottle of brandy beside the teapot. He poured some tea, the delicate amber brown of the brew swirling in his cup. Belatedly, he realized he'd not used the strainer. He scratched his head. Ah, the joys of a civilized life.

He added a lump of sugar and a splash of milk, and gulped the lot of it in one swallow. He wondered if he would make a habit of it. God, for five and twenty of his thirty-two years he'd considered clean water a luxury. He shook his head and almost reached for the brandy before coming to his senses.

It was amazing how spirits could unlock the mysteries of all problems, given enough time and enough firewater. Indeed, the fumes seemed to burn through any complicating factor. The only drawbacks were that the answers were usually fraught with disaster when rational thought returned, with a headache of epic proportions on the side. Besides, he had done so much wrong in his life, he had sworn once he'd left England that he would renounce all manner of sin if only to atone in some small way for his past mistakes.

Sprawled in the leather chair he'd last sat in with Grace, he tried to focus on the plans for winter and spring. He would order seed and then plant ten acres of wheat, barley, and corn aside from the hay fields. And he'd enlarge the flock of sheep. With any luck, within a few years he'd be able to realize his dream of training and breeding horses. Sam had left him three broodmares and a plough team. And then there was Sioux. She would be the first he would breed when he found an adequate stallion.

Why had she been so afraid of horses? He would have enjoyed teasing and goading her into the horsemanship lessons he had suggested. They could have had such pleasure riding the property in the spring. One of the broodmares was docile and the perfect size for her. And during the hot days of summer, they could have ridden to the clutch of apple trees in the north corner near the pond. Or perhaps they would have enjoyed a late-evening stroll with the sparkle of glowworms all about them during the fruitful season.

God, what sentimental drivel.

His mind shuttled away to the cyclical nature of life on this new land of his. The ewes would be dropping young more and more in the coming two months. As would the cows and the two broodmares. He wondered with a heavy heart if, despite his efforts, Grace would grow round with child. With *his* child. And all of a sudden he quite desperately wanted it. He cursed and reached for the brandy, praying for sweet oblivion amid the madness of everything that was Grace Sheffey.

When Michael awoke with a head that felt twice as large as it should, he rubbed his bleary eyes only to find he was wearing brown mittens. His throat cottony, he looked around and his brains sloshed about the inside of his head.

Christ. He had violated the two cardinal rules. The candle was aflame *and* he was three sheets to the wind. He was bloody well going to the dogs.

Yes, indeed, he was as good as gone.

Chapter 9

"Do make an effort, Quinn," Grace insisted quietly. The carriage wheel caught a rut and both Grace and Quinn swayed inside the vehicle.

His face was white with tension. "I do not expect you to accept my apology. Indeed, it seems almost an insult to offer one, as I don't want to ask anything of you. I don't even have the comfort of being able to offer any sort of appeasement."

Grace was in a perverse frame of mind. She'd begged a private word with him at the last posting inn, where the entire party of three carriages had stopped to change horses before they continued on the last leg of the three-day journey to London. Now she wished she hadn't bothered. Gentlemen had no idea how tiresome it was to listen to them blather on about the preservation of their honor.

"I told you, there's no need to apologize. I'm only grateful you and Georgiana admitted your mutual affection before you and I left for the Duchess of Kendale's house party. *Before* we married. Yes, the gossip in town is fevered due to the duchess's tales, but we shall overcome it by standing together. So please,

Quinn, do me the great favor of putting your guilt aside. Otherwise we're doomed to forever feeling awkward."

Across the carriage bench Quinn sat studying her face with care. She watched his Adam's apple bob. "What did he do to you?"

She sighed with exasperation. "If you don't stop this, I'll cut your acquaintance in town after I play the farce of a mammoth ball in your honor and Georgiana's."

He rubbed his brow. "I don't know which is worse— what I did, or what that—that blacksmith did to you. He did offer for you, did he not? And you turned him down?" He continued without waiting for an answer. "Well, at least no one else will ever know of the encounter."

Finally, Grace snapped. Michael's words echoed in her brain. *A man bases his worth on his fortune and station in life.* "All right. I see how it is. I have an idea. You shall direct your steward or solicitor to draw up a bank draft."

Quinn straightened his posture, his eyes alert. "A bank draft?"

"Yes. I've decided the only way you or Luc will ever stop looking at me as though I'm a pitiful creature, is to demand that you each give over an absurd amount of coin."

Quinn's brows drew together, but he appeared ready to acquiesce to anything she asked. "Whatever you desire from me is yours, Grace."

"It's not for me. It's alms for charity. It's the season for it after all, is it not?"

"And what, pray tell, is this worthy cause?"

"A foundling hospital."

The glimmer of benevolent amusement appeared on his face. "How obscene an amount are you proposing?"

"Enough to make you think twice about ever crossing a Sheffield again," she purred with a smile.

"I see," his eyes twinkled.

"No, I don't think you do." It was astonishing how the smile that had once caused Grace to flush with pleasure did nothing to her now.

"I shall double the amount you suggest," he said, his noble smile widening.

"Five thousand pounds."

That wiped the grin from his face. Why, five thousand was enough to keep a great house and all its servants quite comfortable for a year or more.

"Grace, the purchase of Trehallow for Georgiana and her family has put quite a strain on . . ." He sputtered to a halt before continuing. "Would you like my solicitors to deliver the *ten* thousand pounds to—"

"I shall take pity on you, Quinn. I should have clarified that I expect you *and* Luc to divide the burden. I shall not hold you to doubling it."

He exhaled roughly, his face still blanched.

"Oh, and Quinn?"

His posture had finally unbent. "Yes?"

"Thank you."

"No. It is I who—"

"Not for the donation."

"For what then?"

"For marrying Georgiana. For letting me go."

"You've fallen under that heathen's spell, haven't you?"

"No."

He shook his head. "Take care, Grace. I, of all people, recognize the signs now."

"And what precisely are the signs?"

"Decisive one-word answers, for a start."

She laughed. "So you're saying I should prevaricate?"

"Yes. But only if you can do it convincingly." He rearranged her lap blanket. "I only wish there was a true possibility for a future for you with him. But it's impossible. He's not a gentleman worthy of you, my dear. Indeed, he's no gentleman at all."

"Well, I see the entire affair quite differently."

"How so?"

"You think he's not laudable because of his station in life. But, you see, that's not it. I chose not to like him because he's foolish enough to let an illogical notion of pride stand in his way. The man had the audacity to think it wasn't correct to marry a lady with a fortune such as mine when he has so little."

Quinn's lips twitched. "Perhaps it's some sort of dreadful disease afflicting people in the colonies."

"Obviously an advanced case. Lord knows no blue-blooded gentleman I know would ever let a fortune stand in the way of marriage."

Quinn chuckled and Grace couldn't help but join in. And like a giggle in church, the tension had turned and they could not stop until they were nearly out of breath from laughter.

But in her heart, Grace knew the tears on her cheeks were not all from mirth. She finally allowed the full weight of the truth to engulf her.

The Michael Ranier she knew would never have let pride stand in his way if he had truly wanted something or someone. He was like an avalanche, never allowing anything to stop his natural course of motion.

He had not wanted to share a life with her. And so he had conjured up words he thought a rich countess would allow herself to believe.

Well.

Mr. Ranier had forgotten his earlier ludicrous conviction. Perhaps she *was* a Viking at her core—and not an overbred aristocrat. A swell of strength flowed through her for some bizarre reason she refused to examine. She was just too grateful for its appearance.

Grace peered out the small panes of the carriage window and spied the outline of the tallest spires of London in the twilight. They almost looked like the masts of a fleet of vessels.

It was time to go raiding.

It was amazing how nature was able to beautify what man had once destroyed.

Michael sat astride Sioux, gazing at the vast view from the crag of one of Derbyshire's most famous prominences. The wind whipped about him from all directions, but he couldn't feel the cold. The scene in the distance robbed him of coherent thought.

He hadn't seen it in almost two decades. Hadn't thought he would ever have the chance to see it again.

Wallace Abbey—or rather, the charred remains of

one of England's oldest and most beautiful estates— rose up from the faded tangle of winter grasses. Christendom had clearly forsaken the jagged fragments and consecrated this man-made creation to the devil. With the upheavals due to the transference of power from mad King George to the Prince Regent, and the country at war for so long, Prinny and the House of Lords had probably shoved the dilemma of the burned Wallace estate to the bottom of its docket many years ago.

He realized now that some part of him had tried to forget he had ever been born or lived here. The knowledge of what he could have been if he hadn't made so many terrible mistakes was excruciating. But with Wallace Abbey before him, in all its ruined majesty, the magnified horrors of his youth melted away. And he couldn't stop the spark of an impossible dream. In a rush, he wanted to know if the property had reverted to the crown, or if stewards assigned by some unknown authority oversaw the land. And he could vividly envision how the abbey could be rebuilt to its former splendor.

There were a few signs of usage in the distance. Someone either leased the land, or nearby inhabitants had encroached. White dots suggested a flock of sheep and tilled rows gave evidence of past crops. Michael was glad. At least someone was benefiting from the estate.

Lost in thought, he straightened when his mare snorted and pawed the rocky heath, signaling her distrust of the prominence. Michael turned Sioux's head and urged her toward a lone hawthorn tree behind them. Dismounting, he let his horse nibble the sparse tufts of wild grass while he turned to his other purpose for coming here.

He withdrew a letter as he returned to the edge of the crag, unable to stay away from the poignant view of his first home. The note was from London, of that he was certain.

If only it were from her. He had brought it here, far, far away from Brynlow and the curious glances of the kindhearted Lattimers, who appeared determined to hover about him in the barns, and in the house. He was unused to living daily, no hourly, with others.

In his heart he knew the letter was not from Grace. The common gray paper was sealed with a lump of rye dough, and the directions were in a vaguely familiar hand unlike Grace's elegant, sloping script.

She had been gone for only one week, and he had quite effectively sliced to ribbons any chance of continuing the acquaintance. Why, he was the last person in the world she would ever approach again in her lifetime.

But he had learned long ago that hope was an essential ingredient to leading a purposeful life. And so he never pushed it away. Even when there was no foundation whatsoever for fulfillment of wishes, hope was necessary. For without it, without dreams, souls withered and died.

And so, he had hoped the letter was from Grace when Mrs. Lattimer placed it in his hands after her return from the village late yesterday. He had taken the decision to visit a ghost of his past, Wallace Abbey, before he would open the note. And so he had risen at dawn and ridden several hours south to come here.

He cracked the hardened gray dough and unfolded the letter. The wind caught at the edges of the paper, making it difficult to read.

Dear Mr. Ranier,

I pray you have arrived safely. Mr. Samuel Bryn gave me your name as his heir in strictest confidence last spring when he fell ill. Please know all of us at the foundling hospital share in your sadness at the great loss of our devoted benefactor. He was always so very kind to the orphans here, having once lived among us himself. He mentioned you live in a very retired fashion but that you might look favorably on us.

As the mistress of the foundling home here in Lamb's Conduit Fields, I am in the discomforting position of burdening you with a request. In the past, Mr. Bryn was in the habit of organizing and contributing greatly to a Christmas feast for the children.

Please know that we are truly not expecting anything at all. Surely there are many expenses attached to Brynlow. But if, by some small chance, you are able to consider this plea with goodwill, we would be most grateful.

Yours respectfully,
Anne Kane

Michael closed his eyes against the harsh memories of the foundling home. Wind buffeted his body as he imagined the gray lives of the children there now. The nights would be dark and long, the days arduous and often overcast, the sackcloth garments itchy and dull, the bread and gruel coarse and ash colored, and their skin would be almost gray from lack of nourishment. The only thing of color would be their dreams.

And Christmas.

It had been the only day the boys in the west wing and the girls from the east wing were allowed to mingle with one another. The only day their bellies were almost filled. And the only day Michael and the rest of the boys sang the *Messiah* in the overcrowded chapel filled with the fashionable Quality. Grand lords and ladies eased open their consciences and their purses while they listened to the hospital's master play the beautiful organ Mr. Handel had donated sixty years before.

It was the only damned day Michael had looked forward to each year.

He would go back. Go back to provide something of color for the boys and girls at Christmas. He could push back his schedule of progress for Brynlow. There was no hurry, really. For what purpose did he push so hard?

He wondered how Mrs. Kane would react when she realized Mr. Ranier was someone she had known by another name.

Michael folded the letter and stuffed it in his coat, the deeply slashed sides flapping in the wind. He took one long last look at his heritage lost, and turned away.

There was little time. If he was truly to do this, he would have to ride hell for leather to London within the week. And he would have to assemble a plan to secret himself. Well, it wasn't as if he would ever be able to forget the rabbit warren of London's infamous rookeries or the docks or any of the many darker places he could go.

All the while he rode Sioux back to Brynlow, he refused to admit for one single blasted moment, that perhaps, just perhaps, this was actually the excuse he had sought. The chance to see *her* once again.

Clearly it was damned hope, secretly and inexorably, at work. It was all he had left now that her scent had evaporated from the rose-colored shawl he cradled, like a deranged cove, each night.

Chapter 10

It was surprising how quickly Grace found her former daily rhythm in London. Oh, she knew now it had been a mistake to try and return without Ata and the others guarding her flanks. They had been the missing armament a few weeks ago when last she had attempted to reenter society.

It had taken a mere day or two to get settled. She had insisted the dowager duchess, Elizabeth, and Sarah stay with her instead of residing at Helston House or Quinn's Ellesmere House, both on the other side of Portman Square. On the first day, she and Ata had mapped out a calendar with military precision, including invitations to a mysterious masquerade no one would be able to resist.

The dowager duchess had agreed it would trump any doubt of the continued good relations between the three great Portman Square families who had rubbed shoulders for generations. Even Quinn's nine-year-old daughter, Fairleigh, was called to service by taking tea at Sheffield House every day, usually with her new stepmother, Georgiana.

"Georgiana . . ." Grace signaled as the other ladies

in their secret club filed out of the sumptuous front salon, filled with all of the artifacts John Sheffey had collected during his well-traveled lifetime. The other ladies' soft-soled slippers barely made a sound on the beautiful patterned marble hall and entryway beyond.

Georgiana looked down at Grace's hand on her sleeve and then met her gaze. "Yes, Grace?"

"I would ask a favor of you."

"Anything."

"Would you come to my apartments instead of going with the others to the park?"

"Of course." Georgiana's face was grave, so unlike the open countenance Grace had known in Cornwall before her friend had married the man Grace was supposed to have met at the altar.

Grace nodded and they joined the others in the hall. The ladies gathered around as they waited for the carriage to arrive from the mews.

"Grace, dearest," Ata murmured, "it shall be a grand success. And it will be all your doing. Don't think for a moment that you've fooled us. Organizing this lovely event for Georgiana and Quinn is a monumental undertaking. I do wish you'd allow us to help you more."

"Well, you may depend on me begging your aid the morning of the masquerade, when every disaster will strike as they always are wont to do." Grace smoothed her gown and smiled. "Oh, and have you all chosen costumes?"

Fairleigh jumped up and down excitedly. "Oh, I do wish Papa would let me go too."

"My dearest one, I shall promise to organize a ball just for you the season you have your official presentation at court." Grace stroked the blonde curls of the little girl who would have been her stepdaughter.

There were stars in the girl's eyes as she envisioned the future. At the sound of a carriage halting in front of the townhouse, Fairleigh hugged Grace and flew down the steps. After a flurry of well-wishing, everyone took their leave save Elizabeth, who pleaded a headache and retreated to her chamber, leaving Georgiana and Grace alone.

Side by side, they watched the party handed into the formal Berline coach, and waved as the conveyance departed at a spanking pace toward Hyde Park at the height of the fashionable hour. Then silently, they mounted the vast expanse of cold, marble stairs leading to the bedchambers above. Grace had nearly forgotten how convenient it had been to live in a small manor where it took less than half a minute to go from one end of the house to the other.

Once inside her elegant suite of rooms, Grace retrieved a tiny pair of scissors from her embroidery basket. "Georgiana, I'm sorry to ask this of you, but truly, you're the only one I can trust not to lecture me."

"I would never dare to lecture you on any subject," Georgiana said, her eyes downcast.

"I shall hold you to that." Grace presented her back to her friend. "I need your help disrobing."

After a beat, Grace felt Georgiana's fingers working the buttons. She was amused by Georgiana's silence. Under other circumstances, Georgiana would have been full of questions.

The gown and corset loosened, Grace removed them save for her shift, then offered the other lady the scissors.

Georgiana's eyes filled with ill ease and she cleared her throat. "What—"

Grace interrupted. "Take them."

"Of course," Georgiana forced out.

"Oh, don't look at me like that." Grace smiled. "Would you like a bit of brandy? Might make you feel more at ease."

Georgiana's face had lost its color. "No, no. I'm perfectly fine."

"Sounds like something I would say," Grace murmured. Without any of her former reserve, she lowered the front of her shift to reveal the wound under her breast. "I need you to remove the stitches. They are at an awkward angle, and I can't do it myself." The tension in the room simmered, as thick and as awful as Grace's disastrous stew in Yorkshire.

Georgiana's expression brewed with a host of subdued concern. "Grace, what hap—" She stopped. "What I mean to say is, perhaps this would be easiest if you were to lie down."

Grace reclined on the pink toile chaise while Georgiana knelt on the soft Aubusson carpet. The scent of hothouse roses drifted heavy in the air.

Grace covered her exposed breast with a palm and glanced down at Georgiana's pretty head, her brown hair glossy like the dark water of a beck.

Georgiana alternately clipped and removed the threads. It was odd how little it hurt for them to be removed.

Her friend finally straightened and Grace rearranged her shift.

"I doubt there will be much of a scar," Georgiana said. "Whoever ministered to you knew precisely what they were doing and matched the edges perfectly. I wish someone as skilled as this had stitched my injuries all those years ago."

Grace had not forgotten the childhood accident that had damaged and scarred her friend's lower limbs.

"Grace?"

"Yes?"

"I want to thank you."

"Shouldn't I be thanking you?"

"No. Thank you for trusting me with this. I would have thought I'd be the last person you would ever ask to do something as private as this."

"And that is why I asked you, Georgiana."

"Grace, I'm so sorry. So very, very sorry." Georgiana's words came out in a rush. "I should have told you I had been in love with Quinn almost my entire life. It's just that I never thought he would feel similarly. You and he were so beautiful together, and I was—"

"No. You are not to say another word," Grace interrupted. "It is as I said in the letter when I left. My heart was not fully engaged and I think I always knew he loved you. Georgiana, please look at me."

A flush had traveled up her friend's neck, and Georgiana finally raised her eyes. "Yes?"

"I was too distraught to sit through anyone's apologies a month ago—not yours or Quinn's. And a week or so ago, I was in another world, too lost to drown in thoughts of what happened this last autumn. But a week from this moment, if we don't act right now, we will have set a new pattern of living . . . one that is full of ill ease and discomfort. Georgiana, you were my friend once, can you not be again?"

Georgiana's eyes filled with tears and she fell into Grace's arms, her body shuddering in wracking sobs.

Grace stroked the other woman's unruly locks. "You know this is vastly unfair of you. Aren't you supposed to be comforting *me*?"

"But you were always the only one of us who could be depended on for a handkerchief," Georgiana said when she could speak. "I don't know what has become of me, really. I've lately become the worst sort of watering pot. Oh Grace, I've missed you so much. We all have. It's just not the same without you. Luc and Quinn keep threatening to rename our club."

"Really?" She looked at her friend with bemusement.

"Yes." Georgiana accepted Grace's perfectly pressed handkerchief and dabbed her eyes. "In fact, we decided that since you were the true beauty in the circle, it would be deception to call ourselves the Barely Bereaving Beauties without you."

Grace bit her lower lip to keep from laughing. "Deception?"

"Well, you know how Ata is. She's determined to see Elizabeth or Sarah wed this season. And she has this new idea that we should not keep our club a secret any longer."

"But I thought she insisted on secrecy because she was certain no one would want to invite a group of morose widows to any amusement." Grace shook her head. "Correct me if I'm wrong, but I do believe Luc once called us a gaggle of weeping crows, did he not?"

Georgiana giggled.

Oh, it felt so right to laugh with Georgiana again.

"Yes, well, lately His Grace has been in the most foolish kind of mood. Quinn says it's because Luc's finished writing his last book and he's at odds with the world. Ata suggested he start something new. She's even suggested a title." Georgiana's expression spoke volumes.

"And that would be?"

"*The Wicked Ways of Willful Widows.*"

Grace choked and began to cough.

"She had the audacity to suggest in a very mysterious-like manner that *some* in our club are playing it very *fast and loose* lately, or some other vulgar term. Honestly, I don't know where she gets these ideas."

Grace drew in an uneven breath. "I can't imagine."

"Well, she thinks it's a book that would be devoured by the *ton*."

"Lord help us all."

Georgiana's face lit up with happiness. "Oh, Grace. I'm so happy we're all together again."

"As am I." Grace watched her friend's hands drift low to cradle her stomach. Suddenly Grace noticed that Georgiana's physique was slightly lusher than ever before. "But isn't there something else you want to tell me? A secret, perhaps?"

Georgiana's mouth opened slightly and she hesitated.

Grace grasped her hands. "Tell me."

Michael stood in Mrs. Kane's comfortable, small chamber at the foundling home, nearly overcome with memories of his youth. The scent of her precious lavender mixed with musty books wafted through the small room as he gazed at the familiar assortment of trinkets on the lace-covered bureau.

"I beg you to reconsider, Michael. You've the most skill," Mrs. Kane cajoled.

"No."

"But I promise no one will recognize you. It is, after all, a private masquerade," Mrs. Kane continued. "And it's the least you could do."

"I thought the least I could do was provide enough food to feed an army of children," he said dryly.

"Please."

"Absolutely not." He stared at Mrs. Kane. "You of all people know I cannot. Victoria Givan will show the eldest boy how to conduct. She's an excellent organist."

The mistress of the foundling home had learned the art of begging a little too well. But then, she had no doubt acquired the skill nearly sixty years ago, soon after she had been placed in the infamous basket in front of the newly hatched Hospital for Exposed and Deserted Children.

"Listen to me, Michael. I shall secure a cape and domino which will cover almost all of your face."

"I don't know why I dared think you might have changed, Mrs. Kane."

"Well, I like that. And here I prayed for your departed soul for over a decade, and you have the temerity to deny me this tiny favor?"

"I'd hoped addressing your request would buy your forgiveness." He walked a small circle, glancing at all her trinkets and hoping her lecture would end sooner versus later.

"I still can't believe you allowed me to think you dead. How could you not have trusted me? You trusted Samuel Bryn, I see." She snorted. "And what is this name you've adopted? Ranier, indeed."

"It *is* my name—my mother's name. Even you must agree that I had no choice but to find an alias." He couldn't bear to tell her that the original name she knew him by was even farther removed from the truth. "So, is Manning still searching for me?"

She avoided his gaze. "Well . . . he increased the reward. Mr. Jenkins used to announce the new incentive each year, when a runner or two would visit the boys' side. They thoroughly canvassed the west wing every month the first year you disappeared. I still can't imagine how you were able to secure passage to the colonies. I was certain you'd been lost to the filth in the rookeries."

"I tried that route for a few weeks, but was lucky enough to find a job as cook's helper on a privateer's ship. Seems a press gang abducted half the crew." He continued dryly, "So all those endless hours preparing every boy here for a mariner's life proved useful in the end. Our Mr. Jenkins was an excellent master."

"Well," Mrs. Kane said with a frown. "As I'm sure you can guess, there are few who mourn him. I'm sorry for what he did to you and many other boys, Michael. For the beatings, the horrid apprenticeships, the meager food and coal Mr. Jenkins sold to line his own pockets. I'm sorry for so many things."

"No. You musn't be. If not for you, so many more of us would've died. You were a mother to each and every one of us as much as you could be."

"If you truly consider me as such, then you must do as I ask."

He shook his head. "The eldest boy can serve as choirmaster at the event. He has two days to practice."

"But the entertainment is to take place at a private residence. There's absolutely no chance of anyone recognizing you. For goodness sakes, Michael, it's been an age since you disappeared. You barely resemble the boy of five and ten I last saw. You know there won't be runners mingling with the guests."

Preoccupied, he looked away and abstractedly rubbed the edge of his hat. "You've not asked me yet if I did it."

"I don't need to."

"Perhaps you do."

"You've forgotten that I know Rowland Manning and I knew his awful brother, a bad seed in every respect. Every boy who worked there said Howard was a thief. I'll never believe Rowland Manning no matter what he or anyone says."

"Thank you," he murmured, gratitude in every syllable.

"But, I should warn you that his enterprise has thrived. Indeed, Manning has expanded in an astonishing fashion and enjoys the Prince Regent's favor. But, you'll be happy to know that after Mr. Jenkins died, I was finally allowed an audience with the board of governors. The new master takes up his duties in a fortnight. He's cut from an entirely different cloth than Mr. Jenkins."

"I'm happy to hear it," Michael said quietly. "But not happy to hear the other whip-loving bugger is prospering, damn Rowland Manning's soul to hell."

"Michael!"

"Pardon me, Mrs. Kane. And no, I see that look in your eye. I'll not do your bidding to earn forgiveness."

She looked at him silently for a long moment. "You know, I debated with myself as to whether I should tell you this, but I've run out of arguments. When the Countess of Sheffield came here three days ago—"

He interrupted her with a start. "The *Countess of Sheffield*? What in bloody hell was she doing here?"

She ignored him. "She said she had recently made the acquaintance of someone who had been raised here. And me being a woman of sharp intelligence and great perception—"

"And obvious modesty," he drawled.

She continued without drawing breath, "And modesty, you ungrateful wretch. Well, the lady was maddeningly evasive but did admit that the person who influenced her decision to hold a benefit was *someone who was newly arrived to Yorkshire from the colonies.*"

The sweat on Michael's brow turned cold. "She's the one giving the masquerade, isn't she?"

"Well, it was but a moment before I guessed our unwitting aide had been none other than the mysterious *Mr. Ranier.* And by the look on your face, I'm correct, am I not? Well, what I think you should do is—"

"I'll do it," he said under his breath.

"What's that, eh?"

"I bloody well said I'd do it. But don't get any fine ideas about continuing this farce. I'll lead the boys this one time, and you'd best start praying for an early arrival of the new master, for I'll not risk my neck unmasked here before any pitying people of Quality come to hear the *Messiah* in the chapel."

"And I'd never ask that of you," she soothed. "Oh, and Michael?"

"Yes?"

"Allow me to tell you what a fine, grown man you've become, albeit an awfully tall one," she said, a smile crinkling the paper-thin skin around her lively dark eyes.

"Mrs. Kane?"

"Yes?"

"Tell me just one thing."

She waited, her boundless reserves of patience radiating as always from her kindly expression. "Yes?"

"Did she look happy?"

Mrs. Kane tilted her head and Michael endured her scrutiny. "Why do I suspect that you'd like me to reply that she appeared as miserable as you do right now?"

He sighed heavily. Was there a female alive who could answer bloody questions without offering their own ridiculous opinions?

Chapter 11

Sheffield House had never looked quite this lovely, Grace thought, surveying the great hall and ballroom as she welcomed the last dozen guests flanked by Quinn and Georgiana. The pungent scent of laurel and evergreens freshly cut to signal the season wafted through the air to mingle with the perfumes of the guests. Against the pale limestone columns and the light marble floor, a flurry of colorful silks, satins, and velvets presented an astonishing tableau of costumed humanity.

And Grace was proud. Not a single person had declined an invitation. Entrenched traditionalists had postponed early departures to their vast country houses to partake of the colossal entertainment just before Christmas. It was not often a private masquerade was in the offing in town. And this was nothing like others Grace had attended—insipid affairs with everyone dressed of the last century in moth-eaten frocks and towering, powdered horsehair wigs.

No, this was a true masquerade. Tigers and savages and even a somewhat tallish Napoleon paraded about while footmen, dressed as servants to a maharaja, stroked the air with palm fronds.

It was exotic and fantastic.

The whispered taunts Grace had endured last month still echoed in her mind. And so she had taken great pains to produce an event so extraordinary that half the mocking words would be stilled on the lips of the more wretched members of the beau monde. The other half would be subdued by the combined power of Ata and the dowager duchess's friend, Lady Cowper, who possessed boundless consequence as one of Almack's famous patronesses.

Ata had called in a multitude of favors in exchange for the promise of a night to remember. Yes, Grace's easing back into her niche in society was as carefully orchestrated as a coup d'etat.

But it was all worth it. And more important, it would aid the foundling home substantially.

"Come," she said, addressing Quinn and Georgiana, who were dressed as an ancient Egyptian pharaoh and his queen. "I'm desperate for some champagne. Then we've got to go inside that ballroom and begin." She fell naturally and regally into the role she had been bred to, that of a great hostess.

"Grace, I don't know how you managed all this in such a short time." Georgiana's dark eyes appeared huge framed by the black wig's thick fringe.

Quinn tucked each woman's arm against his own and chuckled. "I've recently learned that once Grace has gotten an idea in her head, there's no stopping her. And this plan was better executed than half the peace treaties in Europe."

Grace disregarded the compliment and straightened her Grecian-inspired gold tunic before touching her hair to make certain all the many strands of pearls were still threaded through her tresses. "Botheration. I feel like a thousand snakes are perched on my head."

Georgiana smiled. "Don't worry so."

Grace tilted her half mask back into place and grasped a glass from a passing footman dressed as someone from the bazaars of Persia. She downed the contents and tried to ignore the tickling in her nose. She grabbed another before entering the ballroom. Quinn was still chuckling and Grace could swear he said something about shocking changes in character.

Grace faced the vast swell of the crowd inside and strove for a measure of cool insouciance. With a nod to a servant behind a huge gong, she signaled him to strike the huge metal pan. The shimmering sound quieted the crowd of nearly four hundred guests. All of the members of the Widows Club moved to hover about Grace, Georgiana, and Quinn as the crowd looked toward them with an unmistakable air of malicious curiosity.

"Thank you for coming tonight. Before I introduce a wonderful surprise this evening, I ask all of you to toast the guests of honor—my very dearest friends, the Marquis of Ellesmere and his new bride, whom many of you have not yet met. Please raise your glass to Georgiana Wilde Fortesque, the beautiful Marchioness of Ellesmere, and to the marquis!"

There was a moment of silence before Lady Cowper

lifted her glass followed quickly by her purported lover, Lord Palmerston. Grace heard Luc exhale in relief and mutter, "Thank God, once again, for Emily and Palmerston."

And then one by one, a few of the others who had obviously partaken in enough spirits shouted "Here, here!" There was not a single cutting comment. Even from the corner where the Duchess of Kendale regally stood with her sycophant entourage, there arose not a whisper. Grace had mistakenly counted the pretty duchess as a close acquaintance until she understood it was she who had spurred rumors of Grace's rupture with the Marquis of Ellesmere.

"And since this is the traditional season of giving," Grace continued, staring at the Duchess of Kendale and raising her glass again, "I am certain *all* of you will open your hearts and your *purses* to contribute generously to the Hospital for Exposed and Deserted Children. Their choir is here to offer evidence of the goodness housed behind those walls. Following this, the ball will commence!"

In almost comical unison, with only a few jaded titters, four hundred masked gentlemen, ladies, and beasts turned expectantly toward the vast orchestral balcony far above the gilded ballroom. A quarter acre of young boys of all ages, clad in simple black vestments, faced a choirmaster garbed similarly, with the addition of a black cape, black Venetian tricorn and face mask. He reminded Grace of one of the hordes of revelers she had witnessed during *Carnevale* in Venice the season after Luc had married Rosamunde.

High above them, the master lifted a baton and deftly signaled the choir to begin. An ocean of pure, innocent voices swelled in unison and burst forth in a wave of one of Handel's scores, almost too beautiful in its intensity. For long minutes it seemed as if every last person in the ballroom was struck dumb by the performance, until a voice rose alone in the beginning of a familiar long passage, and then cracked horribly.

Grace's heart lurched in sympathy. The poor boy. His voice betrayed that he had reached the awkward age of an adolescent teetering on manhood. But then her heart filled with something more than sympathy.

The smooth, rich voice of an adult took over, an octave lower than the boy who had faltered. She tried to regulate her breathing as she scanned the crowd. Where was it coming from? It seemed to reverberate from every wall.

It was the voice of her dreams. The one she had heard while perched on a massive horse cradled in the arms of the man who had saved her from herself.

Michael.

And he was in London. Here. *In her house.*

Good God, he had probably been here for hours, closeted with the choir in the musician's chamber beyond the balcony's doors.

Good sense deserted her, as did her good posture.

Luc's haughty figure slipped beside her. "What is it? You're trembling." When she failed to respond, he grasped her arm and draped it over his own.

Spellbound by his haunting soliloquy, Grace tried desperately to regain her composure. The chorus of boy's voices joined his at the crest of joyous music as it drifted to the finale.

A deafening sea of applause broke out as the last notes faded. And then, despite the many calls for an encore, the master ushered the boys from the balcony while a drift of musicians took their place and struck the first chords of a minuet.

Luc shielded her. "Please tell me this is not about who I think it is . . . Grace, if you are half the countess I know you to be, you will snap out of this fog you've entered and remember you've a goodly portion of the most important people in town before you and you've spent a bloody fortune to lure them here. Come, everyone is waiting for us to lead them into the dance."

Grace looked up into Luc's stark sapphire eyes behind a devil's mask and wished she was anywhere else. "Then let's not disappoint them," she replied, cool reason returning with each word. She allowed him to escort her and within moments a flock of couples joined them. Crocodiles paired with ballet dancers while pirates bowed before swans.

Her long years under society's harsh scrutiny stood her well. Woodenly, Grace soldiered on through the movements of the minuet.

"You know," Luc tightened his grip on her hand, "if I discover that bastard is here, I really will kill him this time."

"Of course you won't," Grace replied, finding her voice. "It is my privilege, not yours."

He exhaled. "Thank God. I'd hoped you wouldn't

be missish about this. I should have trusted you'd let good sense prevail."

They bowed and curtsied their way through the dance until the bitter end. At that precise moment, a gentleman dressed as a bear snagged Luc's attention, and Grace disengaged at the edge of the floor nearest the doors.

She made her way inelegantly past all the colorful characters. It was a terrible squeeze until she disappeared behind the ornate double doors. Removing the suffocating half mask and hiking her gown high, she dashed up the back stairs to the private musician's chamber.

The boys, uniformly thin and too pale, were so very quiet inside. Their eyes were like saucers as they filled plates with hearty foodstuffs, all under the watchful gaze of the matron and another young woman.

Grace's skin prickled hot as she scanned the room again. All at once she realized he was not there. And at the same moment the elderly woman from the foundling home rushed forward.

"The boys performed beautifully, Mrs. Kane," Grace said in a voice that didn't sound like her own. "I must thank you again for accepting my invitation."

"The honor was all ours, Lady Sheffield. May I present Miss Victoria Givan? She is our singing teacher at the moment, as the boys' master died not two months ago."

A lovely auburn-haired woman curtsied, her gaze trained on the floor. "We are so very grateful to you for your generosity, ma'am." Victoria Givan finally dared to look in her direction, and Grace could not help but stare at the most vivid green eyes she had ever encountered. Miss Givan was an out-and-out *siren*.

"I'm so glad I could do something to help all of you," Grace murmured.

Mrs. Kane carefully examined Grace over the tops of her spectacles. "I had wanted you to meet the choir-master too, but he's already taken his leave of us, my lady."

Grace noticed Miss Givan glance toward the open window. "Then I shall depend on you to thank him for me when you rejoin him."

Miss Givan appeared very ill at ease, while Mrs. Kane replied, "Of course, Lady Sheffield. Victoria and I should gather the boys and—"

"Oh, please, I beg you to stay. They've not had enough time to enjoy the dinner. And we shall have baskets to take back with you. By the way, you will also receive a great boon of contributions from this evening, Mrs. Kane. I shall personally deliver the monies to you."

"Thank you, ma'am, for giving us such a hopeful, happy season to remember."

Grace edged toward the door, her smile frozen in place. Just before she fully turned to leave, Mrs. Kane wandered toward the open window and murmured something.

"What did you say?" Grace halted.

"Oh, pardon me, my lady. I was just saying it's unusually warm tonight—so balmy after that cold spell." Small gusts of air rippled the edges of the curtains. "It would be a perfect night for a stroll in your lovely garden, don't you think?"

Grace cleared her throat and uttered a few inane niceties before excusing herself to dart back to the lower level of her townhouse.

She rested her hot forehead on the cool limestone in a private corner. He *was not* in the garden. Mrs. Kane had *not* been trying to tell her something.

She was being ridiculous. It was just that she had boiled long enough to concoct the perfect stew of words to ladle over that man's head should she ever have the opportunity to see him again, and she itched for the opportunity. She tugged at a door leading to her garden and hurried into the darkness.

Stud on a leash, indeed.

The tittering voices of a few guests drifted from the balcony. The man had very clearly said he did not want her to stay with him nor had he wanted to go with her. He had wanted a brief affair—a temporary slaking of desire, not an entwining of hearts.

She would never have agreed to it if she had known the intensity of the emotions once desire was roused. She had been far more comfortable in her regulated existence.

Grace leaned against one of the stone archways covered by espaliered fruit trees and closed her eyes. She did not want to go back inside. Oh, she knew she would. Eventually.

She would gather up her tangle of emotions and fold them back into their proper places like the gowns of summer placed between fragile tissues and then locked in the trunks resting in the attics.

Grace finally noticed the sounds of her favorite waltz, drifting from the open sets of French doors above her on the balcony. Her eyes still closed, she swayed to the music, and trained her thoughts on the rest of the evening. She would dance with Quinn for the supper dance. And then she would dine with—

Suddenly, the warm, poignant memory of *his* scent washed over her . . . a smoky moss-and-evergreen aroma. Her eyes snapped open and she whirled around, only to spy an ominous, huge shadow against the wall under the balcony. He appeared even larger than she remembered when he pushed away from the foundation and came toward her, pulling off his domino. Her heart slammed against her ribs as he drew close and blocked out everything in front of her, leaving her nowhere to look except at him.

"Care to waltz, Lady Sheffield?" His voice suggested an intimate caress, all molten charm and heated irony. "Or would you prefer to shoot me?" He leaned closer, and she stepped back and encountered the stone arch at her back.

"Perhaps you're not asking the right questions, Mr. Ranier."

He chuckled. "You've waited a long time for the opportunity to say that."

"Long enough." She quelled a shiver threatening to tease her shoulders and blurted with little finesse what she most longed to know. "Well, Mr. Ranier, what brings you to London? I'd thought nothing could wrest you from Brynlow."

His amber eyes appeared almost black in the low light; harsh shadows carved his prominent cheekbones. "I came for several reasons, *Grace*."

"Really?" This time she couldn't stop the quiver at the use of her given name. And with that, all the words to her well-ordered speech were forgotten, like dreams on a long winter's night.

Michael refused to go on. He meant to drag out this conversation for as long as humanly possible to drink in the sight of her in the moonlight. She was masquerading as an elusive, nubile Greek goddess in that sinfully exotic costume, which showed vastly too much flesh and hinted at everything that lay beyond the golden material. And yet he alone knew of the simple goodness and sweet innocence to be found beneath all the expensive fabrics.

Despite her outward calm, her eyes betrayed her agitation. "Well, are you going to tell me the reasons or not?"

God, her voice was so lovely and lilting. "I came at the request of Mrs. Kane to organize a proper Christmas for the children," he said quietly.

She said nothing, just continued to stare at him, her silver-blonde hair haloing her face in the moonlight.

"Imagine my surprise when I arrived"—his hands itched to reach for her—"and learned of your sudden interest in the foundling home. Sweetheart, you—"

"Don't you dare use that endearment again," she hissed. "I suppose you think all this has something to do with you."

"I would never presume to influence your actions. Mrs. Kane requested I lead the choir tonight."

She raised her chin and looked at him dubiously. "This benefit had nothing to do with you."

"I'm sorry to hear it," he said, unable to keep doubt from lacing his voice. "But I can be reasonable, Lady Sheffield. I won't presume to have had a hand in your generosity if you won't assume I'm here for any other reason than a promise I made."

She appeared vastly annoyed, which delighted him. It was indifference that he most feared. Perhaps he had not managed to kill every last ounce of affection she had held for him in Yorkshire. God, how he longed to pull her into his arms and kiss her until she couldn't breathe.

"Why are you lurking in my garden?" Without waiting for an answer, she rushed on. "You've already discharged your obligations tonight."

He stepped an inch closer to her and was hit by her intoxicating scent. "Actually, I have other reasons for coming to town, and while you try to hide the reasons behind your efforts, I won't," he said, trapping her against the arch. "I came to thank you for the mittens you made for me."

She brushed aside the gratitude with impatience. "It was nothing. Small repayment for saving me in that storm. And the other reasons?"

He would not tell her the real reason. "Why would you think there was another reason?"

"You said there were reasons—plural."

He longed to smooth the fast-beating pulse on her fragile neck.

"Well?"

"Perhaps I missed your cooking, Blue Eyes."

She exhaled roughly. "Surely you can do better than that, Mr. Ranier. Even a—"

Abruptly, several shadows fell from the balcony above. Ladies, at a guess, given their high-pitched giggles. Michael gathered Grace in his arms and swung her under the privacy of the overhang. She made a strangled sound and he released her.

"No," he put his finger to her lips, "don't raise your voice unless you want to be discovered with a scoundrel."

"You know, you don't have to keep telling me what you are," she hissed. "I already know."

"But I think it's only fair to remind the prey before I come in for the kill."

"Oh, pish. You're as harmless as—as . . ."

"As what, Grace?" he whispered, leaning forward. An inch closer and he would drown in her evocative, heavenly scent.

She pushed away from him. "Why are you really here in my garden?"

"For the same reason you are," he murmured.

"Stop it." She looked away.

He was grateful she was stronger than he. No matter how much good sense he possessed, his desire for her trumped his good intentions. "I came because I wanted to know . . . No, I *needed* to know, if you are with child."

Her delicate brows drew together. "I told you before, you needn't worry about that. I'm not like other ladies . . . Oh, this is absurd. I already told you."

"Yes, but there is always a chance when two people engage in—"

She cut him off. "You know, I made an enormous mistake thinking I was cut out for an affair of this nature. I find it unsupportable." She appeared wretchedly self-conscious. "I'm not with child. I had proof of it last week."

A small wave of sadness crashed through him. "There's nothing to be embarrassed about. It's an entirely natural process."

"I don't know why you've come. I promised I would tell you. *I* can be trusted to always tell the truth, unlike other people I've recently come to know."

God, he hated to see the hurt glittering in her angry eyes. "And when have I ever been dishonest with you?"

"When I took my leave of you at Brynlow. And don't you dare make me repeat any of it. We both know you have none of the pride you suggested, and I—"

The sound of footfalls on the stone stairs trailing the side of the balcony made her stop. Four elongated shadows advanced on the short winter lawn beyond the arches. A pair of gentlemen and two ladies strolled into view. The petite elderly dowager duchess was on the arm of a starkly beautiful raven-haired lady. Helston and the marquis swung their gazes toward them and strode forward, the ladies trailing in their wake.

The brandy in Helston's glass sloshed near the rim when he stopped abruptly. "Well, if it isn't the harbinger of tragedy in the flesh. I should knock you down, you bloody—"

"Luc!" the dark-haired lady interrupted, horrified.

"Leave him, Rosamunde," Ellesmere said quietly, the smoke from his cheroot swirling around the party. "Helston's entirely correct. Grace?"

"I'm perfectly fine. I was just about to—"

"He vowed he would leave well enough alone." The duke cut in, his fury uncontained. "I should have known better than to take the word of a turncoat. What in hell are you doing here?"

"The question of the century," Grace muttered.

Michael silently endured their scrutiny until Helston could not hold back any longer and turned to Grace. "It's too bad half the titles in England are prancing about above us, ruining a perfectly good opportunity to drag an answer from his—"

The lady who was obviously Helston's wife interrupted him with a smothered laugh. "Ata said you were tall, Mr. Ranier, but I never dreamed . . ."

"Please escort Ata and Grace to the ballroom, dearest," the duke gritted out.

The dowager turned to her grandson. "But Luc, it's so much more amusing to fraternize with the enemy."

Ellesmere chuckled. "That's why the battle of the sexes can never be won decisively by either side, Ata."

"Damn it to hell," Helston choked, "can we not stay on subject?"

"Luc, our masks are itchy and we need some air. Now, young man," the elderly duchess continued, turning to Michael, "what are you doing here? And why did it take you so long? I think Grace should dance the supper dance with you instead of the marquis."

Michael clenched his hands. That damned ballroom was too exposed. "I'm not here to dance, ma'am."

"Well, none of the gentlemen want to dance, but that's beside the point," the dowager said bluntly before Helston could interrupt. "How are you to win back her favor unless you let her mash your toes?"

Helston's duchess pressed her fingers to her lips to still them.

"As I told the countess, the boys' choir was desperate for a leader and I made a promise."

Grace made an almost inaudible annoyed sound beside him.

"Really?" Ata's one word dripped with doubt.

"Get that blasted torch out of my face, Ellesmere," Helston said to the gentleman next to him.

The marquis smiled and took another puff from his cheroot.

"And what do you find so humorous?" Helston continued. "It's your fault we're in the position of having to hunt down overgrown ne'er-do-wells in the bushes."

"I'm amused because he's fairly competent at deception. Might have been able to use him in the diplomatic corps if his height and features did not make him so recognizable," the marquis replied. "Now, Mr. Ranier, shall we start again? Surely you're here to see the countess. But, why pray tell? I thought we settled everything before. Surely even a man such as you lives up to his promises."

Michael looked at Grace's tumultuous expression and thought quickly. Sounds from her mews nearby filtered through the darkness—a horse nickering for its feed, and another stomping its displeasure. And finally, blessedly, he arrived at an idea. It was entirely derisory, entirely a selfish idea, but it was the best he could do under the scrutiny of five pairs of eyes.

"I'm here to honor another promise. I made one to Lady Sheffield not long ago. I agreed to give her riding lessons when she was my guest at Brynlow."

Grace gaped at him. "I agreed to no such thing. You just conjured that up."

Ellesmere chuckled.

"Do you deny we spoke about horsemanship lessons, Lady Sheffield?" Michael murmured.

"How ridiculous. You might have suggested some far-fetched notion in jest, but everyone knows I detest . . ." She stopped, obviously mortified by the hen-hearted words she was about to utter.

Ata cleared her throat. "I've never understood why you don't like horses, Grace. They are such a necessary part of our lives. I love horses. So do Rosamunde and Georgiana. And I would wager—"

"This is ludicrous," Grace interrupted, her eyes narrowing. "I do like horses. It's just they don't like me. Oh, I refuse to continue this conversation. Mr. Ranier is outrageous. I need to go back to the—"

Ata interrupted her by turning to Michael. "She would need a chaperon and I adore riding. Grace dear, Luc has the most lovely little gray mare from Wales you could try. We could all go. Don't look at me like that, Luc. I'm not suggesting races at Rotten Row. There's a nice little track around the ornamental lake at the edge of Ranelagh pleasure garden. No one ever goes there in the morning. We should go tomorrow with this fine weather."

With the exception of Helston's wife, who was trying very hard not to laugh, the rest of them looked at the tiny dowager with mute horror. The duke clutched his head until his wife whispered to him and pressed a kiss to his cheek.

"Would nine o'clock be too early for all of you?" Michael asked quietly.

"It's too late no matter how bloody early you suggest," Luc muttered, scrutinizing Grace before turning to his wife. "And Rosamunde, I do believe I shall collect on that, uh, bargain you offered . . . *immediately*." His eyes darkened and he glowered before dragging his wife toward the relative obscurity of a large willow tree.

The marquis brought the cheroot to his lips, his eyes half closed, and said not a word.

And Grace? Grace Sheffey lifted her chin and glanced briefly at each of their faces before coming to rest on Michael's. "Mr. Ranier, good manners forbid me from telling you precisely what I think. I don't know the reason behind this absurd charade, but you should know I will not allow myself to be goaded into . . ."

A clucking sound floated from above and Grace sharply turned her head. A short gentleman was briefly silhouetted against the glow of the lanterns decorating the railing before the man returned inside.

If Grace had been the sort of woman who had a predilection for wagering, a person such as her father, she would have bet half her fortune that it had been Mr.

Brown . . . and he had been clucking like a chicken. *To her.* She returned her gaze to Michael Ranier. "Nine o'clock, sharp. I shall leave all of you to figure out the particulars." She then retreated to the stairs alone before she could humiliate herself further.

There would be time for that.

Tomorrow.

At a quarter past nine, sharp, if she had to hazard a guess.

Chapter 12

Grace had come up with a dozen plausible excuses before retiring after the long, successful evening, but when dawn's pink vines unfurled across the sky, all of the reasons to avoid the outing sounded hollow to her own ears.

She wasn't sure what had really brought Michael Ranier to London, but the last thing she'd ever do was let him see how much the sight of him again affected her. Was she not the Countess from the Isle of Ice? Well, now he would see her as such. And then he would return to Yorkshire without a backward glance.

It was how she preferred it.

She was through with courtship, gentlemen, and blacksmiths in particular. And most especially any man with the mad idea of forcing her onto a horse.

Not bothering to ring for her maid, she crossed to her burled walnut armoire, where, after a long search, she found the one and only riding habit she owned. Dark blue with scarlet trimmings and brass buttons, the habit had always made her feel like she should style her hair in two long braids, for then she would truly appear like a little girl playing at captain of the

Royal Navy. She donned the gown, which was uncomfortably stiff, and then sat before the looking glass to pin up her hair and draw down the veil of the modish hat with the long pheasant feather that dipped behind. Both articles had been ordered by the Earl of Sheffield and had never been worn. Grace had hoped to keep it that way.

Looking at her pale countenance, she couldn't decide if she looked more like she was facing the guillotine or ready to do murder. What had come over her in the last few weeks? There was none of the collected elegance gracing her face. She even left off her customary pearls. The long strands catching on some equine paraphernalia was just one more item on the dizzying list of potential disasters in the making.

Why did he insist on continuing the acquaintance? She might have ended it badly, but at least she had ended it. He did not truly want her. If he did, he wouldn't have said what he did at Brynlow. And he did not seem the sort to harbor guilt. He was too plain-spoken for that.

So he was a blackguard, as he insisted. It was one thing to lust after a woman and cast her off. It was altogether something else to then proceed to torment her. He was a rogue without conscience. Well, it was not to be borne.

The smallest voice within her said differently. But then, hadn't small seductive voices always gotten ladies into far more trouble than sensible ones?

A quarter of an hour later, Grace found herself ensconced with Ata, Elizabeth, and Sarah in a dark green lacquered carriage with the Helston coat of arms marking its sides.

"I'm worried for you, Grace," Elizabeth said, tucking in the edge of the carriage blanket. "I tried to warn you most gentlemen can't be trusted to understand the word *no*."

"Oh, botheration," Ata said, smiling, "I, for one, am delighted Mr. Ranier has come. And I would wager he'd go away at the snap of my fingers if he was not in love with her."

"Ata!" Grace moaned. "Don't be ridiculous."

"He might have faltered in Yorkshire, but there he was outnumbered, surprised, and unprepared. Now he is clearly equipped, and has developed tactics."

"One must hope, if this is indeed a battle, that you will take my side," Grace replied with no small amount of doubt.

Ata patted Grace's restless hands, gloved in pink leather. "I will, my dear, I will. Your happiness is paramount, dearest."

Grace had a few conversational tactics of her own, and they included changing the subject when outflanked and outranked. "By the way, Eliza, where were you last night? Rosamunde's eldest brother was looking for you to claim a dance after supper."

Elizabeth looked out the carriage window. "I never promised him a dance. And my costume was ill-fitted—vastly uncomfortable."

Ata examined Elizabeth with skepticism. "You, my dear, have become remarkably skittish since we've come to town. We seem to have lost the lady with the vibrant outlook on life somewhere between Yorkshire and London."

"I'm sure I don't know what you mean," Elizabeth said, evading the dowager's comment by using Grace's tactics herself. "Oh, look, we're almost there."

Ata patted the younger lady's hand. "Don't worry, I won't pester you, Eliza. I rather think I can only successfully badger one of you at a time. And today, we're here to encourage Grace."

Grace rolled her eyes. "I rather think you are here to encourage Mr. Ranier. We all know I never made any silly promise to ride a horse."

"I believe you," Sarah said. "But perhaps you can use this opportunity to have a private word with him. Even if it is only to say a proper good-bye without Luc and Quinn hovering about. My husband always said a good-bye is every bit as important as a hello."

"You must agree, it was a stroke of brilliance on my part to send a note to Mr. Ranier to meet us an hour earlier so we could avoid all that male posturing—although . . . it does feel like dawn, something I've surely never seen," Ata said with a laugh.

Grace pursed her lips. "This will only lead to disaster."

"My darling, haven't you ever noticed that sometimes disaster leads to happiness?" Ata's blind confidence radiated from her petite frame.

Grace conceded a smile. "Well, in that case I, out of all of us, should be radiantly happy shortly."

"Give it time," Ata said, readjusting the angle of Grace's feathered hat, "I have faith, even if you do not."

The carriage lurched to a stop in front of the boxwood hedge separating them from Ranelagh's ornamental lake. Grace peered out the window and spied one of Quinn's smart curricles, driven by Mr. Brown, drawing near. A small gray horse was tied to the rear.

The instrument of torture.

She prayed Mr. Ranier would not come. It was spineless, she knew. But then it would be so much easier. She could simply refuse to see him if he dared lift the Sheffield brass knocker on Portman Square.

All at once, there was a rap on the carriage door and it opened. Mr. Ranier's face was silhouetted against the crisp, pale blue winter sky. His large black mare with the white blaze stood a few feet beyond. It had been apparently too much to wish for freezing sleet or at the very least a miserable drizzle.

He bowed, and looked up with a wink. "Your servant, ladies."

He handed out Ata, Elizabeth, and Sarah, who thanked him graciously. His face reappeared in the carriage.

"Countess?"

"Yes?"

"Would you do me the honor?" He held out his wide, gloved palm.

"Oh, all right."

"Such excitement. Such transports of delight."

"You are lucky I am here." She placed her hand in his only to remember how large and solid it was.

"I know," he purred into her ear as she alighted from the carriage.

A fine mist hovered on the ground, nearly obscuring the great rotunda in the distance as well as the Chinese pavilion. What had always looked like an enchanted castle in the glow of lanterns at night now revealed its man-made small flaws with the daylight.

Mr. Brown was untying the gray horse from the other carriage when Ata gathered the party around her. "Mr. Ranier, Sarah and Eliza will walk the gardens while you give Grace her lesson. And I will try this new team Quinn has so graciously offered for my use."

"I'll drive," Mr. Brown insisted quietly, walking up.

During the long pause that followed, only the sound of two geese honking in the distance could be heard.

"Actually, Charles asked to accompany me," Ata informed him, her eyes steeped in challenge.

"Did he, now?" Mr. Brown placed the reins of the small mare in Mr. Ranier's hands.

"Yes. While *I* take the ribbons."

"Really?" Mr. Brown said, deceptively calm. "Ladies, Mr. Ranier, would you excuse us? The dowager duchess and I must have a word."

Everyone inched away.

"Absolutely not," Ata said, instantly on her guard. "You are all to stay. There is nothing that cannot be said among my friends." She seemed not to notice that Sarah and Elizabeth had managed to disappear, presumably down one of Ranelagh's many paths.

"All right," Mr. Brown said. "Then I am forced to remind you in front of your friends that you made a promise not to drive a carriage ever again."

"No. I promised never to do it *alone* again."

"Is that so?"

"Yes," Ata replied, peevishly.

"Was that after ye nearly killed yourself with a runaway team in Cornwall? The one which left Quinn's phaeton in matchsticks?"

"Yes. Rather like your carriage when you left my dearest girl to die in a blinding snowstorm in Yorkshire."

Grace cleared her throat.

"No, Countess, this is not your affair," Mr. Brown stilled her before returning his gaze to Ata.

Grace met Michael Ranier's glance and nodded to a small domed folly a few feet away. He took the hint and slowly, ever so slowly they backed away from the infuriated couple. But it was not nearly far enough away to avoid overhearing the heated conversation.

Mr. Brown stared at the petite dowager. "Is this truly what is behind your ill humor and behavior of the last month? Is this why you've taken a sudden interest in Beaufort? And here I'd taken to heart your letter. I'd thought you too shy or proud to admit your sensibilities when I saw you again. Your letter said that you might reconsider—"

"I said I would not forgive you if you did not bring Grace back to me," Ata interrupted.

"You did, indeed." Mr. Brown raised his chin, his eyelids at half mast. "You will always be looking for reasons not to forgive me for not meeting you over the anvil all those years ago, won't you? It would be more honorable if you would just have done with it and admit you canna and willna forget or forgive, Merceditas. Och, I'm a fool."

"Now is not the t—ah, there is Beaufort now." Ata's gray curls bounced as she waved to a gentleman astride a horse in the distance.

Grace sensed Michael Ranier's lips near her ear. "Come with me," he whispered. "Please—now's our chance."

She didn't want to go. She really didn't. But she also did not want to witness any more of the heartbreaking encounter between Mr. Brown and Ata. She nodded.

Grace inched ahead of Michael toward the clearing on the other side of the tall, manicured boxwood hedge, while he retrieved the other horse. They were out of sight and out of earshot when Grace finally halted.

"Look, I know I agreed to ride, but really there's no need to play out this farce. I know you just want to speak to me about something. So, say it and then I will return to Portman Square and you can be on your way. In fact, I shan't even require you to beg my forgiveness for your crass words in Yorkshire. I know it was an awkward situation. You wanted me to end what we had begun and I didn't let you off the hook. And so, as a gentleman, you used pride as the tool to avoid being reeled in. Luc or Quinn had just struck you, and obviously insulted you, and—are you laughing at me?"

"Absolutely not, sweetheart."

"You *are* laughing at me."

"Why would I dare laugh at a woman man enough to forgive me for something I've not even had to grovel for? You've even saved me the trouble of inventing excuses."

"Well, Mr. Ranier, most women are pushed to the task as few men ever admit guilt with any sort of finesse. Oh, and by the by, I have not forgiven you."

"I am very willing to admit I behaved abominably toward you. There was no excuse."

She didn't know what to say in the face of such blatant acceptance of blame. "Well, this is inconvenient."

"And why is that?"

"Because I'd planned to rail against you quite a bit longer."

He chuckled. "Do you always chatter on like this, or are you just trying to avoid getting on this horse? You know, you might enjoy riding her."

She would rather endure another failed engagement, truth be told. But she'd also do just about anything to avoid admitting such. "There's no mounting block." She shivered despite the unusually warm winter day.

His face grew serious. "Are you chilled? Would you like my coat?"

"No. I'm perfectly fine, except for the fact that you seem perversely determined to furthering disaster in my life whether we're in Yorkshire or London."

His face eased into a smile and he moved close to the mare. Grasping her waist, he looked down at her veiled face. "Ready?" he murmured.

Grace couldn't breathe, torn between the strength of his hands and her nearly lifelong irrational fear. Her fingers numb, she reached for the front of the side saddle when he lifted her onto the seat. She froze. Her limbs lay in a tangle below the leg horn.

"I would have preferred you to ride astride," he

said, his attention on fitting her foot into the stirrup. "I've always thought it much safer. But this will have to do."

She was dead still in the saddle, unable to move, unable to speak, waiting for an unknown, yet gruesome catastrophe to unfold.

"Grace? Hey . . . hey. Here, let me help you." He was moving her knee over the horn. But maybe not. She really couldn't feel anything. All she could see was the horse's ears lying flat back and she suddenly foresaw what would come next. The horse would run away before she could pick up the reins, and then it would all get worse. A lot worse.

Michael's harsh voice floated through the tunnel of her mind. "Grace, look at me."

She stiffly turned to his voice, unseeing.

Without warning she was blessedly being lifted from the cursed saddle and found her feet on solid ground again. And he was holding her to him. "Christ, I shouldn't have made you do this." He held her tighter. "Grace, I shouldn't have said those things to you at Brynlow." He lowered his voice, "I should've left well enough alone."

His words burned through the fog of her consciousness, leaving her slowly but surely furious. "That's what I've been saying all along, Mr. Ranier." She shoved him away and hissed, "What do you want from me?"

His lids lowered over his golden eyes. "To see you."

"Well, you've seen me." She held her arms out wide for his examination. "Now what? Perhaps the scenery has changed, but the circumstances remain the same." She rushed on, "Or has your neck become itchy? Perhaps the idea of a collar has suddenly become more appealing?"

"Never really liked the idea of a noose, sweetheart."

The small mare pawed the ground in boredom. "You are truly beyond the pale. If you're here because you think I'd consider resuming our—our—" The word stuck in the back of her throat.

"*Friendship*, sweetheart?"

She snorted. "Well, I suppose I should be happy you didn't say something coarser."

"Darling, friendship is all I'm looking for."

"Said the fox to the hare."

He chuckled. "Can a man not be friends with a lady then, Countess?"

She looked at him dubiously. "With enough distance I suppose anything is possible, Mr. Ranier. Perhaps if you were to remove to Portugal and I to Prussia, our friendship would flourish quite nicely."

He scratched his jaw in that familiar way she remembered. "Well, if you really can't trust yourself around me and need that much distance, you'd best begin packing—because I'm not leaving, at least not straightaway."

"You never give up, do you?"

"No . . . It's one of my most endearing qualities, I'm told." He paused. "Now are you going to tell me why you are afraid of horses, or not?"

She muttered something under her breath, unable to hide her exasperation. "Look, it should be obvious I'm no good with horses or really any animals. Always seem to fall off horses. Can't catch a fish. Can't fly a falcon. Fur makes me sneeze. Even Ata's canary always pecks me."

He looked as if he didn't believe her.

Words came from her without thought. "I fell off three times the month my riding lessons commenced as a child. The last time, my foot got caught in the stirrup and I was dragged over half of Mann. But no harm was done—aside from a few scratches and a twisted ankle. My father shot the poor horse, though. Yes, that's when I decided not to ride again."

"I wish you'd told me before now," he murmured.

"Would that have stopped you from insisting I try again?"

"No. But now that I understand the root of your fear, as your *friend*—"

"You are *not* my friend."

"Well, then as your former—"

"No! Don't you dare utter out loud what we once— oh, botheration." She looked at him mutinously.

He tilted up the front of his hat and squinted. Lines furrowed his brow. "Well, you're wrong about one thing, sweetheart. You've got a fine touch with animals. Have you forgotten Pearl? If not for you he wouldn't have survived."

"Pearl is male?" she asked incredulous.

A grin teased the corners of his wide mouth. "He only responds to the name you gave him. And he keeps wandering among the ewes, looking for you, Blue Eyes. He misses you. And Timmy misses you. And I've missed you"—his head tilted—"*terribly*."

"Don't," she whispered.

He took a step toward her and she backed away.

At that moment, she felt something prickly touch her wrist. Grace turned to find the muzzle of Michael's huge black horse sniffing her hand.

"No," Michael said firmly, and the horse swung her massive neck away after staring at Grace with her large intelligent eyes.

Grace was desperate to turn the conversation, tired of playing the charade. "Your horse is very beautiful."

"She's a powerful mix of breeds. Built for endurance and strength—named after the warrior Indian tribe. Only her big, floppy ears give away her gentle nature." He stroked his mare's neck, his smile disarming her as always.

She cleared her throat.

"Yes?"

"I do hate being such a pea goose around horses. And . . ."

"Yes?"

"Well, do you think . . . "

"Think what?"

"No, forget I—"

"Can't."

"No, really, I—"

"Won't."

"Will you stop interrupting me?"

He grinned again. "Only if you're ready to try again."

Without thinking, she rushed on. "I'll do it if only to stop your incessant pestering."

"Smart woman."

Realization of what she'd agreed to do swept through her. Pride kept her from reneging. "I'll only try with Sioux. I feel safer with her."

"All right." He moved his mare into position before she could utter another word. "She responds to *whoa* or *easy* or *steady now*. And she stops on the spot at the word *no*. But if you cluck to her or use your heels, she'll move on. Here, put your hand out, palm up, and touch her muzzle."

She followed his directions and the mare nickered sweetly. Grace was in awe.

"She likes you."

"I like her too," Grace said softly.

"Don't be afraid of her height or her strength."

"I've never been afraid of height or strength." Grace watched Michael's Adam's apple dip as he stared at her with eyes that flared with a poignant mix of hope and sadness.

He finally withdrew a small folding knife from his coat. "We'll have to cut your habit since you'll be astride."

"It's a good thing no one ever appears to come here in the morning," she said dryly.

Grace turned sideways to him and he leaned down to cut cleanly through each of the side seams. She glanced at Sioux and nearly faltered at the sight of the mountain of horseflesh in front of her. The mare's hooves were almost the size of dinner plates.

"Check the girth, first," he directed and then took up her wooden fingers, showing her what to do. "And let's shorten the stirrups."

The mare's neck swung around as she watched their efforts with a baleful expression.

"All right," Michael said with obvious false cheer. "Ready?"

"No," Grace muttered.

He chuckled and locked his hands together in front of him. "Go slowly, now."

She stepped into his hands and he lifted her for an eternity before she saw the top of the saddle.

"Swing your leg over," he commanded and she obeyed.

She could feel him fixing the ball of her boot in the stirrup and then going to the other side to do the same. Out of the corner of her eye, she saw him gather the reins of the other horse to lead her, too. The entire time, a flood of calming words came from his direction. What he said exactly Grace wasn't sure. She could barely breathe, let alone hear properly.

The mare shifted one hoof and it felt like the horse was about to crumple to the ground.

"Steady, now. Grace—you all right?"

She couldn't speak, but she tried to focus on him and nodded.

A moment later, she looked down to find the reins being woven between her fingers.

"You don't have to do anything with the ribbons. Just hold them—or the mane. Now tell me when you're ready and I'll lead you along the path. We're only going for a very short walk."

For a long time they just stood there, the mare pricking her ears up and looking across the lake, the man in front of the two horses, stroking their noses while watching Grace.

"I'm ready," Grace murmured, finally.

A moment later, the mare moved forward, her large shoulders rolling rhythmically between Grace's knees. The slow clop of the animal's hooves hitting packed earth was steady and sure.

"Look up, Grace. Don't look down."

She forced herself to obey.

"How are we doing?" His voice came from somewhere, Grace was not sure precisely where. She was too busy looking forward, beyond the horse's large ears.

"Your seat is excellent. Your back is supple, yet arched, your heels at the proper angle. Lift your hands off her withers if you like."

She didn't dare.

For long minutes, they continued on until Grace chanced to notice how lovely the view of the lake and the pleasure gardens were from this high angle. And, without knowing what she did, she lifted her hands.

And Michael began to hum a tune.

Ranelagh was so beautiful this early in the day. The night frost on the evergreens had turned to dew with the rising winter sun. It was unseasonably warm, Mother Nature being in a particularly fickle frame of mind this season. A flock of geese formed a V in the sky, honking as if to announce their arrival. At the half-mile marker, Michael turned to go in the reverse direction.

That was when Grace realized she had relaxed. She looked at the man in front of her, his shoulders so broad, tapering down his immensely powerful frame to his hips. And yet, despite his great size and blunt humor, he was so very gentle with every living thing. It was all in his eyes, each time he glanced back at her, each time he touched his horse.

After a quarter hour, the mare stopped at his command and he was at her side, disengaging one boot and then the other. "I'm going to lift you off, all right?"

Grace nodded, mutely. And then his large hands spanned her waist entirely and he was swinging her off his horse.

"Can you stand?"

She tried her legs and they felt odd, pudding-like. "Yes, I think I can."

He exhaled sharply. "Good. And how are we feeling?"

"We are feeling perfectly fine. Why?"

"You had me that worried. You said not a word."

"No? Well, I assure you I was having a delightful conversation with myself."

A measure of relief and amusement flooded his expression. "Really? And what were you discussing?"

"I was telling myself that I now understand what you were trying to explain to me, albeit very wretchedly, when I left Yorkshire."

"And what thing was that?"

"That while you enjoy leading someone else about, you are not the sort who can tolerate being led yourself. You don't follow others. And you prefer living alone. I can actually understand that. But . . ."

"Yes?"

"If it's not true, don't tell me. Otherwise, I don't think I could continue our budding *friendship*. You do want to continue on, don't you? Never in the fashion of those days in Yorkshire, but as casual *acquaintances* after today. That's really why you came to see me before returning to Yorkshire, isn't it?"

"Still carrying on both sides of the conversation, I see." There was laughter in his eyes. "You, Lady Sheffield, are the most forgiving, most kindhearted lady I'll ever have the pleasure to know." He pushed back the hat's veil that covered her eyes.

"That's not how I wish for you to remember me," she said archly.

"No? And how would you like me to think of you, then?" His eyes traveled from her eyes to her lips, and her throat constricted.

Inches away from the very thing that brought her such heartbreak, she found she couldn't tell him the truth of it. "Well, I've always thought my restraint quite admirable. I should be given credit for not bashing your head when you threatened me with a horse twitch."

"Actually, I believe I threatened to tie you up like a calf before his ballocks are removed."

She tilted her chin. "What's the difference, really?"

He pursed his lips to keep from laughing. "Well," he scratched his jaw, "I'm sure the calf would have a thing or two to say about it."

She opened her mouth but he stopped her with two fingers to her lips.

"You always change the subject whenever I try to flatter you, sweetheart, which leaves me few options on how to best soften your heart so you will look kindly on a request from Mrs. Kane."

"But, you merely have to ask. There are few things I would refuse her."

"She would like you to do her the great honor of joining everyone at the foundling home for a few hours on Christmas Eve. I'm afraid she has her heart set on it. Victoria Givan and I will be organizing all the activities for the children."

Victoria Givan. How could she have forgotten the ravishing Miss Givan?

"And then there will be the meal, of course."

"Of course," she echoed.

"Well, will you come? Or will you disappoint Mrs. Kane?"

"I don't know."

"You have an odd turn to your countenance just now. What are you thinking?"

"Nothing," she lied.

"You were worried I was going to suggest more riding lessons, weren't you?"

"No."

The light of wry disbelief filled his yellow eyes. "Are you saying you'd actually enjoy another lesson in future?"

"Perhaps, although I don't want you to trouble yourself about it. Actually, I think I know now what I was really afraid of all these years. Everyone thought I was terrified of falling off, of hurting myself, but it wasn't that. It was something else."

"And what was that?"

"I was afraid of being the cause of another innocent

animal's death. Of having to hear the sound of a pistol shot. I think I wanted to ride *your* horse because I knew you'd never blame me or Sioux if I was silly enough to fall off."

"I'd never blame you for anything. I wouldn't even blame you if you never wanted to see me again for the rest of your natural-born life." But there was a glimmer of hope, or perhaps it was just mirth, in his eyes.

"I'll come tomorrow night. If only for a little while. A very little while."

He picked her up and whirled her about while his laughter filled the air. "Come anytime after six o'clock. Oh, and Grace?" His eyes twinkled with amusement.

"Yes?"

"Do you really want to know how I shall always remember you at Brynlow?"

"I'm not sure," she replied.

He leaned in to whisper in her ear. "Your unpracticed seduction will haunt me for the rest of my days."

"I did *not* seduce you." She would withstand this. She took one step away to put distance between them, yet she could not help but take a measure of pride in what he had said.

A grin decorated his face. "No? Well, sweetheart, I beg to differ. And you can rest assured I shall always follow your lead to one place at least."

She snorted in exasperation. "And what place is that, Mr. Ranier?"

"To paradise, darling."

Chapter 13

Michael's feelings of jubilation were soon extinguished when he found himself in the unfortunate position of escorting the Duke of Beaufort back to the edge of Mayfair from Ranelagh a quarter hour later.

"My dear sir," began the duke. "You do me a good turn coming to my aid. Never been to those pleasure gardens in my life. Too much temptation, if you were to ask me. Too many hares, and not enough powder and shot." The portly man guffawed.

"Forgive me for not leading you precisely to your door, Your Grace, but my lodgings are in the opposite direction," Michael replied, full of discomfort. He hated Mayfair, hated the risk he took in coming to this well guarded portion of town. He tugged his tall hat as low on his head as possible.

"No, of course, sir," Beaufort replied. "You were good to accede to my wishes. Especially when I'm certain you've little desire to spend time with me."

"I beg your pardon?" They were nearly a quarter of a mile from Mayfair, and with every step closer, Michael became poised for flight, his knees grinding the saddle flaps.

"It's quite obvious you're smitten with the countess. Would have liked to get in the carriage with her, no?" He winked. "I say, though, you're looking quite high above your station. Knew the earl well. Excellent shot. Very devoted to her. But you'll be delighted to know I shall champion your efforts."

Michael's attention was riveted by three riders, their horses approaching at full gallop. There was only one reason men would set such a pace. His heart leaped to his throat and he swallowed against the knot, barely understanding a word of the foolish man beside him.

"I'm quite selfish in my motives, of course," the duke continued, oblivious. "If the countess will have you, then perhaps the dowager duchess will be tempted to visit my seat in Yorkshire on occasion."

The riders were almost upon them, the cutlasses visible like beacons in the gray dinginess of the cobbled street. *Christ. Bow Street runners.* Michael tried to regulate his breathing. He'd been a fool to risk coming to London. And they were close to Manning's Livery—far too close. He'd sworn never to tread so close as a hundred miles of the place again. And as if the duke could read minds, the pompous man continued his monotonous rant in a new direction.

"Have you seen the new yards at Manning's? Just saw them myself yesterday. Three times the size of Tattersall's now. Who'd have guessed that upstart would grow so far and so fast? From a paltry livery owner to one of the most reknowned men in London.

But for all that, he's still nothing more than a bastard with vulgar pretensions of grandeur. Indeed, can't imagine why he enjoys the Prince Regent's patronage. Richard Tattersall is at least a gentleman if not a lord."

The three Bow Street runners slowed to a trot as they approached to pass, and Michael brought his hand to the rim of his hat to partially shield his face.

"Well, ho!" The duke hailed the runners. "Off to find a criminal, are you? Who are you looking for?"

One man halted as the other two continued past. "A thief, sir. Did you happen to see a grimy boy not above four and ten, running with a sack? He nipped a gen'l'man's greatcoat not twenty minutes ago."

"A hanging offense," the duke said with a grimace. "Why, the idea. We shall be on the lookout for the scallywag. If we find him, shall we shoot him for you?"

"Got to catch up with me mates, sir. But by all means grab the thieving little devil if you see 'im." The runner tipped his hat before riding on.

"Well, I like that. A larcenist in Mayfair. It's the reason I prefer the country. We know how to catch and dispose of riffraff in Yorkshire. You will see how it goes once you've settled there. Why, gypsy vagrants, beggars, and other trash never dare set a hair in our neighborhood, Mr. Ranier."

The man was preening and crowing so much that he failed to notice the tiny waif hiding behind a dung heap in the alley they passed. Michael would have wagered his life that a greatcoat was tucked in the pouch the ragged, thin boy carried.

"And how do you manage it, sir?"

"Why, we shoot first and ask questions later. Saves us the trouble of guarding and feeding them before a hearing. A trial would only to prolong their misery, don't you think?"

"Very enlightened."

"I'm so glad you see it that way, Mr. Ranier. As former Lord Lieutenant of our county, I'm always looking for like-minded gentlemen to recommend for the stipendiary magistrate position. It is good to know I will be able to count on you, sir."

"Oh, you may depend on me, Your Grace. I shall ever and always look upon beggars and vagrants with the same eye I cultivated in my youth."

The Duke of Beaufort glanced at him with a comical mixture of suspicion and arrogance.

"Here we are. Just a few more blocks before St. James's Square."

"And where are you off to now, sir? Where are your lodgings? Surely you have a moment more to join me for a fortifying cup of something stronger than tea? And I will condescend to show you Beaufort House. The armory is not to be missed."

Michael kept a steady gaze on the awful gentleman who embodied everything he most disliked about the aristocracy of England. "Thank you, Your Grace. But I think I shall see if I can find that thief. Wouldn't want you to have to blacken your hands with a rover."

The duke raised his chin and his wattle jiggled. "Good man. Perhaps you should take my pistol."

"No, I won't hear of it. I don't want to put you out." Michael thought he might just shoot the duke between his peepers given the chance. "But if I don't hurry along, I might miss him. You know how wily and difficult criminals are. Especially young, hardened ones."

The man hesitated, confusion battering his small brain-box. "Well, then, I bid you good day, sir."

"Good day to you, too." *You old bugger.* Michael wended his way quickly back to the alley, taking care to employ evasive tactics lest someone saw him.

Noting several shadows of blighted humanity as he searched, Michael finally spied the boy, still hiding behind the dung heap. Returning to London had only served to remind him how powerless he was given the magnitude of the wretched poor lurking everywhere.

"You there," he called to the boy, "come out. The runners are headed south. I have something for you." Michael reached for the guineas in his pocket and tossed the boy half of what he held. "Leave the coat. It will only lead you to the gallows."

The boy was covered in grime; even the whites of his eyes appeared dingy. He bowed his head after retrieving the coins.

"Where are you sleeping?"

" 'Ere and there, guv'nor."

"What's your name?"

"James."

James . . . Christ, it was his own father's name. "And other than thieving, are you employed?"

"Was, sir. Chimney sweep. Got too big fer it. Was turned out well nigh a fortnight ago."

"I see. Well, if I promise you employment, will you come with me?"

The boy lowered his head like a dog. "Are you going ter turn me over?"

"No. Now you will either have the good sense to find your way to the foundling home at Lamb's Conduit Fields, where you will tell Mrs. Kane that I sent you—and where I will meet you later this afternoon—or you will be foolish and end up dead or transported for life. It's your choice, James."

The boy gave Michael a long searching look and then nodded once before dropping the sack and racing back through the alleyway behind him. Michael gave it an even chance of ever seeing the boy again. Trust was something learned, and boys such as James had never been given the chance to comprehend the notion.

As Michael went on to gather the odd assortment of goods needed to ensure a memorable day for the children on the morrow, he wondered if he too was manacled by the past. He questioned if he was an adult version of that boy, unable to trust or to expect the best that life had to offer because he was not grounded properly. In his mind, he struggled to clear a path that would allow Grace into his life despite the clutter of his impossible past. The way appeared mired in far too much danger for her and it left Michael flummoxed.

He had everything he needed, finally—a small property that would prosper in future to ensure his comfort and the comfort of others, such as the Lattimers and that boy James. And yet, he wanted more. He wanted Grace.

Was life always filled with insatiable wanting?

Just then, on the way to a lumberyard for his final purchase, Michael's attention was caught by the jangle of carriage traces at the crossroads ahead. A smart pair of matched chestnuts crossed in front of him, dressed out in the telltale dark blue and gold colors of Manning's Livery. A chill of recognition froze Michael's thoughts.

God. He was such a fool. Why was he leaving everything to such risk? He had to leave. Very soon. He did not want to be one of those reckless sods who lost everything for wanting the impossible. And more important, he could not . . . would not . . . put Grace in peril.

She was being so imprudent about all of this, Grace thought, as she waited for the gatekeeper at the foundling home to open the tall black iron gates for her carriage to enter. Yes, there seemed to be no end to the lengths she would stoop to make a greater fool of herself where Mr. Michael Ranier was concerned.

She should have accepted Quinn and Georgiana's invitation tonight. All of the widows in the club, and their burgeoning families, would be there to celebrate the season. But no, she just couldn't pass up another occasion to see him. To drift ever closer toward further heartbreak, she thought cynically, because really, until she experienced out-and-out disaster a third time, she might never learn that she was not meant to find any sort of happiness with someone else. And, in the end, it didn't matter. She had already decided that she could find contentment all by herself.

Her carriage's wheels crunched the hard-packed sandy path leading to the entryway of the U-shaped structure, the chapel separating the boys' wing from the girls' wing. While she descended, one of the carriage drivers unpacked the provisions she had brought.

"Mrs. Kane," Grace said, when the mistress rushed forward to greet her. "You're very kind to have extended an invitation to me tonight."

"Your ladyship is very generous to have accepted. I'm certain you had far more glorious entertainments in the offing," Mrs. Kane replied. "And once again you honor us with more gifts, I see. I don't know how to thank you properly."

Grace pressed a sheaf of papers bound with ribbon into the lady's outstretched hands. "These are the donations from the other evening. And a little more from my good friends, the Marquis of Ellesmere and the Duke of Helston, as well as, uh, an anonymous donor. I know you will put it to good use."

Mrs. Kane untied the ribbon; her face blanched at the enormity of the bank drafts within.

"Mrs. Kane, you are not to say a word. Tonight it is Christmas Eve, and I've come to help you make merry for a short while."

Mrs. Kane laughed, her eyes bright with unshed tears. "Make merry? Why, I rather think you've just ensured that for the next twelve months if not longer, my lady. Shall we adjourn to the chapel, then? Perhaps I can give you another tour of the—"

"No, no, Mrs. Kane. I don't want to take you away from the children. And I understand there are to be amusements and such."

"Of course. Mr. Ranier and Miss Givan have arranged the games and everything. Do you know Hot Cockles, Lady Sheffield, or Shoe the Wild Mare?"

Grace shook her head. "No, but I should like to learn."

Mrs. Kane smiled and Grace followed the older woman as she bustled down a corridor, her key fob jangling with every step.

A chorus of shouts and giggles met them on the other side of the double doors. Such a scene . . . A crowd of children filled the hall, a circle carved out in the middle. A young girl with a starched pinafore, identical to all the aprons on the other girls, sat in the middle, a handkerchief tied as a blindfold. A boy rushed forward and tapped the girl on the shoulder while the other children goaded her to guess his identity.

The child grinned. "It's Tom. I guess Tom."

Hoots of laughter erupted and she tore off the blindfold.

Michael Ranier strode toward the girl. "And how did you know him when you've not seen one of these boys all year, miss?"

"Half the boys here are named Tom. The other half 're John or Harry." All the girls giggled and Grace could not help but smile too.

At that moment Michael turned in her direction and left the children to their game. "Why, you've come. I feared you wouldn't."

"Well, if yesterday was any example, I would think you'd know by now that I never renege on a promise, Mr. Ranier."

"You're quite right, Lady Sheffield." He chuckled, and Grace was reminded yet again that Michael Ranier could, indeed, be a most devastatingly attractive man when he chose. He had only to turn his full attention on a person and unleash his smile.

Grace searched her pocket for a note. "I promised to deliver this to you." She did not mutter "Lord help me," as she wished. "I shall warn you that it's an invitation from Ata. She would like you to join us at Helston House for dinner tomorrow."

His eyes lit up with amusement. "Would she now?"

"Yes."

"And would *you* like me to come, Lady Sheffield?"

She just could not do it. Her pride would not allow her to put her feelings before him on a platter. "I would not presume to intrude on your time in town, Mr. Ranier."

"I see. And this is to be an intimate family gathering rather than a ball given for half of London?"

Such a strange question. "One never knows with Ata. It should be the former but when she includes extended family and her ducal friends . . . well, I should not hazard a guess."

His expression turned serious. "I'm honored by her invitation but I must decline. I'll be needed here. The children—"

"There's no need to explain," she interrupted. "I'm certain Ata will understand."

He appeared as if he wanted to say more on the subject but changed his mind. "Come. The children must be served a good show. They've waited all year. And you're just in time."

"Really?" She released the tension in her shoulders when she realized the awkward moment had passed.

So he would not accept Ata's invitation. He really

did want nothing more than friendship. The apologies were complete, and they were to part amicably.

"Yes, it's time to drag in the largest Yule log in all of London."

The children overheard his rising voice and erupted into cheers.

She tried to ignore the bruise to her heart. "It sounds daunting. But I'm sure you'll manage it, Mr. Ranier. You always manage everything perfectly well."

"Such flattery, ma'am," he replied wryly. "Although it won't help me move the log."

"Well, if it's advice you're looking for, Mr. Ranier, I'm happy to oblige, although you might not like it."

"Really?"

"Yes."

"Go on."

"Perhaps you should use mind over matter, Mr. Ranier."

"Excellent advice, of course, but then I've always found those who give advice rarely provide what is really necessary."

"And what, pray tell, is that, sir?"

"A helping hand or an encouraging word. Yes, in your case, encouragement is what is most needed. Most wanted." His gaze was steady and Grace wished he would sweep aside all innuendo. She had never possessed a talent for deciphering the difference between dangerous flirtation and the harmless wordplay of "friendship." There was likely nothing behind his words except witticisms meant only to charm.

At the same moment, Miss Victoria Givan joined them, clapping her hands. "Children, make way for Mr. Ranier, please. Oh, Lady Sheffield, you do us a great honor by joining us. Michael? The porter said he would stand by to aid you if needed."

"The only help I will need, concerns the mistletoe. Certainly won't ask for Charlie's help in that corner." He dealt another grin in Grace's direction and then winked at Victoria Givan. The auburn-haired beauty proceeded to raise one lovely arched brow, and a dimple appeared next to her radiant smile.

Dizziness almost overcame Grace as she watched Miss Givan. The lady stared after Michael's powerful figure when he turned his attention to the massive log in the entryway.

Why had she come here? She felt so very alone. She was always out of her element no matter where she found herself. When she had been a child on Mann none of the other children had been allowed to play with her given the fact that her father, the Baron Atholl, was the highest-ranking peer on the island. Then in London, when her family's fortune had disintegrated, she'd been shunned. Even with the other widows in Ata's secret club, she'd felt separate due to her great fortune in the face of the others' near poverty. And now here, she was nothing more than a distraction. The children kept peeking at her and whispering while Mrs. Kane glanced at her and tried to keep the children more orderly.

Grace had formed a list of three or four hasty excuses to take her leave, when the sight of Michael pulling the log arrested her attention. Why, it was nearly larger than he. And he had stripped off his rough-hewn coat, and even his neckcloth and shirt, of all things. He'd replaced them with a leather apron to obviously guard against the ill cut branches, and the dirt and dust on the enormous log.

And then she realized it must be what he had worn in his trade as a blacksmith.

His shoulders gleamed with the effort, and his muscles bunched from the strain. He appeared as a veritable Atlas struggling with the weight of the world, and then all at once the log moved into position in front of the yawning fireplace.

"Stop, stop," the crowd yelled. And the children began to scramble about in an effort to take a turn sitting on the log.

"They want to sit on it for good luck during the year," Miss Givan said to her above the boisterous mayhem.

"Of course," Grace returned.

One of the younger children, a little blonde girl of six or so, stood mutely in a far corner.

"Why is that child not joining in with the others?"

"Ah, that is Lara. Lara Peabody. It's really too bad. She wasn't to return here until after December. The family who took her in during her infancy is having a hard go of it, though. The wife took ill and so the husband had to return Lara early. She's forlorn because she misses them. But have no fear, she'll recover her spirits in a day or two. They all do. I remember it took me merely a week or so before I made fast friends with a half dozen girls when I was returned from the country."

"I see." Grace looked at the courageous expression on Miss Givan's face. "So all the children were placed with families when they were infants?"

"Yes. Then they come back when they are old enough to learn to read and form letters—the boys at least. They're all here to learn a trade. The girls usually become servants in great houses; the boys go to sea or to another trade."

"Such as smithing," Grace added, glancing at Michael still tossing the children on and off the log.

"Yes," Miss Givan replied. "But we no longer send boys to Manning's, as Michael has probably told you."

So he had apprenticed at Manning's Livery. Grace drew in an uneven breath, hurt that he had revealed so little to her. "No, he did not."

"Oh. I'm so sorry. I thought he had confided everything to you."

"Our acquaintance is recent in nature."

"Ah, that is why. Well, I've known Michael ever since he arrived. Even though the boys and girls are not permitted to take classes or dine together, I saw him each week. I was in charge of the wash, and he always helped to carry the boys' items to the washroom, for there was so much."

Grace wished Miss Givan had not drawn her into conversation, but she was too polite to alter the discourse.

"We were very close. It fair near broke my heart when he left. It is so lovely to see him again. And in such good spirits, too."

Without thought, Grace stood up. She couldn't listen

to anymore. She glanced at the dejected little girl in the corner. Large gray eyes looked into her own. "Excuse me, but perhaps I might endeavor to bring a measure of comfort to your newest arrival."

"Oh, of course, Lady Sheffield. You are so kind. But then Michael told us you were always kind to everyone. Michael is very much the same. We are so grateful for your generosity."

Really, what did Grace expect? He was the most charming, virile man she had ever met in her life. And Miss Givan was his equal in vibrancy. Could she blame the lady—or any woman—for being madly in love with him? She glanced at Michael as he seated the littlest children on the log and cajoled the older ones to wait their turn, and was disgusted with herself. She'd never been able to read the nature of a gentleman and a lady's sensibilities toward each other. Victoria Givan and Michael Ranier had known each other since childhood, just like Georgiana had known Quinn. The latter pair had appeared to have nothing more than a deep friendship between them, but, she thought, her heart in her throat, that had been about as far from the truth of it as was Miss Givan's friendship with Mr. Ranier. Why, they were from the same societal sphere and were made for each other.

For the first time ever, Grace felt a vital raw sentiment deep in the bottom of her stomach. She had thought she'd experienced it before, first with Luc and then with Quinn. But no. This was altogether far worse. It made her want to screech like all the pheasants in England.

Well.

She would get through this evening as she got through every unfortunate evening of her life. *With grace.* She could not have been more aptly named than if her parents had given it a second thought.

She tried to steady her thoughts as she walked toward the little girl. "Excuse me, miss, but I'm feeling a bit out of place since I only know two or three people in the room. I saw you standing alone too. Would it be too much to ask if I could sit beside you?" Grace bit her lip. "You would be doing me an enormous favor."

The little girl stared up at her for a long moment, her eyes as gray as the winter skies of Mann. She finally nodded once and then did something that tugged at Grace's heartstrings. Small fingers wormed their way into her gloved hand and tugged her toward a bench nearby. They sat down, side by side.

"What's your name?" the little girl finally asked.

"Grace Sheffey."

The girl peered at her from under long lashes. "Your gloves are very soft." She said it so quietly Grace had to lean down to catch the words.

"Thank you."

The little girl edged closer to her. "I'm Lara."

"Delighted to make your acquaintance, Lara. Would you not like a turn atop the Yule log?"

She shook her head, her expression wistful. "No, I don't believe in luck."

"I don't either." Out of the blue, Grace felt at peace with the world. She didn't need to drum up conversation for the child beside her. And she held on to Lara's hand, wouldn't have let it go for all the world.

Occasionally, Grace looked down at the small head, with the even middle part, and her heart felt less constricted. For the first time in her life, she understood the powerful, unfettered bond a mother might share with a child. She wanted desperately to shelter Lara from any further disappointments and the pain she saw in those sad gray eyes.

At that moment, Michael looked across the room at her and smiled.

She was so very beautiful to him. Like a Madonna. The picture she painted with the little blonde girl seated beside her was almost too painful to contemplate. It reminded him of his dream of her in the apple orchard.

"Michael?"

He turned his head to find Victoria wading through the sea of children.

"Yes?"

"Cook says the food will be ready to serve in a quarter hour. Shall we not proceed to the next game? The children wanted a round of blindman's bluff."

The boys hooted their approval.

Michael laughed. "And here I've dressed for Shoe the Wild Mare. I've even provided the 'horse.'" He nodded toward a beam strung by two cords on either end.

An older girl stepped forward. "But none of the girls ever win Shoe the Wild Mare. It's too hard to stay balanced and tap the imaginary nails. Can't we first play blindman's bluff?"

"Never let it be said that I couldn't be persuaded to

accommodate a lady's wishes." He bowed grandly and pulled a handkerchief from his leather apron. "Who's first?"

One of the more audacious boys called out mischievously, "Miss Givan. We all want Miss Givan."

Michael waggled his eyebrows. "Now boys. Decorum, please. Miss Givan? It seems you've been chosen."

Victoria's face bloomed into a happy smile and she shook her head helplessly. "Oh, all right."

He carefully covered the eyes of the woman who had traded in her former plain features and carrot curls to become a flame-haired beauty. "No peeking, Victoria. I know better than anyone here your penchant for cheating. But happily for me, as your former adversary, I also know all your tricks."

"You're entirely wrong, Michael. I've only ever had a penchant for"—she lunged toward him at the same moment he jumped away from her—"*winning!*"

Michael laughed and put another few feet between them. "Now, Victoria. Just because you occasionally caught me in our youth doesn't mean I'll allow you to win now. You know very well, I'm no good at chivalry." He dodged left then right at every other word, until Victoria appeared to give up her quest.

Michael wended his way to the hidden alcove where he had stashed his articles of clothing. After disposing of his smithing gear, he carelessly donned his shirt and neckcloth before buttoning his coat. He crossed to a pillar on which he leaned, his arms crossed, to better watch the merry scene in between covert glances toward Grace.

He could barely stop himself from walking to her. And despite his earlier reservations, he took the decision to stay just a few days longer—only to see her. Oh, not as long as Twelfth Night, but perhaps, yes, he would depart on the first day of the new year. Surely, few runners would be about during Christmas, Boxing Day, and Childermas.

His brush with James, the former chimney sweep in the alley, who had failed to meet him at the foundling home, had made Michael realize that he was, indeed, too much like the boy. Too untrusting. Gazing at Grace, he knew he could take a chance—trust her. But at the same time, he wanted to shield her from the worst of the ugliness. And so he would merely explain a portion of the true reasons behind his return to Brynlow. And why he could not in future return to London.

A hand clawed his side. *What in hell . . . Oh Christ—*

"I've caught you," Victoria said still blindfolded and out of breath. She'd come up behind him, catching him in his reverie. "Now I must be given a moment to guess who it is."

Michael froze as the children burst into laughter. Victoria dragged her hand around to the front of his body.

"Hmmm. Let me see. Could it be Mr. Wilkes? Or perhaps Charlie Howe? No, wait, you're far too tall and broad to be Charlie," Victoria said with exaggerated uncertainty.

"You're determined to drag out my humiliation as long as possible, aren't you, Vic?" he whispered for her ears only.

The pretty mouth below the blindfold curved into a smile. "Of course. It's the most fun I've had all year."

Michael cleared his throat and addressed their giggling audience. "You can't say I didn't warn you that she cheats. Does anyone not see the gap in the handkerchief? She is looking at my boots. Have you no shame, Miss Givan?"

"None, whatsoever, Mr. Ranier," she replied and then removed the scarf. "Now it's your turn to play the fool."

The children all shouted encouragement. And then Victoria pressed her warm bosom against him as she rose up on her toes to fasten the blindfold around his face.

It was too bad he could not have seen Grace's expression at that moment.

Chapter 14

Michael slid his fingers up Victoria's sides and began to tickle her. She gasped and tried to wrench herself free. "You wretch!" she cried.

"You never could take it, Victoria. Could only ever dish it out," he retorted.

She spun away from him, laughing. "I should've remembered you were a poor loser."

Michael reached toward her voice, his hand finding nothing but air. He swung wildly and heard shuffling feet and muffled shrieks as the children scattered away. But they were no match for him. Within moments he'd caught a boy, whose name, predictably, Michael had not a chance of guessing correctly.

By the time he removed the mask, the dinner bell had rung out, and the mass of exuberant children, long dreaming of the once-a-year feast, stampeded toward the dining hall. Michael turned to escort Grace, only to find she was gone. The pretty girl who had been sitting beside her was now all alone.

He strode across the floor, worry spurring his steps. "Where did she go?" He rushed on, "Did Lady Sheffield leave?"

The girl nodded, clutching something to her tightly, while she silently pointed to the doors away from the dining hall.

Gloves. The child was clutching pink gloves. Good God, she really had left.

Michael raced to the doors, ignoring Mrs. Kane and Victoria's questions.

She was brushing aside the porter's efforts to place her rose cloak about her shoulders. "No, sir. But thank you. I must go, my carriage is waiting."

Michael glared and nodded at the man who scurried away to leave them alone. She took a step toward the entrance and he grasped her arm. "Grace," he said quietly, "where are you going?"

Veiled eyes met his. "To Portman Square. I'm very late. Quinn and Georgiana have arranged such a lovely evening for all of my friends and Ata's family. I must go. Oh, please thank Mrs. Kane for her kind invitation tonight. It was delightful to see the children at play and to see you at your ease with everyone. You must get back to them and—"

He interrupted her. "Are you finished?" Her expression was closed off and he hated it.

"I see you're still refusing to obey the rules of polite conversation, Mr. Ranier."

He pulled her into an alcove overlooking the drive.

"Let me go. My carriage is waiting."

"It'll wait a little longer. Now tell me what this is about. You were to take supper with all of us tonight. Mrs. Kane and others, especially that little girl, will be hurt if you don't stay. Not very polite behavior for someone who esteems such notions now, is it?"

"I will send my apologies to Mrs. Kane on the morrow. And I've already planned a special treat for Lara Peabody. But, I assure you that the others will not be hurt in the slightest by my absence. Victoria Givan will keep everyone's spirits merry along with your help."

He looked at her long and hard. And then a smile teased the corner of one side of his lips. "You're jealous."

"I most certainly am not!"

"Grace," he murmured. "You honor me so."

"You presume a great deal," she muttered. "And don't you dare look at me like that."

"How exactly am I looking at you?"

"Like I'm some sort of disagreeable child to be mollified."

"You've never been very good at reading minds, sweetheart," he said, his voice dropping. "And you know very well I've never thought of you as a child. Far from it."

She said not another word.

It warmed the heart that she still cared, even if she would not fight for him. "I've known Victoria Givan since I was a boy—since the day I walked through these doors." He picked up Grace's bare, delicate hand in his. "She was always exasperating, and always trying to goad me and Sam Bryn into trouble. I've been wondering what sort of miracle Mrs. Kane conjured up to transform Victoria from a willful child to a tireless, caring teacher."

"You don't have to explain. And I do thank all of you for this invitation. But I must go now. It's for the best."

"Well, if I can't convince you to stay . . ."

"You can't, I assure you."

"Then, there's only one last thing to attend to before you go. You see, I promised Mrs. Kane . . ." He escorted her toward the door. Her blonde hair gleamed under the light of the chandelier, the candles lit above the greenery swagged all around. A tiny cluster of waxy white berries peeked out from between the boughs. He blocked her exit at the last moment.

"Botheration. Michael, what are you doing?"

"So you do remember my name," he murmured close to her ear. "Was beginning to worry you'd forgotten it, since you've not said it in so long."

She pushed at his arms as he enfolded them about her.

"Don't ruin the moment, Grace."

"What moment?"

"The moment under the mistletoe."

"Oh, pish," she said, looking up at the greenery. "There are other females here who would help you do it properly."

"Yes, but they're not you." He lowered his lips to hers and she turned her face away. He kissed her temple instead. "You're the one I want. And yes, damn it all to hell, I'll come tomorrow night. I find that where you're concerned I just can't stay away . . . can't get enough of you," he growled.

Startled blue eyes stared up at him, and he seized the chance before she could evade him yet again. His arms tightened about her and he claimed her lips, pouring all the pent-up passion he'd curbed for so long. Ah, she tasted of heaven and sweetness, and pure femininity wrapped in a rosy pink package. Locked tight against her, he deepened the kiss and her fisted hands unclenched against his shoulders. He knew he only had another minute at best before the porter returned, but his head was too full of her. Her elusive scent, her softness, her every last drop of goodness.

His tongue twined intimately against hers; seeking—no, demanding a response. And she did not deny him.

Tentatively, oh so tentatively, she gave back in her own irresistible, shy fashion. As soon as her tongue curled to meet his, he groaned and wound his hands further about her delicate frame. God, how he had dreamed of this. God, how he wanted her—damn his loutish hide.

The problem was that she'd had all the next day to think about what he'd said to her. Nothing could distract her, save for the hour she'd spent finding the only shop still open where she could purchase a Christmas doll for Lara. Packaging it carefully with a note telling the little girl how much she had enjoyed spending a portion of the evening with her, Grace had felt a fissure open in her tightly guarded heart.

But the rest of the day, Grace's mind could not be quieted. She'd dissected every sentence, every look, every nuance of every action of Michael Ranier. And it all came down to the fact that apart from sheer lust, which gripped them both with a vengeance each time they were alone, they had absolutely nothing in common.

Their worlds could not be more different if they tried. And he had made it patently clear that while he desired her, he envisioned no future with her. And the husbands of all her friends had made it equally clear that they agreed. And so Grace deduced that nursing this impossible fascination would only lead to further heartbreak.

Her thoughts shuffled in her mind as swiftly as all the widows dashed about the kitchens within Helston House. Last year's Christmas had also been spent thusly, in a frenzy absent of every last servant save Luc's butler, Mr. Phipps, who had nowhere else to go.

Grace removed the last of the stems from the hothouse strawberries and placed them in a bowl. Ata and the rest of the widows knew better than to ask her to do any foodstuff preparation involving fire. Sarah and Elizabeth were the true geniuses in the kitchen, while Georgiana supplied cakes she had learned to bake from her mother.

"Grace," Sarah said, behind her, "would you mind beating the cream for the strawberries?"

"Of course." Pride swelled in her breast as she took over the task.

"Rosamunde and Georgiana went above stairs to help Mr. Phipps arrange the table. This is the last of it."

Elizabeth came down the stairs again to retrieve a steaming plum pudding on an ornate silver platter. "Goodness. I think we're ready. The wassail bowl has enough spirits to make even Luc happy. The fumes nearly overcame me." She giggled and used the edge of her apron to dab at the cream that Grace splattered on her arm. "He just arrived," Elizabeth informed her quietly.

"I see." She beat the cream a bit faster.

Sarah rushed into the gap. "Is there anything you want us to do while he's here, Grace? Would you like us to keep him slightly apart from you? We can switch the place cards if you like. Or perhaps you would like to speak to him privately again?" Anxiety lined Sarah's kind face.

As Grace glanced between the two women, she realized how very blessed she was by their friendship. "No, that's not necessary. And you are worrying far too much. Mr. Ranier and I are perfectly capable of meeting without any qualms." *Right*. Sarah and Elizabeth stared at her with doubt. "Really. Let's go up now. I think this is done."

The three women looked down at the bowl, only to find the cream overchurned, the peaks now dense and on the verge of turning to butter. "Oh, how ridiculous," Grace muttered.

Elizabeth giggled. "Don't worry, it's not important."

"Well, if you really want to do something," she said, looking at the two of them, "I would ask you never to allow me near a kitchen again after tonight. For everyone's sake. Now please go up before me. I'm determined to try again."

Michael sat on the fragile settee, feeling more than a little like a bull perched on a bamboo fence. How on earth did lords and ladies expect a person to sit on a dainty thing like this without breaking it to bits?

The Duke of Helston paced in front of the fire as he glanced from time to time at his lovely raven-haired wife, who held an infant in each arm. The man finally came to an abrupt halt and then swept the room with an annoyed hauteur, his eyes narrowing as they came to rest on Michael.

Where was she? He wouldn't have come so early if he had known she wouldn't be in evidence.

"Yes, Phipps?" Helston barked as someone entered the doorway.

An elderly man dressed in an elegant style of the last decade stood with a large silver bowl, flanked by two of the widows. "The wassail bowl, Your Grace."

"Very good. Offer it around, if you will, Phipps."

"Oh yes, let's do," said the dowager duchess with a gleam in her dark eyes. She turned away from a beautiful gilded cage, which housed a vibrant canary. "And I must thank you again so much, Charles, for helping me bring Pip from Grace's townhouse. My sweet bird sometimes gets bored staring at the four walls of my private rooms, and it is a holiday."

"Delighted to be of service to you, Ata," Beaufort replied. "Pretty little thing, she is."

"Oh, and she sings so beautifully. Especially in the mornings. You must hear her."

"That would be entirely inappropriate," Mr. Brown ground out. "As I remember, she sings at eight o'clock in the morning. And since you have not risen before noon a day in your life, madam, I find it hard to imagine how the duke will manage to hear your dear Pip sing."

"Well!"

Helston barked with laughter. "He's got you there, Ata."

The petite dowager, who was wearing outrageously high heels for her diminutive stature, tottered over to Mr. Phipps and drained one of the cups he offered. She then gave the cut direct to Mr. Brown, by picking up a second cup and turning her back to him. "My dear Quinn, I know I can count on you to share a bit of this delightful concoction with me."

"No thank you, Ata," the marquis said. "I think I'll refrain."

"You must be joking," Helston said, stopping dead in his tracks again. "Not even on Christmas? Surely, that's blasphemous. Well, Georgiana, may we not tempt you?"

The new marchioness tried to hide a smile unsuccessfully. "Perhaps later."

"Later? Good God, later is never better than the present," Helston said, turning back to the marquis. "Are you hinting that you'd prefer one of those blasted throat torches you favor so bloody much? I was hoping you'd hold off until after dinner."

"No, that's quite all right," Quinn Fortesque replied.

"What's this? Given up those nasty Portugese cheroots? And here after I went through all the trouble to track them down. Spirit of Christmas and all that."

"Your effort takes my breath away. Never knew you cared, Helston."

"This friendship of ours is far more draining than I thought possible. I shall have to reconsider the terms of our agreement if this contrary nature of yours continues."

"It's my fault, Luc," the lovely marchioness murmured.

"Don't be silly. Nothing is your fault," the dowager insisted. "It's the gentlemen who are always at fault." She skirted a glance at Mr. Brown and looked away quickly.

"The smoke leaves me a bit queasy, you see. And Quinn has quite kindly given it up for the time being."

"For the time being?" Helston asked brusquely. "And why is that?" All eyes focused on the chestnut-haired marchioness.

Ata jumped up and rushed to the lady. "Oh, Georgiana, are you?" She left the question to dangle.

"Yes."

Helston's wife looked at her with a warm expression. "Oh, Georgiana, I've longed for this. Our children will be the best of friends in all of the world!"

The duke strode to the wassail bowl, accepted a cup from Mr. Phipps, and passed it to his grandmother. "Well, I'm certain I can count on you, Grandmamma, to celebrate the occasion properly."

The dowager smiled. "Oh, Georgiana! So delighted, dearest. Now I feel better knowing I gave up an entire bottle of my Armagnac for this occasion. Wouldn't want to waste a drop. Mr. Ranier, may we offer you a cup, then? Luc—"

"Thank you, but no," Michael said.

"What? You, too?" Helston said incredulously. "Good God, am I fated to be surrounded by abstainers? When, on earth, did sin go out of fashion? Well," he sighed, "more for me."

Mr. Brown leaned in from the other end of the settee. "You mustn't take offense, Mr. Ranier. Remember, the blacker the scowl, the softer the heart."

"And the harder the apology," the Marquis of Ellesmere murmured.

"What's that, Ellesmere?" the duke muttered. "Can't have you forever talking behind my back."

"Just providing a bit of advice for my new friend Mr. Ranier, here, on the delicate task of forming bonds with a hotheaded sailor."

"Don't worry. I'd never hold my breath waiting for an apology from His Grace," Michael replied.

"Well, it appears Ranier is, indeed, smarter than he looks," Helston said with a dark smile.

"Actually, I was talking about *your* future apology, Mr. Ranier." Ellesmere's eyes were hooded.

"*My* apology? I—" Michael stopped dead when he noticed Grace hovering in the door frame. He unconsciously rose to his feet. Ah, yes. He was glad he had decided to come. It was worth every bit of danger and nonsense within this madhouse for the simple chance to see her again.

She walked toward him and his vision tunneled to only her as she glided forward in a pale pink satin gown, her signature pearls clustered about her slender neck. They lay gleaming against her flesh in a bodice cut lower than Michael had ever seen in his life. The knowledge of what lay underneath all that opulence made his mouth dry.

Grace offered her fingers and he bowed to press his

lips against the back of her hand. He looked up from his bent position. "What's this? Your hand is chafed, Lady Sheffield." The conversation had resumed behind them but he ignored it all, preferring to rest his gaze forever on the angel before him. "Don't say you've been below stairs cooking all this time."

She nodded. "Luc always chases all the servants away for a day or so. But don't tell him I told you. He prefers that everyone think him black hearted."

"He does a fine job of it too."

She smiled, and her face took on the radiant quality that Michael wanted to gaze at every miserable day of his ruined life.

"My dear Grace," the duke said, "do come in and join us. It's so tiresome to pretend not to notice you and Mr. Ranier chatting away as if the rest of us don't exist."

"Now, Luc, we were making progress," Ata replied. "And one would *hope* you would not be so foolish as to pick another fight with such a wonderfully handsome man with the sort of strength only a blacksmith possesses."

"I've always found hope is rarely answered the way one would like," Luc retorted annoyed.

"Well, my tuppence would be on Mr. Ranier, after seeing the results of the last round. You had best just get used to him, Luc."

The Duke of Beaufort broke away from his study of Ata's canary. "A blacksmith? The man's a blacksmith? Won't do at all, I say. Thought he was one of us. Has that look about him."

Michael clenched his hands involuntarily.

"Now, Charles. Mr. Ranier is now a man of property, as you well know."

The Duke of Helston cleared his throat. "Well, if everyone has had enough of this scintillating chitchat, perhaps we should adjourn to table." Without waiting for an answer, he motioned to encourage everyone toward the dining chamber.

Ata ignored her grandson's offered arm and tottered toward Michael. He had noticed she was in the habit of wearing the most outrageous ensembles. Tonight was no exception. Scarlet silk and black lace draped her diminutive frame.

"Mr. Ranier? I have a favor to ask."

He'd liked the petite dowager from the very start. "Anything, ma'am."

She tapped her intricately carved black lace fan on his arm. "I shall hold you to that, sir. The grandson I hold most dear—"

"Am I not still your *only* grandson, Ata?" Helston interrupted with a devilish smile as he herded everyone into the massive chamber.

"As I was saying, Mr. Ranier, the grandson I sometimes hold dear, while other times I do not hold dear a'tall," the dowager said shaking her head, "is to turn another year older and I've planned on—"

Helston interrupted again while everyone seated themselves. "Bloody hell, I thought we'd agreed to stop that annual bit of insanity."

"No, you asked me not to do it and I did what I always do each year, which is not to listen. In any case, pray, may I continue?"

Helston sighed heavily and insisted on taking both

of his infants onto his lap while his duchess ensured that everyone was given portions of the fragrant foods on the table: roast pork surrounded by baked apples, pheasant in gelatin, gingerbread, curried eggs—an assortment of far too much.

"Mr. Ranier, I shall get straight to the point lest I am interrupted yet again," Ata said lifting her napkin to her lap. "My grandson's birthday falls on Childermas and I would like it very much if you would be part of our circle that evening. I should explain that there are three things to entice gentlemen to put in an appearance. Actually, there's really only one thing that has gained a devoted, or rather fanatical follow—"

"Cards. The best game of faro and whist in town," Helston drawled as he kissed with incongruous gentleness one of his progeny. "But then again, Ranier, I don't suppose you play."

Michael kept an iron grip on his countenance. "It can be an amusing pastime."

Grace interrupted. "Luc, please, you're not being fair. I beg you to stop. Truly, Mr. Ranier cannot afford to . . ." She stopped, mortified.

"How deep is the play?" Rainier asked softly.

"Too deep, if you have to ask," Ellesmere murmured, slightly embarrassed.

"Well, I for one am willing—no, by God, I *insist* on staking Mr. Ranier," Mr. Brown said. "I owe you, lad. Owe you for saving Lady Sheffield."

"Then, I shall have to throw support in your grandson's corner, Ata. Dukes must unite against . . . well, dukes must be united," the Duke of Beaufort blustered, narrowing his eyes in Michael and Mr. Brown's direction.

"I suppose it's only fair to remind you, Your Grace," Mr. Brown said with a sour expression, "that Childermas is also Bad Luck Day, and Luc has never been particularly blessed on that one day a—"

Helston interrupted, "Remind me why I invite you to these affairs, Brownie."

The dowager's small mouth *V*'d into a pert smile. "Good. It's settled. Mr. Ranier is to come."

Michael opened his mouth to dodge the invitation, but the dowager refused to notice.

"Come promptly at seven, Mr. Ranier. We start early and play long."

"I shall do my best, ma'am," he said cryptically. "I should tell you it will most likely be the last you will see of me. I return to Brynlow the following day."

He didn't need to turn his head to see Grace's expression, for he sensed her stiffening beside him. If it was the last thing he did, he would find a way to speak to her tonight in private.

Helston's face brightened considerably at the news. In fact, for the first time ever, Michael saw the man smile, one tooth crooked enough to make him appear even more devil-like. How did the lovely duchess tolerate him? At that moment he witnessed a look of tenderness pass from the duchess to the duke, and he idly wondered if it was Helston or Ellesmere who favored billiards tables for seduction. He would bet his last farthing it was the duke.

Michael planned his next move toward Grace as methodically as a pickpocket in the rookeries. While the others sat stuffing themselves like plump chickens, he mulled over the possibilities. Grace refused to meet his eye each time he glanced at her beside him.

At long last, the meal concluded with nary another insult implied or otherwise. The excellent food had lulled even Beaufort into complacency.

Michael grasped Grace's arm as the gentlemen forewent the pleasures of an after-dinner brandy to lead the ladies back to the original salon. "Would you not offer me a tour of the house, Lady Sheffield?" Michael raised his voice loud enough for the dowager to hear. He knew he would find aid in that corner.

"Oh do, Grace. You must show him the gallery. It's much improved with Rosamunde's addition of an imposing lady from her family tree."

Rosamunde laughed. "I vow the Countess Edwina glowers at all who pass except for Luc. For some reason she appears to smile when he walks by."

He sensed Grace's hesitation.

"Please? You would do me a great honor," he whispered in her ear.

Grace looked rather desperately from Ata to Rosamunde to Michael before she relented. "I would be delighted," she lied through her teeth. "But Ata, would you be kind enough to pour my tea? We shall return in but a moment."

"Of course, my dear, of course."

Grace led, or rather dragged him down a long corridor once the others retreated. He stopped short at the first door and peered inside. The library. He allowed her to lead him further down and pulled up at the next door. Some sort of feminine sitting room. He continued along.

"What are you doing?" she asked, eyebrows raised.

"Taking a quick tour. That's what you promised, isn't it?"

She sighed and continued down the gilded corridor, Michael darting glances in each of the rooms as they went along.

He halted again. Ah. It was here after all. He pulled her into the room and closed the door. She whirled around. "What are you doing!"

"This is what I wanted to see. No need to show me the moldy old portraits." He smiled. "All that talk at Brynlow . . . Well, I'd hoped . . ." He backed her against the felt-covered table and with great tenderness looked down at her extraordinary face. "Can you blame me? I was never going to be given a moment alone with you since those lords were watching you like dogs guarding a henhouse."

"And why would you need a moment alone with me? There is nothing that needs to be said without my friends nearby."

"No?" He teased her temple with his lips. "Well, I've never particularly cared for an audience when I wish to be alone with you. Defeats the purpose, don't you think?"

Her eyes darkened with pain and she pushed against him. "Don't. Please, don't make light of everything. I loathe flirtation. And you've done nothing *but*, since you arrived in town."

"That's what happens when you're idle and rub

shoulders with nobs all day long instead of laboring. And here I thought you favored lordly fops."

When she refused to reply, he released her and brutally cut away the façade he'd so carefully cultivated since arriving in London. His voice slowed and became deeper. "I can't continue the farce any longer, Grace. I've decided you would be happier knowing the truth about my past."

Grace took a step away from him. "Look, this isn't necessary. You're leaving in a very few days. You just said you were. And I would like us to part amicably, since you've made it abundantly clear that is what you want and there cannot be, ultimately, anything more. I feel precisely the same way. I really think it best if we refrain from any more of this, this . . ."

"This what?" Michael asked.

"Nonsense," she finished, brokenly.

"Nonsense?" He wanted so badly to have her come to him, but she would not, and he could not blame her. "I think I liked it better when you called it connubial bliss."

"I can't stand this." Her lower lip was caught between her teeth and he longed to soothe it, but instead he forced himself to say what he had come to say.

"Grace, I wanted a moment alone to explain why I cannot offer you marriage."

Hurt eyes darted to his. "It's not necessary."

"It absolutely is necessary. And I beg you to accept my apology for not telling you—for not *trusting* you enough to say all of it before you left Brynlow."

She must have seen something in his expression for all at once, her blue eyes softened. "What is it, Michael?

I know you don't bestow your trust easily, but I owe you my life. And I promise, despite everything, that I won't let you down."

"Grace," he said so quietly she leaned in. "I—I . . . God. You see, the thing of it is, I've committed a terrible crime . . . I'm a fugitive from justice."

Shock registered in her expression but he continued. "A warrant and a huge reward were issued for my apprehension many years ago."

"But what did you do?" she whispered.

He forced the words past his teeth. "I killed someone."

"I don't believe it," she breathed.

He drew back from the evidence of horror in her expression; bitterness invaded his soul. "Well, you should. I'm guilty and on a list for the gallows. It's the reason I left England. I would still be on the other side of the ocean if not for Sam's will."

Her shoulders slumped. "Oh Michael."

He rubbed her arms. "There. Now you know the truth of it. Now you can say good-bye to me and be glad. And you can understand why I must return to my corner of Yorkshire. And why you will continue on here. And I shall promise to never invade your circle of friends again—or see you—much as I would like to do otherwise. It was foolish of me to come. But Grace . . . God, I just couldn't stay away from you. I had to see you to try and take the hurt from your expression. To make you understand that you are cherished—even if it isn't worth much being adored by a bloody murdering blacksmith."

He edged away from her and moved to the edge of

the billiards table, picking up two of the ivory balls and absently sending one of them skidding across the felt surface. "You should return to your friends now. Let us say good-bye, then. I can see my way out. Give my regrets to Ata about that gathering. Your tea is probably cold." He stared at the second ball as he sent it cracking into the other one, which shot into a corner pocket. He came about the end of the table to retrieve it and Grace's slim arms circled him from behind.

"Michael . . . you cannot make me go away that easily."

He went still and dropped his head.

"You don't have to tell me what happened. There's no need. I'm certain you had a very good reason for what you—for what happened. And I'm equally certain you're not to be blamed for it. Any of it. It was surely an act of self-preservation."

He felt an involuntary twitch in his jaw. "Don't fool yourself. I killed someone, plain and simple. And if I'm ever discovered, I'll taint anyone caught in my circle. You hate scandal, Grace. You were running from it when I found you. Believe me, two broken engagements will look like child's play compared to being found cavorting with a murderer. You'd never be able to hold your head up again in any drawing room in town. And even if I was never caught, can you really see yourself buried in the back of beyond with only me for company? Although, if I may say"—he tried valiantly not to show how much the conversation affected him—"the thought does hold some appeal."

"Stop it! Don't make light of this." She hesitated but

a moment. "I'll never believe you black hearted. And, Michael, I understand why you don't place your trust in anyone—you've probably had too many people disappoint you when it came to the point." She quickened her words, "You told me a while ago not to trust people, but you see, I placed my trust in you the day I allowed you to pull me on top of your horse in the middle of a blinding snowstorm. And I cemented it when we were together. And I'm not afraid of the future, because— my God, Michael can't you guess what I feel for you in my heart?"

His mind went blank. And then he moved her soft hands away from him. "Don't become a tragedy, Grace."

"Don't you dare tell me what to do or what to feel. Don't you know how tired I am of everyone trying to protect me? It should be my choice what I'm willing to risk."

He burst out with pent-up emotion, overwhelmed by her courage and her faith in him. "Grace, you've had a mere quarter of an hour to think about something I've lived for a lifetime. Don't be a fool about this."

She ignored his attempt to divert the conversation and searched his face. "We could find a way to sort through all of it. Perhaps if you were willing to confide in Luc or Quinn, they might be able to secretly help you find a solution."

"I rather think they'll secretly arrange to string me up using your pearls. Even you must see they are aching to escort me back to Yorkshire." He whispered it into her ear as he wound his hands into the silvery locks of her soft hair. "Grace, you don't understand I made my choice seventeen years ago. And while there have been times when I wished that I had been of a more mature mind when fate knocked on my door . . . ah, Grace, I regret very few things. I regret having to tell you all of this. But I assure you that if there was the slightest chance of giving you a normal life I would grab it. There is not."

Grace hung her head.

"Darling, don't be sad. I'm happy I've finally told you. Now you will understand why I said the things I did, and why I've acted as I have. And now I want you to do me one last favor."

"But Michael, I'm certain if I—"

He touched his forefinger to her lips to silence her.

"What is it?"

"I want you to promise me you will not speak of this to anyone. And I want you to promise me that we will endeavor to see one another at least one last time before I return to Brynlow, because I'm just that selfish to want one happy memory of you—without any discussion of my past and without any falsehoods. Grace, I want you to remember me with fondness, if that is possible after I've told you about my unsavory past. But I also want you to let the memory fade in the half light of time and go on to a better life, a happier life with someone your equal in every respect."

"You wouldn't say that if you really—"

A tap on the door interrupted her words. And the dark-haired duchess slipped her head around the corner. "I'm so sorry to intrude, but Luc is breathing fire and is threatening—well, I shall try to keep him in check for another few moments."

Michael gripped Grace's wrist and pulled her to the door. "We'll be right behind you, ma'am," he said then leaned against the door when she was gone.

He pulled Grace into his arms and looked down into her wistful eyes. "God, how did I ever find you? How did I ever deserve you—even for just this little while?" He swallowed painfully against the ache in his throat and claimed her lips with his own. He tried desperately to imprint the memory of this moment on his mind. They had so very little time left. He must not waste a minute of it. Must not waste a single fragment of a single second with her.

Chapter 15

Two days later, in the privacy of her beautiful suite adjacent to her bed chamber, Grace dipped the quill into her inkwell and circled a notice in the *Morning Post*. Abstractedly, she feathered the soft end of the quill against her chin as she pondered her predicament.

Michael had asked her to make the most of the handful of days before he left for Brynlow and she would do as he bid, the mystery of what he had revealed to her still swirling in her head.

She had pieced together all the conflicting actions and conversations they had shared in the North, all he had said in their bitter parting, and all his words here in town. And the more she thought about it, the stronger her convictions became, and the more she wanted to be everything he needed her to be. He needed for her to be as strong as he had been for so long.

And she would rise to the occasion. Because she was almost sure she had seen the truth in his eyes . . . that he cared for her, truly cared. And she was even more certain he was as innocent as the day he was born.

She looked down at the advertisement before her. It had taken two days of scouring the morning and afternoon papers before she had found a cottage villa not forty miles from Hyde Park corner. The solicitors in London offered immediate tenancy but required a one-year term. She would let the modest Berkshire dwelling, even though she would not need it nearly so long, all for the chance to be with him in secret while they planned their ultimate departure. It was the only solution given the circumstances.

As she wrote a letter accepting the conditions and noting her early arrival date, she also planned how best to ask her loyal maid, Sally, to deliver it furtively to the solicitors with the requisite number of gold guineas.

She paused for a moment before she signed the letter using her given name coupled with her mother's maiden name, *Roijen*. Grace caught the edge of her lower lip between her teeth. She might very well have to endure a new name if Michael was ever discovered in future. Since he was a commoner and could not escape the charges, they'd have to flee, have to go away for a lifetime. But she could easily afford to buy a new life with him, far away from everything they both knew. It was too dangerous to return to Yorkshire given the unfortunate garrulous new connection with the Duke of Beaufort. Perhaps Mr. Brown would help them find an isolated property in Scotland if it came to the point.

And how could they marry given the danger of the public reading of the banns for many weeks? Grace buried her face in her hands. It appeared so impossible. All of it. She hated deception and that's what all of this was. She finally understood what Michael had been trying to tell her.

And yet . . . it made her want to fight the injustice of it all the more. It would take endless hours to convince Michael to allow her to go away with him. But she would explain how she'd come to a decision today, on Boxing Day, when she'd endured a stream of the same people she had always known parading through Sheffield House while they boasted about their annual offerings. She didn't care about any of these people.

At the sound of a light tap at the door, Grace quickly finished sanding the letter and hid it beneath a book on her escritoire. "Yes? Come."

Rosamunde flew inside her chamber, a smile of mischievous delight on her face. "Well, are you ready? I'm half surprised to find you here. Thought you were trying to play a prank."

Grace grabbed her veiled riding hat and swept the heavy skirt of her habit behind her as she rose. "You should know me a bit better than that. Have I ever played a prank on anyone?"

"No, but there's always a first time."

Grace arched a brow. "How very true. Come to think of it, I might just surprise you after all. And it might be very soon."

As he had done every cold dawn for the last several days, Michael swung his leg over Sioux and carefully wended his way through the half-dark maze of London's streets.

He told himself he did it to find the chimney sweep. To find *James*. But he knew deep in his heart, he did it in fear. He felt far too restless no matter where he was: in the foundling home, in the great houses of Grace's friends, even in the very streets he now tried to lose himself in. He had to go away. He only stayed because of the request he'd made to see her one last time.

He pulled the edges of his long slashed riding coat about himself to ward off the chill. His mare tossed her head at the sight of an expanse of grass in front of them and he let her have her head. Sioux lengthened her neck and her stride and broke into a gallop. Yes, even his horse was trying to tell him they needed to get out of the cramped spaces of London and return to the open moors of Yorkshire, a place that promised relative obscurity.

By the time they reached the other side of the park, his mare had released her energy and relaxed into a fast trot. And the exertion had also released the worst of Michael's own doubts. He could do this. He could stay and attend Helston's small celebration, stay for a last chance to snatch forbidden happiness with Grace, stay until he could say good-bye properly.

So deep was he in his thoughts, he did not hear the approach of a carriage along the street bordering the park. In the instant the driver passed him, their eyes met and Michael recognized him. Gordy Lefroy, grown much older, just as surely as Michael. Without thought, Michael turned his head to look back at the familiar dark blue and gold markings of Manning's Livery, and Gordy's head peered around the edge of the carriage in that same moment.

Fear clawing at his belly, Michael turned Sioux in the opposite direction and urged her away as fast as he dared. His mare sensed his fear and galloped as if all the Indians of the Carolinas were come to steal her from him.

Good God. Would Gordy say something to Manning? He prayed not. Gordy had been one of the best stable hands at Manning's; he'd have known who was in the wrong even if he hadn't witnessed the accident. But Michael knew better than to count on him. The lure of a reward might prove too strong for his former acquaintance.

Within the hour, runners might be sent in search of him. Hardening himself to the bitter possibilities, Michael knew what he had to do, what he would do until he saw her tonight at Helston House, the last place the runners would ever search for him.

He would hide all day today, damn it all. If there was one thing he knew how to do well, it was hide.

Time had run out and there would be no waiting until the first of January. He forced the bile of dread back down his throat.

"Grace, dearest, do come in. Gracious! Where have you been? We were beginning to worry," Ata clucked as Grace entered Helston House's grand entranceway. A bevy of footmen ushered the last of the guests to the supper chamber or card room beyond as Ata gathered all the widows in a corner of the great hall.

"I'm so sorry," Grace replied. "It took longer than I thought to take Lara to the circulating library and then to feed the ducks at the Serpentine."

"Goodness, you've spent a lot of time with that little girl," Ata said with a smile.

"You are to be commended, Grace," Georgiana continued. "Your notice of her no doubt means the world to her."

"No, it's nothing, really. I assure you I receive more pleasure watching her eyes light up with joy than she does," Grace murmured.

"*Brrrr . . .*" Ata interjected. "It's so very cold tonight. I wonder if it will snow. It would play havoc on driving tonight. Remind me to have Phipps lay down straw if it does. Well"—she sighed—"I suppose winter will have its day after all, and of course it would happen on Bad Luck Day, would it not? Now Rosa, come, you promised to be my partner, yes? I'll need you on my side if I hope to finally win a few shillings from the Countess of Home."

"You obviously enjoy a challenge." Rosamunde smiled and smoothed the folds of her deep crimson gown. She was so lovely with her vivid aquamarine eyes and shiny raven hair that Grace could not help but feel like a pale doll in comparison.

"I shall stay in the supper chamber to make sure your guests are in comfort if that is all right with you, Ata." Sarah, dressed in a simple dove-gray gown, looked expectantly toward Georgiana and Ata.

"I know better than to try and cajole you otherwise, Sarah. But where is Eliza? She should be here already." Ata turned toward Grace. "You will want to know that Mr. Ranier arrived two hours ago and disappeared with Luc, Quinn, Mr. Brown, and the Duke of Beaufort. Luc has been breathing fire for two days. If Ranier wins more than Luc at faro, I rather think my grandson will scorch a path all the way to Yorkshire to help him on his way home."

"Oh, I do wish they hadn't dreamed up this nonsense," Grace uttered in vain.

Ata patted her arm. "Come, come . . . boys will be boys."

Rosamunde twisted her lips in mirth. "Well I only think it fair to admit that girls will be girls, too, Ata. Did you not just tell me you were going to fleece the Countess of Home tonight like a sheep in summer?"

"No. I said earlier I wanted *Grace* to fleece that gossiping magpie, the Duchess of Kendale. I simply plan to gull our neighbor until she coughs up some vowels."

Georgiana pursed her lips to keep from laughing. "Ata, your language has certainly taken on bold, new colors."

"And I'd stake my future winnings tonight that we have the Duke of Beaufort to thank for that," Rosamunde murmured with a smile.

"Ata, I already told you I won't play," Grace inserted. "I'll stay with Sarah and Georgiana."

Ata and Rosamunde exchanged knowing looks and then moved in the direction of the card room. Grace sighed heavily and glanced at Georgiana and Sarah. "Well, I know I can depend on you both not to plague me. Now, shall we?"

In deference to the Devil of Helston's birthday, not a trace of holiday greenery dripped from the opulent sconces, chandeliers, or balconies of Number Twelve in Portman Square. Instead the bold black-and-white checkered parquet floor gleamed opposite the glorious yet brutal battle scenes of heaven and hell painted on the ceiling by a master.

Grace, Georgiana, and Sarah linked arms and entered the milling crowd in the wood-paneled dining chamber flanked by enormous yawning fireplaces, which were often likened to the infamous entrances to hell. The door to the card room lay on the opposite side of the room from Grace and she could discern the green baize card tables. A coldness raced in her veins. She wasn't sure she had the nerve to go to him. She just couldn't bear to see him gaming.

She feared he'd be wearing the expression of an inveterate gambler. It was always the same; agitated visages, some absurdly jubilant, others in despair, and all feverish with the addiction to play . . . like her father's face.

She wished Michael hadn't taken the bait to play the game. It irked her that with so little time left in London, he had chosen to spend it in that room, even if it was with the very gentlemen whom Grace had secretly nurtured a hope—it seemed a very long time ago now—he would form lasting friendships. Now it was all such wasted effort.

She stiffened her spine to mingle with the crème de la crème of the beau monde who had been lucky enough to receive the coveted invitations to Helston's Bad Luck Birthday. And as Grace perused the room, she noticed, not for the first time, that many of the bejeweled guests appeared somewhat absurd. Their heads held all in the same condescending manner, their chins high, their shoulders low, and their cheeks sucked in as if tasting lemon ice. And most noticeable, the darted glances and whispers punctuating every banal conversation were all conducted with practiced looks of boredom in their eyes. Truth be told, they mostly appeared like some sort of royal school of lemmings. Why had she ever coveted spending days on end among them?

Grace skirted the edge of the room, conscious of several pairs of eyes watching her progress. Unable to stop herself, Grace tilted her head to try and catch a glimpse of Michael.

Her gaze flickered over a dozen of the new arrivals forming the last few tables before she found Michael, whose hand was working the knot of his cravat as he glanced at the flood of people arriving. "I thought you said this was to be an informal family gathering, Helston," he said loudly enough for her to hear.

"One can always hope," Luc said, annoyed as he counted the meager amount of markers in front of him. "But when you've spent more time around my grandmother you'll learn that she considers any social occasion a rare chance to trot forth the eligible ladies in her Widows Club."

"Actually, I've always called them the Barely Bereaving Beauties," Quinn Fortesque added to Michael beside him.

Grace could see Michael's lips move but could not hear his words.

"Eh, what's that you said, Ranier?" the Duke of Beaufort asked while parceling out a heavy enameled marker on the faro table.

Michael appeared very tense as he repeated, darkly, "I said 'Masquerading Mares at Market' would be better. Is that not how cosseted ladies are presented by their relatives in the Assembly Rooms all over England? Damned primitive ritual if you were to ask me. Yes"—Michael nodded to the banker—"*parlee* my bet."

"That's the running limit, sir," replied the mustached dealer.

Michael nodded absently.

"Really, Ranier?" Luc said, stiffly. "And how do the revolutionaries in the colonies approach foisting ladies into the arms of unsuspecting gentlemen?"

"In a more rational fashion, I assure you. Women are chosen for their ability to maintain a home and raise children in often harsh conditions, and not for their ability to waltz and gossip. But above all else, there must be similar stations in life, mutual respect and, of course, affection."

Quinn coughed and all the gentlemen looked up to find Grace observing them.

Michael raised his large frame partway out of his chair and Grace stepped back from the doorway. He cared for her, didn't he? He had said so, had said he wanted to marry her if not for his wretched circumstances. But perhaps he thought her nothing more than a pampered aristocrat, incapable of being a good wife to a man such as he. She had never felt so unsure in her life.

She looked up from her frozen stance a few steps from the doorway only to find him coming toward her, his shoulders rolling in time to his long, heavy strides that ate up the distance between them. His face was grim, ill ease in every line of his furrowed brow as he came toward her.

The crowd in the dining chamber halted its every movement at the sound of a single sentence.

"Good God above, is that . . . why, it's *Wallace*."

Michael halted and turned to a silver-haired gentleman whom Grace recognized as the very rich Scottish laird of the Palmer clan.

"By God, 'tis you. But, how is it possible? Oh, my dear friend . . ."

"You are mistaken, sir," Michael replied swiftly as he tried to turn away from the elderly Scot. "My name is Ranier."

A woman, probably the gentleman's wife, gasped, and moved forward to clutch Michael's arm, forcing him to stop. "Glory be, it canna be. 'Tis"—her voice lowered to a whisper—"nay, it canna be."

The distinguished laird closed his faded blue eyes for but a moment before they opened again. "I'll eat my sporran if you aren't Wallace's boy. You've got that look about you—the identical physiognomy of your sire."

"And pray, Lord Palmer, what would that be?" Luc asked. He and Quinn and a host of gentlemen from the card room had seeped into the room.

"Why he's got those odd yellow eyes, and that shock of hair, and that mouth with that voice. Why I would bet he can sing like an—"

"Pardon me, Palmer, but I hadn't thought brown eyes, brown hair, and the ability to carry a tune was all that rare a bird." Luc plucked an invisible bit of lint from his sleeve.

Ata tugged on her grandson's arm. "What have I been telling you all along? It *is* him. I knew it the moment I saw him. He is one of us. He's the Earl of Wallace. I recognized him the moment I first saw him." Her eyes were moving in an alarming "play along with me if you treasure your hide" manner.

Lord Palmer continued, "And every man in creation is the size of two lumberjacks and a mountain, Your Grace? But, yes, I know how to prove he's James de Peyster's lad." He turned to address Michael, whose expression was as white as the snow on a lumberjack's mountain. "Your father always said that you both had a pinprick mark on your left ear. Joked that it was made by Satan's pitchfork."

Michael's hand crept up to his ear as Luc blinked.

"Is it true then, son? Were you stolen by the gypsies the night of the fire? Do you know who you are? Do you remember?"

The Scottish lord's wife interrupted, "Give the poor lad a moment to collect himself, Thomas." She turned again to Mr. Ranier, a look of motherly concern overspreading her wrinkled face. "Why, you're the lost heir of the moors, Michael. That is your given name, isn't it? I remember you as a little boy, when we'd come to visit in the summer. You were forever galloping across the green dales of Derbyshire, always—"

"I am not who you say," Michael said flatly. "My name is Ranier, and I'm certain you can tell by my accent that I'm not from Derbyshire. I am a commoner."

"I believe him," Luc said with force, and a seriousness Grace had never seen before. "You are mistaken, Palmer. Forgive me, Lady Palmer."

Ata sputtered in protest, until she dared to glance at her grandson's expression.

Quinn sidled up beside Michael, casually. "I can vouch he speaks the truth too, Palmer."

Lord Palmer shook his head. "Well, I must respectfully disagree with all three of you. You'll never convince me and I plan to look into this further. Good God, this is an occasion for rejoicing. I lift my glass to you, Michael. Everyone, to the Earl of Wallace, may we all warmly welcome him back to the ranks of the upper ten thousand tonight!"

A few glasses rose in the air while whispers dodged about from all corners of the room. Grace moved slowly backward, toward the doors to the main hall, all the while taking care to avoid notice.

How he had lied to her.

He was a living, breathing *earl*.

The Earl of Wallace, for God's sake. She knew it with each ounce of her being. With every quiet word, every expression, every movement, he had given away the fact that he knew it too. And so did Luc and Quinn. The only one who wasn't certain was Ata. Her insistence proved just the opposite.

Grace had to get out of Helston House. She was suffocating. Her feet itched and she wanted to run into the teeth of the icy wind outside. She wanted to be anywhere but here. Anywhere else than under the gaze of his mendacious eyes.

Grace edged beyond the doorway, her heart in her throat and her breathing labored. Only a dozen more steps at most to the main doors. Her wrap forgotten, she numbly took the icy steps to the street slowly, to avoid notice. It had started to snow, and as she wended her way past the drifts of blanketed horses and carriage drivers awaiting their masters' pleasures, Grace's emotions swirled in a fashion as dizzying as the snowflakes spiraling ever downward.

And then she was free of the choked mass of animals and humanity, free of the confining crowd of her past, and she was running toward the locked gate of the garden of Portman Square. She fumbled with the key in her pocket, and then she was inside, the gate clanging shut.

The cold eased her. It instantly cleared her mind and ordered her thoughts as she walked quickly along the path toward the other side of the square, to her beautiful, pampered world in Sheffield House, where she could lock out any and all. She would have given anything at that moment to have been able to block out all memories of that man—Michael Ranier, Michael de Peyster, Michael whoever-he-was.

And then, unbidden, came some hard-to-grasp memory, a few remarks here and there over the years about a lost heir . . . Why, even Mr. Brown had mentioned the wind howling between Derbyshire and Yorkshire was the sound of *the lost boy of the moors*.

Why, oh, why had he hidden something so vitally important from her?

He had said he trusted her, had said he'd told her everything. And yet he hadn't.

God, she didn't know this man at all. He was a wholly nonsensical equation and had proved his duplicitous nature down to the bone. And she had been about to give up her home and all her friends to create a new life for them both far away from here.

Her thin slippers were no match for the wet snow, and were soaked through in moments. She dashed down the path in the black shadows of the trees, whose bare branches reached blindly toward the clouded dark heavens. And a thousand more doubts trickled through her.

Why had he lived in an orphanage? Had gypsies, indeed, taken him? If he had killed someone, why hadn't he used the power and the immunity of his title to protect himself? But then again, perhaps he hadn't killed anyone . . . Oh, perhaps he had lied to her so she would let him go.

A little piece of Grace withered at the wretchedness of the idea. It couldn't be so. None of it made a drop of sense. But no matter how hard she tried to stop the thought, it weaved its way into her conscious like an unwanted vine in a garden.

She heard the distant rattle of gates behind her and she turned to see an enormous figure trying to bend the iron hinge to his will. Grace dodged into the shadows and quickened her pace. She was nearly halfway to the other side.

A thud sounded, and then loud steps closed the space between them. Her heart nearly bursting, she pulled up her skirts to run faster. And yet, she knew she would fail to evade him. Had she not failed at nearly everything she had set out to do? And she was particularly incompetent at running away.

She reached the marble statue in the center of the garden, when his hand caught her waist and pulled her to face him.

Chapter 16

"**D**on't you dare touch me, you—you, *my lord*! This is a private garden."

"Nothing . . . no guard, no key, and no bloody gate will keep me from you, Grace," he said, breathing hard. ". . . not even myself."

The snow was falling on her blonde tresses, leaving her head dark and her face deathly pale.

"You are without morals, your character is as black as . . ." she sputtered to a stop before she whispered, "I never believed it before, but now. Well, I . . . Oh, just let me go."

"No. You already know I don't possess any bloody pride. I don't care if you think me the devil himself, but I will talk to you whether you like it or not. So you choose, sweetheart, will it be here in the freezing open air, or will it be in your warm apartments?"

"Say what you have to say, right here, Mr. Ranier. Oh, pardon me, I mean *Lord Wallace*. As you know, I *love* the cold . . . all that Viking blood, don't you remember? So unlike the lying, conniving, dishonest, black-hearted hot blood of, of . . . a *blacksmith*."

He laughed, the sound awful and hollow to his own

ears. "Aye, you'll need Norse strength to bear this."
And the heart of a saint to believe it.

He stopped and tried to steady his thoughts and his
words as he kept a firm grip on her arms. He had not
a doubt she would run away if he let go. He possessed
not an ounce of gentlemanly behavior at his core and
he would not release her until he had finished.

"Grace . . . I," he hesitated but for a moment, "I'm,
indeed, the Earl of Wallace—Michael de Peyster. My
mother was Lavinia *Ranier* de Peyster." He tried to encounter her expression through the thick flakes floating in the air. Her gaze was trained on the freezing
ground. "She died when I was born and I was raised at
Wallace Abbey until I was seven. But then there was a
great fire, and everything was lost, as I told you."

"Is this when you suggest you killed someone or,
no, I remember, you were spirited away by gypsies?"
she asked, her voice heavily laced with disbelief.

"No," he whispered, his hands loosening without
thought. "I was never taken by gypsies. I went away
voluntarily . . . gratefully."

"And why would you do that, Michael?"

"Because I started the fire," he shouted, his hot,
guilt-laden breath swirled in the freezing air. "I was
spoilt and headstrong and oftentimes slept in the
stable and sometimes forgot to extinguish the lantern.
And everyone at the abbey knew it. My father died in
the inferno. The stable master, Howard Manning, told
me I was to blame." He stopped, the horrible scene—
the sight, smell, shouts engulfed his psyche.

And then he noticed she was tugging at his coat
sleeves. Shaking him, really. So hard he nearly fell

over. The weight of his guilt had robbed him of balance. "What, Grace?"

"Answer me, damn you," she said hoarsely.

Through the heavy snowfall, he finally noticed the trace of tears streaking her cheeks. "What did you say?"

"You know a young child would never be condemned for a calamity of this nature."

His jaw hardened. "Yes. But when you are seven years old and a person of authority says he saw you light a lantern that you remember lighting, and when you awake with blinding smoke filling your lungs, and the screams of horses soon after filling the air, it's not hard to believe you are entirely to blame."

He closed his eyes, his voice fading. "And when that person, the stable master, who had only ever been sensible in the past, offered me a way to escape the persecution he insisted would soon follow, I jumped at the opportunity. Grace . . . you know when you told me you were craven? You know when you suggested that you always run away from everything?" He took a step away from her. "You know nothing of it."

And then he took another step back.

"Don't you dare walk away from me," she said ominously.

"You want me to stay?"

She walked up to him and poked him in the chest. "You do not walk away from me until you answer my questions. Do you understand?"

"Whatever you want, Grace," he said quietly. "I'll do anything you want for the rest of my godforsaken life."

She grabbed his arm with her small fingers in a surprisingly strong grip. "You are coming with me right now. It's obvious there is more to this and I won't rest until I drag every last drop of the truth from you. I will not allow you to make a fool of me thrice over, *my lord*."

Feeling very much the cat being led by the mouse, he allowed her to drag him toward the far gate; candlelight from her opulent townhouse glittered in the widows on the other side.

She marched them both up the limestone stairs, her door swinging open. To his credit, the footman on duty said not a word as she proceeded to walk up the center of the staircase with him, shaking off snowflakes with every step.

He dragged his feet behind hers, wholly reluctant to involve her further in the misery that was his life.

She lowered a brass door lever on a third floor chamber door and entered. The shocked eyes of a maid registered his presence before the frail-looking miss lowered her gaze.

"Sally? Please leave us."

"Yes, my lady." The maid dropped a curtsy and the night rail she was laying out, and then disappeared.

"Grace . . ." he whispered.

"No," she stopped him. She walked to an intricately sculpted pink marble mantel and knelt with the obvious intent of seeing to the fire, which needed building.

"Please, allow me," he said, coming up behind her. He longed to find a shawl to warm her.

"No. I am perfectly fine. And perfectly capable of tending my own fire."

It took her forever and a day to rearrange two logs, but Michael watched her with pride. God, how he loved her. She had no idea how much. Nor would he burden her with it, for he was terrified she would rise to the challenge of loving his wretched and unworthy hide back, and thereby ruining her own life in the process.

She rose and spread her fingers in front of the fire, but refused to look at him. "Now, you will tell me what really happened. And you will tell me why, when you were old enough to realize you would not be blamed for a fire you *might* have *accidentally* set, you did not come forward and claim your rightful place in society. A place, by the way, that would have given us similar stations in life, would it not? Did I not hear you tell Luc that that was required?"

"You have very good hearing."

"Yes. So how long were you going to continue this farce? How long were you going to pretend that you are not part of the barbaric pack of gentlemen who send their *mares to market* or allow themselves to be led about like *prize studs* in exchange for a fortune?"

He felt strangling laughter shudder in his throat. "Uh, I was trying for forever."

"Damn you. Tell me why you are living a falsehood."

"Grace . . . how to begin?"

"I have all the time in the world."

He ran his hands through his hair. "I'll admit there's a part of me that wanted you to remember me as a sod less black than I am. There's another part that has never been able to trust anyone. I think I completely lost that ability soon after the master at the foundling home allowed Rowland Manning to apprentice me when I was eleven. I was to learn a farrier's trade in his livery stable, a struggling, mean enterprise at the time. You see, Rowland was the older brother of Howard Manning, the former master of Wallace Abbey's stables."

"Yes?" She still refused to look at him and he stood a few feet away, ready to leave as soon as she asked.

"Howard went to work for his brother after the fire . . . after he took me to the foundling home, where Rowland knew the master."

"But why would Rowland Manning apprentice you a few years later?"

"Actually, I learned later it was Howard's idea. He probably wanted to keep a closer eye on me." It was so hard to get the words past his lips and his rasping voice probably betrayed his emotion. "At first when I was apprenticed, I had hoped the Mannings would . . ."

"Be kind to you?" she said in a more gentle tone.

"Suffice it to say, they did me a much greater favor instead," he said with no small amount of contempt. "They taught me everything I needed to know about trust and envy and blind familial loyalty and yes, the rest of the ways of the world. Do you require more details?"

"Michael, there are to be no more lies between us." She put more space between them by going to stand behind a pretty chaise longue, but at least she raised her beautiful eyes to meet his. "I'm going to tell you something I did this morning, but only after you tell me truthfully, this time, why you are in hiding. Surely, there is a great misunderstanding."

He stood stock still, his heart pumping furiously in his chest. Good God, what had she done? "There's no misunderstanding, Grace. I told you I've had Bow Street runners looking for me for many years. They have an excellent incentive—five thousand pounds. Make no mistake, Rowland Manning will parade out the older men still in his employ to bear witness that I am guilty."

"But you would have all the privileges of rank to protect you, to help you. This is truly nonsensical, Michael. The House of Lords would never allow one of their own to walk to the gallows for an accident."

He strode over to face her on the other side of the chaise longue, the back of which he gripped in his hands. "Grace, this isn't about my father or the fire."

They stared at each other in silence before Michael clutched his temples to ease the tension. "When I was older, I began to wonder why Howard insisted I go into hiding. I've never been sure, but I think he might have been stealing horses from the estate." He returned his hands to the seat back, forcing himself not to reach for her.

"You see, my father, while ever involved with every part of the estate, might not have noticed if a horse or two went missing. We had a tremendous number. Indeed, Wallace was known for its stock.

"The abbey was everything to my father, who followed generations of great men. Every day, he worked himself to exhaustion, constantly adding, enlarging, bettering every aspect of the estate." He paused before adding quietly, "There was a sadness to my father that I never understood, but it's what drove him."

"Why was he so unhappy?"

"I'm not certain. I was too young to understand most of it. But I remember hearing him cursing sometimes late at night behind the doors of his private chambers. He kept calling for Maura."

"And who was she?"

"I don't know. I told you my mother's name was Lavinia."

"Go on."

"Well, perhaps my father caught Howard Manning in the act. Perhaps it was Howard who set the blaze." Lost in the memory, he paused before continuing. "To be honest, it's more likely I've fabricated the entire scenario in order to avoid blame."

Her expression pained, she whispered, "Do you have any sort of proof?"

"The thing of it is that I remember seeing Howard Manning lead a few of our horses to a dark-haired wiry man as I emerged from the smoke-filled stables. I'd never seen the man before. Howard gave him the horses and then, as the other left, Manning turned and spied me. As dozens of servants emerged from the great house, he rushed me away and effectively convinced me of my guilt. I watched helplessly as the blaze consumed the stable and moved along the shared walls to the abbey." His voice was nearly gone. "I tried desperately to go to my father as someone pulled his lifeless body from the ruins of the stable, but Manning wouldn't let me go—he rushed me away. The image has haunted me every day of my life."

Grace said not a word, but compassion illuminated her face. He hated having to tell her the rest.

"I told you I killed someone and then fled. It was Howard Manning, and I was five and ten years old. I refuse to natter on about it. The fact of the matter is that a man died by my hand, even if it was an accident—something Rowland Manning would refuse to believe and the other apprentices and men he employed would have been too afraid to suggest, lest Rowland cast them out. Howard was his only family and Rowland wouldn't tolerate any truths about his brother." Michael finished softly, "The accident ruined any chance I had of ever living a normal life or of discovering what really happened the night of that fire."

In the growing silence that followed, he watched her eyes soften. "I believe you, Michael."

Her faith in him was staggering. "You shouldn't, darling. I keep trying to warn you off blackguards."

"And I'm beginning to think you know nothing of the matter. Believe me when I tell you I've become quite the authority. You are but a scape-grace, finding trouble and disaster wherever you go. Luc and Quinn are more advanced cases, hardened hellions, if you will. You may only earn that rank if you allow a lady to think you will ultimately lead her to the altar. You never led me to believe that. Just the opposite, actually. You always made it abundantly clear I was not to pin my hopes on you."

His hands were shaking and he gripped them behind himself to hide his nervousness.

"I suppose I should warn you I've decided that since it's obvious I am only capable of surrounding myself with varying forms of less than ideal gentlemen for as long as I live and breathe—with the exception of my dear Lord Sheffield—I might as well stop trying so hard to lead a respectable life."

"Grace, don't even think it, please. Now, I've told you everything—the whole sordid story. Tomorrow, if not sooner, I will have to disappear again. But I'm prepared. I took the precaution earlier this week of securing a large portion of what Sam left to me. I had a notion . . . And no, I won't tell you where I'm going. If I'm very lucky I might even be able to surreptitiously sell Brynlow without revealing my whereabouts."

"Michael?"

"Yes, my love?"

"I've never risked a single ha'penny in my life. You know that, don't you?"

"Yes, but what does that have to do—"

"We are both going to have to risk something—give up something that is integral—if this is to work."

"If you think you could ever offer up something to force Rowland Manning to drop this matter, you know nothing about the nature of the man. I would sooner see you face a pit of vipers than have you come within a thousand feet of the sort of malice Manning is capable of. He is a man bent on revenge. I know this because he's increased the reward for my apprehension over the years." He shook his head. "Grace, you are not going to risk a bloody thing."

"I think it's really you who is afraid to risk something, Michael. But I will make an allowance for that. I would probably feel similarly if every person I'd depended on had led me toward disaster. I've at least had Lord Sheffield, and Ata, and my friends."

Her words were killing him, and he finally understood her disdain for pity. He wanted none of it. He opened his mouth but she stayed him with her hand.

"And, Michael? Don't you dare tell me what I can and cannot do. It's already done. And I don't want to hear a single one of your arguments. You lost that right when you lied to me—all for your noble reasons. There is only one condition I require. If it is met then you owe me the courtesy of following through with my plans."

He knew the whole bloody mess was his fault. "What is the stipulation?"

"Your heart must be fully, irrevocably, and truly engaged. And don't think you can lie to me again. I swear if you do, I shall stand next to Saint Peter at the pearly gates and call the hounds of hell myself if you arrive after me."

The horrible urge to laugh and cry came over him. "Sweetheart . . . this is but another indication that I'm a very bad influence on you. You're losing your trusting nature, and you're also hinting of terrible risk. Are you not the young lady who detests wagering of any sort? Please don't suggest you're contemplating driving toward disaster with me."

"Actually, I'm contemplating *riding* toward disaster, since everyone would recognize my carriage."

"Grace, will you tell me what you did? I would go before the House of Lords or to gaol itself before allowing you to place yourself in harm's way."

"No. It's out of the question for the moment. I had thought we would have to go away—quite possibly for good. I'd thought we might leave everyone we knew behind us if you were ever discovered. Everything, except for my fortune, that is. We might have made a new life for ourselves. I was even thinking about Scotland. Had thought you would be very safe there. But now . . ."

"Yes?"

"Well, I don't think you fully understand the power behind your title if we can manage to have it restored and if we can find evidence against the Mannings."

"Don't you think I've thought about this every bloody day since I was old enough to figure Howard Manning might be at fault? Grace, it's impossible. It would be my word against Rowland Manning's—who, may I remind you again, is one of the most influential men in England. In the end, two facts stand out—any remaining servants from Wallace Abbey would admit that I had been reprimanded for leaving lighted lanterns in the stable, and secondly—Manning hands would say that I killed Howard. More importantly, I do not want to ever publicly admit my true identity."

"But why?"

"If I did, a terrible blot of shame would rest forevermore on the honorable Wallace name. My beloved father would not have wanted me to sully the published family records of generations of indomitable Wallaces with my terrible history. And above all else I won't tarnish your name by association. As it stands, the murder charge was issued using the name Howard and Rowland invented for me when they took me to the foundling home. And Rowland has every reason to keep my true identity a secret. In fact, it's the only thing we agree on."

She stared at him for a long moment and then ignored every last thing he had just said. "We might not have to go away forever. But we need time alone—away from here to consider all of this very carefully."

Michael could stem the desire to reach for her no

longer. "Grace, please darling, no more. I can't argue against you any longer. I'm no good for it. For Christ sakes, at the very least stop using this chaise as a barrier to keep me from you."

"I'm not using it to keep you from me."

"Then what are you using it for?"

"To be able to continue standing."

"Pardon me?"

She reached behind her to retrieve the *Morning Post* and handed it to him. "After I wrote a letter to the solicitors for this cottage villa outside of London to secure it for us, Rosamunde took me to Ranelagh gardens again to go riding since I needed the practice if we're to ride away from here. I hadn't realized how sore my limbs would become. Oh, and I used an alias when I arranged to lease the cottage for a twelve month."

It was as if she were speaking a foreign language. And she was far too calm.

"You know, for a sheltered female who was raised to live with propriety and restraint, you've certainly displayed a masterful hand at deceit and trickery. An alias, sweetheart? Running away with a fugitive to—" he glanced at the folded paper "—Ivy Cottage in Berkshire? What next?"

"I think that will do quite nicely until we decide if we shall fight this or leave permanently."

He would never let her leave her world forever. He wasn't even sure if he could let her leave it temporarily. But he wasn't such a saint that he could leave her here right now.

"Grace . . ."

"Yes?"

He walked around the chaise and finally enfolded her in his arms, whispering into her hair, "Thank you. No one has ever . . ." The words stuck in his throat.

"I guess that means I've earned your admiration. Finally. Well, I was certainly never going to do it in the kitchen."

"Grace, you've never had to try and impress me. I've been in awe since the day you let me sew you up with nary a peep. Well," he smiled against her rose-petal-soft skin, "perhaps there was a wee word of protest. But there was not a single tear."

She turned in his hawkish embrace and raised her arms, barely tall enough to reach around his neck.

"Grace?"

"Mmmm?"

"I would like more than anything to stay here and forget the outside world. But perhaps it would be best if you returned to Helston's party. Perhaps, I should go."

"No." She dragged her soft, soft lips across his.

"And here I was hoping for a biddable partner."

"You have no one to blame but yourself. You've taught me to think like a man." She pulled his head down until his lips were within inches of her own. "Now kiss me."

"If you insist, Lady Sheffield."

"That's *Mrs. Roijen*," she whispered.

He drew back slightly. Her eyelids were heavy with longing, but a smile played about the corners of her lips.

"Mrs. Roijen, eh? Sounds like someone from the frozen north."

As she pulled him back, she whispered, "I know."

Lost in each other, Michael gripped her to him and lifted her as he seated himself in the overly plush chaise longue. He arranged her in his lap, unable to make himself leave her.

In the heat and golden glow of the fire he stroked her cheeks . . . and knew happiness—the joy born of revealing all of one's oldest fears and past to another only to be accepted despite so many sins and flaws.

He felt a tugging sensation and realized her hands were undoing his damp neck cloth. And then her delicate fingers were working his vest and disappearing under the top edges of his shirt.

"Darling," he breathed in the heavenly scent of her hair, "you said your limbs were sore from riding. Here, now," he whispered, lifting her again to rearrange her legs. "Turn away from me. Let me ease your poor muscles. That's it. Lie against me."

Her back to his chest, her knees demurely closed atop his, Grace relaxed as Michael's large hands surrounded the clenched muscles through the layers of fabric and then pressed into the knots. It was heavenly. He nuzzled her neck. "That's right. Relax against me."

"Oh . . ." she sighed. "That feels wonderful."

"Delighted to hear it."

"You're very good at that."

His hands worked their magic. "Well, I've had a good bit of practice."

Her eyes opened wide. "Why am I not surprised?" There was no small amount of annoyance in her voice.

His hands had stopped moving and he pressed a kiss to the side of her head. "I was referring to the horses I was employed to rub down, sweetheart."

Foolish relief filled her. "Of course you were." She knew she should be on her guard. But she was so tired of holding back, so tired of all the complexities they would have to face in the harsh light of the days to come. All she wanted was this one moment to celebrate their future together, in whatever form it would take. He cared for her. She was sure of it. She didn't want to examine any of the tiny cracks of doubts that might surface.

He began to work his hands along the full length of her limbs. "The animals especially like it after a long hard day's work. Does it hurt here too?" His fingers were prodding her bottom hidden under the fine cotton undergarment and silk evening clothes she wore.

She was too shy to respond.

"I hope you don't mind, but," Michael pulled at her gown until it was above her legs, "this way is easier and will feel better."

She could barely breathe.

"You pushed yourself too hard. I can feel it," he whispered as he nuzzled the side of her neck. That essence of him reached her senses and made her dizzy with longing.

He had removed his gloves and she sensed warm, calloused palms through the undergarment. She looked down and saw his strong bronzed arms and hands working her pale thigh above her stocking tied with ribbon.

Oh, the pleasure of the overly tight muscles releasing their stiffness to his skilled hands brought such relaxation. And something she was still too shy to say out loud. For many minutes the only sounds she could hear were the rustle of material and their mutual labored breathing.

He finally leaned forward and whispered, "Would it hurt if I arranged you in this fashion?" He grasped one of her knees and placed it over the padded arm of the chaise longue. Her other limb still lay alongside his own long legs.

She trembled.

"Relax now, and let me take care of you." His hands moved over the pantalets in a slow, workmanlike fashion, easing the taxed muscles on the tender inside of her thigh. But Grace felt horribly exposed.

He moved to the small of her back and massaged her spine through the silk and whalebone until, without a word, she felt him unbutton the gown and ease it from her. He made short work of the corset, muttering something about cursed iron cages of England. And then his fingers returned to the small ache in the arch of her back. "Tell me about riding today."

It was so hard to concentrate when he touched her as he did. Had he any idea what she was feeling? "That is so lovely," she murmured. "I mean, *it* was so lovely. Rosamunde showed me how to use the ribbons, and I trotted for a little after walking a good distance. She didn't have to lead me."

"What horse did you ride?"

"Fairleigh's pony, but . . ."

"Yes?" He untangled her many strands of pearls and

once unclasped, he slid them in a heap in front of her.

"I would have preferred Sioux."

He chuckled and slowly moved her other leg to the opposite arm of the chaise. "Is this all right?" he murmured as he began to kneed the inside of her other sore thigh.

"I'm perfectly fine like that," she said in a hushed, bashful tone.

He groaned and it was such music to her.

After long moments, his fingers lost the edge of labor and turned to long, lush caresses. "Relax with each stroke," he said into her ear. "No, don't move. In fact . . . yes, just like that . . ."

She held her breath.

"So soft," he murmured in her hair. With each supple movement, she wondered if he would dare to reach beyond the slit in her pantalets. And the knowledge that he might was unbearably erotic. The tension made her clench her tender muscles each time he slid an inch closer.

"Relax, darling."

She choked. "I rather think that's impossible."

He kissed the column of her neck. "Perhaps then, you would prefer me to stop?" His hands stilled and she could not stop the moan from escaping from her throat.

"Or . . . perhaps you would prefer a very little more?" At that moment his fingers slid the final inch past the thin fabric to caress the sleek folds at her center. She bit her lip to keep from shouting.

"Christ, you are magnificent," he whispered harshly. She swelled with pride, and he did something wicked with the tips of his fingers. "Sweetheart . . . so soft, so perfect."

She tried to turn toward him and he stopped her. "No, don't move. I've missed you, and after everything I've done—after everything that's happened, Grace, for once, I need to do something right, something for you."

She bowed her head forward.

"Will you allow me, darling?"

Her throat was too constricted to be able to speak. Instead, she nodded and he exhaled roughly, and eased away the last remaining barrier between them, her chemise, and then pulled her back against his chest.

She watched his hands move up the sides of her body and curl protectively around her breasts. Her breathing hitched.

Pleasure-pain rocketed to her womb when he gently pinched the tips.

She felt his fingers trace the edges of the recent scar. "Does this still hurt you?"

"No, not really," she whispered.

"God, you smell so good. Like woman, and fragrant flowers in the spring rain. You know I have a shawl you left behind." Through half-closed eyes, she watched his hands find the mound of pearls in front of her. "I'm afraid I hadn't the heart to return it to you."

He grasped the ends and drew the pebbled strands across her breasts, teasing them. "Do you like that?" His deep voice rumbled from his chest.

How could he talk so rationally when she couldn't form another word to save her life? Her breath came in tatters.

"I thought you would. Perhaps, darling," he murmured, "you'll like this too."

He wound the many strands around his fists and drew them lower, until she nearly choked in embarrassment. She jerked the slotted ends of her soft pantalets closed and Michael chuckled, ignoring her shy protestation. He then dared to do something unspeakably wicked, rocking the pearls against her veiled flesh until she teetered on a pinnacle of pure pleasure. When her breath caught, he stilled and immense waves of pleasure crashed all around her.

When she could think coherently, she asked softly, "Michael?"

"Yes, sweetheart?"

"That was . . . well, unbearably pleasurable."

"Yes, but? I sense a but . . ."

"It's just that I prefer when I can please you, too."

He stilled, and then groaned.

She eased herself from the chaise and turned to nod toward her bedchamber beyond the connecting door. He muffled an exclamation and then lifted her to carry her beyond.

It had always been her favorite room in the townhouse. Pink and white toile covered the walls and the window coverings, while pillows and downy bedcovering lay piled on her bed. It was clearly a lady's domain.

Michael deposited her in the center of the bed and removed the last of his clothing and hers before joining her in the soft jumble. "Mmmm . . . this is just far too tempting," he said with a growl.

She'd never really seen his length so clearly, and it

was a little unnerving. His desire for her was beautiful, yet she was glad she had not seen it so vividly the first time. She might have lost her nerve. "What do you mean?"

"This opulent, soft life of yours. Almost makes me want to be tamed . . . will you insist on a jewel-encrusted collar?"

She threw a pillow at his head and he dodged it before wrestling her back against the bed.

God, what a vision she was . . . her golden hair haloed about her head, mirth dancing in her bonny eyes, a sweet, innocent smile gracing her lips.

He couldn't hold back any longer. It had taken his every last shred of control not to lever her onto his arousal when they had been sitting on that blasted chaise.

He released her arms and she drew her soft hands to his face and then allowed them to fall, ever so slowly down the hills and valleys of his chest and abdomen. Her fingers were so pale and slim against his coarseness. She used both hands to fully encircle him and he started to shake with the effort to bring himself under control.

He uttered a curse and stayed her hands with his own. "No, sweetheart. I'm sorry, but I can't be counted on to go slowly if you do that."

She smiled, her obvious pride and happiness in bloom. "Do most gentlemen talk so much when they are in a lady's bed?"

He rumbled with mirth. "This man does. Is that a problem for you?"

"No," she said in a whisper.

"Lie back," he commanded, and then stared at her with such a pure ache of happiness. "You know, if we are to go away together, I'm thinking it might be a good idea if . . ."

"Yes?"

"Well, all this soft living . . . all this feminine opulence. Perhaps in our new bedchamber we could consider a billiards table to offset some of the frippery." Before she finished laughing, he continued, "But, I suppose we'll just have to make do for now." He looped his arms under her slender limbs and gently eased her open to him. The vision nearly made him explode.

He dragged his length along her slick folds and hesitated but a moment. Pulsing against her, he finally allowed the engorged end of himself to enter her.

Oh God, oh God, oh God. She was so tight, and so hot. He'd forgotten. He heard her deep sigh of passion and it urged him to test her. With care he eased farther inside of her. His taut shoulders ached with tension, his muscles completely fatigued.

He pulled back to see her face, flushed with desire, and then felt her hands move to clutch him closer. "Yes, my darling," he murmured, and then edged in and out of her just the slightest bit.

And then she said something that nearly made him lose all control.

"I want to be on top."

"What did you just say?"

"I want to be on top. It's only fair. You said this was all for me, didn't you?"

His arms shook from the tension of desire and his

pent-up laughter came in short gusts. "That was before. And you were supposed to be so lost to pleasure now that you wouldn't question what I did to you."

"Yes, well . . . I'm almost lost, but not far enough along to not know what I want."

He exhaled, his voice nearly gone. "I suppose I should have known what life would be like with a wench from the frozen regions." With wrenching effort he disengaged himself and rolled to his side before pulling her on top of him. His beautiful miracle now sat astride his thighs with a comical, uncertain expression on her face.

"I suppose you need a bit of help? Guidance?"

"No, I'm perfectly fine."

He chuckled. "You know every time you say that, I know you are perfectly not. Darling, let me show you." He encircled her tiny waist with his hands. "Now, try to control this. Be careful. I won't let you hurt yourself," he insisted.

Her eyes wide, she slid down slowly to take half of him before she stiffened.

"That's it. Now ease up."

She set a tempo, and he kept his hands on her waist to not let her eagerness get her in trouble. But then she grasped his hands and placed them over his head; a siren intent on having her way, and God help him, but he let her.

Looking at the incandescent wonder of the woman he wanted to give the world to, his arousal abruptly thickened, his release poised in the heavy shaft. "Grace . . . wait. No—"

She bent forward and kissed him, his words lost in

a vortex of potent desire and longing. And suddenly she slid down in an inexorable long motion and he felt her fully seated. She had dared to take all of him inside of her and her face radiated ecstasy as she cried out with pleasure. The excruciating sensation broke his every last restraint, and he couldn't stop the great pulsing waves from breaking inside of her. And he didn't want to.

For he had found safe haven at last. Once and forever.

It had taken a strength of will that he hadn't known he possessed to tear himself from her arms after she fell fast asleep. He scratched out a few words to her—words telling her to rest and a promise to send word to her at first light on how they were to proceed. And he had signed it . . . *Mr. Roijen.*

His heart lighter than it had been for years, he carefully peered from the upper-story windows to look for signs of potential trouble. He had calculated that it could be as soon as an hour before Manning might hear of his reappearance. Why, two or three of the carriages waiting in the huddle outside of Helston House had borne the Manning colors.

Michael slipped out of one of the ground-floor side windows, dropping the last few feet into a crouch.

He regained his footing, but the crunch of many footsteps on pea gravel surrounded him and he knew with sickening finality that his meager reserves of luck had finally run out.

Chapter 17

*G**race was so happy riding Sioux over the cobblestones of the small village toward Ivy cottage. Her heart swelled when she looked down to find Lara Peabody, from the foundling home, riding a pony beside her and wearing Grace's pink gloves, which were too large for her small fingers.*

The sound of the two animals' hooves echoed sharply until Grace finally woke from the surreal dream to find that the sound was instead someone insistently rapping on her bedchamber door.

She sat up and turned sharply to find herself alone in the vast bed.

He was gone . . .

But a note on her table next to the bed caught her eye. Grace clutched the bed coverings closer and cleared her throat. "Come . . . Come in." She hid the note in her hand.

Sally entered, red-faced, and bobbed a curtsy. "Pardon me, Lady Sheffield, but I can't put them off any longer. The dowager duchess and her friends are belowstairs and threatening to, uh, *disturb* you."

"Help me then, please, Sally?"

The little maid rushed forward with two morning gowns.

"Yes, the dotted silk . . ." As Sally set aside the other gown, Grace hurriedly read the note he had left for her, and she allowed a smile to blossom on her face.

"Where are your pearls, Lady Sheffield?"

Grace could feel a mottled flush rise from her neck as she hastened to retrieve them. "I have them." Fastening them behind her neck, Grace stepped behind a screen and onto thick toweling to splash soap and water over as much of her person as possible, while Sally set out her articles of dress.

The maid murmured, "I shall see to your tea as soon as I take my leave, my lady."

But before Sally could do up the last of the gown's buttons Ata's tiny wizened face peered around her door.

"Ah, you *are* here. Thank heaven."

Rosamunde rushed past Ata along with Georgiana, Sarah, and Elizabeth.

"And why wouldn't I be here?" Grace said, trying to push her usual mantle of complacency into place. "Thank you, Sally." Her sweet maid disappeared.

Rosamunde's face was ashen as she placed the *Morning Post* into Grace's hands. She glanced at the folded section, the familiar swagged "Fashionable World" column exposed. The first words jumped out at her . . .

Their Royal Highnesses the Duke and Duchess of Helston entertained a party of fashionables last eve, for the annual celebration of the Devilish Duke's Bad

Luck Birthday. In keeping with the theme, an earl long lost was found only to be lost yet again! Ah, but the mysterious Lord W's gigantesque figure should not be hard to find for the Countess of H insists she spied him entering a townhouse with Lady S, she of the recent spate of ruptured matrimonial engagements. La! What a to-do in Portman Square . . .

Grace lowered herself onto a chair Elizabeth had hastily brought behind her. With no emotion, she stared sightlessly out the window to see a pattern Jack Frost had etched on the panes.

"Is he here?" Rosamunde asked cautiously.

"Of course not," Grace replied.

In the silence, Sally hurried in bearing a tea tray with an array of biscuits, buttered toast, and apricot preserves.

"Thank you, Sally."

The maid began hesitantly, "My lady, will you be receiving today, as usual? It's Thursday."

Ata inserted herself, "Absolutely not."

"No, Ata," Grace contradicted, cool reason now restored. "Of course I will be receiving at the usual hour, Sally."

The maid nodded and retreated from the room.

"Are you out of your mind, Grace?" Rosamunde asked. "I should warn you that Luc and Quinn are riding hell for leather to the foundling home this very moment. Mr. Brown at least saw fit to wake me before he went after them himself."

"We must pray that Quinn will restrain my grandson," Ata said.

Georgiana was pacing, her limp obvious. "While I would like to spare you this, I do believe it will be Quinn who will need to be brought to heel. I've never seen him in such a state. He left without a word, ignored my every protest to wait for me. I . . . I . . ." She covered her face and burst into tears. "I think he's going to challenge him to a duel."

Grace, with great tranquility, attended to the tea tray, pouring, straining, and preparing each of the cups precisely as her friends liked their tea. She then poured her own and took a small, delicate plate. Placing three pieces of toast on it, she carefully slathered jam on each one before taking a large bite of the first. Grace looked up from her task to see all of her friends staring at her. "What?"

Elizabeth giggled. "Well, I rather think we all expected that at the very least, your appetite would be off."

"She's in shock, I tell you." Ata harrumphed.

"No, I'm not. I'm not worried about Luc or Quinn finding Michael for I'm certain he's long gone." She took another leisurely bite and a sip of tea. "And I'm going away to join him, so none of this matters. I wasn't going to tell you before I left, but I don't want any of you to worry."

"Oh God, she's running away again," Ata moaned.

"I'm not. I'm *going* away. There's a difference."

"Yes, rather like the difference between ham and bacon, don't you think?" Rosamunde followed with a moan very much like Ata's. "Oh, Grace, you can't go away. Please. If only for all of us. We can withstand this again if we face them together—but we have to do it straight from the start. You can't leave again."

"Rosamunde, my dearest friend, I hadn't thought I'd quite used up all of my pity chits yet."

"But this is such nonsense," Georgiana continued. "If your Mr. Ranier really and truly is the lost Earl of Wallace, you can be married and within the week everything will be forgotten."

"It's true, Grace," Sarah said, coming forward. "And we will put it about how romantic your courtship was."

Grace looked at her friend with doubt. "Look, it's far too complicated to explain it all right now, but suffice it to say that we need a bit of time and privacy to sort out a few, um, problems of a delicate nature."

"Time and privacy?" Ata huffed. "I rather think you've had a bit too much of both with that man, and I don't care what modern thoughts have gotten into your head, missy. You cannot continue down this wicked path, no matter how tall he is or how seductive his eyes are."

Rosamunde bit her lower lip to keep from laughing. "She's right, Grace. None of us recognizes you any more. Not that I don't like this new version of you quite a bit."

Ata rolled her eyes. "Do not think you can just go away again without telling us precisely what level of madness you are considering, Grace."

She glanced at the concerned expressions from her dearest friends in the world and finally consented, pouring out a small portion of Michael's past, and her future. She had promised not to reveal the name of the influential man who had leveled the murder charges and she did not mention the name given to Michael at the foundling home.

"But surely there is some sort of terrible mistake," Rosamunde said, crumpling in a heap at Grace's feet. "Surely Luc and Quinn, and also Lord Palmer will band together. Under their combined influence, and others, Lord Wallace will be fully restored with time, and then this man's accusations will be discredited and dismissed."

"I don't know, Rosamunde. That is what should happen, but would you want to expose the man you cherish"—she choked a bit on the word and Sarah and Elizabeth rushed toward her—"no, wait, I'm perfectly fine. He and I both agree that we must disappear for a short while, so we can consider the best course of action. And no, I won't say where we are going, but I will write to you."

"But Quinn may be able to—" Georgiana was interrupted by the sound of footsteps in the hallway.

A quick rap and Sally entered and bobbed a curtsy. "I'm sorry, ma'am, but a Miss Givan is most insistent and—"

"Please show her in." Grace crossed the room to greet the exuberant beauty. Her hair and gown in disarray, Victoria Givan rushed forward.

"Oh, Lady Sheffield, I'm sorry to intrude, I'm sorry to—"

"What is it, Victoria?"

She finally took notice of the other ladies in the chamber and stood silently clutching her hands. Grace led her to a settee and they both sat.

"It's Michael," she whispered. "He's . . . oh, he's been taken to Newgate." The woman burst into tears. "Gordon Lefroy, a former foundling who is still employed by Mr. Manning, came to warn us this morning."

Grace felt the room spin on its axis until the gnarled hand of Ata grounded her. "Good God, this involves Rowland Manning? He's so terribly powerful. Shall I fetch salts?"

"No, no," Grace whispered brokenly.

Rosamunde and Georgiana were conferring, but Grace could make little sense of their hurried words. God, she had to go to him. Straightaway.

"Grace?" Rosamunde broke through her tangled skein of thoughts. "Georgiana and I will find Luc and Quinn. They will sort through this, I promise you."

A course of action now forming in her mind, Grace moved methodically to the door. "I know. Victoria, thank you for coming to me. I fear I must look like a wretch. May I beg you to excuse me while I finish my toilette?"

Ata nodded. "Very good idea, my dear. So rational you are. We should all take a lesson from you."

The ladies rose en masse and thinned into a two-by-two queue out her door, Sally leading the chattering group toward the salon below.

Grace gathered her reticule, her cloak, and gloves as she counted to twenty. And then with spurious vigor born of ungodly fear, she rushed from the room, down the spiral servants' stair, and into the teeth of the winter morning. She dashed inelegantly from Portman Square and hailed a hack for the first time in her life. Scuttling inside, she directed the hansom cab to the infamous prison.

She could barely breathe as horrid visions tumbled in her mind—of Michael straining against heavy manacles, being dragged in chains to the deepest dungeons of hell right in the heart of London. She gulped and dragged air into her tight lungs, fighting back the paralyzing effect of powerlessness.

Nearly flinging the fare at the stunned driver, Grace flew from the confines of the hackney and stumbled in her haste to reach the grim and imposing stone entrance to Newgate.

The terrible stench of unwashed and untended humanity assaulted her senses once inside. Gaol keepers, turnkeys, and men who brought others to justice milled in a confusing mass. An elderly woman carrying a child pleaded with a jailer to see her son, while a manacled criminal attempted to pick another's pocket. At long last, Grace worked her way past a group of leering and overly bold characters to face a man with a dirty wig seated at a long, rough-hewn desk with many ledgers.

"Aye?" the man said without glancing at her.

"I understand a gentleman was brought here today, and I wish to see him."

At her cultured voice, the man looked up, his eyes nearly black but displaying a sign of intelligence. "Yer ladyship?"

"I demand to see a gentleman who was brought here this morning," she repeated more forcefully.

Perplexed lines appeared on his forehead. "Gen'l'men are not brought 'ere, yer ladyship."

"I realize that, but he is being wrongly held. He is, indeed, a gentleman."

A few cackles of laughter floated in the air and the man before her scratched his head, leaving his wig slightly askew.

"And ye be?"

"The Countess of Sheffield," she said with no small amount of irritation.

He skimmed the page in front of him. "Yer ladyship, only one man was taken within this morning. A large bloke. Saw 'im meself, I did. Now what would a charming lady such as yerself want to be doing with the loikes of that murdering smithy?" The man's jowls trembled as his cockney accent threatened to overtake his words. " 'e's too dangerous by half, that one. Took down four men within these walls, 'e did. I'm under strict orders from the magistrate not to allow anyone closer 'an fifty feet from 'is cell."

"Then I want to see him fifty feet from his cell," she said, the tension crumbling her fortitude more than a little. "Oh please, sir, tell me how he fares. Tell me what I must do to see him. Is it money you want?" She thrust out her reticule and the man began to mop his florid face.

"Well, fer the moment, 'e be in the hold, as we're a bit overcocked. The next session at Old Bailey starts a fortnight after the New Year, yer ladyship. If you'll pardon me for sayin', ma'am, you're far too foine a lady to be crawling about 'ere, but I'll tell ye something." He motioned her closer with his fat fingers.

She leaned in despite his fetid breath. "Yes?"

"If you're determined, you'd be better served going

to the man who paid the runners to find 'im. Rowland Manning be 'is name—of Manning's Livery—yer ladyship. Oh, and ma'am?" His voice was barely audible.

"Yes?"

"You'd best be advised to bring that with you." He pushed away her reticule and winked. "Sometimes blokes who bring charges can be persuaded to see reason—although Mr. Manning promises to be a tough 'un."

Grace nodded once. "Sir, I thank you. And I shall mention to the magistrate how very kind and organized you are here, Mr. . . . ?"

"Fawkes," the man said with a rickety picket-fence smile.

"Mr. Fawkes. But I should also warn you that if my acquaintance is harmed in any way during his stay here, I will personally come to condemn you and anyone else who has a hand in it." She drew herself up as tall as she could. "Do I make myself perfectly clear, Mr. Fawkes?"

"*Perfectlee*, ma'am." The man's smile grew as Grace expertly transferred a hidden sum to his hand.

Lord, she was taking to the life of bribery with sinful ease. Would wagering and thievery be far behind? She prayed to God she would have the nerve to see this through.

Not two hundred yards beyond several reinforced locked doors and fifty feet below street level, Michael prayed to God just the opposite.

Chapter 18

The sound of water dripping on stone just inches from where Michael's head lay was driving him mad, but not nearly as mad as his worry for Grace.

God, she was too innocent of the ways of man. He greatly feared she would go to Rowland. His hands half clenched at the thought. But there was no fight left in him. A gang of gaol keepers had seen to that with extraordinarily effective methods. Experimentally, Michael tried to ease open his mouth and pain ricocheted in his head. At least his jaw still worked and he could see. But then again the jailers had probably left him his sight so he could see the dank reality of the here and now. That, or he was too bloody tall for them to reach his eyes. His knees and torso were another matter altogether.

All around, the sounds and stench of imprisonment radiated. He guessed more than fifty men were squashed into the holding cell.

All at once, a small face hovered above his.

"Don't bother. They took it all," Michael growled through clenched teeth.

"You're him—the nob," a boy's voice said, with obvious anger.

"You can see well enough to know I'm no bloody nob."

"Nay. You be the nob what had the runners waiting for me at the foundling 'ome."

Michael closed his eyes against the pain in his skull. "James?" he whispered.

"I should kick you."

"Go right ahead, lad. Just do it on the top of my head will you?"

"You're bloomin' daft, sir."

"Know it," he returned, conserving his words. "James?"

"Yes?"

Michael noticed the boy sounded exhausted. "I'm sorry I asked you to risk meeting me. You'd probably be far away from here if you'd not listened to me."

Silence reigned for a while before James replied sagely, "It was only a matter of time 'afore they'd 'a got me. At least you're here now an' maybe we can trade turns at watchin' an' sleepin'."

Michael forced himself into a seated position, ignoring the never-ending points of blinding pain that radiated from his frame. "Lay your head here, James. I swear I won't let you down this time."

The second hackney cab was far harder for Grace to find. She walked six blocks from Newgate in the miserable sleet, her cloak and gloves barely able to keep out the wet cold. She arrived in front of the offices of the venerable solicitors who had guarded, tended, and grown the vast Sheffield fortune for generations.

"Mr. Williamson." Grace nodded as she was ushered before a tall, thin gentleman of nearly white hair, who bowed deeply.

"What a lovely surprise, Lady Sheffield. I am honored you thought to condescend to visit our offices, but you know I am always available to come to you, madam."

"Thank you, sir. But, this is a matter of grave urgency and I was hoping, well . . ." It all sounded so awful, so lurid, she couldn't force it past her lips.

Robert Williamson cleared his throat and indicated a chair across from his massive desk. "Lady Sheffield? Please permit me to offer whatever sort of confidence you might desire, ma'am, such as I did with Lord Sheffield. What is it? Perhaps a gaming debt or an unpleasant business transaction of some sort? I am at your disposal . . . with discretion." The concern reflected in the gentleman's gray eyes nearly cracked Grace's tightly held emotions.

"I would ask you to come with me straightaway. I have business which cannot be delayed. I will need to have a contract drawn up if all goes well. And yes," she said, training her gaze on a point beyond his thin shoulders, "I will need it done with the utmost discretion."

Mr. Williamson nodded, and when learning she had not brought her carriage or her maid, sent her a brooding look but, gratefully, said not a word. The elderly man, whom Grace received for quarterly meetings at Sheffield House, arranged for his carriage, gathered his affairs and accompanied her to the Warwick Lane entrance.

Grace leaned back against the plain but gleaming black squabs of the solicitor's carriage after murmuring their direction. She silently wondered how she would convince Mr. Manning to release Michael.

"Mr. Williamson?"

He immediately leaned forward. "Yes, Lady Sheffield?"

She licked her lips. "May we review my fortune at present?"

"Your annual interest or your entire fortune? Including an estimate of the unentailed Sheffield House?"

"Yes. I mean absolutely everything. Has there been any significant change since last we met, sir?"

He blanched and then chose his words with care. "No, madam. We applaud your conservative nature, and that of the late Lord Sheffield, and well, there is relatively little change. Your fortune, together with Sheffield House, which might be valued roughly at twenty thousand, unless you consider the paintings, the furnishings—" He stopped. "Pardon me, Lady Sheffield, but may I offer my—"

"No," she said politely, "thank you, sir." She said not another word as they turned a corner to drive the last few blocks toward Manning's Livery. Mr. Robert Williamson was about to be rudely awakened by her new incautious ways. The solicitor's team slowed to a walk.

Grace's heart plummeted as she studied the vast, sprawling enterprise, far grander than she had envisioned. Three immense stone structures of elegant, classical lines fronted a series of other buildings—stables and enclosures—teeming with horses. Why, this was many times the size of the famed Tattersall's at Hyde Park Corner, although this address was not nearly so fine.

"Oh, I had no idea," she murmured to herself.

"Magnificent, isn't it? Manning hired John Nash, himself, to design it. Of course, it's not quite finished yet, but when it's complete it will rival the grandest liveries and riding schools in all the world," Mr. Williamson informed. "May I ask if madam is considering purchasing a new team? May I offer to negotiate for you, since, as you must be aware, ladies are not generally admitted to, uh, places such as—"

"Mr. Williamson, thank you, but I would ask you to request a private audience for me with Mr. Manning. You may tell him it is extremely urgent and it concerns Mr. Michael Ranier. I shall wait inside your carriage, sir."

He looked at her steadily before tipping his hat, and making his way toward the open enclosure with many columns along the three sides. A marble fountain in the center stood empty and silent in the cold winter afternoon, long shadows dragging on the corners of the imposing structures before her. Grace felt faint and she realized that amid the turmoil of the day, she had had naught but two bites of toast that morning.

Oh God, this place was not at all what she had expected. She had thought Manning's Livery would be sprawling, yes, but rickety and unkempt. Slovenly, even. This boded far, far worse.

Mr. Williamson braved the gusting cold walk back to the carriage. "Take my arm, Lady Sheffield. Mr. Manning said he would be honored to see you.

Today's auction and primary business of the day has concluded, ma'am. " Grace nodded and accepted Mr. Williamson's support.

Two men dressed in dark blue and gold livery flanked the inside entrance as a third walked forward and indicated that Mr. Manning awaited her in the next chamber. When Mr. Williamson would enter with her, Grace halted.

"Sir, I would ask you to wait for me here."

His faded eyes sharpened. "But Lady Sh—"

"I'm sorry. I insist. But I shall require your aid shortly."

Before he could say another word, Grace strode forward, past the paneled doors, into a majestic chamber. The ornate door closed out the rest of the world with solid finality.

Beyond the bronze figurines of horses, and an endless stream of past and present champions captured within the gilt frames of masters, a solitary man sat at an orderly, large wooden desk without ornamentation. As Grace approached, he raised his head, and she nearly stopped in surprise.

The man was charismatic in a brutal fashion. He could not be much older than forty, yet his thick raven hair was shot through with startling silver streaks. That barely tamed hair, his bronzed skin, and pale green eyes combined to radiate ruthless power and keen intelligence. He slowly stood, and Grace was nearly overwhelmed by his presence.

Oh God.

"Lady Sheffield?"

She nodded and offered her hand. He brought it to

his lips and kissed the back of her hand. "A pleasure, Countess."

She had meant to provoke him, humiliate him, and, if necessary, beg him to release Michael. What she had not planned to do was be overawed by a man who had done everything in his power to destroy the one man who meant everything to her. "Actually, this will most likely not be a pleasure, sir, for either one of us."

He chuckled. "Oh, but you are mistaken. It is not often a beautiful lady such as you condescends to visit a mucked-out male bastion. Shall we?" He indicated a bow window facing the neatly manicured rear grounds.

Two new leather armchairs faced each other on either side of a low table and Grace seated herself in one, feeling immediately dwarfed by the overtly masculine furniture. Casually, Mr. Manning pinched together two crystal glasses on a side board and brought forward a bottle of brandy as well. He raised his brows. "So sorry I cannot offer you tea, Lady Sheffield, but I do believe this might be more in keeping with the tenor of our meeting, don't you agree?" His tone and smile brimmed with intimacy. "May I?"

"Thank you, but, no. I've come to discuss—"

"Oh, but Lady Sheffield, I insist." He poured great dollops of amber spirits into the two glasses and raised his own to make a toast. She reluctantly followed suit.

He grinned, one side of his smile rising a bit higher than the other. "What say you? Shall we toast Michael, possessor of far too many aliases? Dare I hope that he is finally to bring me good fortune instead of bad?" The man had the utter audacity to wink.

Grace suppressed the urge to toss the drink in his face and instead swallowed the contents. To her credit, she did not reveal the fact that a flood of fire had just entered her throat.

"Oh, *very* good, Lady Sheffield. You are a revelation, Countess." He reached for one of the many newspapers on the low table. "And here I was expecting a wilting, tearful dab of a miss . . . *'Lady S, she of the recent spate of ruptured matrimonial engagements.'*"

So much for polite small talk. "Mr. Manning, precisely how much money will it require for you to withdraw your complaints?"

"My dear Lady Sheffield, how very vulgar. And you a proper member of the ton and all. Are you attempting to buy my integrity? A man's word is everything, is it not?"

With a start, Grace remembered Michael saying the Mannings had taught him everything about dishonesty, cruelty, envy, and something else, which eluded her. She pondered her answer as she rearranged her gown's skirting. She was no good at wit and innuendo. She was no good at negotiation or compromise. He would either take her money and release Michael or not.

Grace cleared her throat again. "Mr. Manning, you and I both know Michael Ranier is the Earl of Wallace. As soon as this is brought to the attention of the House of Lords—indeed, the Prince Regent himself—he will be released."

"I would not wager on it." He scratched his jaw. "I daresay the criminally minded Mr. Ranier has little if any proof of his identity now, does he? Other than his apparent uncanny resemblance to the former earl. And, my dear Lady Sheffield, I suppose it only fair to tell you that half the lords in Parliament owe me favors and the other half owe me substantial blunt. I did say a man's word is everything, did I not? And the Prince Regent? Well, suffice it to say that I supply him with some of his more *interesting* amusements. Shall I tell you about them?"

Her imagination brimming with horrid ideas, Grace did not dare to ask for clarification. Instead, she used her last bargaining chip. "I am prepared to offer you twenty-five thousand pounds in exchange for your signature on a document clearing Michael Ranier of any and all murder charges."

"Hmmm. He's worth only twenty-five, is he? That's vaguely insulting, don't you think? Then again that lovely auburn-haired vixen, Miss Givan, offered but a pittance in comparison. Perhaps if I wait a bit more other women will appear with even higher bribes in the offing."

Grace thought that if she held a dagger, she might indeed be provoked enough to plunge it in his heart. She lifted her chin. "I am prepared to offer you fifty thousand pounds, *sir*." She would have given an extra thousand all for the chance to call him what she really thought of him.

Mr. Manning raised one of his sweeping black brows and then leaned forward. Refusing to move away from him, Grace sat, her back arched, on the edge of the massive seat. Mr. Manning's fingers caught the long strands of pink and white pearls at her neck, and he twisted them, almost forcing her to leave her seat. "Fifty thousand, eh? But that's not such a hardship now, is it my dear? *Seventy-five* thousand is a much more interesting number, don't you think?" He released the necklaces and sprawled his large frame inelegantly against the padded leather. "You are fortunate that I find myself tempted, as you've come at a convenient time. I'm swimming in debt from these new buildings and that sum will come in quite handy. Yes, I think even Howard would agree his murder adequately avenged for that tidy sum."

Rowland Manning uncrossed his legs and recrossed them in the other direction. "I'm actually a very generous man, Countess. You might live comfortably on your reduced yearly income as long as you release your servants, forego new frocks, and economize most ardently. Ah, but that is not my affair, now is it?"

She really couldn't breathe. She might very well deflate if she opened her mouth to say a single word.

"Oh, and I think I would fancy those pearls, too, madam. They'll be such a lovely reminder of our impromptu afternoon interlude."

"You are as vile as I've been told." Grace's hands were trembling as she unhooked the heavy pearls and allowed them to drop into his outstretched hands. This was proof positive a man could not be judged by his physiognomy. Rowland Manning was as terrifyingly beautiful as his soul was ugly.

"My dear, you are entirely correct. I assume Mr. Williamson accompanied you to prepare the necessary documents? I am sure you will understand if I ask you to wait with your solicitor as he draws up everything in the private outer chamber? Can't abide solicitors or their endless rationales. But I shall await *your* return with great anticipation, Lady Sheffield." His smile was as frosty and benevolently charming as a newly minted aristocrat with charity on his mind but not in his heart.

Grace decamped, furious at being dismissed in such a cavalier fashion, and furious at herself. But that was nothing compared to the abject feeling of despair she endured as she explained to Mr. Williamson what he must do. There were far too many protestations, and far too many mentions of Grace's dear husband and how Lord Sheffield would disapprove.

"Mr. Williamson, I'm ordering you to do as I ask. I appreciate all your fine advice, but I shall never waiver and Lord Sheffield left me this fortune to do with as I see fit."

He looked at her with such pity, and yet for the first time, Grace didn't care what he or anyone else thought of her rash actions. She kept picturing Michael in misery, straining against chains, hungry and freezing, cut and bleeding. Each time, she would urge the solicitor to write faster.

After an eternity, documents in hand, Grace rapped loudly on Mr. Manning's door.

"Come."

The footmen closed the heavy door behind her and she approached his desk where he was once again ensconced. With nary a look at her, he accepted the documents, motioned blindly toward a chair across from him and became engrossed in the sheaf of papers for the next quarter hour.

"Could we get on with it, Mr. Manning?"

"Impatient, aren't we?"

"Will you ever stop asking redundant questions?"

He laughed and the sound was different from the cynicism she had heard before. It was richer and deeper, and she hated it because she was determined to hate everything about this man who had hunted Michael unjustly for so many years.

And then, after a final perusal of the documents, he signed the letter to the magistrate clearing Michael of the murder charges for Howard Manning. He tossed the document back to her and retained the extraordinary promissory note.

"Thank you, my dear. It has been a pleasure to do business with you. Please feel free to bring your cattle here for auction. I can guarantee an excellent price, especially since it's you, Countess." He came around the desk and stood before her.

"I'll use Tattersall's, you black-hearted monster."

He smiled. "You know, Lady Sheffield, even though you will not believe me—and I daresay you shouldn't—I feel it my duty to warn you to take better care the next time you choose a lover."

Her gloved hand cracked against his massive jaw before she could think. She'd never struck a living thing in her life, and here she'd slapped two men in less than two months. She was utterly justified, but still . . . Her hand throbbed with pain.

He chuckled and wiped a tiny speckle of blood from the corner of his mouth. "Michael is a lucky sod. Such fire under such elegance. It's too bad I did not find you first. Are you sure I can't tempt you to favor a different suit—with the additional lure of my new fortune?"

She ignored his audacious words. "Why? Why do you hate him so much? He didn't murder your brother and you know it."

"Take heart, you're not the first to be taken in nor likely the last. He always had such an honest air about him. But don't fool yourself, my dear. Your devoted Saint Michael is a gambling, unprincipled sod in disguise. And may God preserve those who best him in a wager."

Grace's words of denial stuck in her throat and Mr. Manning continued. "He killed my brother. Lost two quarters' worth of wages to Howard at dice and then plotted to murder him. And he carried out the plan right under my nose, in a boxed stall not fifty feet from my office. I blame myself. I should have known that boy would be nothing more than a replica of his nob of a father, the greatest debauching, depraved aristocrat I've ever known. His offspring did not fall far from the tree."

"And how would you know anything about the former earl?" she asked stiffly.

"Why, my dear." He smiled grimly. "I know more about the elder Lord Wallace, may Satan eternally torture his soul, than your dear Michael does."

"How could that be?" His calm, certain, cold expression infuriated her.

His laughter held not an inch of humor. "Haven't you guessed, sweetheart?" he asked dryly. "The former Lord Wallace was my sire too, sad as I am to admit it."

A few pieces of fractured knowledge fell into place with sickening perfection.

"He was a giant, profligate, rutting nob, he was—

despite everything your Michael always had to say about the grand Earl of Wallace. Seduced my mother, a maid in the abbey. She was but sixteen. He made her pretty promises but did nothing to protect her when she found herself with child. *With me.*"

"And so you blame Michael for his father's sins. May I ask when this occurred, sir? You are many years Michael's senior, are you not?"

"A man's character is fixed early on. My sire was a randy heir of fifteen, and apparently went on to fool everyone that he was a modern-age saint living a virtuous existence in and around the sacred abbey's walls."

"But surely it was your father's *parents* who cast out your mother."

He glared at her, his dark eyes burning with anger. "You can fabricate your version, and I shall choose my own."

"And what of Howard Manning?"

"My mother was sent away and after much hardship, found work as a seamstress in London. A year later Howard was born. I don't know who Howard's father was and I never asked. Even though you've lived a sheltered life, Lady Sheffield, even you must know the sordid things that can happen to a woman who is not offered protection."

Bile rose in the back of Grace's throat. "What was your mother's name?" God help her, but she could guess . . .

"Why, it was *Maura* Manning. Buried her many years ago in the potter's fields and then I sent Howard to Wallace Abbey with the lovely signet ring my father gave her. The one she refused to sell. My father had enough of a conscience to at least employ my brother, while I apprenticed for a livery stable here in town. But I'm not complaining, mind you. I think I did rather well for myself, don't you?"

"I'm sorry for what you and your family suffered." She struggled not to feel sorry for the man before her. "But I would hope your current station would help you forget the past."

"Did it help you?"

"I beg your pardon?" she asked.

"I remember your own family's downfall. Was the talk of the town. I even bought one of the horses at auction. Did Lord Sheffield's wealth ease you? No, I see it did not. It rarely does, you know, although there is one recourse that does have its merits. *Revenge.* It's even better, I've learned, when one has to wait for it."

Her anger flared anew. "Well, I hope you choke on it. There is nothing that will erase the stain of evil on your soul for persecuting an innocent man for so many years. Michael did not kill your brother over money. It was done in self-defense, at a guess."

"At a guess?" He lifted his brow. "Never say he got you to fork over seventy-five thousand pounds without ever telling you what happened? Backed my brother into a stall and stuck a pitchfork in his belly to ensure a slow and painful death. He then retrieved the wagered blunt and ran away like the murdering thief that he was. My brother had plenty of time to tell me the whole of it before he died. And, of course, there were witnesses . . . my most trusted stable hands."

Grace withered under the harsh man's impossible words uttered in such blinding certainty. Shaking, she hid her hands behind her. "You are wrong. I will never believe what you say. Howard Manning started that fire at Wallace Abbey. The only question I have is whether he was stealing the earl's horses and giving them to you or selling them to the gypsies. Are you a liar, a blackmailer, and a thief, sir?"

His eyes flared for a moment before they returned to their earlier cool appraisal. "That's all right, sweetheart, you are probably better off believing as you do. You'd be a simpleton to gamble a royal fortune unless you believed him with your whole heart. You and he should rub along well together—both of you wagering fools. Of course, you'll die penniless, just like your parents. I thank the good Lord above for my mother's practical Irish blood every day of my life."

Her own blood had nearly stilled in her veins at a sudden thought. "Michael doesn't know you're his half brother, does he? You took him in as a young apprentice and never told him."

His heavy-lidded gaze raked over her. "My dear, do I look like the sort of man who would claim a sniveling arsonist as a relation? I would not trust Michael Ranier or any of the other names he hid behind, within an inch of my life. I was generous to give him the same start in life that I had myself." His mysterious, penetrating eyes bore into hers. "And you may tell him that if he ever dares to set foot on my property, I will shoot his bloody head off without question."

Chapter 19

Grace was grateful for the steadying arm of Mr. Brown as a footman announced their presence to the occupants of the elegant Helston House front salon later that evening.

"Ata, whatever is the matter?" she said as soon as the footman retreated. The dowager was mute with grief, tears streaming down her face as the Duke of Beaufort stood looking out of an open window, the cold air swirling into the room. Mr. Brown brushed past her to go to Ata.

"He . . . he . . ." Ata stumbled. "Charles must have misunderstood that—"

Mr. Brown strode over to the duke and poked the much larger man in the chest. "What did you do to her? Why, I'll strangle you with the bell cord if you've harmed a hair on her pretty head. What in hell is going on?"

Grace glanced at Ata's gilded birdcage, the little door hanging open. "Oh, Ata . . . where is dear Pip?"

She moaned. "She's gone. Flown away, and in such weather."

"It was a little mistake," the duke blustered. "She insisted the bird loved her and would never leave her. But everyone knows birds don't give a damn about anyone. They can't when they have a brain the size of a pea."

"And then?" Mr. Brown said ominously.

"And then she insisted the bird always flew to her when out of its cage so I opened it to see if she was right. I thought it more sporting to give the bird a choice so I opened the bloody window."

"You will not blaspheme in front of Her Grace." Mr. Brown emphasized each word with additional pokes to the flustered duke, who was forced to take a step back with each prod.

"I don't know what you mean. She always blasphemes."

"Yes, but she's a lady and it's her right to do as she pleases. You, however, are not permitted to do anything to alarm her. Opening that window was a capital offense," Mr. Brown barked. "Do you understand?"

The taller gentleman was finally against the wall and his face became nearly purple with rage. "I'll tell you what I understand. You are nothing more than a minor peer of Scotland whereas I am the royal Duke of Beaufort, seventeenth in line to be king, you miserable piece of plaid-colored lint. If you dare to touch my person again I shall call you out. Now step away, sir."

Mr. Brown whipped off his glove and slapped the duke's face. "There. I've saved you the trouble. Swords or pistols? Or perhaps you'd prefer those barbed truncheons from your armory?"

Ata shrieked her distress and Grace gripped her arm to stay her diminutive friend from running to the odd-matched pair butting chests. "No, Ata. You must let them settle this. Don't you remember what you told me at Brynlow? Just think of the pleasure we'll take in reminding them later of their stupidity and how much they deserve every last injury for not listening."

"This is not the time to throw my idiotic words back in my face, Grace. Do take pity on me. He's far too old to do this anymore. He might get himself killed."

The duke cleared his throat. "There's absolutely no need to worry about me, Ata."

"I was talking about John, not you—you bloody scoundrel."

John Brown stepped sideways to block the duke's attempted retreat. "I'll have your answer now, if you please, *Your Majesty.*"

Beads of moisture had materialized on the duke's upper lip and forehead despite the freezing draft. "You are fortunate, sir, that I refuse to duel demented souls who are beneath my notice."

"Just as I thought," Mr. Brown said with disgust. "It's always the same with bullies. All puffery and no grit. Get out of here. And by the by, if I ever hear of you inconveniencing Her Grace again I shall round up every poacher in five counties and lead them to your bloody Beaulieu Park with an engraved invitation to hunt you down."

"Now see here," the duke blustered, backing toward the double doors, "I shall have the magistrate take you up on—"

"What's this?" Luc asked as he nearly collided with

the duke at the doorway. Quinn stood at his shoulder as their glances moved from each member of the group to the empty cage and open window.

"Not your affair, Luc," Mr. Brown said in a clipped tone. "Just let the imbecile go before I change my mind."

The Duke of Beaufort did not wait for a "by your leave," but retreated as fast as any prey under scrutiny.

Ata crumpled onto a settee and covered her wrinkled face with one hand as her gnarled one rested uselessly in her lap.

Mr. Brown offered her his handkerchief and settled into a chair next to her. "There, there, my love. Take this."

Luc's eyebrows had nearly risen to his hairline. "Will the goings-on in this house ever cease?" Luc pointedly shot a glance at Grace before he strode to a glass-fronted figurine case. Upon opening it, he extracted a bottle of Armagnac from a large Grecian urn while Quinn secured the crystal.

Ata sniffed. "Luc, I shall require a larger glass, if you please. And, by the way, you are not to blame Grace for any of this."

In the lengthening silence, Quinn coughed discreetly while he poured the Armagnac.

Luc paced the room restlessly. He stopped, and turned to Grace. Downing the contents of his glass, he glared at her. "She's absolutely right. Actually, where Grace is concerned, I am fully to blame. I let you down, my dear. I should have followed my instincts and killed that man when I had the chance."

"Killed him?" Ata restated. "Well, perhaps that's a bit severe. I am guessing John would have merely shot His Grace's foot as punishment. Although—"

"I'm not referring to that idiot Beaufort. I'm speaking of Ranier, or de Peyster, or Wallace—whatever you choose to call that criminal."

Grace's hand drifted over her heart as Luc extracted a letter from his pocket.

"Grace, please tell me that this outrageous letter, begging for my aid—a bit too late if you were to ask me—from a Mr."—he glanced at the bottom of the note—"Williamson is a hoax. Dear God, there must be some mistake. You did not squander seventy-five thousand pounds, indeed, nearly your entire fortune, to save that murdering blacksmith from the gallows." She had never seen Luc so stunned.

Ata moaned and Mr. Brown glanced at her with worry in his eyes.

"We missed you at every opportunity today, Grace," Quinn murmured. "If we had not gone to the foundling home before Newgate, we might have had the chance of intercepting you at Manning's and putting a stop to this insanity. But you are part of our family. We protect what is our own and we will shoulder this as—"

"Stop," Grace insisted. "There's no need to argue. What is done is done and cannot be undone. Not that I would choose a different course. That said, I came to ask a favor of you both. It will be the very last request, since I am well aware that I have outstripped anything either of you ever owed me."

"My dear," Quinn said, his desire to please her in

great evidence. "What do you require? What do you want us to do for you?"

"Would you personally deliver this letter to Old Bailey tomorrow at first light? It's from Rowland Manning officially withdrawing the complaints against Michael. I would ask you to see it through for me—see that he is, indeed, released."

"Of course I will do it. Newgate and Old Bailey's is no place for a lady."

"It's not that. I returned there not two hours ago but the guards said it was too late—that all matters would have to be addressed tomorrow. And . . . well, Mr. Brown and I are leaving straightaway, that is"— she turned to her old friend—"if you are still inclined to leave tonight, sir?"

Mr. Brown nodded in the tense silence.

"What?" Ata sat up abruptly and glanced from Mr. Brown to Grace. "Not that nonsense again. But with Michael to be released, and surely his title to be eventually restored, well, surely there's no need . . ." She anxiously looked from Grace to John Brown. "Where are you going?"

"To Scotland," Mr. Brown said firmly as Grace cleared her throat nervously.

Ata snorted. "Really?"

"We haven't precisely come to an agreement," Grace admitted. "Look, I told everyone I was going away and I haven't changed my mind. If anything, I have no other choice now after that gossip column. And I must retrench immediately if I've a chance to live independently. Besides, I've no desire to stay to play the martyr while all of you try to resurrect my nonexistent standing in society all over again. It's a complete waste of time and effort. Elizabeth and Sarah have kindly agreed to oversee the closing of Sheffield House. And Mr. Williamson will see to selling everything. I am only sorry you will all grieve for it. But I beg you not to."

"But Grace," Ata said. "What about Mr. Ranier, or rather, Lord Wallace? He will come after you—marry you. Why will you not wait for him?"

"Ata, in my heart, I know what is best. Lord Wallace told me himself that men base their worth on their fortune and station in life, and he will want to see to restoring both when he's released. That, in addition to Brynlow . . . well, he will have much to do. And I must see to my own affairs. Perhaps, after we've had adequate time to reflect on our wishes for the future, we shall find we will not suit. When we first spoke of going away, it was to hide, but now he has no reason to go away—and every reason to stay and take his rightful place here."

Luc made an exasperated sound. "Grace Sheffey, are you determined to ruin the peace of my dotage? You have clearly lost your mind."

Grace smiled. "Yes."

"The hell of it is that even I can't decide if it would be better to strangle Wallace, or Manning, or you. And none of those options will restore your fortune. Perhaps, it will, indeed, be the most satisfying to watch you live in poverty, raising chickens and such with that Wallace fellow."

"Oh, please. No more reproofs," Ata said to her grandson. "We all know why you're in such a black mood. You should have taken my idea of writing about all of us instead of some fusty tome about naval warfare. I keep telling you—you must write about the here and now, not the past. Then the creative process will unfold naturally, my love."

Luc stared at his virago of a grandmother, his left eyelid twitching. "I require your solemn oath, madam, that you will never, ever, ever form another secret society without my express permission."

"May I interrupt?" Grace's smile had faded. "I had wanted to try and explain this one thing to all of you to lessen your worry. I finally realized during the carriage ride back to Sheffield House that I should be grateful for everything that has happened."

Ata spoke up, "And why is that?"

Grace looked into the dark eyes of the dowager. "Because it took giving away almost everything to understand the ease of being free from all the obligations and trappings of before. The guilt of seeing so much of humanity living in squalor as I lived like a princess, the guilt of maintaining appearances—the horrendous expenses of fashion, frivolity, balls, furnishings, carriages, dozens and dozens of servants. Enough. I've had enough. And now that most of it will soon be gone, I also feel less cowardly. I'm glad I spent the money as I did. I'm proud of myself. I had a moral obligation to fight injustice. Before, I always withered from confrontation. I didn't this time."

Ata rose from the settee and grasped her hand. "I was never more proud of anyone, Grace. But won't you let me go with you?"

Mr. Brown shuttered his faded brown eyes, and

Grace responded. "Thank you, Ata, but no. You will miss your great-grandchildren too much. You've not been happy staying at my house instead of here. And Georgiana will need your help with her lying in. And Sarah and Elizabeth will require your good counsel. They're packing your affairs and their own at Sheffield House as we speak."

"John?" Ata questioned, her voice strained to breaking.

"I made a promise to take Lady Sheffield to the North several months ago, and I won't let her down again."

"This has nothing to do with that old promise. I want to come with you."

John Brown cantilevered his stiff form from the chair. "I think it best if you stay."

Ata's eyes narrowed. "Well!"

"You do like to live dangerously, old man," Luc murmured.

"I guess it comes from warming my bones too close to the Helston fires," Mr. Brown muttered.

Grace walked to Luc, and instead of offering her hand, she hugged him to her breast and kissed the taut hollows of his cheeks. "Please don't worry. I shall be much happier this way. And I won't be a burden. I was not stupid enough to give away everything. I shall live quite comfortably—the way I did on Mann—simply and close to the land. I will be perfectly happy."

"And perfectly poor," Luc said gruffly, hugging her hard to his chest. "Have no fear, Grace, I shall probably only let you live in squalor for two months before I send the marquis to retrieve you. It should only take the remainder of a cold winter for you to learn your lesson. The true luxuries of life are to be revered, not mocked, my dear. We shall hear enough of the reverse nonsense when we are tossed before our maker in the end."

With equal parts tears and good wishes, Grace and Mr. Brown said their good-byes to their friends. There was only one person who refused to see them off from the columned splendor of Helston House's entrance. Ata.

And there was only one person who noticed. John Brown.

Grace gazed at the forlorn image of her traveling companion across from her in the carriage. "Mr. Brown?"

"Yes?"

"There is one last thing I must see to before we cross the bridge."

"And what is that, Lady Sheffield?"

"Just a very little thing—an invitation, if you will."

"Och, lass, I'd thought you finished with the trappings of society."

"Actually, this is more like offering someone a wager."

He shook his head. "Wagering's an addiction, lassie. One you can no longer afford. You should know that better than anyone."

"But this, I promise, will be my very last one."

"Spoken like a confirmed gambler."

"Good God," Ata said three mornings later, nearly stumbling down the last three steps of Helston House's grand staircase. "Leave him!"

Four liveried footmen, appearing every inch like identical tin soldiers and about as effective, released the various appendages of the purported Lord Wallace. Or someone who might be Lord Wallace if he'd been dragged through the streets and had the bloodied body and dirty clothes to prove it.

With horror, she rushed to him. "Is it you?"

"No." Michael refused to smile. It hurt too much.

"It absolutely *is* you!"

"No. It's only me if Grace is here."

"And why is that?"

"Because if I were Helston I would have borrowed, loaded, sharpened and readied all of Beaufort's weapons, including a few cannon, which I'd point at that door just in case I ever decided to stop by for a dish of tea."

"Well," Ata said sidling up to him, "he might have suggested such."

"Where is she? And why will no one answer the door at her townhouse?"

"You smell."

He chuckled and abruptly stopped, clutching his jaw. "Are you ever going to tell me where she is?"

"No. Not until you bathe. Phipps? Have water heated for Lord Wallace, send someone for his affairs at the foundling home, and arrange one of the chambers for his use." She stopped the butler. "Oh, and Phipps?"

"Yes, Your Grace?"

"Make sure it's very far from my grandson's apartments but close to mine." And then, Lord help him, she winked at Michael.

Perhaps the dowager duchess had been right, Michael conceded as he steeped in the largest, most impressive hip bath he'd ever seen in his life not an hour later. Christ, he felt almost human again. And yet, despite the hot water, the perfumed soap, and the clean clothes draped over the screen, his fears eddied through the corridors of his mind on well-worn pathways. For so long he had been living a half life, always hiding. He wondered if he'd ever be able to lead a normal, relaxed way of life—if he'd ever stop feeling hunted. He had a primal desire to find Grace and hole up in some godforsaken corner of nowhere and never leave. He plunged his head under water.

But, now that she had met Rowland Manning, there was every reason to believe she would never want to see Michael ever again. For surely Manning had told her his version of what had happened. And surely Grace had paid dearly to buy his release from Newgate.

Michael stood up, a rush of water sluicing down his toughened, bruised form. He was not a pretty sight, and would not be suitable for viewing for a long while. He needed to do so much, and yet, there was only one thing he wanted to do. To find her. To find out what had happened. He reached for the soft toweling as a familiar bark of irritation funneled from beyond the cracks of the door.

Without warning, the door banged open, Helston and Ellesmere gusting inside. The duke's eyes squinted as he addressed the marquis. "Please tell me my eyes deceive me. Pray tell me the dirty dog did not have the audacity to trot here?"

Ellesmere merely raised his eyebrows and sighed heavily, while Michael donned the clothes that had been neatly pressed and laid out for him.

"Look, I have only two questions for you. How much did she pay him? And where is she?" He limped to the other side of the screen.

The duke traded glances with the marquis. "Everything she had." Helston smiled viciously.

Michael staggered back, his arm flailing, only to catch the screen. Both man and panel crashed to the ground.

"Come, come," Ellesmere said. "Take care. You're not allowed to die on us quite yet, Wallace."

"And why is that?" Michael asked, his voice raspy.

"Why, because you owe Lady Sheffield too much money." Ellesmere offered his hand to ease Michael from the floor.

"There's that," Helston growled, "and the fact that he owes *us* far too many favors."

"What sort of favors?"

"The ones that involve recalibrating the delicate balance of power among our peers, all in an effort to see your title secured in the most efficient way possible. You know, the sort of debt that is nearly impossible to repay."

"I shall repay you."

Helston snorted. "Wallace, don't be ridiculous. You have little chance of repaying us in ten lifetimes. And since you've used up nearly nine lives to get to this point, I do think you should just give up all pretence to noble intentions."

The sound of his true name coming from both gentlemen nearly broke him.

The marquis pursed his lips and cleared his throat. "A plan is already in motion. Lord Palmer and Helston have secured the support of more than half the peers in the House of Lords. We are waiting for answers from the other half. You certainly were cutting it close, Wallace."

"What do you mean?"

"Another few years and the land might have reverted to the crown, although I haven't had the time to study the matter closely enough to be certain. As it stands, the lands were left in the hands of trustees, and the title was left dormant since you were presumed alive but taken up by gypsies who were seen in the vicinity. While the abbey and the attached stable all burned, as you know, the authorities who investigated the fire noted a few inconsistencies. In addition to you, there were a number of horses missing—and chickens."

"Chickens? I see you've taken it upon yourself to research the matter," Michael murmured, overawed that these gentlemen had made such efforts on his behalf. "I fear I owe you both a great deal, indeed."

"Oh, but this is just the beginning," Helston said in a bored tone.

Michael's chest ached. Gratitude was an emotion he had so rarely felt, he wasn't even certain it was what was welling up inside of him. "I am honored by the yoke of friendship you both so willingly took up," he said, quietly.

"*Friendship*?" Helston said, his eyes darkening with horror. "Oh, Christ, no. Ellesmere, you never said we'd have to befriend him. I took on just about as much friendship as I can tolerate in one lifetime when I agreed to befriend you."

Ellesmere chuckled. "Wallace, you can help by giving us the names of any people who knew you when you were a child. People who might remember you well—servants, the vicar, anyone. Or names of peers who knew your father—or any other incontrovertible proof. I've already sent my steward to Derbyshire to ask about the neighborhood. We'll need all the ammunition we can secure to have you officially declared the right and true Earl of Wallace."

Michael scratched his jaw. "While it's impossible to tell you how grateful I am for everything you've done, my lords, you still haven't told me what I really want to know."

"How very demanding of you, Wallace," Helston replied dryly.

"I want to know where Lady Sheffield is. And I also want to know about her meeting with Rowland Manning."

"And why would you need to know that?"

"Because I mean to get her fortune back, of course. You didn't really think I'd sit here and do nothing, did you?"

Helston, exasperation dripping from his expression, sighed. "We're coming to that. But you'll have a better chance with the power a title confers."

"I don't need a title to kill the bastard. And I'm not going to wait another day. Manning will secrete away or spend her fortune in a fortnight, if not sooner."

Ellesmere gritted his teeth. "Don't be a fool. Do you really want to revisit the underground gardens of Newgate so soon? I would think one tour would be enough for anybody."

"Actually, I was hoping since we're friends, that—"

"God help me . . ." Helston muttered.

"Perhaps you would come with me. I would of course do the primary work. But it would help if I had you both stand as sentry."

The duke and marquis exchanged glances.

Ignoring the blaze of pain in his jaw as he grinned, Michael continued, "Since you've been good enough to expend your varied talents to my benefit, I was thinking I might show you some of mine."

"And what talents would you possess, Mr. Jack-of-all-lowering-trades?" Helston asked, exasperated.

Michael raised a single brow. "Entering without breaking for one, finding but not taking, for another. Unless it's Grace's money, of course."

Ellesmere examined his fingernails. "I suppose we should have guessed it would come to this."

"Undoubtedly," Helston replied. He dragged his hands down his face. "Good God, I'd thought my days of plundering over when I resigned my commission. And when were you proposing we—God preserve us—pay a 'social call' on Mr. Manning?"

"At three o'clock," Michael replied. "Tomorrow morning."

Helston shook his head. "I hear Ata coming up the stair. Let's decamp to plan this properly. Won't waste a moment letting her expound on all your fine attributes. I would prefer to keep my dinner, thank you."

The three men strode to the door, and nearly collided in the effort to file out at the same time. "Blast it all, Wallace," Helston gritted out. "It's dukes before marquises, and marquises before earls. Please tell me we are not going to have to waste our time teaching you the elementary rules of polite society?"

Michael attempted a contrite expression. The duke sighed heavily as he preceded Ellesmere out the door. Michael followed his new friends down the back hallway. God, were they really that to him? The last time he'd enjoyed that bond had been with Sam Bryn. It had been a long time ago. A very long time.

But it felt good. It felt very good.

Chapter 20

Nine weeks later . . .

"**J**ames," Michael said to the boy riding alongside him in the flat lands of Berkshire, "I have a good feeling about this place."

"Sir, you've said that the last three times." The former chimney sweep's small gray gelding trotted a bit faster to keep up with Sioux.

Michael chuckled and tried to ignore the pain in his one arm. "I know, lad. It's just that I've had a good feeling ever since we left town. Anticipation is half the joy, don't you think? Lower your hands, and ease off the bit. Yes, that's exactly right."

The boy showed such promise. He'd taken to riding like a bird takes to flight. Michael glanced at James's noble profile and open countenance, so different from two months ago, when Michael had arranged his release with much difficulty. Ah, the adaptability of youth.

Michael halted Sioux at the crest of a small rise, James following suit. "Glory be, sir," he said with wonderment. "Never seen anything like this in me life."

The magnificent view beckoned them, the air thick with vernal evidence—shy snowdrops nodded their single clasped blooms while enjoying the shade of the burgeoning tree branches heavy with bud. Daffodils and gorse competed to show off the brightest yellows of the season, and everywhere, new life was in evidence. Tiny lambs bleated for their mothers in the vast pastures dotted with wisps of lost wool that appeared like remnants of snow.

Nestled in a little bit of wilderness, with a stream running nearby, lay an ivy-covered cottage complete with gables and a tile roof. Two outer buildings stood behind. When he spied the very uneven lines of a newly laid kitchen garden, Michael grinned and tipped back his hat. "James?"

"Sir?"

"I'll wager evening chores this is the one."

"Why, you know I'll do whatever you ask, sir." The boy looked so happy. "And you know I never gamble, sir."

"Except that one time."

"Yes. Except that one time."

"I've not said it, James, but I thank you for placing your trust in me, son."

"I'd go to the ends of the world for you, sir," the boy said quietly.

Michael leaned down to place his hand on James's shoulder for the briefest moment. "And I think you just about did. But I've good news. We've arrived."

James studied the landscape. "It sure is pretty. How long will we stay?"

"Not sure," Michael said, clucking to Sioux to continue forward. "It might not be as long as I'd like." Michael did not mention that this was the point where expectation turned into uncertainty.

"Sir?"

"Yes, James?"

"Tell me again what she's like."

Michael smiled. "Like the first ray of sunshine after a long blizzard. Brilliant and pure. And her eyes are like bluebells and violets and as clear as a sapphire, untainted by any other hue of a rainbow."

"Can't imagine it, sir. But tell me about her goodness."

He'd asked so many times to hear about Grace's character. Michael knew it was all due to the boy's fear. He would never voice it, but Michael guessed long ago that James was terrified she wouldn't accept him. What James did not know was that Michael was a thousand times more worried that she wouldn't accept the larger of the two of them. She'd had two months to regret the horror of what she had done, two months to doubt him, and two months to learn she could go along very well without him.

"Her goodness, James, is as pure as an angel from heaven. Her generous heart is unparalleled; her spirit, kindness personified. You do know what those words mean, don't you?"

"It doesn't matter, sir. It sounds better than anything I can imagine. So shall I water the horses and let them graze, like at the other places?"

Michael nodded. "Yes, here near the stream." Michael swung off, removed Sioux's bridle and replaced it with a halter, James mimicking his motions with the other, smaller horse.

He strode toward the cottage, James's words floating behind him. "Good luck. And sir?"

Michael stopped but didn't turn around. She was so near. "Yes?"

"Don't worry so. If she won't take ye in, we can al'ays go back to Brynlow. Or if she takes ye, I could go to work in the stables of the Duke o' Helston, like his worship said."

"James, I would as soon as part with you as I would lead you back to the rookeries. You'd best get used to it. You're stuck with me. Always. And I'll remind you of it every day of our damned lives until you tell me you're sick of hearing it. Agreed?" He glanced behind him just in time to catch James bob his head and turn away to hide his emotions. Michael swallowed against the knot in his throat. "And James, if it becomes too hot, I spied shade trees on the other side of the cottage. I'll return as soon as I can."

Michael continued on but his footsteps slowed as he approached the lacquered door with the black cast-iron winged hinges. He knocked, his belly churning. Counting to twenty, he knocked again, and then tried the latch, which gave way.

Michael called out, "Lady Sheffield . . ." He cleared his throat, his voice strained to the point of breaking. "Grace?" The floorboards creaked as his heavy boots crossed the room. He poked his head in each of the four small rooms.

Evidence of her was everywhere he chanced to see . . . he recognized her even stitches in a small pile of mending. A simple pink wool shawl lay on the back of a worn armchair near a grate. But more than anything, it was her elusive scent he caught once or twice, which sent his mind spinning.

Blinded suddenly by the overwhelming need to see her, he took the steps on the narrow staircase three at a time, now calling her name with increasing urgency. But she was not to be found in any of the bedchambers above. This was not going as he'd expected.

Where in hell was she? Had she hid herself when she'd seen him coming? He chastised himself. Fear always led to absurd thoughts. He let himself out the back of the cottage and scanned the small garden and structures beyond.

A loud squawking erupted from one and he broke into a run toward the enclosed yard. Without bothering to knock, he entered the henhouse.

Feathers floated in the air and a clutch of birds intent on mutiny surrounded her. She was everything he remembered and so much more. Christ, she was his whole world. Her hair was pinned back and gleamed in the shaft of light from the sole window. He would never be able to describe her no matter how many times he tried. For she was perfect. Even her damned imperfections were perfect because they were part of her.

He coughed. "You know, sometimes it's easier to collect eggs when you distract them with feed outside."

Grace whirled around, her eyes widening. She dropped the empty wire basket she carried. "Oh. It's you."

Leaving the door open, he walked forward, the chickens scattering into the yard behind him.

He leaned down, retrieved her egg basket and placed it in her hand.

"Thank you." Her gaze remained on the basket.

"You're very welcome. Grace, I'm sorry I star—"

"It's lovely to see you, my lord," she interrupted, her tone now even and calm.

He stared at her, terrified of her formality.

She brushed a lock of her hair back into place and finally raised her eyes to his. "If I'd known you were considering a call, I would have prepared better for your visit."

Her eyes were so very warm, their blue depths startling. He longed to wrap his arms around her and crush her to him, and yet it was obvious she would not welcome it. Not in the least. "May I offer my help?"

"No, this will take but a moment." She strolled the aisle, plucking eggs from the various nests until she circled to the door. He stood watching her silently, feeling every inch the awkward lumbering giant in the cramped space. Christ, what had he been thinking? He should have just walked up to her straightaway and taken her in his arms instead of standing there like a silent fool.

He followed her as she left the henhouse, her apron flapping in the spring breeze. Michael rushed forward and opened the gate for her and then, fifty yards later, the back door of the cottage. In the small kitchen, she placed the basket on the simple, rustic table and swung a black pot filled with water over the fire.

She appeared as if she had lost weight, and it filled

him with ill ease. Made him want to force her down in the chair while he prepared a feast for her and hand-fed her with a spoon. Instead, he found his voice. "I'm sorry I gave you no notice. I assure you it was not for lack of effort."

Her eyes lifted to his. "May I offer you something to drink? Perhaps a cup of—"

"Tea would be lovely," he interjected.

A faint blush crept up the prim edges of her simply styled gown. "I'm afraid there's no tea. May I offer you water or perhaps milk, Lord Wallace?"

He couldn't forget how her plush lower lip was like soft petals in the rain and he wanted to cry for the damage she was doing, worrying her bottom lip with her teeth. "Water would be most welcome. Grace, please let me—"

"And may I offer you a biscuit?" she interrupted. "They are freshly baked."

"Thank you." Would she ever let him speak? He was near to breaking as she placed water and several biscuits before him.

He stared at them, wondering where to begin.

"Well, are you going to try them? I've made a bit of progress. Cooking, I mean," she said.

He bit into the fragrant, flaky biscuit, his appetite nil, his jaw working only to please her. He finally registered her effort. "Grace, this is bar none, the best biscuit I've ever tasted."

"Thank you." She finally lowered herself into the chair opposite him, and brushed a crumb into her apron, her eyes avoiding his. "What happened to your arm?"

He looked down at his forgotten sling. "Nothing much. It's just a scratch."

"I remember you once telling me the same when Luc and Quinn fought you. Did they strike you again?"

"No. This was courtesy of Rowland Manning, although I assure you I fared better than he."

Her eyes flew to his.

"Really, it's nothing."

She jumped up and came to his side of the table. "I want to see it. Is it a broken bone or a flesh wound?"

He was so happy to see her concern, he would have let Rowland Manning shoot at all his limbs if he had known it would encourage her to touch him. He leaned his head back and closed his eyes. He let himself drown in the gentle sensation of her fingers working the sling from his arm and unwrapping the bandage.

Her breath hitched and he finally opened his eyes to see her staring at the raw scar on his forearm. Before he could stop himself, his other hand reached to stroke the ends of her hair so gently she didn't register the fact.

"Won't you tell me what happened?"

"Grace . . . none of this matters. I've come to ask you something. I'm sorry it's taken me so long, it's just that, well . . . I couldn't find you."

"Pardon me?"

"I've toured half of England and Scotland looking for you. First to Brynlow, then to Mann—where I assure you it is indeed, cold enough to please any Viking, only to be surpassed by Scotland in February. By the by, Mr. Brown's estate is quite lovely, even when covered by three feet of snow."

She said not a word as he continued. "And did you know that there are at least six dwellings known as Ivy Cottage in the county of Berkshire?"

Grace looked into his clear golden eyes and prayed for control. She closed her eyes to stop herself from falling toward him. It had taken so long to force hope from her mind that she dared not ever hope again, after the agony of the last month of winter.

In the beginning, she had taken secret nourishment from the idea that he would rush to her the moment he was released from Newgate, like a grateful prince coming for his bride. But after the first three weeks, hope had slowly strained and become tinged with fear. And fear had continued unabated with each passing day, when no letters ever appeared from London. It was obvious that even Ata had given up hope, had not been able to bring herself to write of any happiness, and so had not written at all. Endurance replaced hope with shattering reality. And yet, self-reliance had brought the warm glow of pride to her heart. And *Lara* had fanned the flame.

Unexpectedly, she registered his large, warm hands circling her wrists and pulling her onto his lap.

"Your arm," she whispered.

"Is fine—as long as it is holding you."

She bit the inside of her cheek to keep from crying at the overwhelming feel of his warm embrace. "Shall I find a fresh bandage for you? Or perhaps you'd prefer a poultice?"

"Still asking the wrong questions, I see," he murmured close to her ear. "Aren't you ever going to ask me why I'm here?"

She swallowed against the lump in the back of her throat, and tried to pull away. "My lord, I had thought—"

"Are you trying to torture me, Grace? Because if you don't stop referring to me as 'my lord,' or 'sir,' or 'Lord Wallace,' or whatever else you dream up, I think my heart will never recover."

"And how would you propose I address you?"

" 'Michael.' And shall I tell you how I should like to address you?"

She shook her head, her throat tight.

" 'Lady Wallace,' or more intimately," he whispered, " 'Mrs. de Peyster.' Yes . . ." He nuzzled her neck, sending shivers down her spine, "either of those names would serve, don't you think?"

Her mind swirled with ill ease. "But—"

"No good comes from a sentence that starts with *but*. Start again, if you please."

"Michael, I really think—"

"Say it again . . . the first part."

"Michael?"

"Yes. I kept dreaming of you, whispering it over and over again as you did the last night I saw you. I think it was the only thing that kept me from going mad the four days I spent at Newgate."

"Four days? But Quinn promised—"

"And delivered. But I wouldn't leave without arranging a young friend's release as well. It took more than a little doing, but your former fiancés were very accommodating. Well, one was a bit more courteous than the other. Oh God, Grace . . . I have to kiss you. I'm sorry I can't wait any longer."

She struggled against him. "Michael . . . wait."

He sighed and stared at the lengthening shadows in the kitchen. "Grace, I struggled before leaving London. Do you want to know why?"

"Yes."

"I struggled between the desire to come after you and the necessity of staying there, to secure that bloody Wallace title, the land, and any monies due. And do you know why?" He didn't wait for her answer. "It was to make myself more worthy of your notice. But in the end, I couldn't wait. And so, I took one day to do something I had to do and then I went after you. And by the by, if you ever contemplate the idea of leaving again without telling someone precisely where you can be found, I do believe I will have to fashion a twitch to . . . Well, this blasted Norse wanderlust has got to be reined in, I tell you."

"But I did tell someone. Mr. Williamson knew precisely where I was. Although, I didn't know there were six Ivy Cottages in this county. Perhaps that's why I never received any letters." She swallowed. "What was the one thing you had to do?"

"I refuse to tell you until you give me an answer."

"To what question?"

He looked at her grimly. "I found a letter waiting for me at Mr. Brown's estate in Scotland. Helston and Ellesmere informed me that the House of Lords has indeed looked favorably on the request for restitution of the patent letters of nobility and all Wallace lands, although, Grace, I must warn you that there is virtually nothing in the coffers save for a portion of the meager rents the trustees collected each year from the tenants. The abbey is in ruins and will most likely stay that way forever. But I can at least offer myself to you as a gentleman, and no longer as a fugitive. And I do own Brynlow."

"What are you asking of me?"

He took up her hand in his. "I would ask you to condescend to marry me, much as I do not deserve a person of your good character, your integrity."

"Oh, Michael . . ." She burst into tears.

"Is that a yes, my love, or a no?"

"I know why you are asking. You feel honor bound to offer for me. But you see, it's as I told everyone before I left. I'm grateful for what happened. I'm happy here with Lara. Did you know I went to the foundling home before I left and asked her if she would like to come away and live with me, despite my reduced circumstances?"

"Mrs. Kane informed me."

"Well, you do not need to worry about me. I will be perfectly fine here with my little angel. And when the lease runs through, I might very well continue on here, or Lara and I might live simply yet comfortably on Mann. We shall see."

He stared at her. "Grace, will you come with me for a moment? Trust me?"

She nodded and stood up. He offered his arm and she placed her own lightly on top of his, her chapped fingers resting on the back of his hand. Michael led her outside, toward the little bit of wilderness on the side of the cottage.

"Who is that?" Grace asked, looking toward James and the two horses by the stream.

"Just a deserving boy. He's been searching for something—or rather someone—for most of his life. I invited him to come with me when I left London."

"Really?"

"Yes. He reminds me of me, you see. He's been searching a long time for someone he can entrust with his heart."

"Michael, this isn't very fair of you."

"I know and I don't care." He raked his hand through his hair. "Grace, I'm that worried you won't have me and I don't know how to convince you. Please, my darling, I beseech you to find it in your heart to love me, as I love you. Do you think you would ever be able to do that?"

"You know," she replied softly, "if you had just said that part at the beginning, I would have agreed straight away. Haven't you guessed I'm in love with you . . . and will never stop loving you, ever?"

And suddenly she was flying in the air. He had snatched her off the ground despite his injured arm and swung her in an arc about him. And he was laughing as if he would never stop. And then he was clasping her to his immense chest, and she was lost in his embrace. He whispered in her ear. "You must promise me, then. Promise you will marry me soonest."

Emotion robbed her of speech. She arched away to show him her feelings instead.

"Well, do you? Do you promise to marry me?"

"You know I will, Michael. Why won't you trust me?"

"Because I need to tell you something else, but I must have your word first."

"Well, again, I must say you aren't playing fair. I would think you should do the gentlemanly thing and tell me if there is something that might influence my decision."

He blinked, unmoved by her reproach.

"Well?"

"Will you have me or not?"

She sighed. "I said I would. Now what is it?"

Michael reached for her fingers and extracted four long strands of pearls from his coat, using his uninjured hand. Grace watched as they coiled, overflowing into her waiting palm, and suddenly realized how little she had thought of them once they were gone. "How did you ever . . ."

"Consider them a wedding gift from Rowland Manning, if you will. And this"—he extracted a worn document from his coat—"is from me."

Grace allowed the forgotten pearls to slip from her fingers when she spied the document. *The promissory note to Rowland Manning.* "What did you do . . . ?"

"You didn't really think I would let that blackguard ruin your life, did you? I would have killed him before I let him collect your fortune, Grace. And I would have hung for it. Gladly. But I will not let you live in poverty because of me. I coerced Helston and Ellesmere to go to Manning's with me. As they stood guard, I climbed through a window in the middle of the night to steal the promissory note."

Good God. "And?"

"And he was waiting for me."

"*And*?"

"And I convinced Rowland to return the note."

Ill ease filled her. "And how did you do that, Michael? Perhaps you forget that I met the man."

"I told him he could have my head, but not your fortune. During the course of our gentlemanly disagreement, I parted Rowland from his pistol at the same moment his pistol parted with its ball, hence the injury."

She swallowed awkwardly.

"Gordy Lefroy appeared at the sound of the discharge. He was an old mate from the days when I apprenticed for Manning. When Rowland ordered Lefroy to fetch a pitchfork to kill me, Gordy refused. He did me a great favor, actually. He finally had the courage to tell Manning the truth, that I had accidentally killed Howard, who was beating a horse in a senseless rage after losing a large amount of coin to me. I had entered the stall with a pitchfork when I heard the horse screaming. The stallion swung about and reared when he heard me, probably assumed I was come to hurt him too. I raised the pitchfork to protect myself only to have the horse change direction in midair when he saw who I was. But the force of the horse's shoulder landing against mine propelled me into Howard Manning. Gordy had seen it all, but Rowland's rage at finding his brother near death was such that he would have killed anyone who contradicted Howard's falsehoods. I don't blame Gordy. He would have been relieved without recommendation and would have had nowhere to turn. Gordy and the others had urged me to run, had even emptied their own pockets to help me get away. All of us knew Rowland would blame me, would not hear the truth."

"Oh, Michael," Grace moaned.

"Helston and Ellesmere came in behind Gordy, and heard it all, even the damning part. Gordy said Howard had once hinted that he'd stolen a string of nobs' horses in the North Country to line his pockets."

"But how did you get the promissory note from Rowland?"

"Helston and Ellesmere threatened to expose all to the peers Rowland depended on for his business to thrive. That's when he relented. But not before he wounded me more deeply than he had with a pistol ball."

"He finally admitted you were his half brother."

"Yes. Christ, Grace . . ."

She stroked his arm when she saw the sadness in his eyes. "But why didn't you tell me about meeting Rowland when you arrived here?"

"Because I thought I had a better chance convincing you to marry me if you thought your only options were living in modest comfort at Brynlow or living as an egg and dairymaid here. I figured I had little chance of tempting one of the richest and most beautiful women in England to do my mending in Yorkshire. Just consider the family of scoundrels you would be forced to marry into."

Grace felt her lips twitching. "You are a very foolish man."

"I suppose I should be completely honest with you, should warn you of one last thing."

"And what is that?"

"As part of the bargain in retrieving your fortune, Rowland insisted he be the one to walk you down the aisle if we are wed. Suggested outrageously about having the right, since he was providing the *dowry*. Even had the audacity to suggest you might prefer him over me." He leaned in to add, "Said he liked your fire. Imagine the nerve."

"The trait does appear to run in your family," she whispered with a smile. Grace studied the document in her hands. The idea of being in possession of the Sheffield monies again felt nothing so much as a burden all over again. "Michael? What would you think if I told you I don't want this fortune anymore? If I suggested that it never brought me any sort of happiness?"

He looked at her, earnestness filling his face. "I would ask you what you propose to do about it."

She gazed beyond his shoulder to the sight of a boy leading two horses with one hand and a young girl— Lara—with the other. "I would like to use a good portion of it to rebuild your family's estate, and to offer the use of Wallace Abbey to the foundling home. The children could live in the countryside where they would have a better life, where we could also provide better food, better everything. Oh Michael . . . please say yes."

"You would want to do this, truly?" he asked, amazement warring with adoration in his eyes as he pulled her behind the privacy of a sturdy oak tree.

"Yes."

"Then you must do it, Grace. For you will create a far better place than I ever envisioned."

"What place was that?"

He turned to see what she was staring at around the trunk of the tree. As he watched Lara and James laughing together in the distance, he gently clasped her to his warm chest and whispered, "Why, paradise. Now I see it's anywhere you are, my love."

Grace stared up into the golden eyes of the only man who had ever inspired her to reach beyond her carefully cultivated orderly life, and very inelegantly pulled his head down to hers. "This is when you're supposed to kiss me."

He dazzled her with a grin, and plucked a chicken feather from her hair. "I was trying very hard, just this once, not to rush you."

"But I want you to rush me."

He stared at her, waiting. And so she took matters into her own two hands and rose up the last inch to meet his lips.

And then, only then, did he let himself loose on her, prowling, and growling, and nuzzling and nipping to make sure she fully understood the depth and breadth of his love—forevermore.

Epilogue

⌒◯◯⌒

Dear Mr. Brown,

I am writing to thank you for the new love of my life. I don't know how you managed it, but a dear little dog, whom I have named Attila, was delivered to Helston House almost a full month ago. He has stolen my heart, quite recklessly, you see, despite the sentiments I still retain for my late husband's large dogs. Luc tells me his breed has a God-given talent for dragging vicious badgers from their holes, but if he understands any of my late-night whispers, he will develop a taste for portentous, bloodthirsty dukes in their armories. Right now, however, he excels in lap sitting and bed sleeping.

John, I'm certain you will realize how difficult this is to admit, but it was very wrong of me to act as I did this winter. While a proper apology does not include excuses, I beg you to consider my explanation. I have never told anyone why I feel as responsible as I do where it concerns Grace Sheffey, who if there is any right in this world will soon become Lady Wallace. I *would beg of you not to tell her, but it was my terrible husband who convinced Grace's father to invest in that foreign canal scheme that failed so miserably. And Luc compounded Grace's misfortunes by breaking her heart. Truly the Helston family has brought nothing but suffering to a young lady whose character is far greater than anyone else's I've ever known.*

When you left her in your wrecked carriage in the middle of a blizzard, I didn't blame you. I blamed myself. I held myself liable for not having gained her trust. She turned to you in her darkest hour, not me. That pained me terribly. I had been determined to fix every evil the Helston family had ever done to her.

But I have learned something. I've learned that I must stop assigning culpability for other's mistakes. And I've also learned that I must accept blame for my own wretched wrongs.

This is all to tell you that I am determined to change. I have never believed advancement in years may be used as an excuse for ill behavior. I do not blame you for going away without me this last time. I only ask that if you still possess the smallest shred of regard for me, and I am praying that Attila is a testament to that fact, then you will one day forgive me—just as I shall forgive you for suggesting that Attila, who is far more snout and teeth than leg and hair, reminds you of me.

Lastly, I wanted to inform that I am contemplating a possible return to Cornwall. While I had thought to remain in London this spring to broaden Elizabeth and Sarah's prospects for happiness, it has become blindingly obvious that Elizabeth is everything but happy here. Indeed, she has changed from the fearless, outspoken lady we all knew. And I cannot fathom why. Sarah continues on as always . . . determined to revere the memory of her heroic husband. And so, I am undecided about remaining in London.

I am, however, determined to put off the decision until I hear news from you. Please tell my dearest girl that if she decides to run away yet again, that it had better be with Michael, the most perfect scoundrel I have yet to meet. And there is to be no talk of special licenses. They had best come to London, for I am determined to arrange a proper wedding at St. George's with all the trimmings.

Your perfect hoyden,
Ata

At Avon Books, we know your passion for romance—once you finish one of our novels, you find yourself wanting more.

May we tempt you with . . .

- **Excerpts** from our upcoming releases.
- Entertaining **extras**, including authors' personal photo albums and book lists.
- Behind-the-scenes **scoop** on your favorite characters and series.
- **Sweepstakes** for the chance to win free books, romantic getaways, and other fun prizes.
- Writing **tips** from our authors and editors.
- **Blog** with our authors and find out why they love to write romance.
- **Exclusive content** that's not contained within the pages of our novels.

Join us at
www.avonbooks.com

AVON

An Imprint of HarperCollins*Publishers*
www.avonromance.com

Available wherever books are sold or please call 1-800-331-3761 to order.